The Ramtalans

Species: Book Three

The Ramtalans, Species: Book Three

Previously published by Escargot Books and Music as Two Brothers: Species by Sofia Diana Gabel.

ISBN: 979-8-9893356-8-8

Dedicated to Alexandra, Olivia, and Andrianna.

Chapter 1

Citadel, Ramtalan Headquarters on Earth
Command Center

After receiving an onslaught of photometric pulses from his aunt, Galena, as punishment for losing his orb weapon to the renegade Dachel brothers, Aridesian Stargaard cowered on the floor in the corner of the Command Center. His gut burned. He was certain he had internal injuries.

It was only after the brothers had sought refuge with Commander Jampara in the court room that Galena discovered that Argus and Tai had broken through the adjoining walls between their apartment and Ari's. Even worse, they'd stolen the weapon. Ari knew it wasn't his fault they had the orb, but Galena wouldn't listen to reason. She blamed him.

Galena ordered an extra security detail to monitor activity on the mainland of Labrador, where the Settler Guardians were gathering to battle for control of the Citadel. She was furious, and Ari was scared.

"Ari," she said sternly.

He struggled to his feet as the other Ramtalans in the room stared at him. "What? Are you going to fire on me again?"

She glared at him. "There's no point. You know your place now. You will work on opening the court room door. I want the Commander *and* the boys. Now."

Ari rubbed his midsection. "Can I go to medical first? I'm hurt."

Galena's eyes flashed brilliant blue. "You are such a disappointment to both me and your father. Argus and Tai are braver and more intelligent than you'll ever be. How you can be related to them is beyond me." She turned around. "Go to medical, but I don't want to see you again until you've found a way into the court room."

Ari stumbled from the Command Center and made his way to the medical wing. He was fed up with being Galena's puppet. He was Argustine

Lenox's firstborn son. Where was the respect? Once inside the medical room, he lay down on a hover-stretcher and closed his eyes as the robotic medical personnel began the examination. If it was the last thing he did, he'd make sure Argus and Tai Dachel never saw the light of day. Without them around, he'd be the only son once again.

CITADEL, COURT ROOM

Argus Dachel wandered around the Citadel's court room, unsure of what to do. He and Tai had successfully delivered Ari's orb weapon to Commander Jampara and the Commander managed to replace Galena's shield around the room with his own, but nothing else was happening. The Commander stood, actually floated a few inches off the ground, doing nothing but holding the orb.

"Arg, sit down. You're driving me crazy." Tai motioned to the chair next to him. "Sit."

"I'm too wound up to sit. Why isn't anyone doing anything? We both heard Aunt Celeste say hundreds of Guardians were getting ready to storm the Citadel. But they can't get through the Citadel's shield. And now we have the orb weapon, but the Commander isn't doing anything. This is crazy." Argus finally sat, but he couldn't stay still. His nerves were jangled. It was like waiting for a bomb to drop on their heads. "Commander?"

Tai nudged Argus. "Leave him alone, Arg. He's probably doing some Ramtalan meditation thing or something. You should try it, maybe it'll calm your ass down. Look, Aunt Celeste said she was waiting for Neb. Maybe he hasn't arrived yet."

"I guess. Tai, I was thinking about something."

"Of course you were. You never stop thinking." Tai got up and stretched. "I'm getting kind of antsy, too. So, what are you thinking?"

Argus wrung his hands together. It had to be the collective energy of the Citadel that had him jittery. That, or the idea of impending war. "Lenox knows we crash-landed his ship on the field at Highland High. He can go and get it any time."

Tai groaned. "Well, shit. I wish you hadn't reminded me of that. Hey, how long have we been in here?"

Argus shrugged. "Not sure. Maybe four or five hours. Why?"

"That means it's daylight in Palmdale. There'll be no missing the ship when school starts."

"Oh, ah, Lola and I sort of took care of that." Argus smiled at the thought of the ship disguised as a Homecoming float. "I was put on the float committee."

Tai stared at Argus. "What? What in the hell are you talking about?"

"Lola had this great idea to put Christmas lights and tissue paper all over the XTRA-A1 to make it look like a float. It looks pretty good. It was fun." His smile only lasted for a moment. "But that doesn't change the fact that Lenox or AURA can still get it."

"Unless I can get there somehow and fly it again." Tai raised an eyebrow. "Once Aunt Celeste deactivates the shield and overthrows Galena, we can shift to Palmdale and take the XTRA-A1 before Lenox gets to it. Easy."

"Easy? Nothing's been easy so far."

Jampara floated over to them. "Boys, we must prepare for attack."

"Excuse me?" Tai got in front of Argus. "What do you mean? What's going on?"

Jampara settled to the ground. "Tai, you can relax. I did not mean anyone was going to attack right now. As a Defender, you are driven to defend your brother from harm, but this could ultimately be your downfall. Argus, as a Protector, you will always seek to sacrifice yourself for your loved ones. While these qualities are admirable, you must learn to suppress them in battle."

Argus stepped out from behind Tai. "I don't understand. How can we suppress the way we feel? I've tried and I can't do it."

"Yeah, me either." Tai sighed loudly. "This whole thing sucks. Why are we just waiting around to be overrun by Galena and her herd of Invaders? We should go on the offensive."

Jampara's slit of a mouth turned up into a smile. "Tai, we *will* be on the offensive, but not yet. Boys, there are ways to overcome your feelings and emotions in a battle. You will do no one any good if you worry needlessly about one another."

"Needlessly?" Tai's eyes flashed blue. "Keeping my brother safe isn't a needless act, sir."

The smile faded from Jampara. "As I said, you both have admirable qualities. However, those qualities are detrimental in a battle situation." He held out the orb. "This weapon was designed to disrupt one unique gene sequence found in New Breeds. Argustine Lenox built it to target our New Breeds in an emergency situation. If the New Breeds became faulty, it would kill them instantaneously to prevent any suffering. I believe he planned to use the weapon to eradicate the planet of New Breeds and he wanted you two, and Aridesian, converted so you would not be affected. This would allow him to power his ship with your combined energy. But I am not certain anymore if that is his true intent or not. We must prepare for anything as we will be going up against Lenox *and* Galena, the two most powerful and merciless Invaders known to us. Any weakness on your part will be discovered and used against you."

Argus didn't understand how he could change his feelings and forget about protecting Tai, Lola, or anyone else he cared about. It was impossible. But Jampara was right about it being used against him. Lenox had already done that back at Lake Elizabeth, when Lenox realized how important Lola was and then attacked her. "Okay, sir, what do we do?"

Jampara cast the orb into the air, where it rose up near the ceiling and hovered. "While the orb was designed as a weapon, it contains Ramtalan energy that can be tapped and manipulated. We do not have long before Galena counteracts the shield I put around this room, so I will begin your training right now."

"What training?" Tai glanced at Argus. "You're going to use the energy in the orb for something?"

"You will train for war," Jampara said as he motioned to the orb. "Your suits contain a weak energy source within the metallic bands. The orb will conjoin with that energy to create a simulation program that I prepared a moment ago."

Argus now understood what Jampara was doing when he was in the corner of the room. "So you programmed the orb? Is it still a weapon?"

Jampara shook his head slowly. "Not in its current state. If it is infused with additional energy, it can again be weaponized. It is depleted somewhat now. Prepare for simulation."

"What does that mean?" Tai asked, looking over at Argus. "Do you get what he's—?"

In a flash, they were no longer in the court room, but standing on an ice-covered field. Argus looked around. The wind whipped around him and blowing ice stung his face. He shielded his eyes. They were surrounded by pure-forms, all with their arms extended, ready to fire photometric pulses.

"Arg! Where are we?" Tai shouted.

"No idea. What are we supposed to do? Are these guys real?" He crouched, pulled Tai down with him, and assessed the situation. There were ten pure-forms, Invaders obviously, in a circle around them, maybe twenty feet away. "Tai, shoot them with a pulse. I'll try to use a plasma burst."

"You got it." Tai raised his hands and fired one pulse after the other, but each one was deflected by the Invader he aimed at. "Shit! Is this a simulation or real?"

"That's what I want to know." Argus concentrated on collecting his energy into the pit of his stomach, and released it in one shock-wave burst. He knocked one Invader backward, but the rest of them began closing in. "We're screwed, Tai."

Jampara's voice echoed, "Try again, Argus, but release the burst in a wider array. Tai, once you fire at a target and the pulse is deflected, fire immediately at the same target before it can react again."

"Damn, Arg, this *is* a simulation. But how come I'm freaking freezing? What sort of simulation gives you frostbite?"

Tai's words played in Argus's head. "Oh, no. Tai, I just had a thought. If we can feel the temperature, maybe we can get hurt." He kept his eyes on the encroaching Invaders.

Jampara again, "Very good, Argus. While you are in a simulation, all things are simulated to represent reality. Do not allow the Invaders to hit you with a pulse."

"Great." Argus concentrated again and imagined his burst spreading out more than usual.

Three of the Invaders' palms glowed blue, which meant they were gearing up to fire a pulse. They were aiming at Tai and instinctively, Argus jumped up and put himself between them and Tai. Within a heartbeat, he was struck with a direct hit to his stomach. He flew backward, right into Tai.

"Bro!" Tai recovered and dragged Argus to the side.

Tai got to his feet, now blocking Argus from the Invaders.

There was a barrage of pulses fired at them both. Argus was struck at least four times, each one feeling like a punch to the gut. Tai wasn't doing any better.

"What sort of simulation is this?" Tai yelled. "Commander!"

There was a blue flash and they were back in the court room. Tai stomped over to Jampara, but Argus grabbed his arm and held him.

"Tai, stop. It's over." Argus let go of Tai. "What was that supposed to teach us, Commander? We didn't stand a chance."

Jampara floated backward a few feet. "Because you are still acting like a Protector, Argus. And you, Tai, are behaving like a Defender. You must learn to work as a team, not one out to save the other. You are outnumbered and only have limited abilities. Use what you have. Are you ready?"

"What? Again?" Tai groaned. "Don't you have body armor or something for us?"

There was no answer. Instead they were back on the ice and this time, there were twice as many Invaders. Argus already felt defeated. There was no way they could fight against so many pure-forms. Or could they?

"Tai, I've got an idea."

"Tell me, because I've got nothing."

"Okay, we stand back-to-back. I'll fire a burst and knock down as many Invaders as I can and turn so you can shoot them while they're on the ground, and while you're doing that, I'll shoot a burst at the next group. We'll keep firing and shooting until we knock them all down."

Tai nodded. "Sounds good to me."

They stood with their backs touching and when Argus released a plasma burst, he turned so Tai could fire his photometric pulses at the downed Invaders. It wasn't perfect, and they were shot at least six or seven times each, but after a few minutes, they had most of the Invaders down.

The remaining Invaders, however, anticipated what they were doing and flew up and over their heads. Argus tried to aim a burst upward, but it didn't work and the Invaders crashed down on top of them.

Again, they appeared back in the court room with Jampara. Argus lay on his side, trying to catch his breath.

Jampara smiled. "Good job, boys. I will give you a moment to recover and then we will return to the simulation."

Tai rolled his neck. "Oh, good. I was worried we wouldn't have another chance to get our asses kicked."

Argus sat up. "Yeah, Commander, could we maybe take a break? My stomach hurts and one of those guys cracked me over the head pretty good."

Instead of sympathy, Jampara's voice rose in volume, "You do not get a 'break'. This is war. Do you think the Invaders will take a break and drink a cup of coffee so you can rest? Continue."

The training went on, one simulation after the other, each session slightly different. Sometimes there were more Invaders, sometimes there was a different setting. One time it was the desert, another on a beach where they were trapped between the ocean and a platoon of rabid Invaders.

Argus did his best, but after a while, he was too exhausted to continue and simply put his hands up, shouted *I give up* and allowed the Invaders to hit him with multiple bursts. He returned to the court room, but Tai wasn't with him this time.

"Sir, where's my brother?" He looked around, but Tai definitely wasn't there. "Is he still playing? You left him there without me?"

Jampara's eyes were searing black. "This is an unexpected problem."

"What is? Where's Tai?"

There was a long pause as Jampara moved around the room, glowing blue. "Argus, your brother is lost in the simulation."

"What does that mean?" Argus went to Jampara. "What the hell does that mean?"

Jampara floated out of reach. He motioned to the orb and it descended into his hand. "Someone has intercepted the program. They have trapped Tai inside the simulation."

Chapter 2

Max Jackson, having ridden in a cramped van from the airport to some frozen wasteland in Labrador, couldn't stop shivering, even though he wore a down-filled parka, a woolen scarf over his mouth and nose, and stiff, puffy gloves that wouldn't let his fingers move. He stomped his feet, hoping to avoid frostbite. Neb, that mercurial alien who both threatened him and treated him nicely at times, stood with Celeste, the Dachel brothers' aunt, and a gathering of other Ramtalans, discussing something that apparently wasn't worthy of saying in front of an ex-AURA agent.

According to what Neb said before, Galena, another of the angry and hostile aliens, took over the Citadel, the alien headquarters on Earth, and had their Commander hostage. Nobody had seen a sign of Argustine Lenox, head honcho bad guy. That was the only good news Max had heard so far. After a few more minutes, he couldn't take the cold anymore and waved his arms around to catch Neb's attention. Neb noticed and came over.

"What is it, Max?" Neb's eyes were softly glowing blue. "We're sort of in the middle of something."

Max's teeth chattered. "I'm freezing to death."

"Yeah, sorry about that, but this is our staging area." Neb pointed to the group of aliens. "We've been deciding on our plan of attack."

"Don't care. Neb, why am I here? I can't do anything. Why can't I go home?" Max stomped his feet again. "I can't feel my toes. I think one's fallen off."

Neb placed his hand on Max's shoulder. "I've told you before, you know too much. I can't take the chance that you'll talk to your boss or anyone else. What's happening right now is critical and if any humans find out what's going on, it'll cause a global panic. We need to prevent that." He squeezed Max's shoulder. "I'll transfer a small amount of my energy into you. It'll warm you."

Max felt an instant warming sensation right where Neb's hand was. It spread throughout his body until he was as comfortable as if he was basking under the summertime sun. "Cool trick, Neb. So what am I supposed to do? Stand here with my thumb up my ass?"

"Actually, I have a little job for you that doesn't require your thumb. You and your friend, Gretchen Manheim, are going to be our lookouts. Can you do that?"

"Gretch? Where is she?" Max looked around. "I don't see her." He'd assumed Celeste had let her go.

Neb pointed behind Max. "She's waiting for you. Max, when I implanted her with a monitor, she fought the procedure. I warned her not to fight. And now, she hates the sight of me. That's why I need you to deal with her and keep her in check."

There was nothing in the direction Neb pointed except snow and ice. Where was Gretch and what did Neb do to her? Max took a step toward Neb and poked him in the chest. "You lobotomized her?"

Right away, Neb's eyes flashed and he had Max by the throat. "Don't ever make a hostile move toward me. Gretchen is fine. It just caused her some discomfort. It was not my intention to hurt her. I'm rather fond of her spunk. You'd better get going, because the energy I shared with you will wear off in a few minutes. Go." He let go of Max.

Max rubbed his throat. "You've really got an attitude problem. Go where? I don't see anything."

Neb extended his arm and made a beckoning movement. A moment later, a snowmobile, without a driver, came into view and stopped about ten feet from Neb. "Go to Gretchen."

"What?" Max went to the snowmobile. "Where is she?"

Neb came over and patted the seat. "Get on, follow the GPS and it'll take you to a cozy little cabin. Gretchen will give you instructions. She has her orders. Remember, Max, you've both been implanted and if you try anything, I'll know."

Max climbed onto the snowmobile. He'd never ridden on one before, but he'd managed to drive the Lamborghini, so how hard could it be? "Are we going to be safe from Lenox in this cabin of yours?"

"You'll be safe enough." Neb pointed to a bank of clouds closing in. "Better get moving, there's a storm coming."

That was an understatement. There was a shit-storm coming that involved crazed Invaders, bullying Ramtalans, and possibly the end of the world.

Max gripped the handlebars. "I'd really rather go home to Los Angeles."

"Not going to happen, Max. You have the throttle on the right and brake on the left. Good luck." Neb turned and strode back to his cohorts.

"I hate aliens." Max tested the throttle and took off a little too fast, but soon got the hang of it. He followed the directions the GPS display gave him and after a few minutes, just like Neb said, the warmth left and he was soon freezing cold. Now he officially loathed two climates; the miserable desert and the equally miserable tundra. What was wrong with the Ramtalans? They either liked it hot or cold, nothing in between.

The GPS led Max up a slope and back down into a small valley where there was a dinky wooden cabin with a trail of smoke rising from a chimney. The thought of a blazing fire made him accelerate, right to the front door. He shut off the snowmobile and knocked as best he could with the puffy gloves.

The old woman, Lucia, from the Acoma pueblo opened the door and stared at him. "Well, come in before all the heat goes out." She slammed the door shut as soon as he was inside.

"What the hell are you doing here?" Max looked around, but didn't see Gretchen. "And where's Gretch?"

Lucia pointed a bony finger at his parka. "Take that off. You don't need it in here. Your friend is in the bedroom, resting."

Max stripped off his gloves and unzipped his parka. "Do you have any coffee?"

"I'm not your maid, AURA man." Lucia wandered off to a small kitchen.

"Never mind then, I'll make it myself if you have a coffee pot." He went to the bedroom and opened the door a crack. "Gretch? You in here? It's Max Jackson."

The door opened wider and Gretchen peeked out. "Jackson? How did you get here?" She motioned him in. She was wearing a fluffy pink robe with matching slippers.

"Are you okay, Gretch? You look good."

"Yeah, well, I wasn't so good after that asshole stuck that alien shit inside my head. It gave me a raging migraine and I was puking for hours. I can't wait to get my hands on him. I can't believe I thought he was hot."

Max felt that pang of jealousy he did last time she said that about Neb. "He's a menace. Like all of them. Hey, why is that old lady here?"

Gretchen closed the door and sat on the bed. "I don't know. She's weird. Nice, but weird. Always talking about Neb like he's God's gift. So, ah, why are *you* here?" She raised an eyebrow. "I figured that Lenox character got you."

"Gee, Gretch, you don't sound too upset about that thought." Max sat next to her and ran his hand down the sleeve of her robe. "Where'd you get this? From Neb? You two have a thing now?"

She glared. "If I ever get my hands on that alien prick, he'll wish he'd never met me. It's not from him. Lucia has a whole closet full of clothes. I told you, she's nice."

"Okay, so what are we supposed to do? I don't even know where we are. Neb said you have orders. What does that mean?"

"Oh, that." Gretchen got up and went to a laptop on a small desk. "This is an outpost, directly on the path from the Labrador airport to the staging area. I wasn't expecting you to show up, but it makes more sense now that you did. Neb said I'd be working with another person. Guess that's you, eh, jackass?"

"Really, Gretch? After all we've been through, it's still jackass?" Max kicked off his boots and shrugged off the parka. "What exactly are we doing here, Gretch?"

She logged onto the laptop and pointed at the screen. "We're monitoring human activity, specifically AURA. See this, that's LA and this view is Edwards. Those freaking monitors in our heads are plugged into the Ramtalan monitoring system so we can control the views. Get it?"

"Not at all." Max sighed and looked over her shoulder. The laptop screen was a checkerboard of different views like she said. He recognized Edwards in the top left box, the Federal building in LA was on the top right. "How are we controlling any of this? Aren't these views from security cameras?"

Gretchen turned and stared at him. "Security cameras? We're dealing with aliens here, Jackson. Their technology and that freakish energy source of theirs allows them to zero in on whatever they want with their minds, or something like that. What we're programmed to monitor are these views on the screen. I don't know how the views are generated, and I don't really want to know. If we see any hostile deployment or movement, we report it. What don't you get about that?"

"Ah, well, how we can do that. We're not Ramtalan."

"No, we're not, but we have those damn implants that are hooked into our brains. Look, Jackson, I'm not pretending to understand it, but Neb gave me orders and I have to obey them. So, either get on board and help me or stay the hell out of my way." Gretchen opened the door and leaned out. "Lucia! I'm hungry!"

Max felt the back of his head. He had to find a way to get rid of the monitor so he could contact Stone, or Angel and John at Edwards. No way was he going to go along with being used as a security guard. He was a skilled AURA agent. He owed his allegiance to the United States government, not a bunch of renegade aliens. He'd wait until Gretchen and Lucia went to sleep, then he'd make a getaway on the snowmobile. Nobody was going to make a fool of Max Jackson.

Chapter 3

Argus paced around the court room, waiting for Commander Jampara to say something. Anything. Tai was missing and Jampara wasn't doing a single thing. Argus knew his eyes had flipped, and his temperature rose even though he was doing everything he could to maintain control. If he wasn't careful, he'd release a plasma burst.

Minutes ticked by. Finally, Jampara floated in front of Argus. "You must regulate your energies, Argus. Remember, your abilities are amplified at the Citadel."

"Yeah, well, that's a little hard right now. Is Tai okay? Is he alive? Can't you restart the simulation? Where is he? I thought we were still in the court room during the simulation."

"You were, but not on this plane. The simulation takes place within a higher plane projected by the orb's energy source. It is what you could call an alternate reality. Do you understand?"

Argus tried to comprehend what Jampara said, but it didn't make sense. He'd never learned anything about alternate realities, whatever those were. "No, I don't understand. At all. And you didn't answer me before. Is Tai all right?"

Jampara tossed the orb into the air where it floated and glowed. He stared at it for a moment and caught it when it descended. "The simulation program has been disabled."

"What does that mean? Where the hell is Tai? How can I get him back? You told us not to protect each other in the simulation and now look what's happened? Who's behind this? Galena?" Argus trembled all over. "Sir, I can't control my new ability. I think I'm going to fire a plasma burst."

"Do not! Not in here. If you jeopardize the shield I have on the room, we will be vulnerable. Focus. Suppress your anger."

He closed his eyes and took a few deep breaths, but it did nothing. He didn't want to calm down. Tai needed help. What Tai didn't need was a brother who did nothing. "No. I have to do something. I have to find my brother."

Just when he felt the plasma burst start, he felt faint. He couldn't breathe. It was like something had cut off his oxygen supply. He collapsed and tried to suck in a breath, but he couldn't. As fast as it had started, the sensation ended and he could breathe again. What the hell?

"Argus?" Jampara knelt beside him. "What is it?"

"I don't know. Wait, I've had this sort of thing before. Aunt Celeste calls it a physical premonition. But I never know who's being hurt. I couldn't breathe. It's Tai, it's got to be Tai. Does that mean Tai can't breathe? Please, we have to help him. I'll do anything. I don't care if Galena or Lenox win anymore. I'll give my life for Tai's." He jumped to his feet and shouted, "Lenox! If you can hear me, stop this. Tai's going to die. Take me and let him go."

The room lit up with a bright blue flash that came from Jampara. He grabbed Argus and threw him to the ground. "You will not call to Lenox. I do not know if he can hear you, but we cannot open a channel to him. You risk exposing all of the Settler Guardians and New Breeds to his venom."

Argus hit the ground so hard, the wind was knocked out of him. "I'm sorry, sir, but if Lenox or Galena did this to Tai, then they're the only ones who can undo it. I won't let my brother die." He struggled to his feet only to be slammed down again.

Jampara hovered over him. "I am the Commander of the Citadel and you must obey me. You are a child and you know nothing of strategy and war. I have experience in both and have lived through the Ramtalan-Malaris wars. Invoking Lenox will end in devastation. Remain where you are and it is me who takes care of negotiations."

Before he lost control completely, Argus squeezed his eyes shut and breathed in and out slowly over and over until he'd calmed down somewhat. How did Jampara expect him to do nothing at all?

Jampara kept his eyes on Argus, but motioned for the orb to come to him. He spoke to it, "Galena Helios, if you are the one responsible for capturing Tai Dachel, I order you to release him." He clutched the orb.

There was a loud bang on the door, followed by Galena's voice from outside the room. "Commander Jampara, you are no longer in control of the Citadel. Release the shield."

Argus got up. "Galena! Don't do this to Tai. Let him go."

Again, Jampara reached out and shoved Argus to the ground. "Mind your tongue, boy." He floated to the door. "Galena, you cannot win. If you allow either of the Dachel brothers to die, you will incur not only the wrath of Ramtala, but of Lenox."

Galena again, "I will kill Tai personally unless your remove the shield immediately."

"No!" Argus jumped to his feet, staying away from Jampara. "Galena! I'll do whatever you want me to, but let Tai go."

"Argus, your brother is dying. Remove the shield." Galena's voice was harsh, angry. "I need the orb."

"I can't do anything."

Jampara turned and faced him. "I ordered you to remain silent, yet you continue to disobey me."

"I don't care. I'm not going to let her kill my brother." Argus ran forward, grabbed the orb from Jampara and threw it as hard as he could against the far wall. It shattered into pieces, releasing colored sparks that shot out in every direction. Jampara attempted to catch the pieces, but they exploded and disappeared.

"What have you done, Argus?" Jampara zoomed toward the door. "You have killed us all."

Argus looked at Jampara. "Did that destroy the shield? Galena can save Tai. She saved him before and now she won't get the orb."

"You may think you have saved your brother, but you have surrendered Earth to Argustine Lenox." Jampara settled to the ground, his entire body glowing brighter and brighter. "I can no longer predict how this war will end."

What did that mean? Argus watched Jampara and had a sinking feeling that he'd made a huge mistake thinking Galena would do anything to help him or Tai. Once again, he'd acted like an impulsive Protector.

The door to the court room slid open and Galena, Ari, and about ten Ramtalans stormed in at the exact time there was a blinding flash and a shock wave that threw everyone off their feet. Galena was the first to recover, but Jampara was nowhere.

She screamed out in fury, "No!" She grabbed Argus by the front of his jumpsuit and pulled him to his feet, holding him off the ground a few inches. "All you've done is delay the inevitable." She dropped him and turned to Ari. "Jampara is gone."

Argus looked around. Did Jampara die in the bright flash? "What happened to the Commander? What did you to do him? And where's Tai?"

She glared at him. "Tai is suspended within the orb's energy source. Where's the orb?"

Argus's gut tightened. "I smashed the orb to break the energy shield so you could get in." *And to keep it away from you.*

Her eyes widened. "Didn't you think the orb was important? You knew the Commander used it for the simulation program. You're turning out to be as worthless as Ari. Can't my brother have just one intelligent son? Tai is now trapped in the simulation plane and the Commander has abandoned the Citadel." She slapped Argus across the face. "Without the orb, I can't retrieve Tai. My brother needs all three of you pathetic creatures."

What? What had he done? Argus felt sick. He sank to the ground. "I don't...why can't...I thought you—"

"Stupid, stupid child." Galena slapped him again. "Once you destroyed the orb, the energy field went with it and took your brother at the same time." She turned and motioned to the others in the room. "Secure the remainder of the Citadel. No mercy. If there is resistance, kill on sight."

"You can't do that, Galena." Argus ran and blocked the doorway. "You can't kill anyone."

"I can do as I please." Galena pointed to Ari. "Ari, take Argus to his room and if he gives you any trouble, do whatever is necessary, with the one exception of killing *him*. I have to find a way to free Tai." She strode from the room, followed by her cohorts.

Ari smirked and aimed his palm at Argus. "I'll fire on you if you give me any trouble. Remember, my pulses are lethal."

"Galena said not to kill me, Ari."

He shrugged. "Did she?"

Argus sized up the situation. He was trapped in the Citadel with Galena, Ari, and the other Invaders, and without the Commander or Tai. The only good thing was that he only had Ari guarding him. It was one-on-one.

"Move, Argus." Ari stepped into the hallway and waited for Argus to comply. "You know, you and your brother have caused me nothing but grief." He lowered his voice, "If you both die as a result of this war, I won't give it another thought."

Argus swallowed and walked slowly down the corridor toward the lobby. Was Ari planning on killing him and Tai? "Ari, listen, you told me that you never forgave Lenox for what he did to you and your mother. So why are you betraying your planet? To make Lenox happy? He doesn't care about you. He doesn't care about any of us. Help me get Tai out of the simulation before it's too late. We're your half-brothers. Doesn't that mean something to you?"

There was a pause. "Yes, it means something. It means I wasn't good enough, so Father created you."

Wrong thing to say. Now he knew Ari wasn't going to help, too bitter and consumed with anger to know what the right thing was. They got to the lobby and went down the corridor to the sleeping quarters.

At the apartment, Argus stopped and turned around. "Ari, please help me find Tai. I had a premonition that he's going to suffocate. I know you hate us both, but please, we share a father."

Ari waved a strip of gold and silver metal over the door panel and it opened. "The shield is still active on your apartment. You cannot leave." He stepped aside and motioned Argus to go in. "Just because we share a father doesn't mean a thing to me. If I could, I'd put you in the ground right now. And you know what else?"

Argus went into the apartment. "No, what?"

"I'm going to do everything I can to delay things so Tai *does* suffocate." Ari waved the metal over the panel and the door slid shut.

"Ari!" Argus banged his fists on the door until they hurt. This couldn't be happening.

Chapter 4

Max curled up on the floor of the bedroom because Gretchen made it perfectly clear he wasn't welcome in the bed. When he heard her breathing slow down and fall into the rhythm of sleep, he sneaked out of the room.

Unfortunately, Lucia was still awake and stoking the fire. She turned. "Why are you up? You should get some sleep."

"Can't sleep." He sat down on the fireplace hearth and warmed his hands. "So, if I may ask, what's the deal with you and Neb?"

Lucia sat down next to him. "Neb is a good man. You should listen to him."

"A good man? He's a damn alien who stuck a device in my head. How can I feel anything but hate for someone like that?" He glanced around. "Hey, where do you sleep?"

"I sleep where I make my bed."

Max stared at the old woman. What in the hell was she talking about? He needed her asleep so he could make a break for it. He forced a yawn. "Well, it's getting late. Why don't you sleep in the bedroom with Gretch? I'll stay out here."

She slowly shook her head. "Neb says you'll try to escape. You sleep in the room. There's no window in there for you to sneak out. Go now."

"I hate Neb and I'm starting to hate you, too." Max shuffled back to the bedroom.

Gretchen sat up in bed, rubbing the back of her head. "Jackson, I don't want to do what Neb said, but I have to. It's like he's controlling my brain. What the hell is this thing in my head?"

He shrugged. "I don't know, Gretch. But I don't have the same compulsion to help Neb or any of them. And I have no intention of doing what they want."

"Then why do I have to? It's pissing me off." She patted the mattress next to her. "You can lie down here if you want. But don't even think of trying anything."

Under any other circumstances, he probably would try to make a move, but this wasn't the time for that. He lay down and took her hand in his. "Gretch, we'll get through this. I haven't given up on our plan to capture these assholes. That Lenox character is going to try to take over our planet. And if he doesn't, Neb and his gang of freaks will. I don't know about you, but I'm not going to let that happen."

"Wish I could say the same, but I'm on Neb's side whether I want to be or not. I tried to stop him implanting me, I really did. He was upset and told me to stop fighting. Why did this happen to me, Jackson?"

"Because we're human and these Ramtalans treat humans like toys, to be used and mistreated at a whim. Well, I'm nobody's play thing. I'm going to fake it 'til I make it." He gave her hand a squeeze. He couldn't believe it, but he actually felt sorry for her. Pity usually wasn't his strongest emotion.

She squeezed his hand and lay down. "I'm glad I'm stuck here with you."

"Yeah, me too. How about we look at this with fresh eyes tomorrow?"

"Sure." She leaned over and rested her head on his shoulder. "Night, Jackson."

"Night."

He closed his eyes and thought about what he could do. A desperate thought flashed into his head. What if he got rid of Lucia and forced Gretchen to come with him? Even if she was being controlled by aliens, she was still Gretchen. He could knock her out and tie her up if necessary. Once he was back home, he'd find someone who could disable the monitors and then he'd mount an attack on Neb. In time, Earth would belong to the humans again and the Ramtalans would be strapped down, chopped up, and put on display. And it would be Max Jackson who'd collect the admission price for the exhibit. He smiled and drew in a relaxing breath. He'd sleep well tonight.

Chapter 5

Argus slumped against the apartment door. He'd screwed up everything. Now Ari wanted both him and Tai dead, Galena had the Citadel, and Jampara fled to who-knows-where. Not to mention that Tai was still stuck inside the simulation program and nobody seemed to know how to get him out. Argus looked across the room and saw how the hole he and Tai had made into Aunt Celeste's room was now patched up with a panel of the silver-gold metal. He was stuck, no chance of escaping through Aunt Celeste's room anymore.

He thumped his hand on the door. "Damn it! Why did I break the orb? I'm so sorry, Tai."

"Mr. Dachel."

Argus jumped up. "Who's there?"

"I have a message to convey." The robotic waiter came out from behind the kitchen counter and hovered.

"What message? Who from?" Argus waited as the lights on the robot flashed. "Come on, what message?"

"Commander Jampara stored a message for you. The Commander has initiated a destruct sequence throughout the Citadel that will disable the energy shield for a short time. He requested you utilize the time when the shield is down. Use your abilities to locate the Guardian faction on the mainland and go to them."

"What? Are you serious? I'm not leaving without Tai." Argus walked away from the robot. "Commander? Can you hear me?"

The robot floated over to him. "The Commander has left the Citadel to bring reinforcement troops. I repeat his request. You are to use your abilities—"

"I'm not leaving." Argus ran to the door and tried to open it, but of course, nothing happened. "Damn it!"

The robot flashed its lights. "Galena Helios has not removed the protective shield around your room, but it will fall once the Citadel shield is disabled. The countdown for the shield destruct sequence will begin...now. You will have four planetary seconds to escape the Citadel before the shield is reactivated. The countdown begins now. Ten, nine, eight, seven..."

Argus shook his head. How could he leave Tai? "I'm not going." He went to the breakfast bar and sat on a stool, resting his head in his hands.

"Six, five..."

Tai was probably already dead. What would be the point in dissolving? He didn't care what happened anymore.

"Four, three, two..."

Of course there was Lola to think about. And all of the New Breeds.

"One. Deactivation has commenced and will reactivate in four, three..."

Argus concentrated and saw the blurry image of Aunt Celeste dressed in a white parka.

"Two, one...shield is reactivated."

The image was gone. He'd been too slow. He slammed his hand on the counter. "I can't do anything right!"

"Argus," came a whisper.

Argus looked around. It sounded like Aunt Celeste, but he was still in the apartment. He hadn't dissolved to her. "Hello?"

"Shhh." Aunt Celeste appeared right next to him. She kept her voice low, "When the Commander said the shield would go down, I took a chance and shifted here. Neb is on the mainland with the other Guardians. Are you all right? Where's Tai?"

Tears welled up in his eyes. He wiped them away quickly. "It's all my fault."

"What's your fault?" She went to the door, listened and came right back. "What's going on, Argus?"

He couldn't hold it in any longer and let the tears fall as he explained what had happened. Aunt Celeste's eyes shone and when he finished, she nodded solemnly.

"What can I do, Aunt Celeste? Because of me, there's going to be a war and Tai might already be dead. I have to fix this." Argus took a breath. "I felt him suffocating."

"We'll find Tai. There was going to be a war anyway. It's not your fault. Lenox has been preparing to go to war for years. While you did compromise the Commander's safety, he managed to escape and deactivate the shield. I would have preferred that you complied with the Commander's request to escape yourself, but that's a moot point now. As much as I don't like the idea, I have to ask for your help in finding Tai."

"Anything." Argus got off the stool. "Tell me what you want me to do."

She gave him a pat on the shoulder. "Since you're now more Ramtalan, we can merge our energies."

"What does that mean?"

Aunt Celeste ran her fingers over the metal bands on the sleeve of his jumpsuit. "You have to change out of the suit. These bands block your full potential."

"Full potential?" Argus looked at the suit. "Tai said this helps us control our abilities. What'll happen if I take it off now that I'm converted? And what do you mean by merging our energies?"

"Your abilities will be magnified once the suit is removed. That's why you have to take it off. It's restricting you. We can merge our energy sources and with the collective energy in the Citadel, the merger will be even more powerful. The only problem is..." she paused. "It'll drain my energy very quickly. Yours is still somewhat locked up in your human body."

Argus shook his head. "Whoa, hold on. You said Ramtalans...die when their energy is used up."

"Correct. But I have no intention of using up all of my energy." She smiled. "I have a job to do and almost a hundred Guardians under my command."

"Under your command? I don't understand?" Without any warning, Argus felt like he was choking. He couldn't breathe at all.

"What's wrong?" Aunt Celeste took him by the shoulders and shook him several times. "Is this another premonition?"

He nodded. After a few seconds, he drew in a breath. "Does that mean Tai's still alive?"

"I would think so. We have to get him out. There's no time to waste."

Argus agreed completely, but how could they find him? "We don't have the orb."

Aunt Celeste thought for a moment. "The Commander used the kitchen helper to communicate with you and activate the shield destruction." She pointed to the robotic waiter. "It's an artificial intelligence device infused with Alpha 2a energy. We can try to use it."

"Okay." He crouched near the robot, not sure exactly what Aunt Celeste was talking about, and looked up at her. "Aunt Celeste, are you in charge of the other Guardians?"

"We'll talk about that later. Right now, I have to find a way to merge our energy with the kitchen helper's. Then I'll have to create a simulation program similar to the Commander's. With any luck, both simulation programs will merge into one and I can recall Tai."

Argus groaned. "I don't understand a single thing you're talking about."

"Yes, you do. I taught you about computers and artificial intelligence. Now, go and change out of that suit."

He put his hands on the robot. "You wait right here. We need you. Don't you dare leave." He ran up to the loft, slipped off the jumpsuit, and put his jeans and tee shirt back on.

"Are you ready?" Aunt Celeste called from downstairs.

"I guess. Wow, my energy's buzzing." He hurried down the stairs. "If this doesn't work—"

"Positive thoughts." Aunt Celeste motioned to the couch in the sunken living room. "Sit on the couch. This might hurt a bit."

"Like when I first did the molecular shift?" It didn't hurt anymore to do a shift, but at first, it felt like his body was tearing apart. He sure wasn't looking forward to that sort of pain again, but he'd willingly do anything to get Tai back. He sat on the couch.

Aunt Celeste sat next to him. "I'm not sure what pain you felt, but this could be the same, or worse."

Great. "Okay, I'm ready."

She held her hand out, palm up. After a moment, her blue energy ball rose up from her palm. "My Alpha 2a energy, that's the Ramtalan energy source, will pass into you and comingle with your Alpha 2a. I will then recall it. We will both have half of each other's Alpha 2a. Once we have shared energy, we will both combine with the kitchen helper's. Are you ready?"

He really wasn't, but he nodded and closed his eyes. Within a heartbeat, his body felt like it was on fire. The burning was so intense that he screamed out. Next came the sensation that his insides were being twisted in knots, tighter and tighter. Would it ever stop? "Aunt Celeste!"

"Almost done. Hold on."

He couldn't take it anymore. "I can't..." He opened his eyes and saw red. Everything was red. He felt Aunt Celeste's hand on his shoulder.

"It's over, Argus. Breathe slowly." She got off the couch. "Are you all right? I've never seen...how do you feel?"

He drew in a couple of deep breaths. The pain was gone, although he felt like a bolt of electricity had gone through him and left him tingling all over. The redness faded until he saw normally again. "I think I'm okay. That was the most awful thing I've ever been through."

"I'm very sorry. I wasn't sure what it would feel like. This procedure has only been done twice before and that was between two pure-forms."

He jumped up, feeling incredibly angry. "So you weren't sure if it would kill me or not?"

She stared at him and backed away. "Calm down, Argus. I would have recalled my Alpha 2a if it became dangerous to you. Are you sure you're feeling all right?" She hadn't taken her eyes off him. "Do you feel different?"

"Actually, I feel pretty good now. Just kind of agitated. Why?"

"Please don't be alarmed, but your eyes are glowing red."

Red? Not black? No. That couldn't be right. Lenox had red eyes. Argus knew his energy was building inside, ready for a plasma burst. "How could that happen? Is it another physical premonition?"

"No," was all Aunt Celeste said.

He ran to the bathroom and looked in the mirror. Just like she said, his eyes were bright and blood red. It was like looking at Lenox in the mirror. And that was the last thing he wanted to see.

Chapter 6

Max woke up with a start. There was a strange noise, like humming or droning. What the hell was it? He sat up. Gretchen still slept beside him. Stealthily, he crept from the bed and peeked into the living room.

"Jackson," Gretchen said from behind him.

He spun around. "You startled me. Don't ever sneak up on me like that."

"We're on." She dashed to the laptop.

"What the hell does that mean?" He watched her as she logged on. "Gretch? What's going on?"

"We've got company." She pressed a button on the side of the computer and spoke, "This is Gretchen Manheim. I've detected movement heading to our location."

Neb's face appeared on the screen. "Good work, Gretchen. I will arrive at your location shortly with a small battalion. Give Lucia advance warning of my arrival. She'll know what to do. Max?"

"Yeah, what?" Max moved closer to Gretchen.

Neb gave a brief smile. "Ah, there you are, Max. AURA has found you. Do you have a tracking device on your person? I didn't detect anything on the plane ride here, but if you hid a device from me, it won't work out so good for you."

Max checked his pockets. There wasn't anything there. "I don't have anything on me. Don't blame me for your slip-up."

Neb's eyes flashed. "There is no slip-up, Max."

The computer monitor went blank. Gretchen got up and went into the living room. "Lucia! Neb's coming."

Max followed and was amazed when Lucia opened up a crate and lifted out a box full of dynamite. She placed it on the old couch, dusted her hands off on her apron and sighed. She pointed at Max. "You brought AURA here?"

"No. No, it wasn't me. I didn't do anything. So, ah, what's that for?" He went to the dynamite. "Is it safe to have it in here?"

She shrugged. "Neb says it's safe, so it's safe."

He backed away from the box. "Well, does it have to be in the house?"

Neb appeared next to Lucia. "Yes. Gretchen, how far away are the intruders?"

She held up four fingers. "Four miles."

"We're cutting it close." Neb glanced at Max. "Go and wait on the snowmobile with Gretchen. Lucia, bring me the detonators."

"Hold on, Neb." Max took another step backward. "You're going to blow up the cabin? What's that going to do?"

Neb picked up a stick of dynamite. "It's a distraction. It'll give us time to assess the situation and move in on the targets. Is that all right with you?"

Max shook his head. "Not really. What am I supposed to do?" Of course, if Neb was off fighting AURA, there was a chance to make a getaway with Gretchen on the snowmobile. Maybe there was some hope of escaping after all.

Lucia came up to Neb and grabbed the dynamite out of his hand. "You don't touch it, Neb. It's delicate. Can't have you getting hurt."

Neb smiled at her. "I'm a pure-form, Lucia. I can't be hurt by dynamite. You know that."

She frowned. "I don't care. You don't touch it. Now, go to your friends and I will set the detonators."

Damn, for a small, frail woman, Lucia was plucky as hell. Max went to Gretchen. "Come on, Gretch, get your coat."

Gretchen hesitated. "Neb?"

Neb turned to Gretchen and put his hand on her forehead. "Pack up the equipment and go with Max. Follow the GPS to Location 2 and wait for instructions."

Max waited as she blinked a few times and nodded, went into the bedroom and came out a few minutes later with a duffle bag. She handed Max the bag and his parka, slipped on her coat and went outside.

The bag was heavy, heavier than if it was only the laptop. Max glared at Neb. "This is bullshit. You've got Gretch trained like a circus animal. You can't do that to us. Humans belong here, not you aliens."

Neb got in his face. "This is a shared planet, Max. Get used to it. We're not going anywhere. I'm here to protect the human race from Lenox and his band of Invaders, in case you haven't noticed. Don't test me. You'll lose."

"Threatening me, Neb? I'm a government agent. You can't push me around like you do with Gretch." Max threw his shoulders back. He wasn't going to let anyone treat him like crap.

In a flash, Neb had him by the front of his shirt. "It amazes me how ungrateful you are, human. If not for me and my fellow Settlers, you humans would have ended up enslaved by the likes of Lenox years ago. We've protected this planet from invasion several times because we need it safe for our New Breeds. Now, go with Gretchen before I lose my temper."

Max pulled away from Neb. "So this is you under control? You don't need me. You've got your trained Gretchen-monkey. Take the monitor out of my head and I'll be on my way."

"The monitor stays. And you stay. Ramtala is a friend of Earth, Max. Get on board." Neb opened the front door and shoved him out into the cold. "Put your coat on. Oh, and Max, don't cross me." He slammed the door shut.

There was a flurry of snow in the air and wispy flakes swirled around. Max slipped into the parka and found Gretchen already seated on the snowmobile, waiting. Wherever they were going, one thing was certain, he'd find a way to get word to AURA. The aliens had to be overthrown, even if it meant siding with Stone to get the job done.

Chapter 7

Argus stared at his reflection. It wasn't him in the mirror, not anymore. He rubbed his eyes, but they stayed red. He tried everything; regulating his heart rate, calming down, breathing in and out slowly. Nothing worked.

"Aunt Celeste!"

She came up behind him. "It's all right. I'm here. There's got to be an explanation, but we don't have the luxury right now to figure it out. We have to find Tai."

He felt sick to his stomach. It was bad enough knowing he was related to Lenox without having to look like him now. What would Tai think? He'd be repulsed. "Tell me whatever you need me to do to find Tai. I don't care anymore what it does to me. Look at me. I'm a freak. *More* of a freak."

"Don't talk like that." Aunt Celeste put her hand on his shoulder. "Come back to the living room. We'll create a triad of Alpha 2a energy sources; yours, mine and the kitchen helper's. Maybe your eyes will revert back after some time."

Argus took a final look in the mirror and turned away. "Is this going to hurt, too?"

"Not at all. But you will experience an influx of thoughts and memories from everyone in the triad. It will be confusing. Try not to break the connection though. I'll take care of creating another simulation program. You can do this."

He wasn't so sure, but he followed her back to the living room and sat on the couch again. He didn't feel nervous, but he had so much energy running through him, he could hardly sit still. Aunt Celeste called to the kitchen helper robot and ordered it to stay in front of the couch. She held Argus's hand and placed her other hand on top of the robot.

Nothing seemed to happen for a long time, until the entire apartment filled with blue light. A few seconds later, he stood in the desert. The sun beat down on him and a strong, hot wind blew. Aunt Celeste was nowhere.

"Hello?" he shouted. "Anybody here?"

"Argus?"

"Who's there?" Argus wandered around as sand flew in his face. "Talk to me."

"How are you in my mind, son?"

What? Now he recognized the voice. It was Lenox! "I don't understand. I'm looking for Tai."

"Tai is with me, son. Have you come to join us?"

Argus peered into the distance. There was something out there, a structure of some sort. He took off in a full run and got to the building in a few seconds. It wasn't really a building, but more like four brick walls, not quite connected. There was a miniature version of the XTRA-A1 at the base of one of the walls and a tombstone near one of the other walls. He went to it and read the inscription: Here Beneath Lies Gaia Dachel, Beloved Mother and Wife, Rest in Peace.

What the hell? That was his mother's name. Argus stumbled backward. "What are you playing at, Lenox?"

There was silence. Then, "You are in my memories, Argus. But that is not all. This is intriguing. You have tapped into my Alpha 2a via...are you at the Citadel?"

"I don't know where the hell I am. Where's Tai. Show me my brother."

"Arg?" Tai suddenly appeared next to him, on all fours, straining to breathe. "Get me out of here, bro."

Argus dropped to his knees. "I'm going to try to shift us back to the Citadel."

"Arg, I'm still in the simulation. I can't find a way out. Why did you leave me here?"

"I didn't. Galena did something and trapped you. Come on, take my hand." Argus reached out, but Tai vanished. "No!" He jumped to his feet. "Lenox!"

"Argus." Lenox, in the form of the apparition, walked toward him. "This is imaginary. None of this is real. Tai is with me. He is safe. You must break away from Celeste. Allow your Alpha 2a energy to return to you. Concentrate on Galena. You can go to her if you break free. She will bring you to Tai. Do it now."

Argus shook his head. "I can't. Isn't Tai stuck in the simulation? He just said he was."

"No, son. That was part of your memory." Lenox stopped and spread his arms. "Argus, you and Tai belong together, with me. We are a family. You know that." He took a step closer and wrapped his arms around Argus in a hug.

A flood of emotion surged through Argus. He could feel Lenox's arms around him. "Dad, what do I do?" He hugged Lenox back and felt like a lost child who'd finally found his home.

"Say the word, my son, and I will help you break free from Celeste."

Should he? If he went with Lenox, what would happen to Tai? Lenox said he wasn't in the simulation, but could that be true? Aunt Celeste said not to break the triad, and she said there would be memories and thoughts that he'd see. Could Lenox's appearance be one of those? Maybe he wasn't really there at all.

Lenox loosened the hug. "My son, your brother is waiting."

"I can't." Argus pulled away. "You're not real. None of this is real. That brick structure, that's part of my memory of your lab. And Mom's tombstone...you killed her, didn't you?"

The image of Lenox wavered. "Gaia served her purpose. If you will not willingly break free from Celeste, I will force you to."

Argus shook his head. "You don't frighten me and you can't make me do anything I don't want to do. I'm in control here, Lenox. You can't have my energy. Release Tai. Now."

Lenox's eyes burned red. "Your brother's death will be your responsibility." He faded away into the desert landscape.

"Wait! Come back!" Argus collapsed. The wind roared in his ears and the stinging sand bit into his skin. It sounded like whistling, no, a voice, coaxing him to get up. He struggled to his feet and was instantly standing in the living room in his Citadel apartment. He fell to his knees with an overwhelming sense of loss, both for Tai and for his mother.

"Argus! Breathe." Aunt Celeste shook him gently. "Breathe."

He drew in a deep breath. "Lenox said Tai's going to die." He wiped his brow.

"Bro, I'm here," Tai whispered.

"What?" Argus looked around and saw Tai standing next to Aunt Celeste. "How?" He stood on shaky legs.

Aunt Celeste supported him. "What did you experience? You saw Lenox?"

Argus nodded and gave Tai a shaky fist-bump. "Yeah. Lenox was there and said I was in his mind. He told me to break the energy triad and concentrate on Galena. Tai, you have no idea what a relief it is to see you. I thought—"

Tai rolled his eyes. "Well, it was no picnic being in that freaky wasteland. I could hardly breathe and I couldn't use my abilities. I was wandering around in this dark space. Then I heard Aunt Celeste tell me to find our house. It was dark, but I found a light in the distance and when I got to it, it was the house. I opened the front door and bam! Here I am."

Argus fell onto the couch, exhausted. "I saw Mom's grave."

"You did? What else...?" Tai paused and sat next to him. "Bro, Aunt Celeste told me about, ah..." He pointed at Argus's eyes. "It doesn't mean anything. I know you probably think it does, but it doesn't. You can get some cool contacts to cover them up."

"You mean my eyes are still red?" Argus ran to the bathroom again. "Aren't they going to change back?"

Aunt Celeste called from the living room, "I told you I'll investigate when there's time. We still have a lot of work to do. Like locate Galena. Argus, tell me exactly what Lenox said."

Argus turned away from the mirror. Red eyes didn't mean a damn thing. He wasn't like Lenox. He couldn't be. He took a last look in the mirror. The reflection was Argus Dachel, not Argustine Lenox. But still, everyone on Earth would blame the two Dachel brothers for whatever Lenox did because they were his sons. So much for being the popular football heroes at school. There'd be no more cheering crowds in the bleachers shouting *Dachel, Dachel, Dachel.*

Lenox didn't care about anyone but himself. That hug meant nothing. Argus peeked out of the bathroom. Tai sat at the breakfast bar and Aunt Celeste paced. There was only one thing to do.

He drew in a deep breath. "Aunt Celeste, in the simulation, Lenox told me to concentrate on Galena. He said if I broke away from you, I'd be able to go to Galena. Why don't I try to use my ability to find her now? Maybe Lenox knew that with our energies comingled, I'm stronger and can get through the shield around the room. He got into my mind in the simulation, so maybe the shield isn't as strong as we think."

"Whoa, bro. Hold up. That comingling thing is what changed your eyes." Tai slid off the stool. "You can't use your abilities until Aunt Celeste figures out what happened."

Aunt Celeste came toward him, shaking her head. "Tai's right. If anyone attempts to break through the shield, it'll be me."

Argus held up his hand to keep them quiet. He didn't want to hear any more. If he didn't try, he'll be riddled with guilt his whole life. "We really don't have time to stand around arguing. You didn't see what Lenox did back at the lake, Aunt Celeste. He killed a boy and hurt other kids. I saw it. That's *my* father who's doing this and now everybody knows it. I have to fix it before he hurts anyone else."

"Damn it, Arg, he's my father, too. I'm responsible as well. Those red eyes of yours are making you talk crazy. Sit down and we'll figure something out." Tai motioned to a stool. "Whatever we do, we'll do it together. Remember our pact, victory or death?"

Aunt Celeste's eyes flashed. "What?"

Argus sighed. "It's okay, Aunt Celeste. How can I ever be among humans again? Look at me. I'm Lenox." Argus felt a build-up of energy coursing through him and he couldn't control the overwhelming need to protect Tai and all of humanity. The memories of Lola getting hit with a pulse from Lenox and Todd flying through the air, dead, were burned into his brain. Enough was enough. He ducked into the bathroom, locked the door and concentrated on Galena.

He had to work hard at ignoring Tai banging on the door, but once he blocked out the noise, the image of Galena formed. He was behind her. She sat with Ari in front of a bank of computers, both of them dressed in Citadel jumpsuits. Galena held the Wand of Ramtala in one hand and moved something with the other.

Argus changed his view point so he could see what she was doing. She used a touchpad to move triangular symbols around on one computer screen. Another screen was full of names and addresses. As he looked closer, he saw how the objects were being positioned on a map of the world. He knew right away what she was doing. The objects were Invaders. Galena was going to send Invaders to wherever the New Breeds were. But the Guardians had shields around the houses, which meant Lenox would need his XTRA-A1 ship to disable the shields.

Ari suddenly turned around. "Galena."

She nodded. "I sense it, too. Strong energy. Argustine? Is that you? Are you here?" She looked around.

Argus held his breath. He'd actually dissolved and was invisible. They knew he was there. He had to act fast. He reached out and grabbed the wand, wrestled it from Galena's grasp and concentrated on the apartment. It wasn't easy to shift because the wand seemed to anchor him, preventing him from leaving the room. But after a struggle, the shift began and he appeared back in the bathroom of the apartment. The door had been broken in and Tai stood in the doorway.

Tai stared. "Bro, you've got the wand."

"I know." Argus smiled and pushed past Tai. "Aunt Celeste, let's win this war before it starts!"

Chapter 8

Left with no choice, Max climbed on the snowmobile behind Gretchen and put the duffle bag on his lap. She didn't say a word, just started the engine and took off. There wasn't much to look at since the landscape was blanketed in white, with the occasional pine tree breaking up the monotony. It smelled like Christmas because a faint pine smell seemed to follow them. Freezing snow was worse than the blazing desert in Palmdale, and Max was miserable.

"Gretch, where are we going?" he shouted above the engine noise.

Silence.

"Gretch? Can you hear me? You ignoring me? Did Neb zap your brain?" Max bounced in the seat when she went over a bump.

"Shut up, Jackson."

"So you did hear me. Come on, Gretch, talk to me." He tapped her on the shoulder. "Talk to me or I'll toss this duffle bag into the next snow drift."

She slowed the snowmobile and turned her head. "I don't know where we're going. Neb controls me and he puts these thoughts in my head. It's like it's not me who knows what's going on, but some other part of me that doesn't tell me anything. I don't know how to explain it." She turned around and opened the throttle again.

What did that mean? She'd been taken over by the aliens? If so, then she'd have to go as well. All of the alien scum and any remnants of them had to go. "Well, wherever we're going, I'm about to turn into a popsicle."

She turned the snowmobile into a forested area and drove alongside a half-frozen river. "We're almost there."

"Almost where? I don't see a damn thing."

She didn't reply this time, but kept driving right in between two columns of trees. The space between them was so narrow that they clipped a few branches on one side, one smacking Max on the thigh. Just when the trees closed in even more, she stopped, shut down the snowmobile, and hopped off.

"Follow me, Jackson," she called, waving him forward.

Max climbed off with the duffle bag and looked around. Nothing but snow and trees. "Ah, sure. This looks like a lovely spot for a picnic."

He followed her into the woods and shuffled through the soft snow banks that had collected at the base of the tree trunks. Hopefully she knew where she was going because much longer in the freezing weather and he'd lose his toes for sure.

"We're here, Jackson." Gretchen stopped.

Max looked past her. There was a clearing and the outline of a domed structure the same color as the snow. It was pretty darn big, maybe thirty or forty feet around and ten or fifteen feet tall. "Gretch, what is this place?"

She shrugged. "Don't know for sure. I think it's an offsite stronghold."

"It's a freaking igloo." Max shuffled after her.

Gretchen looked at him and shook her head. "Not an igloo made of ice, Jackson. And there's someone waiting in there for us."

"You mean Neb. I hate that guy on a molecular level."

"No, not Neb." She walked around the dome and placed her hand on a gold and silver panel about five feet off the ground.

Max touched the structure. Like Gretchen said, it wasn't made of ice, it was metal. "Gretch?"

"Here we go, Jackson."

Go? Where? "What are you...?" Before he could say anything more, a weird sensation washed over him, like he was plunged underwater and couldn't breathe.

When he could breathe again, he wasn't standing in the forest, but inside the domed structure. It was quite warm, with strange machinery embedded in the rounded walls. Not computers, at least not like any computers he'd ever seen, but metallic panels like on the outside of the dome, with wavering lights flickering over the surfaces. The structure was partitioned into several rooms at one end and Gretchen stood in front of one of the rooms.

He got a bit closer, but backed away when the dome took on a blue glow. If there was a way out, he'd hit the road in the blink of an eye, with or without Gretchen. Was this another nest of aliens? He was about to chew out Gretchen for dragging him to yet another creepy Ramtalan fortress, but didn't have the chance. One of the aliens, a weird blue ghostly-looking thing with black eyes appeared in front of Gretchen.

"I wasn't expecting you, Mr. Jackson."

Max knew the voice right away. It was Jampara. The Ramtalan commander. "Yeah, well, I wasn't expecting to be here either. Exactly where am I?" He dropped the duffle bag.

Jampara floated a couple inches off the ground. "Think of this as a secured storage facility."

"Sure. What's stored here?" Max went to Gretchen and tapped her on the shoulder. "Gretch? You okay?"

Jampara answered, "She is in stasis until I need her. Mr. Jackson, while Ramtala is not in the habit of using humans, in this instance, we require it. You and Ms. Manheim have a specific purpose. As humans, you cannot be detected. Therefore, you will be our delivery service."

"I'm nobody's delivery service, you blue moron. Let me go."

"I cannot do that, Mr. Jackson. Not right away. You will be released from service once you have made the delivery." Jampara floated to the other room, vanished and reappeared with a gold box in his hands. "This is what you must deliver."

Max eyed the box. It was about the size of a shoebox. Was it solid gold? How much would that be worth? Thousands, maybe millions. "What's in the box?"

"That is not your concern. You must take the box to Nebulon."

"Really? I was just there. Why didn't he come here and get it himself? Better yet, why don't you do that disappearing act and go to him yourself?" Max shook his head. "I'm a government agent, you can't force me to do anything."

Jampara's eyes flashed bright blue. "I can do anything I desire. With the wave of my hand, I can destroy you and no one would even know you were here. Do you wish to try my patience further?" He held the box in one hand and extended his other hand toward Max. "Say the word, Mr. Jackson."

Shit. Max hoped Jampara couldn't hear his thumping heart. "Ah, no, I'll take your package all the way through the damn freezing snow back to Neb. But you have to let Gretch come with me."

"No. She stays here with me now. I have another job for her. Take this, do not lose it. Do not get caught by AURA. They are close by, coming by snow vehicles and helicopters, and have far more powerful OEEDs now. Should I leave this bunker, I will be detected by them and by the Invaders. Remember, Mr. Jackson, you still have the monitor attached to your brain. Only I can remove it safely, so it is in your best interest to obey my orders. You diverge from my directive to deliver the box and I will set your internal monitor to destruct. Do you understand?"

Max nodded. "Yeah, I understand. You're a prick and you made us come here so you could keep Gretchen. Give me the box." He reached out and grabbed it from Jampara. "Hey, what's in the duffle bag? I think you owe me an answer, considering you just threatened my life."

Jampara picked up the duffle bag. "A communication system. Now, go. Reverse the GPS and it will guide you back to Nebulon."

"Whatever. Say, how do I get out...?" He was outside again before he got the rest of the sentence out. "I hate aliens." He climbed onto the snowmobile, cradled the box on his lap, pushed a button on the GPS that said *reverse* and started the engine. Not only did he now want the Dachel brothers and Neb on a slab, but Jampara as well. His alien autopsy list was getting longer and longer.

Chapter 9

Argus held the wand tightly, not wanting to let it go. Galena was sure to come looking for him. "Aunt Celeste, what exactly does this thing do?"

Aunt Celeste's eyes were smoldering blue. "How did you take the wand? A converted New Breed wouldn't have the energy required to possess it and our comingled energy should have faded by now. This makes no sense."

"Well, I do have it, so what does it do? Is it a weapon like the other orb or a time-controlling device like Tai said?" Argus touched the orb on the top of the wand. It pulsated and made his fingers tingle. It wasn't actually solid like the other orb, but more like a ball of electricity. "What is this thing?"

Aunt Celeste held out her hand. "Give me the wand, Argus."

He didn't want to. "Maybe I should keep it."

She shook her head. "No. You shouldn't have it. In fact, you should never have had it. Just give it to me and...go sit down with your brother."

Argus wanted to do as she said, but he also felt like he should have the wand, that it was a part of him. "I think I have to..." His heartrate got faster and he felt hot, sweaty.

Tai came over. "Bro, come on, what are you doing? Give her the wand. Um, your eyes are...weirder than they were before. Red with silver...sparks. Aunt Celeste."

"Argus, focus on my voice." Aunt Celeste put her hands on Argus's shoulders. "Let go of the wand. Now."

Argus closed his eyes and concentrated on what she was saying. Why did he feel so strange? What was happening? "Here." He handed the wand to Aunt Celeste and the second she took it, he felt normal again. "That wand did something to me."

Aunt Celeste held the wand behind her back. "Yes, I'm sure it did. Sit down so I can check you over. Tai, take him to the couch."

"Come on, Arg." Tai pulled on his sleeve. "Your eyes are back to solid red. They had these silvery sparks through them, from the pupil to the outer edges. What the hell was that?"

Argus sat down and leaned back against the cushions. "I have no idea. It was like I belonged with the wand. Aunt Celeste, can you explain?"

She came over, without the wand, and knelt in front of him. "One moment." She put one hand on his forehead and one on his chest. "Your energy levels are a bit high, but still within the normal range for a converted New Breed. It's impossible that you could hold the wand."

"Why?" Tai paced. "Is he okay? Did that thing do something to him?"

"I feel fine." Argus sat up when Aunt Celeste removed her hands. "There's nothing wrong with me."

Tai continued pacing. "Well, something made your eyes all whacked out."

Aunt Celeste stood and ran her fingers through her ponytail. "The orb on the wand isn't like the orb weapon. The Wand of Ramtala contains a purified energy particle. It's almost pure Alpha 2a energy. Only a pure-form can come in contact with the wand since the energy sources are compatible. You, Argus, don't have a compatible Alpha 2a source. The wand should have killed you."

"What?" Argus jumped up.

Tai looked Argus up and down. "Whoa, Aunt Celeste, what are you saying? That somehow Arg has a compatible energy source now? Other than those disturbing red eyes, you look the same to me, bro."

"Thanks, Tai. That makes me feel a whole lot better. You know, Galena thought it was Lenox in the room with her. Is that because my energy's changed?"

Aunt Celeste pointed to Tai. "Go and wait upstairs in the loft. I need to perform a test on Argus."

"The hell you do!" Tai shouted. "That's my brother and you're not doing anything to him."

"Control your Defender impulses," Aunt Celeste said sternly. "Go upstairs. You can't be close, just in case something...goes wrong."

Argus took a step backward. "What?" He sure didn't want any tests that might "go wrong". "Why don't we think about this first, Aunt Celeste? I feel fine now. I got a little crazy about the wand, that's all."

Aunt Celeste motioned for Tai to go upstairs. "To the loft, now."

"Okay, but I'll be watching. If anything happens to Arg, I'm coming back down." Tai charged up the stairs and peered down over the railing. "You going to be okay, bro?"

Argus nodded. "I hope so."

"Argus," Aunt Celeste was near the kitchen and had the wand again, but held it away. "Have a seat on the stool and be still."

He complied and sat, but he couldn't stop trembling. His energy level was high, maybe too high. He waited while Aunt Celeste slowly brought the wand closer, an inch at a time. When it was about a foot in front of him, the orb sparked inside and he reached for it. Aunt Celeste moved it away before he could touch it.

"Argus, tell me exactly what you feel." She brought the wand close again.

The wand was right there in front of him. "I want the wand. It's like it belongs to me, or maybe I belong to *it*. Can I just touch it? I need to have it." He reached for it again, but Aunt Celeste pulled the wand away. "I need it."

She shook her head. "No, you can't have it. Concentrate on the loft and do a shift."

"Okay." He closed his eyes and imagined the loft, but the image wouldn't form in his mind. He focused harder and heard Tai scream out. He opened his eyes. "What happened?" He was still sitting on the stool, but Tai was next to him.

Tai slapped him on the arm. "Damn it, bro, you shifted me! That hurt."

"I did? How?" Argus looked at Aunt Celeste.

She blew out a puff of air. "That's incredible. Something must have happened when we comingled our energies. It seems like you've developed a very powerful ability to transport people to you. And I think you've connected somehow to the Alpha 2a energy in the orb. Almost like your body is craving more energy."

"Wait." Tai glared at Aunt Celeste. "You said the orb is pure Alpha whatever. Isn't that dangerous to Arg?"

Argus sort of understood what Aunt Celeste meant because he did feel like he needed the wand. It was a craving. "I don't think it's dangerous, Tai. So what does it mean, Aunt Celeste? *Is* the orb's energy going to hurt me?"

She shrugged. "I don't know what's going to happen just yet. I have to discuss this with Neb. He knows more about the effects of Alpha 2a on New Breeds than I do."

Tai slammed his hand on the counter. "Neb's not here."

"I told you to calm down, Tai. I'm well aware that Neb's not here. We don't have much time before Galena comes here to investigate the missing orb. We have to gain control of the Citadel so we can get to Neb. Unless..."

Argus had a feeling he knew what she was thinking. "Unless what?"

She held the wand behind her back again. "You've broken through the shield before, Argus. Let's see if you can do it again. But this time, concentrate on Neb. If this ability of yours is strong enough, it might allow you to transport Neb through the shield. We have to act quickly before Lenox arrives at the Citadel."

Tai got in front of Argus. "Lenox is coming here? Gee, that's fantastic news. And what if this ability hurts Argus? Did you stop to think about that? You don't even know what this ability is."

Argus shoved his brother. "Can I say something here? My whole life has been screwed with because of Lenox. Now I'm not even who I thought I was. My eyes are red and I want that damn orb like a drug. If I can do anything at all to fix what's going on, I'll do it. I don't care if it hurts me or even kills me. All I want is for my family and all of the humans on the planet, *especially* Lola, to get through this alive." He sat down on the stool, feeling exhausted. His heart raced so fast it felt like it would burst through his chest. "Let me do this. I have to do this."

With a scowl, Tai rolled his eyes. "Fine. You want to play the hero, go ahead. I'll do what the Commander said and push my Defender feelings aside so I don't interfere with your suicide mission. Go on, risk your life while I stand here and watch." He folded his arms across his chest.

"I don't plan on dying, but I have to do this." Argus closed his eyes and thought of what Neb looked like. The image of Neb's face came into focus, but it wasn't clear. The shield distorted it. Damn. He couldn't do it. But if he didn't, then Lenox would come to the Citadel and the Invaders would undoubtedly find the orb. That meant nobody would be safe. He couldn't live with that. "No!" He thought of how Lola had already suffered. Her life had been screwed with, too. She should be allowed to live her life in peace. It wasn't fair. "No!"

"Bro!" shouted Tai as he shook Argus by the shoulders. "Arg!"

"Argus, stop!" Aunt Celeste yelled.

Argus opened his eyes. He whole body shook and he fell off the stool. From the ground, he saw Aunt Celeste crouched beside someone. It was a struggle to sit up, but he managed. "What happened? What did I do? Is Neb all right?"

Tai was beside him in a flash. "Easy, bro. Take a breath. Just...stay here." His expression was between concern and fear.

"Tai, what happened? Did I do it? Is he okay?"

"Arg, I don't want to upset you, but..." Tai looked him in the eyes. "It's not Neb. I don't...I mean...Aunt Celeste is doing what she can."

Argus tried to stand, but Tai pushed him down. "Let go of me. If it's not Neb, then who?"

"Don't panic, Arg. I'm sure she'll be okay. You brought Lola here with a shift."

Argus couldn't stop his heart from fluttering and racing. "But humans can't go through a shift."

"Yeah. Let Aunt Celeste try to...you know." Tai kept pushing Argus down each time he tried to stand.

"Lola!" Argus lashed out and knocked Tai half-way across the room.

Chapter 10

Max followed the GPS on the snowmobile, loathing the entire Ramtalan species as he drove over the frozen landscape. His hatred kept his mind from freezing along with his body. Just when he thought he was lost, he came to a clearing he'd gone through with Gretchen. It was disgusting how the alien assholes used her like she didn't matter. She did matter. Kind of. He took a moment to think about what it would mean if she wasn't around. Without her, all of the credit for capturing the Ramtalans would go to him. Okay, so maybe losing Gretch wasn't such a bad thing after all.

He slowed down and checked the GPS. Still four miles to go. With the engine idling, he heard a familiar sound, a whomp-whomp coming closer. The sound of a helicopter. He shut off the snowmobile and listened. If it was AURA coming, he should signal them. No, wait, he couldn't because Jampara said he would set the monitor to destruct.

Max tried to get the snowmobile going but it wouldn't start. "Shit!"

The helicopter was close, real close. He jumped off, put the gold box on the seat and attempted to push the heavy snowmobile. It wouldn't budge. The helicopter, a military copter, zoomed in over the clearing, kicking up swirls of snow. Now what?

"Stop! Don't move!" came a voice from a loud speaker attached to the helicopter.

Max would have made a run for it if the helicopter didn't have two turrets with heavy machine guns pointed right at him. Without a choice, he raised his arms and waited. He had to be the unluckiest man in the world. Why couldn't one thing go right?

While the helicopter hovered, two ladders lowered and four guys, dressed in white head to foot, climbed down and aimed machine guns at

Max. He was ordered through the speaker to lie face down and not move. As if he would move with machine guns pointed at his head.

Max complied and lay down, wishing for a merciful death. When he was poked in the back with the business end of a machine gun, he got to his feet, hands still in the air. "I'm an AURA agent. Max Jackson!" he shouted above the helicopter noise.

The four guys with the guns didn't say anything. They just stood there looking stupid. What were they waiting for? With the snow blowing around, Max was certain he'd freeze to death unless they let him climb up into the helicopter.

Might as well try to reason with them. "Yo! It's fricking cold. Do you hear me?"

Then came the one voice he didn't want to hear. Stone's. "Yeah, I hear you, Jackson." He shuffled into the clearing. "You're a long way from home, aren't you? Are you a traitor now, Jackson? Working with the aliens? What's in that golden box?"

Oh, hell, the box. Max lowered his hands. "Listen to me, Mr. Stone, you have no idea what's going on here. Get me out of here and I'll explain it to you."

"Uh-huh, sure, but what's in the box. A bomb? A secret alien weapon? What?" Stone moved closer to the snowmobile.

Max shook his head. "Don't touch it, sir. I don't know what it is, but I was warned that if I don't deliver it to a destination, I'll die. I don't really feel like dying today, Mr. Stone."

Stone went to the box and motioned to one of the gun-toting guys. "Take this to base camp and don't let anyone but me near it. Understand?"

The guy nodded, slung the gun over his shoulder and picked up the box. Before he took a single step, the area glowed blue and a shock wave shook the ground. It knocked everyone off their feet and made the helicopter wobble in the air and move away with the ladders dangling and catching on the tree tops.

"Oh, Max, what trouble have you gotten yourself in now?" It was Neb standing over Max.

From the ground, Max shrugged. He motioned to the helicopter and the men lying on the snow. "Neb, did you make that earthquake?"

Neb didn't answer, but went to Stone and lifted him off the ground with one hand. "You're Stone, aren't you? Chief of AURA?"

Stone nodded. "Yeah, that's me. Put me down or you'll regret it."

With glowing blue eyes, Neb shook his head. "I rarely regret anything." He dropped Stone and motioned to the gold box that the gun-toting guy still had in his hands. "That package is for me. Put it down and move away."

The guy refused, got to his feet, clutched the box to his chest and began backing away.

Max called out, "You better do as he says, guy. These aliens don't mess around."

"So you are a traitor, Jackson," Stone grumbled. "Working with the enemy. I knew it!"

Max could see that Neb was fed up because his eyes were getting brighter and his lips were tightly pressed together. He got up. "I don't work for anyone except AURA. You rehired me, remember? But I'm telling you from experience, these blue-eyed freaks are crazy and have these weird powers that—"

"That's enough, Max," Neb warned. He pointed to the man again. "Put that box on the ground before I have to do something that you'll all regret."

"Stone, make him do what Neb says." Max pointed to the box.

Stone yelled, "You worthless piece of alien-loving shit, Jackson. I'll have you up on charges and I'll make sure you rot in prison."

Max glared at Stone. "Neb, do me a favor and zap Stone for me, please? And make it hurt."

"Traitor!" shouted Stone.

Neb ignored him, disappeared and reappeared next to the gun-toting guy with the gold box. "I won't tell you again, human, give me the box."

This time the man offered the box to Neb. "Take it."

"Thanks." Neb grabbed the box and motioned to Max. "Go on, get moving back to my cabin." He shot a bolt of electricity from his hand to the snowmobile and the engine started.

"Sure thing." Max climbed onto the snowmobile. He accelerated slowly and glanced back to see if Neb would do anything to Stone, but when Neb frowned and motioned that he should continue on his way, Max did just that. He had to stay on Neb's good side so he could get a look at whatever was inside the gold box. He mumbled, "I'm not a traitor and I sure as hell won't be bossed around by you, Neb. Watch your back."

Chapter 11

Argus ran to Lola and dropped to his knees. She wasn't moving, her face pale, deathly pale. Aunt Celeste had one hand on Lola's forehead and one on her chest, and looked up. "Argus, I'm so sorry."

"What do you mean? You have to keep trying. You can heal her." Argus cradled Lola's head in his lap. "She can't be dead."

Aunt Celeste stood. "Nobody can heal a human who's gone through a shift. The shift destroys—"

"Don't. I don't want to know." Argus lifted Lola into his arms. "I'm going to take her to Galena."

"Argus, no. Even Galena can't heal a human." Aunt Celeste shook her head and motioned to the couch in the living room. "Why don't you put her down?"

"No." Argus looked at Lola's sweet face. He didn't ever want to put her down. How could he have killed her? "I don't accept that there's nothing that can be done. Ramtala is more advanced than Earth, right? Then someone can bring her back."

Tai rushed over. "Wait, someone can. At least I think so. Aunt Celeste, before Galena took away my computer time, I remember reading something about how the scientists on Ramtala had experimented with humans early on, and accidentally killed them when trying to merge the Ramtalan DNA with human DNA. It wasn't an easy process. Right?"

Aunt Celeste nodded. "You're right, Tai. Boys, I didn't want to tell you that part of our history, but perhaps there is a possibility that—"

Argus blurted, "Whatever it is, Aunt Celeste, I'll do it. I can't let Lola die."

"Bro," Tai paused. "She's already dead."

"But didn't you say there might be a way to bring her back?" Argus glared at Tai. Was he going back on what he'd just said?

It was Aunt Celeste who answered, "Yes, Argus, there might be a way. But it's not something we can do easily. And it might not work. The only pure-form I know of here on Earth who has enhanced knowledge and abilities of healing humans is Lenox. Even Commander Jampara can't help with something like that."

Argus looked at Lola again. "Then I'll go to Lenox. I don't care anymore. He can have my energy for the XTRA-A1. It won't kill me now that I've been converted."

"Arg, you can't. We still don't really know what he's planning. I know you care for Lola, but use your head. What if you get Lenox to help and then the XTRA-A1 kills you and me, and all of the New Breeds? Will that be worth it?" Tai glanced at Aunt Celeste. "Tell him it's not a good idea. Sorry I opened my big mouth."

Aunt Celeste shook her head. "It's definitely not a good idea. Argus, please put Lola on the couch and let me think about this situation more fully."

"Of course it's worth it, Tai. We have to do something now." Argus felt his temperature rising. "You might be willing to let her die, but I'm not."

"Argus!" Aunt Celeste shouted. "Control yourself. You won't do anyone any good if you lose control. There *is* a time limit for healing a deceased human, but we still have time. To summon help from Lenox would be a mistake. He preys on our weaknesses. Your weakness, Argus, is Lola and your concern for humans. He knows that and he'll use it against you."

Argus clutched Lola close. "How much time?"

"Put Lola down on the couch and let me calculate how much time she has." Aunt Celeste motioned again to the couch. "Argus."

He nodded. "Okay." Carefully, he placed Lola on the couch and stepped back while Aunt Celeste knelt beside her. It would be worth giving up everything to see Lola alive again.

Aunt Celeste placed a hand on either side of Lola's head. A blue aura settled over Lola's entire body. "The shift has caused internal damage, cellular damage. I would estimate we have no more than ten planetary minutes to revive her." She removed her hands and the aura faded. "I'm sorry, Argus."

"Bullshit." Argus ran to the kitchen and found the Wand of Ramtala leaning against the wall. Just seeing it made his heart race. He grabbed it and immediately felt a rush of adrenaline and energy surge through his veins.

"Argus." Aunt Celeste was beside him. "The Wand is a powerful extension of Ramtalan energy. Even Galena has to be careful, and she's fully comingled with it. You're not. Give it to me."

"No." Argus held it tightly and rushed back to Lola. "I'm going to use it to heal her."

"Bro, you don't know how." Tai put his hand on Argus's shoulder and took hold of the Wand. "Give it to Aunt Celeste."

Argus glared at Tai. "Take your hand off the Wand, Tai. I do know how to use it. I'm a part of the Wand. I don't know how to explain it, but it's like the Wand is telling me what to do. Get your hand off it and stand back." He knew his brother was trying to help in the only way he knew how, but he didn't understand the Wand. "I won't tell you again."

"Arg, you're scaring me. Your eyes have those freakish sparks in them again. That Wand's going to kill you. I can't let you do this." He tightened his grip on the Wand.

The energy inside Argus built up and he knew he was about to throw a plasma burst. "Let go, Tai."

Aunt Celeste came over. "Tai, do what he says."

"No. You'll have to kill me, Arg." Tai raised an eyebrow. "I hope you don't, but that's the only way I'm letting you do anything with this Wand."

"I..." Argus couldn't control it any longer. "I'm sorry." The plasma burst he released caused such a shock wave that Tai flew across the room and slammed into the wall, leaving a deep impression.

"Argus!" Aunt Celeste shouted.

Argus turned back to Lola and held the Wand directly over her body, head to foot. A moment later, a red curtain of light drifted down and wrapped around Lola like a blanket. He felt strange, like he did when he and Tai were flying the XTRA-A1, but he didn't care. The Wand forced him to continue, assuring him that he was doing the right thing. He kept his eyes on Lola, willing her to open her eyes.

"Argus," came a firm voice behind him. "Argus, break your connection with the Wand." It was Galena.

He couldn't. Even if he wanted to, he couldn't. "No," he rasped.

She continued, "If I have to break it, you and Lola will both die. Break the connection."

"I can't." Argus's hands felt like they were on fire, almost as if they were melting into the Wand. In fact, his whole body was hot, but it felt right. He was the Wand, with all of its power, all of its abilities. Everything poured into him and he welcomed it.

"I'll help you. Listen to my voice." She got close and put her hands over his. "Search your mind for a time when you were in complete control of your actions."

Argus struggled to listen to Galena because his thoughts swirled, were scrambled between the need to save Lola, no matter what, and remembering his life in Palmdale. A fleeting memory hit him, it was of the first day of school, when Justin teased Lola. He stood up to Justin. He was in control then. "I have it, Galena, but I don't want to release the Wand."

"You have to. Now focus on that memory. Make it clearer and clearer in your head. Don't lose it. Now, slowly separate your mind from the Wand. Pull away like you're stripping off a piece of clothing and leaving it behind. Are you doing that?"

Argus kept the image of Lola at school in his mind and concentrated on letting go of the Wand and walking away from it. It was hard to do, because the Wand kept telling him to stay. "I can't. Galena, I can't do it. It's making me—"

"No, Argus, it's not making you do anything." Galena took one arm and crooked it around his neck, pulling him backward. "I'm in charge now. You listen to me, not the Wand. The Wand is killing Lola, not healing her. It wants the energy that remains in her. Do you understand? Release your hold on it. Now!" She tugged him backward.

His grip on the Wand loosened and he tumbled to the ground on top of Galena. In an instant, he felt cool again, weaker, and rolled off. "What happened? Lola!" He got up and stood over her. The Wand had fallen on top of her.

Galena sprung to her feet. "Don't touch the Wand, Argus. Walk away and go to Celeste."

He turned and saw Aunt Celeste with Tai in her arms. He wasn't moving. Argus ran and checked his brother for a heartbeat. There wasn't one. "Is he...? I killed my brother?" It couldn't be true. He'd forgotten completely that he'd shot a plasma burst at Tai. "He can't be. This isn't possible."

Aunt Celeste shook her head. "He'll be fine, Argus. Galena will heal him as soon as she's done with Lola. Unfortunately, we're captives now." She motioned behind her to about a dozen Ramtalans who'd just filed into the apartment. "I had to call for Galena to help Tai and get you away from the Wand."

Argus sat on a stool at the breakfast bar and lay his head down. What had he done? He'd ruined everything; jeopardized humanity and put the New Breeds in danger. And he'd killed Lola and Tai.

After a moment, Galena came to him and pulled his head off the counter by the back of his shirt. "Stupid boy." She peered at him. "Judging by your eyes, you've had a secondary conversion. I can't believe you're alive." She released him and went to Aunt Celeste.

"You comingled your Alpha 2a with him? You're not qualified for actions like that, Guardian." Galena motioned to one of the Ramtalans. "Take Tai to the medical wing."

Argus slid off the stool. "Wait! What about Lola? Take her, too."

Galena strode to him and poked him in the chest. "You have no idea what you've done, do you? A secondary conversion has changed you, genetically. You were already more Ramtalan than human after the first conversion. Now you're a full Ramtalan. A pure-form in a host body."

"That's not possible, Galena," Aunt Celeste said. "He received an influx of Alpha 2a, but that didn't make him a pure-form."

Argus held out his hands. "Of course I'm not a pure-form, I have my body. Don't try to screw with my brain, Galena."

"Perhaps you'd prefer to hear it from your father. He'll be here shortly." Galena spun around and shoved Aunt Celeste. "You go with Tai, because Argus shouldn't be around any other pure-forms right now." She waited until everyone left the room and the door slid closed before she turned back to Argus. "You managed to heal Lola before the Wand had time to take her remaining energy. She's alive. But she's not the same. We have to leave the Wand on her until it has completed restructuring her genetics. The Wand is not to be used for healing purposes, Argus. Ever. It's a very powerful device, but not designed for that."

Argus glanced over to the living room. "I'm not a pure-form. I don't know why you're saying that. And what do you mean by Lola not being the same? She's alive, right?"

Galena nodded. "She is. The shift infused her with a little Alpha 2a, which the Wand wanted, but it had to heal her before taking it. You broke away just in time. There are severe implications to what you've done. Number one, your guardian is now our prisoner, and number two, you're a twice-converted New Breed, and number three, Argustine might not be able to initiate his plan now. Argustine and I have worked hard over the years to perfect the eradication of the New Breeds and now a foolish boy might have undone everything." Her fury made her eyes shine brighter.

"How can you blame me for wanting to stop Lenox? Every New Breed on the planet is like a brother or sister to me. Just because I've been converted doesn't mean I care about them any less. Plus, Lenox doesn't give shit about humans. He'll kill anyone in his way. I can't stand by and let that happen." He went to Lola and sat on the floor next to the couch.

Galena was there in the blink of an eye. "Don't you ever walk away from me. You might be a pure-form, but you still have a ridiculous attachment to humans. What a pity." She put her hand over Lola. "The restructuring is complete." After lifting the Wand off Lola, she tamped it twice on the ground. "We're back to planetary time and the Wand has been deactivated. Argus, you must stay in seclusion for a time now as your body adjusts to its new form. Lola can stay with you as I believe she will keep you grounded and I doubt you would ever do anything to hurt her."

"Of course I won't hurt her." Well, he already did, didn't he? "Why do I need seclusion? What's happened to me? I mean what's really changed inside me?" He brushed a strand of hair behind Lola's ear. "And what's happened to Lola?"

With a sigh, Galena pointed to his eyes. "You have the eyes of your father, Argus, and have more in common with him than you can imagine.

Back on Ramtala, Argustine had the most abilities of any Ramtalan and a superior intellect. I'm not his full sister. We had the same mother, but different fathers. It's best he tells you the rest. For now, do whatever you normally do to relax. Watch movies, work out, read a book. I'll come back when your father arrives. And don't worry about Tai, I can heal him easily." She motioned to Lola. "Lola will need rest. You might notice changes in her, so be prepared. The Wand had to repair the cellular damage. But she's alive and that's what you wanted." With that, Galena took the Wand and walked to the front door shaking her head.

After she left, Argus sat on the edge of the couch and held Lola's hand. She was warm and breathing. No matter how'd she'd changed, she was still Lola, and that's all that mattered. He did what he had to and surely she'd understand that.

Chapter 12

Max zipped the snowmobile in and out of trees and followed the GPS back to where he'd started. To his utter dismay, there were even more Ramtalans now. Too many to count. Where'd they all come from? The planet really was crawling with the vermin.

He pulled over to one side, shut the machine off, dismounted, and looked for Neb. Max smirked. Once he got his hands on the gold box, he'd high-tail it back to Stone, reclaim his dignity as a human instead of an alien stooge, and become the hero he dreamed of.

"Max." It was Neb, right behind him.

"Damn!" Max spun around. "Don't sneak up on me like that. So, ah, what happened back there?"

Neb gave a half-smile. He didn't have the gold box. "Did a little memory manipulation." He slapped Max on the shoulder. "You've been a big help. But I think it's time to part ways. You don't want to be around for what comes next. Trust me, you don't."

"Why? What's coming next?" Max swallowed. Did he really want to know?

"War, Max, war. And it's going to get ugly. When Invaders are involved, it's always ugly." Neb looked toward the group of Ramtalans. "I'm going to cut you loose."

"Change of heart? I thought you said I knew too much." Max swallowed again. What if "cut you loose" meant death? Neb could make the monitor self-destruct. Oh, hell. "Wait, I can still help you. I'm sure I can. I know how the government operates, how they think."

"Max." Neb sighed. "The governments of Earth are inconsequential at this point. No human on the planet can stop the Invaders. And we're beyond trying to hide our New Breeds from the people. I told you, we're at war and this isn't the type of war you can help with. There are much bigger things to worry about than you."

"So what, you're just going to kill me? That's it, no gold watch for my dedicated service?" Max backed away.

"Gold watch? Oh, the proverbial retirement gift." Neb laughed. "I said you were a big help and I meant it." He took a step forward and lowered his voice, "I know you, Max. I know you're trying to think of some way to capture us all and imprison us. But hear me, that will never happen. If I ever encounter you acting in a hostile manner toward me, my people or our New Breeds, I will kill you." He stepped back. "And that's why the monitor will remain in place. Oh, I almost forgot." He grabbed Max by the front of his jacket and pulled him in close.

Max struggled, but it was useless. He couldn't get free from Neb's grasp. "You are going to kill me."

Neb shook his head. "I said I wouldn't unless you cross me. Relax, you're not going to die. But I'll know every move you make." With one hand still grasping the jacket, Neb took his other hand and placed it palm down on Max's forehead. "Sweet dreams, Max."

Max felt a pulse of electricity shoot through his entire body, like he'd been struck by a bolt of lightning. Even his toes tingled. Then, everything went black.

Chapter 13

Lola looked peaceful in her sleep, and since Argus didn't want to wake her, he crept into the kitchen for something to drink. His head spun from everything that had happened, especially with Tai. How could he have done that to his own brother? If Galena hadn't been around, his brother would be dead, permanently. Argus got a glass of water and noticed the dent in the wall where he'd thrown Tai.

"What have I done? I hurt everyone around me." He leaned against the kitchen counter. He was racking up quite a list; Tai, Lola, and Aunt Celeste, who was now Galena's prisoner. "Damn it!"

"Argie?" Lola whispered in a hoarse voice.

He rushed to her side. "Lola? Are you all right? How do you feel?"

She sat up, still very pale. "Where am I? What happened? Your eyes."

He sat on the couch, covered his eyes and took her hand. "This is a place called the Citadel. The Ramtalan headquarters on Earth. But you're okay. I accidentally brought you here."

"Oh. But what's wrong with your eyes? They're red."

"I know. Don't freak out. It's nothing. Should I put sunglasses on?"

She shook her head. "No. I'll get used to it. It kind of looks like you had a bad night, a *really* bad night." She gently pulled his hand away from his eyes. "Wow. Do they hurt?"

"No." He sighed. "I've sort of inherited my father's eyes. Are you sure you're not freaked out?" He looked away.

"Argie, at this point, nothing about you freaks me out. So what exactly happened? I was at school, on the field with the spaceship and then I felt like something was tearing me apart." She burrowed her head against his shoulder. "It was horrible."

"I'm so sorry. I would never have done that to you on purpose. It's called a molecular shift. Are you sure you're okay?" He stroked her hair. "I'd die if anything ever happened to you."

She leaned back and wiggled her hands and arms. "Nothing seems to be broken. How does a molecular shift work? Did it make me invisible like you said it makes you?"

How much should he tell her? Well, obviously not too much since he didn't fully understand how a shift worked. "It, ah, dissociates your molecules, or something like that. But then they all come back together." He gave a little shrug. "It stops hurting after a few times."

Lola nodded. "Well, I don't want to do it again. Ever. Is your brother here, too? And your aunt?"

"Yeah. But..." How could he tell her he'd brought her right into the middle of a war and that Lenox was on his way? "I don't want to talk about it right now."

"Oh, okay. Family drama. I get it." She took his hand. "Hey, before I forget, everyone loves our spaceship float." She smiled and drew in a deep breath. "Rumor has it that we'll win best float."

Argus found himself smiling, too. "Cool. I love you, Lola."

"You better," she whispered.

He gave her a kiss on the cheek and stood. "Lola, Lenox is coming here."

She jumped to her feet and crumpled to the ground. Argus was quick to help her up.

Her legs trembled, but otherwise she seemed okay. "What? I hate that guy. Sorry, I know he's your dad, but really, I hate him. Can we leave and go home before he gets here? Where exactly are we?"

"Labrador. Under an island. And we can't leave. I tried to bring another Ramtalan here, but I accidentally brought you. I don't want to try to do anything else that could...hurt you." He looked at her carefully. She didn't seem any different. Maybe Galena was wrong. "You sure you feel okay?"

She walked around the living room. "Yep, I feel pretty good in fact. Galena's coming."

"What? What did you say?" Argus went to her. "Lola, how do you know that?"

A moment later, the door opened and Galena, with Ari in tow, walked in. She didn't have the Wand. "Argus, I need you to come with me. Tai's asking for you. Hello, Lola."

Lola came forward. "You're Galena, aren't you? How do I know you?"

Instinctively, Argus dashed out in front of Lola. "Lola, it turns out that Galena is my real aunt. And Ari over there is my half-brother."

"You have a very complicated family, Argie."

He nodded. "I know. Galena helped...I mean...when I brought you here, she sort of..."

Galena groaned. "Nice to see you up and around, Lola. Argus, go with Ari. Lola and I need to have a talk."

"Wait." Argus shook his head. "I'm not leaving her here with you."

Lola put her hand on his shoulder. "It's okay. I think I need to talk to her."

Argus turned and faced her. "I can't leave you, Lola. I mean, I really can't. It's that Protector thing in me."

"Argus," Galena said firmly. "I will not harm Lola, but I must evaluate her. You need to leave. Tai's fighting with the medical team and won't settle down until he sees you. Lola will be here when you get back. Understand?"

"Lola." Argus leaned down slightly and kissed her on the lips. It felt like the first time he'd ever kissed her; warm and sweet. "I'll be right back."

Ari waited by the open door with a scowl on his face. "Hurry up, Argus, I have more important things to do than babysit you and your brother."

Argus went to Ari and shoved him out of the way. "Nobody babysits either of us, *brother*." He strode through the doorway and into the corridor.

Within a second, Ari had caught up and pushed ahead. "I don't like the idea that we're brothers any more than you do. But it's a fact we have to live with. Oh, Tai's rather upset at you."

Of course he was. Who wouldn't be upset? "I figured he would be. But *he's* my real brother and he'll forgive me." Argus followed Ari to the medical wing and found Tai pacing around the surgical room.

"Argus," Tai growled. "You asshole." His eyes burned blue.

"I didn't mean it." Argus stood with his back to the wall so Tai couldn't dissolve and appear behind him. "It's the Citadel. It's screws with us, remember? Sorry I kind of flipped out. Galena fixed you."

"Really? *Kind of* flipped out? You lost it, bro, and you took it out on me. *Me*. How can I just forgive and forget a thing like that?" Tai pounded his fist into the wall and made a long crack all the way down to the floor.

Ari spoke up, "Calm the hell down, both of you. Father will be here shortly and if you two are acting like spoiled brats, he'll be the one who'll *flip out*. You are the sons of Argustine Lenox, the greatest Ramtalan ever born. You *will* treat him with the respect he deserves."

Tai turned to Ari. "Shut up. I'm sick of your voice and your face." He raised his hand and fired a pulse at Ari, but it fizzled out before reaching him.

"Your pulses won't work in here. The medical wing has an energy shield." Ari motioned to the doorway. "Galena says you can leave if you don't make trouble with Argus or anyone else. Do I have your word?"

Argus went to Tai. "I am sorry. Really, really sorry. You can shoot me with a pulse once we're out of here if it'll make you feel better."

Tai rolled his eyes. "No, I guess your weak-ass apology is sufficient to ease my troubled mind." He smirked. "You're still a gigantic asshat though."

The old Tai was back. Argus held his fist out. "We good?"

Tai fist-bumped Argus. "Yeah, I guess. But I get to kill *you* next time." He walked to the doorway and purposely knocked his shoulder into Ari. "Oh, sorry, Ari."

"I really detest you both," Ari mumbled.

Argus went into the hallway. Tai seemed okay, like nothing had happened. It was weird to think that only a few weeks ago, they were both normal high school kids who only worried about being outcasts and thought death was a permanent thing.

Tai nudged Argus. "Oh, hey, bro, how's Lola?"

"She's okay, I think. Galena might be screwing with her head though. Get this, Lola knew when Galena was coming to the apartment." Argus stepped aside when Ari elbowed his way past them. "Pardon us for being in your way, Ari."

Ari turned, glared, and kept going.

Tai snickered. "I hope Lenox takes Ari with him back to Ramtala."

"That'd be sweet." Argus grabbed Tai by the arm. "Wait for a sec."

Tai stopped. "Why?" He shook Argus's hand off.

"I don't want Ari to overhear. So, what are we going to do? The stakes are even higher now that Lola's here. We have to find Aunt Celeste and get out of here."

"Oh, really?" Tai rolled his eyes. "Of course we do. But you delayed everything by bringing Lola here and by killing me."

"How many times can I say sorry?" He motioned for them to keep moving when Ari spun around and yelled at them to "stop dawdling".

In a whisper, Tai said, "You can make it up to me by letting me have the Lambo."

"Done." Argus jogged to Ari. "Where are we going, Ari? And where's Aunt Celeste? I have to get back to Lola, you know."

They got to the lobby.

Ari stopped right on the spiral galaxy logo and sneered. "Don't pull that Protector bullshit on me. You'll see Lola when, and if, Galena says you can. Your Guardian is in the court room under a new protective shield since you destroyed the old one when you smashed the orb, so don't go thinking you can get any help from her."

Tai went on the other side of Ari. "You're an galactic-sized prick, Ari. And you didn't answer my brother's other question. Where are you taking us?"

"You two don't listen very well, do you? I told you Father is coming here soon. If he didn't need you both, I swear...we'll wait for him in the Control Room. Now go." Ari pointed to the last corridor. "All the way down the hall to the golden door."

Argus walked with Tai, and ignored Ari who stomped behind them. As they approached the end of the corridor, there was a gold door, just like Ari said. It had three panels of silver-gold in a column to the right of the door. Tai waved his hand over the panels, but nothing happened. Argus decided to try it now that he'd been converted, but still, nothing.

"It's a secured door, boys," Ari said smugly as he came over, pressed his palm to each panel in turn, starting with the top one. "You don't have access."

Access? Argus glanced at Tai. "How do you get access?"

Tai shrugged. "Who knows."

The door slid open. Galena waited just inside. "Take a seat, boys." She pointed to a couple of chairs that looked a lot like the chairs in the XTRA-A1, except these were missing the depressions in the arm rests. "Ari, prepare the energy deflectors in case Neb gets it in his head that he can break through our defenses when Argustine arrives."

Ari went to the chairs and knocked on an arm rest. "She said sit down." He turned back to Galena. "The shields will only be down for a split-second. Neb won't have time to do anything."

"You don't know Neb, Ari. You didn't see him during the Malaris wars. He's capable of a lot more than you think." Galena raised an eyebrow. "Prepare the deflectors."

Ari's eyes flashed blue, but went right back to normal again. He went to a computer monitor that was directly in front of the two chairs, and sat down heavily on a stool.

Argus got close to Tai and kept his voice low, "Did you hear what she said?"

"What, am I hard of hearing? Of course I heard it. Whatever the deflectors are, we have to disable them." Tai motioned to the chairs. "We've got ring side seats and can watch what Ari's doing."

"Right." Argus went to one of the chairs and sat. "Galena, where's Lola? If you hurt her—"

"Why would I hurt her?" Galena shook her head. "Just sit there and don't talk. Let the grownups handle things."

Tai flopped into his chair. "Well that's a little insulting, *Auntie*."

She glared at him. "I said be quiet."

"Tai, be careful." Argus leaned to one side so he could see what Ari was doing. The monitor was filled with wavy lines running horizontally. Every now and then, the lines would straighten and Ari would slide his fingers around on the touch pad and the lines would go wavy again. "What the hell is he doing?"

Tai shrugged. "No idea, bro."

Ari spoke, "Galena, the deflectors are stabilized and on standby. I'm also picking up a slight buffeting of the energy shield."

Galena nodded. "That's Argustine. He's here."

Chapter 14

Max woke up feeling cold and groggy, but he remembered everything. Thankfully Neb didn't mangle his memory. He blinked and realized his scarf was still wrapped around his nose and mouth and his beanie was pulled down over most of his eyes. He yanked the hat off and saw a few overhanging tree branches passing by above him, bent under the weight of snow. He was moving.

"Gretch?"

Gretchen drove a snowmobile that towed him behind on a stretcher. She slowed the machine and turned around. "About time you woke up, Jackson. I was getting lonely."

He gripped the edges of the stretcher and sat up. "Stop. Where are we?"

She eased to a stop, shut the engine off, and hopped off. "We're in Newfoundland."

"Where the hell is that?" Max got to his feet and looked around. Nothing but a frozen wasteland. "Gretch?"

"Labrador." She touched the back of her head. "I've still got that damn monitor thing in my brain. Neb has me programmed like a damn machine. More than anything, I want those damn aliens off my damn planet."

"Well, yeah, so do I. Get us to habitation, Gretch, and I'll call in the military to blow those bastards back to Ramtala."

"Wow, weren't you listening?" She pointed to her head. "I have that damn monitor wrapped around my brainstem. I can't unprogram what Neb programmed. I'm an alien puppet." She wiped her teary eyes. "I don't like this, Jackson. I've always known exactly who I am, what I believe in. But now, I've lost control of myself. No more free will."

Whoa. Gretchen was crying. He went to her and gave her a pat on the shoulder. "This is why we can't let them win."

"How do you propose to beat them? You've got a monitor, too. We stray off the path Neb set for us, and he'll know. We're screwed." Gretchen sniffed and wiped her eyes again. "Damn it, he made me cry."

Max would have liked to hug Gretchen, but knowing her, she'd take it the wrong way and probably cold-cock him. "Neb said they're at war. Do you honestly think those blue-eyed alien dicks are going to be watching us? We're the least of their worries. So, what are we doing in Newfoundland?"

Gretchen sniffed again. "There's a helicopter waiting to take us to LA."

"LA? That's the best news I've had all day. I'll call Stone and tell him to call off his attack and get the Air Force, the Navy, the Marines, and the damn Army involved. Once the Ramtalans are under wraps, we'll get the best surgeons to remove the monitors and that'll be that. Hey, Gretch, how long was I out?"

She got back on the snowmobile. "About four hours. The helicopter's a mile from here." She unhooked the stretcher and started the engine. "Do you really think we'll be okay? I'm not sure I want to live like this."

"Easy. I can't have you suicidal. I need you and we have to focus on showing these aliens who's the boss of planet Earth." Max got on the snowmobile behind Gretchen. "Let's go to LA and bring back a firestorm. Everything is going to be fine. You'll see."

She nodded and accelerated, dodging between several evergreen trees. Max wrapped his arms around her waist and hung on. He wasn't a hundred percent sure he could rally the entire military to eradicate the Ramtalans, but he wanted Gretchen to be on board. She was the only one who had experienced everything he had.

After maybe half an hour of driving up and down over small hills and in between skinny trees, Gretchen pulled the snowmobile up to a raised helipad in the center of a clearing. There wasn't anything else around, just a Jet Ranger helicopter and a bright orange windsock off to one side. Max's stomach muscles clenched. He felt uneasy. What if Neb had been lying all along and the helicopter wasn't taking them to LA? Maybe the pilot was one of them and would disappear from the cockpit and let the copter crash.

Gretchen shut off the snowmobile. "Well, Jackson, I hope you're right about everything turning out okay."

"Trust me, Gretch. They'll pay." He forced a smile, got off the snowmobile and headed to the helicopter. It would take them to freedom or death. He hoped for the first one.

Chapter 15

Argus watched Ari's computer. Each time the wavy lines straightened, Ari worked the touchpad until they became wavy again. That had to mean the deflector was unstable when the lines were straight. That was the opportunity to disable it.

"Tai," Argus whispered.

"I know. I worked it out, too. When Lenox appears, we have to destroy the deflectors and contact Neb."

"No talking!" Ari shouted. He turned and scowled at them. "If you're thinking that you can do something to stop Father from coming, you can't."

Galena approached and stood behind Argus. "Argustine is in his pure-form state, which means he can arrive in an instant once he brings down the shield. It'll be back up before you can take a breath. You can't stop him, boys." She walked to Ari. "Get ready to engage the deflectors."

There was a brilliant burst of blue that filled the room. Argus closed his eyes for a split-second, but there wasn't time to waste, so he opened them and lunged forward, knocked Ari from the chair and slammed his fist onto the computer. The screen shattered. Ari shouted and Galena grabbed Argus by the arm.

"Tai!" Argus yelled, "Find Neb!"

"Don't you dare...!" Galena screamed.

Argus looked behind him, but Tai was gone. Hopefully he'd made it out of the Citadel.

The blue faded and Lenox appeared and floated toward Argus. "Galena, release my son."

Galena shook her head. "No. Your *son* just destroyed the deflector system. Someone could have made it through. And your other son escaped because this one disabled the deflectors."

Lenox looked around and his eyes flashed bright red. "Galena, there are no hostiles here. I detect nothing. If Tai did escape, he did not return with the Guardians. The shield is restored and we no longer need the deflectors to disrupt incoming energy sources. We are safe, but I will require Tai at some point."

Argus pulled free from Galena. "I won't let you hurt my brother. Tai got away and he'll bring help. You might as well give up, Lenox, and go back to Ramtala. Leave us alone."

"Do not disrespect me, Argus. I have shown you leniency because you are my son, but my kindness will not continue if you behave defiantly." Lenox's red eyes glowed steadily as he stared at Argus. He came closer. "Galena, what has happened to my son?"

Galena shoved Argus. "Celeste. She did something that altered his genetics further."

Argus backed away. "I might look like you now, Lenox, but I'm nothing like you." He concentrated on bundling his energy for a plasma burst.

Before he could fire the burst, Lenox vanished and reappeared behind him and encased him in a blue veil. "My son, I can always anticipate your desire to harm me."

The blue veil paralyzed Argus from his neck down. He couldn't move at all. His energy dissipated and he felt weak. "What are you doing to me, Lenox? Let me go." It was similar to the feeling when the XTRA-A1 used his energy.

Lenox circled around Argus. "You have been placed in stasis and you will stay this way until I need you." He went to Galena. "Have you successfully signaled our compatriots?"

Galena glared at Argus for a moment. "Of course. But with Tai on the outside blabbing about our plans, they'll have trouble getting through. We can't deactivate the shield because Tai has undoubtedly told the Guardians that Argus smashed the deflectors. I know you don't want to hear this, Argustine, but perhaps Tai should be forfeit. I can send word to Corona or Hadron and they can take care of him. They're waiting in Iceland."

Argus struggled, but was held firmly. "No! You can't do anything to Tai. He's done nothing. Take me, do whatever you want to me, but leave my brother alone."

"Ah, my son, so very brave. I will not allow anything to happen to Tai. Do you understand me, Galena? Nothing will happen to Argus *or* Tai."

Ari ran to Lenox. "What about me, Father? Did you forget that I'm here?"

"Aridesian, you are my eldest son and as such, you know what importance I place on you. Do not accuse me of ignorance. Mind your place."

"Yes, sir." Ari went to Argus. "Father won't hurt Tai. We're all going back to Ramtala like he promised. We'll be a family and Ramtala will be restored once the New Breeds are gone from here. Pure-form babies will once again be born. You'll see."

Was Ari really that delusional? Argus wanted to slap some sense into him. "Ari, killing New Breeds isn't going to solve anything, because Ramtalans can't reproduce. You know that. Lenox has lied to you all along."

"No, he hasn't." Ari turned to Lenox. "Tell him, Father. Tell him how you'll take us to Ramtala with you. We'll be happy there. We will."

For a moment, Argus felt sorry for Ari. "It's all a lie, Ari. Deep down, you know it is."

"No." Ari took a few steps backward. "It's not a lie. Father, you'd never lie to me, would you?"

Without answering, Lenox flashed blue and disappeared. Galena lunged at Ari and grabbed him around the throat.

She lifted him off the ground a few inches. "I'm getting sick and tired of your whining. A son of Argustine's should not be whiny and weak." She dropped him.

"I'm not weak." Ari rubbed his throat. "What do you expect from me?"

She glared at him. "I expect you to do your job."

Argus spoke up, "She wants you to carry out Lenox's orders without complaining. She doesn't want you to think for yourself. You're his puppet, Ari."

Ari's eyes glowed brightly. "I'm nobody's puppet." He vanished.

Galena groaned. "You need to learn how to keep your mouth shut, Argus."

"Can't you let me out of this stasis thing, Galena? I'm not going anywhere with the shield up. I need to see Lola." If Galena would release the veil, he could try to find a way to disable the shield and find Tai.

"You'll stay right where you are, so I know exactly where to find you." She checked the broken computer. "Your strength is dangerous while you're at the Citadel and I can't trust you to keep your abilities under control." She turned and faced him. "I'll look in on you shortly." She flashed blue and disappeared.

It seemed like nobody bothered using the doors anymore. Maybe the collective energy of the Citadel allowed them not to deplete their own. If that was the case, would *they* also have enhanced abilities? If so, what did that mean? *Think, Argus, think*. The blue veil—the stasis—had him trapped. But how? When Aunt Celeste used the invisibility veil, it came directly from her energy source. So if this veil came from Lenox, how was he projecting it and controlling it?

He closed his eyes and fought against the feeling of weakness. He willed his energy to build and felt a strange sensation, like he was tapping into a power source and getting a boost. Is that what Lenox did? Use the collective energy to somehow project his own?

The harder he concentrated on collecting more energy, the easier it became, like he'd turned on a faucet and the energy flowed into him as if it were water. His strength was back before long and he focused on firing a plasma burst. It took a couple of tries, but in the end, the burst fired and the veil vaporized. He was free.

Chapter 16

Max sat in the back seat of the copter next to Gretchen, with his fingers clutched tightly on the edge of the seat. The pilot hadn't said a word, not a single damn word. Gretchen seemed comfortable with the whole deal and strapped herself in without a hint of concern, even when the copter lifted off and climbed into the clouds.

"Gretch!" Max shouted above the sound of the engine. "Are you sure we're going to LA?"

She turned and stared at him for a moment. "Neb doesn't lie, Jackson. Just sit there and shut up. We'll land at the LA airport."

"LAX? That's a huge, busy airport, Gretch. Do these aliens understand about clearance and how we humans fly around? Is Neb sending one of his buddies to meet us? I don't want to get arrested as a terrorist. How can you expect me to go along quietly with whatever those aliens have in mind? Wake up. Snap out of it. Where's the ballsy Gretchen I know? You've got to be in there somewhere."

"Wow, Jackson." She smacked him on the arm. "Do you have to keep reminding me that I'm a prisoner? If I could get this monitor out of my head, I would. I thought you were going to help me."

"I will. It just gives me the willies that you trust Neb so completely." Max took her hand. "We're the good guys, Gretch, not them."

She shook her hand free. "Yeah, I know. But, Neb's a good guy, too. He sent us away so we wouldn't get hurt. And so we wouldn't be in his way. This war of theirs could jeopardize Earth. That much I know. The Settlers don't want this war, but they have to protect the New Breeds. I actually understand that. I sort of feel what Neb feels. He's very protective, almost like a father."

"Whatever." Max turned and looked out the window. A father figure was the last thing he needed. His own father was a great man who worked hard up until the day he dropped dead from a heart attack. Neb was definitely *not* like his father.

So it looked like Gretchen was an alien sympathizer. Great. She wasn't reliable anymore, and worse still, she was probably a spy who would report everything back to Neb. How had everything spun out of control? What started out as a simple snatch-and-grab of the Dachel brothers had now become an all-out war of humans against Ramtalans.

If only he'd been successful at keeping Argus Dachel under wraps at Edwards, everything would have worked out perfectly. It was all that damn kid's fault. Well, no alien was going to get the best of Max Jackson. But it was going to take careful planning. Maybe he could use Gretchen to feed false information back to Neb and catch him with his guard down.

Max smiled and turned back to her. "Hey, Gretch, what are you supposed to do in LA?"

She blinked a few times. "Report to AURA headquarters."

"What? Is that what Neb wants you to do? I don't get it. Why?"

"What do you want from me, Jackson? You asked me a question and I gave you an answer." She leaned against the seat and closed her eyes. "We have a long flight. Get some sleep."

Sleep? Who could sleep? Why would a Ramtalan want his two monitored puppets to report to AURA? What was the point? Would Stone be waiting? Come to think of it, what had happened to Stone? Neb said he'd take care of him, but what did that really mean? Was Stone an alien puppet, too?

Max watched Gretchen for a while. She looked so peaceful, her breathing was calm and it seemed like she didn't have a care in the world. How could that be? Planet Earth was on the brink of annihilation and she was taking a nap. Worthless woman. Best to ditch her as soon as they landed in LA. Oh, well, he knew all along that she was expendable. He preferred to work alone anyway.

Chapter 17

Argus ran to the door and listened but didn't hear anyone. He had to get help, but how? Maybe he could try to get through the shield with a molecular shift. If he'd brought Lola through, then *he* should be able to get through. But he couldn't leave her.

Okay, so he had to get to Lola first and then find Aunt Celeste, all without Galena, Ari, or Lenox finding out he was free. With any luck, they wouldn't come back into the room for a while. That'd give him time to go to Lola. He closed his eyes and concentrated on her until her image came into view. She was still in his apartment, sitting at the breakfast bar.

He opened his eyes and appeared beside her. "Lola, are you all right?"

She slowly turned to him, apparently not startled at all that he'd just appeared. "I'm fine, Argus."

"Are you sure?" He reached out for her, but she leaned away.

"Yes, I'm sure." She got off the stool. "Galena explained some things to me."

He tried again to reach for her, but she moved away. "Like what?"

"Well, she said that when you brought me here to the Citadel, it killed me. *You* killed me. Galena brought me back to life by doing something with my body, my DNA." She stared at him. "Ever since I met you, I've been in danger from the government, from these aliens and from you. Your father is a good man and he's trying to get rid of the Settlers and the New Breeds so he can give the planet back to us. Why are you fighting him, Argus?"

"I'm fighting him because he's...did you say he wants to give the planet back?" He realized Lola was no longer looking at him the same as she did before. There was no love, just an accusatory look. "Lola, you know nothing about Lenox. He's not good. He'll kill every human, as well as his own people. Do you want your mom to die, and your friends?"

She shook her head. "Lenox doesn't want to kill anyone, especially the human population. He simply wants to send all of the Ramtalans and New Breeds back to Ramtala. What's wrong with that?" She glared at him. "You're the one who's a bad person."

He sat on a stool and leaned on an elbow. "How can you say that? I never meant...can you ever forgive me? For everything. I never meant to hurt you or drag you into all of this. I love you so much. You have to believe me."

"How can you expect me to forgive you? I was dead, Argus. If Galena wasn't here, I'd still be dead. When we met that first day at school, I thought you were so kind and sweet and I couldn't wait to find out more about you. Now, I regret ever meeting you." She slid off the stool and walked to the living room.

He wanted to go to her and hold her, tell her again and again that he was sorry, but he knew it would be a waste of time and time was a luxury he didn't have. Lola seemed fine and it wasn't like Galena was going to hurt her. The priority now was to find Aunt Celeste.

"Bye, Lola. I love you." He concentrated on the court room and in an instant did a molecular shift and appeared in the corridor right outside the room. The shield around the room was too strong to shift through. He rapped on the door. "Aunt Celeste? Can you hear me?"

There was no answer. If only he had another orb, he could use it to break through the shield like he did before. He knocked a couple more times, listened at the door and focused on Aunt Celeste. It wasn't any use, he couldn't locate her because of interference from the shield. So what now? What other options did he have? Standing in the corridor was dangerous, he'd get caught sooner or later.

He thought of Tai and hoped he'd made it to Neb. Neb would know what to do and how to get into the Citadel. After a few seconds, Tai's face came into view. He was smiling. That was odd.

"Bro," Tai whispered.

Argus spun around and saw Tai right behind him. "Where'd you come from?"

With a smirk, Tai replied, " I used shared-sight and found you."

"What? So you never made it through the Citadel's shield?" Argus checked the corridor. Nobody else was around. "I thought you'd made it outside to Neb."

He grabbed Argus by the arm. "Shift with me, bro. We can't stand here in the open."

"Shift where? You didn't answer me." Argus pulled free. "I'm not going anywhere until you tell me what's going on."

"Fine. We'll just stand here and chat for a while until Lenox and Galena arrive. Well, let's see, when you broke the deflectors and Lenox disabled the shield for his entry into the citadel, I dissolved to Neb and he and I shifted back to the Citadel. Really quick. Neb's amazingly fast. Apparently Lenox didn't put the shield back up as instantaneously as Galena thought. What else would you like to discuss, bro? Politics? World peace? How Lenox wants to use our energy for his insidious plan?"

"Shut up." Argus thought for a moment. There was no way Tai could have come with Neb into the Citadel. "Wait, Lenox said he didn't detect any 'hostiles' in the Citadel. Are you kidding around or something?"

"No, Argus, he's not," it was Neb, right next to Tai. He glanced around. "Take Tai's hand. Tai take mine. I'll initiate a shift and you'll all come along. We're certainly not safe here."

Argus hesitated until Tai grabbed his hand and before he had time to think, they'd all shifted and appeared in the apartment. Immediately, Argus rushed to the living room and found Lola on the couch watching a movie on the TV.

She jumped up. "What's going on?"

Neb came over. "Don't worry, everything's fine. Just keep watching your movie like nothing's wrong."

She glared. "Don't treat me like an idiot. This better not be a move against Lenox."

Argus groaned. "Lola, Galena brainwashed you. Lenox wants to use me and Tai for whatever he has planned. It'll kill us. I know you're mad at me, but you don't want to see us both dead, do you?"

After a pause, she shook her head. "No, of course not. Look, Galena told me everything about how Lenox can repair Ramtalan DNA so you can all have kids again. That's why he wants to stop the New Breed program. There's no point keeping half-Ramtalans around anymore."

Neb whistled. "Little girl, Lenox is pushing for genetic purity, the exact thing that got us into this predicament in the first place. If Ramtala had mixed our DNA with our neighboring planets through marriages, we would have been genetically stronger to resist the effects of the irradiation. Our neighbors weren't affected, but we were." He sat on the couch and sighed. "About a hundred and fifty thousand planetary years ago, Ramtala was involved with a series of wars with a species very similar to our own. The Malaris. The wars went on for close to a hundred thousand planetary years."

Argus sat next to Neb. "A hundred thousand years? Really?"

"Bro, that's in Earth years. Not so long in Ramtalan years." Tai sat on the arm of the couch.

"Oh. Was Lenox involved with the wars, Neb? I don't understand why he's so bent on killing the New Breeds."

Neb hesitated for a moment. "Lenox was born some years before the war started. Once the war began, his father, your grandfather, was rumored to have been killed by the Malaris as a prisoner of war. The details are sketchy and nobody seems to know much about his father, but let me tell you, that death affected Lenox on a deep, deep level. He withdrew from society and was obsessed with making Ramtala into a fortress. His intelligence was, and is, greater than anyone else's and when he sets his mind on something, he accomplishes it. He invented an energy veil that he placed over the entire planet to protect us from enemy intrusion."

Tai sighed. "That's a good thing, isn't it?"

Neb continued, "Not really. Unfortunately, we all had a false sense of security and when the supernova exploded. We took it for granted that we'd be protected from everything, but the veil wasn't equipped to prevent the irradiation. The veil weakened and everyone on the planet blamed Lenox. As you can probably guess, that made him a little crazy. When my mother had me, she couldn't bear any more children and I, like everyone of my generation, was affected in the same way. For another ten thousand Earth years, Celeste and I fought side-by-side in the wars." He stopped talking and gazed off into the distance.

Tai got up, stretched and sat on the floor. "What was it like, Neb? The war, I mean."

"Boys, I'm not proud of what we did." Neb stood and paced. "The Malaris were an old species. Been around a lot longer than Ramtalans. Their only mistake was having no negotiating skills whatsoever. They refused to surrender."

Lola leaned against the cushions. "You said they 'were' an old species, like the Malaris aren't around anymore. What happened to them?"

Neb stopped pacing. "The whole thing started when the Malaris found out they were in jeopardy. Their planet couldn't sustain them anymore. They wanted to settle on Ramtala, but went about it all wrong."

Argus took Lola's hand, and she let him. As much as he wanted her to know everything about him, Neb's story didn't sound like it was going to end well and might make Lola want even more distance between them. "Maybe we *should* talk about this later, Neb. We have to find Aunt Celeste and stop Lenox and Galena."

"Seriously, bro? I want to hear this. Go ahead, Neb. Ignore my brother."

Neb motioned to Argus. "Argus is right, we have to stop Lenox. At all costs."

"Thank you." Argus got up. "Let's go."

Lola pulled him back down onto the couch. "No, Argus, I want to hear this, too. If Galena lied to me, I want to know. She said Lenox is trying to save Ramtala, but nobody will listen to him. Is that true, Neb?"

With a heavy sigh, Neb shook his head. "Not true at all, young lady. At the very beginning, the Malaris sent a fleet of vessels to Ramtala, but instead of making a formal request for help, they stormed in and attacked. In that first attack, we lost more than half a million of our people. The Malaris took up residency, keeping our people as prisoners and slaves. Of course, Ramtala was unprepared at first because we were a peaceful planet. But in secret, our elders put together a fleet of our own. You see, children, Ramtalan pure-forms have a more complex energy source than the Malaris, so when Lenox developed weaponry, the orbs, that draw on our Alpha 2a energy, we were able to defeat and kill the Malaris on Ramtala. Lenox was young at that point."

Argus couldn't believe it. Ramtala defeated the enemy by using the orbs. And now Lenox was going to use the same thing to kill New Breeds. "Neb, if Ramtala killed the Malaris in the first war, why were there more wars?"

"That wasn't the end of the first war. That was Ramtala's first wave, designed to eradicate the Malaris from our planet. After that, our fleet attacked first and laid waste to half their planet. This war went on for over thirty thousand planetary years. It ended in a stalemate. That's when Lenox really stepped things up. Records show that even as a child, he was devious and hyper-intelligent. The perfect killing machine. He developed incredible technological advancements throughout the wars. It just went back and forth, them attacking us, us attacking them. Each side created better killing weapons. It was only during the last war that Lenox implemented the energy veil. When the supernova exploded, about half of the Malaris fleets around Ramtala were destroyed, and those surviving were hunted down and...they only lasted another fifteen thousand planetary years after that. At that point, Lenox wasn't only thinking of Ramtala's safety. He was out for revenge and he used Celeste to kill off the Malaris. It was her unyielding ability to...we really should rescue her." He stood. "There's a shield around the court room and I can't wander the hallways or I'll be detected."

Argus waved his hand for attention. "Wait a second. How come Lenox didn't detect you before?"

Neb winked. "Tai concealed me. New Breeds, even converted ones, are hard to detect."

"What?" Argus turned to Tai. "What's he talking about?"

Tai smirked. "Remember how I told you that I learned some cool tricks when I was here last time? Well, one of those tricks is to project my energy source into an invisibility veil, sort of like the one you said Aunt Celeste covered you with at the airport when you hid from DeAlba. I covered Neb until we came to you."

"So do it again and then Neb can—"

Neb shook his head. "Can't. It takes too much energy and even with the Citadel's collective energy, it'll drain Tai too much, similar to how the XTRA-A1 drained you. Both New Breeds and pure-forms can only project a veil for a short time. We have to conserve as much energy as we can. Remember, pure-forms die once our energy is depleted, and I don't plan on dying any time soon. I can't tap into the Citadel's collective energy or they'll trace the signature and find me. This apartment is safe because of the shield around it. I can't be detected as long as I don't leave. But, I have a plan."

Argus stood with Tai. It was up to them to save Aunt Celeste and once they did, they'd have two battle-hardened pure-forms in the Citadel to fight Lenox and Galena. Now the trick would be keeping Lola safe while all of this went down. Even though he'd probably lost Lola's love forever, the thought of anything more happening to her hurt him to his core. Would life ever be normal again? All he wanted was to be with Lola, kayaking on Lake Elizabeth, sitting in *Marco's* eating pizza or dancing at the Prom. He glanced sideways and couldn't imagine a life without her. No matter what, he had to get her out of the Citadel and back home to her mother, who must be worried sick. What a mess it all was.

Argus straightened his shoulders. "What do you need us to do?"

Chapter 18

Max woke when the helicopter engine noise changed and he peered out the window as they descended into LAX. Jets were parked at the terminals, nose first, waiting for their passengers to disembark or board and fly off to some destination. None of those people knew anything at all about the impending Ramtalan war. They were the lucky ones.

He glanced over at Gretchen, who stared out her window. The helicopter flew over one runway to the other side of the airport and settled near a hangar. The rotors slowed and the pilot held up a hand.

Gretchen nudged Max. "That's our cue. Time to leave."

Max undid his seatbelt. "Ah, okay." He checked out the window again. There didn't seem to be anyone waiting for them at the hangar, so what were they supposed to do, take a cab, rent a car?

Gretchen opened the door, hopped out, waited for Max and then pointed to the hangar. "Neb said there's a car waiting for us."

When they got to the hangar, the helicopter lifted off and flew off toward the ocean, then made a sharp right turn and climbed into the clouds.

"A car?" Max found a metal door on the right side of the hangar and worked the handle. "Gretch, I want to know everything Neb said to you." As soon as he opened the door, a light came on and illuminated a shiny black Mercedes sedan. Damn, those Ramtalans sure knew how to live.

"Jackson, you drive." Gretchen went to the Mercedes and got into the passenger seat.

Max hesitated. He'd rather go it alone and get away from Gretchen. All he had to do was contact John and Angel at Edwards for help. Screw Stone, he was either dead or had his memory erased, and either of those scenarios meant he was useless. Once in the driver's seat, he turned to Gretchen.

"Why are we going to AURA? Stone isn't there. He's still in Labrador. What's at AURA?"

"Neb wants me to recover something from the AURA laboratory. Something that's locked away in a secret vault."

"A secret vault? I don't know of any vaults. Neb's crazy." Max started the car and noticed a remote control on the dash. He pressed the button and the huge hangar door started to roll upward like a giant garage door. "Trust me, Gretch, there's no vault in the lab."

"Well, there is. We just have to find it. Now drive, Jackson." Gretchen snapped on her seat belt, leaned back and pointed to the open door. "Go."

Go? She ordered him around like he was nothing. Yeah, it was Gretchen who had to *go*. "Sure." Max accelerated fast and slid the car on the pavement as he turned outside the hangar. AURA was only a short distance from LAX, which wouldn't give him much time to ditch Gretchen. Once he was free, he'd go and find the secret vault and bingo! He'd have whatever it was Neb wanted so bad. Maybe Neb used his freaky powers to read Stone's mind and that's how he knew about the vault. *Well, Neb, you'll never get your alien hands on whatever's in it*. Max smiled to himself. That'd be the bargaining tool he needed. Remove the monitor or lose the prize. *I've got you now, you alien asshole!*

He drove to Wilshire Boulevard, pulled into the employee parking lot under the Federal Building and used his ID for access. "You ready for this, Gretch? I'm *persona non grata*, so if Stone has security on the look-out for me, we'll be in deep shit."

"Whatever. Neb gave me orders, so yeah, I'm ready. I can't go against what he said. I wish I could, Jackson, but I can't. You'd better keep out of sight then, because I'm not about to get in any deep shit." Gretchen frowned.

The parking structure was full, meaning there were tons of employees at work and that was going to complicate things. Max climbed out of the car and jogged toward the stairwell, trying to think of some way to get rid of Gretchen. A low-tech escape plan tickled his brain. He swiped his ID and the door unlocked, but before Gretchen got there, he ducked into the stairwell and pulled the door shut. Gretchen didn't have an ID badge. She was stuck and he was free. Sometimes low-tech worked best.

Chapter 19

While Lola walked around the apartment mumbling to herself, Argus sat with Tai and Neb in the living room, discussing Neb's plan to get to Aunt Celeste. What Neb wanted seemed impossible.

Argus shook his head. "Neb, we can't get through the shield that's around the court room. I can't even do it. I tried. Besides, I don't know for sure if Aunt Celeste is really in there or not. Plus, Galena and Lenox must know I'm not in the command center any more. They'll be looking for me."

With a sigh, Tai nodded. "He's right. Even with the collective energy, there's no way to break through the shield. We had the orb last time, so unless you happen to have another one in your back pocket, we're screwed."

"Well," Neb started, "I will have another orb, but I'm not about to waste it on breaking out Celeste."

"Seriously?" Argus jumped up off the couch. "I thought Aunt Celeste was your friend. I don't think rescuing her is a *waste*."

Neb's eyes flashed blue. "She is my friend, Argus. Don't ever accuse me of not caring about my friends. The energy orbs aren't something you can pick up at your local convenience store, they're hard to come by. Therefore, Argus, when I get my hands on one, I plan to use it to deactivate the entire Citadel shield. You and Tai have to get to Celeste without an orb. Understand?" He didn't even try to hide his anger.

"Sorry." Argus felt small. He knew nothing about war or Ramtalan weapons. "How do we get to her then?"

Neb's eyes dimmed to normal. "I didn't mean to lose my temper." He got up and gave Argus a pat on the arm. "We friends again?"

Argus nodded. "Of course."

"Good."

"Glad we're all friends, but..." Tai exaggerated a shrug. "Where's this new orb of yours?"

Neb sighed. "It's getting retrieved."

Argus looked at Tai, who rolled his eyes. "Ah, okay, I get it, you don't want to tell us. Fine. Then how do we get into the court room?"

After giving Argus another pat, Neb motioned to Lola, who was now sitting at the breakfast bar. "Your girlfriend is going to help us."

"No." Argus stepped away from Neb. "The only thing Lola's doing is going home."

"I've got to agree with Arg on this one, Neb." Tai pointed to Lola. "She could get hurt. She's human and we're not supposed to hurt humans."

With another, deeper sigh, Neb lowered his voice, "You're both very young. Sometimes we have to do things, bend the rules a little, when there's no other choice."

Argus took a few breaths to calm the energy that was building up. "You mean bending the rules like mixing Ramtalan DNA with human DNA without asking humans if that was okay? Isn't that pretty much the same thought process the Malaris used? They invaded Ramtala without asking if they could live with you. What's the difference between you and the Malaris?"

Neb's eyes flamed. "Early humans were incapable of understanding what we were doing. What we did was nothing like what the Malaris did. We didn't kill or destroy. And we didn't merge our DNA with *all* of the early humans, only the strongest. But, yes, Argus, you are right about one thing. For our species to survive, we came to Earth without asking permission. If we hadn't, you and your brother wouldn't be standing here. Or is that your point, you want to martyr yourself and end it all? Sacrifice yourself and all of the New Breeds to Lenox?" His whole body shimmered blue.

"Whoa, dude." Tai backed away. "You're glowing blue, Neb."

Neb stepped back and pressed his palms together. "Stand back, both of you. I'm inadvertently reverting to my pure-form state. I need to stop it."

"What?" Argus grabbed Tai by the arm and pulled him farther away. "What do you mean? Why are you...?"

Tai yanked his arm free and whispered, "Bro, did we make him do that?"

"I think it was me. I didn't mean to accuse him of anything." Argus saw Lola. "I have to protect Lola." He ran to her, scooped her off the stool and carried her behind the kitchen counter. She struggled until he put her down.

"What are you doing, Argus?"

"Duck down. Please." He gently pushed her to the ground behind the counter. "I don't know if it's dangerous of not, but I can't have you get hurt."

She didn't resist. "Okay. But what's the danger?"

"I'm not sure. Promise me you won't move."

"Okay." She slumped against the cabinets. "I hate all of this."

"I know. I'll make it up to you one day. If it's the last thing I ever do, I'll make it up to you." He gave her a quick kiss on the cheek and rushed back to Tai.

"Bro, he's freaking out." Tai motioned to Neb.

Neb's entire body was encased in a translucent blue cocoon that vibrated and pulsated. There was no way to know exactly what was going on, nobody had ever explained the process of using a host body or going back to the pure-form state.

"Tai, what happens if he goes pure-form? Did you find any information on the computers?"

"You mean from before? No. I never thought to look. But this looks like a metamorphosis, doesn't it? Like he's wrapped in a cocoon."

Argus nodded. "That's exactly what I was thinking. He said he was going to try to stop it, but maybe he can't. Damn it, what are we supposed to do, stand here like idiots while he pupates or whatever?"

"That's a little insulting, bro. He's not a bug."

"Sorry, I didn't mean it like that. But seriously, what should we do?"

"No idea." Tai took a step forward. "Neb? Can you hear me?"

The cocoon began to fade away starting at the center. Argus watched as Neb slowly appeared, still in his host body, but he was standing very still and his skin was blue all over. After a moment, he opened his eyes and blinked a few times.

"Neb?" Argus asked. "Are you all right? I'm sorry if I caused this."

When the cocoon dissipated completely, Neb drew in a breath. "Not your fault, Argus. Is everyone all right?"

Argus nodded. "Yeah, nothing happened. Are you sure you're okay?"

Neb rolled his neck and stretched his arms above his head. "I'm fine. I suppressed the change. Sorry for losing control, but there's too much going on and too much collective energy. It strained my emotions to the breaking point. I apologize, boys, if I scared you."

Argus shook his head. He had been scared, but he didn't want Tai, or Lola, to know. "No, it was a bit weird, that's all. I'll be right back." He ran to Lola. "It's okay now, you can come out."

"Argus, Galena's looking for you." Lola shrugged. "I don't know how I know that."

"I don't either. I'll find out though and we'll figure it all out. I have to talk to Neb and Tai. Are you going to be all right here for a few minutes?" Argus took her hand in his and gave it a gentle squeeze.

She pulled it away. "Sure. Go."

Would she ever forgive him? He rushed back to Tai and Neb. "I had to make sure Lola wasn't too scared. So, Neb, I've been wondering, what exactly is a host body? I was going to ask Aunt Celeste, but never got the chance. And she never offered to tell us."

Neb kept stretching. "Oh. I assumed she told you. I have to rest for a few minutes anyway to allow my body to readjust. If you think you can handle the details, I'll tell you."

With a roll of his eyes, Tai groaned. "Of course we can handle it. We're not little kids."

Neb continued, "No, you're not. You already know that our pure-form state is our natural body, made up of purified Alpha 2a energy. By the way, the Malaris have a form of energy called Zeta 40, but we'll save that for another time. To move around on Earth, we adopted the use of a host body. At first, we didn't bother, but as the humans became more evolved, they began asking questions and couldn't handle beings that looked so different. Mythology is made up of stories about us in various forms. Again, we can talk about that later." Neb moved to the couch and sat down.

Tai spoke up, "Aunt Celeste already told us that most of the myths about gods were really about Ramtalans."

Neb nodded thoughtfully. "Those were good times. Before humans had the desire to hunt us down. But, I digress. You know how we can manipulate genetics, well, that's what we do when we take a host."

"Take a host?" Argus glanced at Tai. "You kill someone and take their body?"

Tai looked shocked. "I thought you couldn't hurt humans."

"Boys, we don't exactly kill the human." Neb stretched his legs out. "We find a human who is about to die, then we create what you just saw, an Alpha 2a energy isolation field that unites the human body with our pure-form state. The human, for all intents and purposes, is gone and we remain. This cannot be done without the human giving us permission. That's why it's difficult to find a host. Most people want their loved ones to bury their body. Anyway, once we're united in the host body, it sort of morphs into a reflection of the pure-form Ramtalan. We're all taller than the average human, so the host body increases in height. Our personalities are incorporated into the body. Lenox was the one who came up with the technology to do this so the host body would never look exactly like it did originally. We couldn't have friends or relatives walking up to us, now could we?" He stopped and stared at them. "You understand?"

Argus let it all sink in for a moment before nodding. "What would have happened to the host body if you, ah, reverted?"

"It would have vaporized. Like I said, that's not a good thing because it's really hard to get another one. That's one reason Settlers stay on Earth for so long. If we went back to Ramtala in our pure-form state and then came back to Earth, we'd have to start all over again. Plus, it uses a lot of our energy to travel back and forth. And now with agencies like AURA snooping around, being a pure-form isn't as easy as it once was." He stood and worked his shoulders. "All right, I'm good. Now, you boys have to go and get Celeste."

"Wait." Argus pointed to Lola. "Lola said Galena is looking for me."

"Hmmm." Neb stepped out of the living room. "That's an interesting side effect. Lola, can you tell where Galena is now?"

Lola glanced at Argus, then back at Neb. "Did she make me one of you?"

Neb went to her. "You're human, Lola. You're not Ramtalan. But it appears as if you have a slight connection to Galena. That could work to our advantage. Try to concentrate on her."

"This isn't fair." Lola pouted. "I don't want any alien abilities. I just want to be me."

Argus wanted to hold her and wrap her in his arms, tell her everything would be okay and that she had nothing to worry about, but that's not what she wanted, at least not yet. "Lola, I'll figure something out. Maybe Galena can undo what she did or it'll wear off."

With a sideways glance, Neb gave Argus a slight shake of his head. "We'll talk later about genetics and trace Ramtalan energy, but for now, I need Celeste. Lola, because you're not Ramtalan, Galena can't track you, which means you can move around the Citadel unseen. Now, concentrate on Galena."

With her pout deepening, Lola closed her eyes. "I can't see...wait." She opened her eyes. "I saw her. How can I see her?"

"Don't freak, Lola." Tai came over and put his hand on her shoulder. "The first time Arg and I found our abilities, it was kind of weird, too. Just go with it."

"Go with it?" She groaned. "Whatever. Galena's in a room with white walls and blue lights, but she's not alone."

Neb's eyes were softly glowing. "Is she with Lenox?"

"Yes." Lola closed her eyes again. "They're in a room, an apartment. I can see a kitchen...it looks a lot like this room."

"What?" Argus looked at the wall separating them from Aunt Celeste's room. He lowered his voice, "Neb, could they be..."

Without answering, Neb sprinted to the connecting door between the rooms and placed his hand flat against it. A moment later he shook his head. "I don't sense any Ramtalans. Okay, enough delay, we have to spring Celeste and get the hell out of here."

Tai let out a breath. "No argument from me. Lola, if I tell you where the court room is, can you—?"

"I said she wasn't doing anything." Argus ran in front of Lola. He had to protect her and keep her safe. Nothing was more important. "You're not going to use her. I'll go."

"Argus," Neb said sternly, "You're Ramtalan. Galena or Lenox will locate you as soon as you step out of this apartment. I'm not risking either you or Tai getting caught."

Argus continued to block Lola. "Just why is he so hell-bent on killing the New Breeds? I still don't get it. He was the one who came up with the plan in the first place, right? To save Ramtalan DNA? Why does he hate us, I mean, them? It doesn't make sense."

Neb ran his hands over his hair. "I don't have an answer for you. All I know is that we need to stop him. This planet is all we have. Because you boys are the key to his plan, I'll protect both of you up until my last breath."

"And Lola." Argus turned to face her. "Don't worry, I won't let anything happen to you."

Her eyes narrowed. "Yeah, you've done a great job so far." She spun around and stormed into the living room.

"Bro, I don't know how you can possibly patch things up with Lola at this point. But there's always Sandra at Marco's." He raised an eyebrow. "She's into you."

"I'm not sure I'm into her." Argus sighed and sat on a stool. Nobody got to him like Lola did. Sure other girls were pretty and he was attracted to them, but Lola made him feel normal, like they had a special connection. Was that love?

"Not into her? Really? Arg, you're her date. Did you forget?"

"Shit. Yeah I did forget." He chuckled lightly. "Dating is the last thing on my mind right now."

"Date?" Neb shook his head. "We're at war and your old life is history. Wake up, boys. Your abilities and genetics have changed you forever. There's no going back to being regular, football-playing, girl-chasing teenage boys."

Argus glanced at Tai. That's all they ever wanted to be. Tai had been so excited to go to high school and meet girls. He'd been happy, right up to the point where Galena altered his DNA. Was Neb right? Had everything changed so much that they'd never be allowed to live like regular people? And what about Lola? Her life had been turned upside down for sure.

Neb let out a sigh and wandered into the kitchen, which gave Argus the opportunity to get his brother alone. He tugged on Tai's sleeve and motioned for him to go up into the loft and once there, Argus put his finger to his lips and kept his voice low.

"I don't think Neb has our best interests in mind. All he cares about is defeating Galena."

"Totally agree with you, bro. He's a mercenary and mercenaries don't care about anything but winning. He's got a vendetta against Galena." Tai glanced down at Neb.

"How do you know anything about mercenaries and vendettas?"

"Seriously, Arg?" Tai rolled his eyes. "I've watched movies. He's so desperate to get Aunt Celeste and capture Galena that he doesn't care about us or Lola."

"You're wrong about one thing. He does care about us, but only because Lenox needs us. I think he wants to use us as bait. We've got to get out of here. With Lola." Argus peeked over the railing and saw Neb rooting through the fridge. "What about if we try to use the robot waiter to disable the energy shield around the Citadel? Commander Jampara did it. Once it's down, we can shift back to Palmdale with Lola."

"And do what? You don't think Neb and his minions will come after us? Arg, think." Tai paced. "Hold up. What do you think'll happen if Aunt Celeste does break out of the court room?"

"I'm not sending Lola out there and put her in danger." Argus sat on his bed.

Tai continued, "What if we go with her?"

"With Lola? Are you crazy? Galena will detect me. Detect us."

"Exactly. Neb said he's got someone bringing another energy orb weapon thing, so what if we wait until he has it, give it to Lola and send her to the court room. Then we follow a few seconds later. Galena will find us, but she won't be looking for Lola. We'll be the distraction that will let Lola get to Aunt Celeste."

Argus shook his head. "No. Using Lola is exactly what Neb wants. And then we'll be captives of Galena and Lenox."

"I didn't finish, bro. You always jump to conclusions before you let me finish. Anyway, as soon as Aunt Celeste is free, Neb can then use the orb to disable the shield. When that happens, we'll shift, with Lola, back home."

"Tai, the shift killed Lola."

"I know, but that was before Galena did her Ramtalan magic. They share something, and that something is protecting Lola."

Argus shook his head. "You don't know that. You're guessing."

"I'm not." Tai smirked. "Neb let it slip. He said Lola had a trace of Ramtalan energy. That's going to let her make it through a shift."

"I don't know." Argus checked over the rail and watched Lola.

Tai continued, "Galena won't know Lola has an orb because we'll be the ones she finds."

That sort of made sense. "You think Galena's guard will be down? But how's Neb going to get the orb in the first place? The shield's up now."

"Well, damn it. I didn't think of that." Tai smirked. "Hey, Neb! How are you going to get the orb since the shield's up?" He turned to Argus. "Sometimes being direct works."

Neb appeared in the loft, holding two cartons of orange juice, which he handed to them. "Commander Jampara is going to help with that. A mutual friend of ours, Gretchen Manheim, is going to bring an orb to the Commander. Trust me when I say the Commander knows what to do. He's not very happy about this little insurrection of Galena's."

Argus paced. "So he'll use the orb to destroy the shield? Then how do we get Aunt Celeste? Won't the orb get destroyed?"

"We'll use the orb, but not in the way you think. Once the Commander has the orb, he'll combine his Alpha 2a with the orb's and..." Neb paused. "It doesn't matter. All you need to know is that we'll have the Citadel back and all of Galena's energy shields will fall." He smiled and winked.

"Wait a second." Argus replayed everything in his mind. "You said you wanted Lola to go to the court room and get Aunt Celeste. Why? That doesn't make sense. You don't need her at all, because you just said the orb will break down the shields."

There was a strange expression on Neb's face, like he'd been caught in a lie. "It's all strategy, Argus. I told you that you don't understand strategy."

"But *I* do." Tai came forward and poked Neb in the chest. "You want to use *Lola* as bait. You'll make sure she gets caught trying to break into the court room, providing you with a distraction so you and Commander Jampara can attack. You're a major dick, Neb. You don't know what might happen to Lola. You've been playing us all along."

"Playing you?" Neb's eyes steadily glowed brighter. "I never play. But you caught me, Tai. I do need Lola to be a distraction. Whatever Galena did left a trace of Alpha 2a within Lola's DNA, enough to be tracked. Galena will know when Lola's on the move and will track her, taking her concentration away from what we're doing on the outside. We only need a few seconds for Galena to stop monitoring us so Jampara can merge his energy with the orb. That's going to show up as a spike of Alpha 2a, but if Galena's not looking..."

So much for their plan of going with Lola. Argus felt his energy collecting in the pit of his stomach again and more than anything, he wanted to fire off a burst right at Neb. "I can't believe you'd do that to Lola."

In an instant, Neb had Argus by the shoulders and slammed him onto the floor, straddling him. "Let me put this in words you can understand. She's your Kryptonite, your weakness. You don't see straight or think straight around her. I need her out of the way and I need that distraction." He got up and glared at Tai. "Don't try anything, Tai, or you'll force me to act. I need you both unharmed."

What the hell was going on? Argus jumped up and stood with his brother. Was Neb a traitor or was this how mercenaries acted? Whatever he was up to was unacceptable. Argus felt his energy dissipate. "You're not using Lola. I won't let you."

Tai raised his palm toward Neb. "And don't you ever touch my brother again."

Neb lunged forward and slapped Tai's hand away. "What part of *war* don't you understand? I'm doing what's best for Ramtala and Earth. I'm not the enemy, but if you insist on acting like *my* enemy, I will treat you as such."

"You have been playing us." Argus drew in a deep breath. "Why couldn't you tell us the truth instead of screwing with us like this? We're not stupid punk kids, Neb. We get it. We know what's at stake. Be truthful and we'll help. But if you lie, we won't cooperate."

Neb turned to Tai. "Is that how you feel, too?"

With a nod, Tai clasped his hands together. It looked like that was his way of controlling his impulse to fire a pulse at Neb. Part of Argus wanted him to fire. Their whole lives were filled with lies and deception. It was time for the truth.

"Fine." Neb shrugged and sat on the floor at the foot of the bed. "You don't know everything about me. Or Celeste for that matter. Be certain you're ready to hear this."

"Go ahead." Argus was done with being kept in the dark. He wanted full disclosure from Neb.

"All right, here goes." Neb sat cross-legged with his hands on his knees. "War sometimes brings out the worst in people, boys, and survival is a very primal instinct. That said, there are times when war is necessary."

Argus understood. "Like when the Malaris attacked Ramtala."

Neb nodded slowly. "Precisely. My people, our people, had lived in peace with our neighbors for eons. Our ancestors traveled the galaxy and learned much from other species. They all worked together to set up a sort of information network where everyone benefited from this shared knowledge. Earth was in the first stages of being able to support life, but was still a volcanic mess. Nobody gave it a passing glance as it wasn't even considered a viable planet at the time. Funny how things changed later on. Anyway, back to my story. Ramtala never dealt much with the Malaris because they rejected the invitation to join this union of planets. We didn't consider them hostile or enemies. We left them alone and they left us alone. There are millions of other planets in our galaxy that also wanted to be isolated, like the Malaris, and the union paid them no mind either."

"Millions?" Tai sat on his bed.

Neb continued, "Ramtala had never been at war with any species until the Malaris. We were ill equipped to handle hostility, as I said before."

"Yeah, I know." Argus peered downstairs and saw Lola sitting at the breakfast bar with a glass of ice water. He went and sat with Tai. "So what's this secret about you and Aunt Celeste?"

"Not a secret. I just didn't think you'd want to hear it." Neb stretched his legs out. "Celeste is an expert at interrogation. She always gets what she wants. No matter what it takes."

Argus swallowed. What did that mean? "Like what, Neb?"

"You already know that Celeste can alter genetics like Galena can, but not as nearly as good. Celeste has another gift as well. She's a close second to the Commander in synaptic readjustment."

"What the hell is that?" Tai leaned forward. He breathed heavily.

"Please don't think any less of her, boys." Neb smoothed his hair. "She interrogated multitudes of Malaris by extracting their thoughts and memories. The problem was, since they contain Zeta 40 energy, her techniques left them, well, it was a one-way trip for them."

"They died?" Argus felt his stomach clench. "She killed them?"

"I warned you that you might not want to hear this." Neb stood.

Argus regretted insisting Neb spill the truth. He got up and hurried downstairs. Nothing was the same anymore, except for one thing; Lola. He went to her and wrapped his arms around her. She was what he needed. She was his comfort, not his Kryptonite.

Chapter 20

Max pressed his ear against the cold metal of the door of the parking garage and listened as Gretchen cursed, kicked, and banged. He'd screwed her over and she wasn't any too happy about it. Too bad. He had to find the vault himself so he could own Neb's ass once and for all. Whatever Neb wanted was important and that meant it could be used as a bargaining tool, or even better, his destruction.

But the fuss Gretchen was causing with her assault on the door would draw attention to herself and get her arrested. Well, maybe that'd be a good thing. Nobody would believe she was with him. He turned away from the door and hurried down the stairs to the AURA lab. He had to find the vault before Neb got wind of the double-cross.

As luck would have it, there wasn't anyone in the corridors. They were probably all locked away in some secret meeting to discuss Stone's disappearance, and his replacement. AURA never wasted time replacing employees when they were burned out or terminated. Hopefully Neb had taken Stone completely out of the picture. Then they'd need a new chief and who would be better to replace him than Max Jackson, professional alien hunter. With the Ramtalans at his mercy, they'd promote him without a second thought.

Max smiled and used his key card to access the lab. The lights were on, not surprising since it was the middle of the day, but he'd need to be stealthy. He crept around, peering at the racks of glassware and weird bottles of colorful reagents. Where would something Ramtalan be hidden? He checked the walls for hidden compartments, but found nothing.

Maybe it was a floor safe. After checking every inch of the floor, underneath cabinets and tables, he came up empty. Where was the damn vault? The lab supervisor had his own office down the hall, maybe there was something in there.

He jogged to the office and rapped twice on the door. "Hello? Dr. Allen? You in there?"

Nothing. He tried the knob and found the door unlocked. Cool. He slipped inside and had to take a couple of seconds to take it all in. The office was huge with a couch and recliner to one side and a mini-bar across the room. Max's office was maybe a third the size of this one. After shaking off his jealousy, he wandered around, but like the lab, there wasn't any vault. Did Neb send them on a wild goose chase?

"Jackson."

Max spun around and saw Gretchen in the doorway. "Gretch? How'd you get down here? You don't have an ID badge." How could he explain his way out of locking her out of the stairwell?

She turned her hand over and showed him a small blue dot in the middle of her palm. "I don't need an ID badge. That creep, Neb, put something in my hand that circumvents human technology."

"Human technology? You're talking like one of them, Gretch. You're human, not Ramtalan."

"Yeah, like I don't know that. Oh, and thanks for ditching me." She motioned for him to leave. "The vault's not here, by the way."

"Then where the hell is it?" It looked like he was stuck with her, for the time being anyway.

She stepped into the corridor. "There's a secret vault, down a level."

What was she talking about? There wasn't another level. "Gretch, this is the bottom level. You've got your intel wrong."

She shook her head. "No, I don't. I'm Neb's puppet, remember? He commands me where to go, so I go. He says there's a lower level, and that's where we're going."

Max followed her down the corridor to an unmarked door without a knob or security key pad. "How do we get in there, then? There's no way in, except by breaking it down. Besides, the elevator stops on this floor, so do the stairs. There isn't a lower level."

Without answering, she pressed her palm against the center of the door. "What part of *secret* vault don't you get, Jackson?"

The door slid open and Gretchen stepped inside with a smile. "Secret elevator that leads to the secret vault."

"Holy, shit. I had no idea this was here. What other secrets does AURA have that I don't know about?" He stepped in.

"Probably a ton." She pressed her palm to the right side of the door and it slid closed. The elevator jerked and descended. "It's so freaking weird how I know to do this stuff. I think this was designed by Lenox in the 60s. At least that's what's churning in my Ramtalan-manipulated brain."

"You're weirding me out." Max held onto a rail and watched Gretchen. She was a Ramtalan informant and that meant he couldn't trust her. Once she found whatever Neb wanted, he'd make sure she never made it out of the vault.

Chapter 21

Argus held onto Lola until she gently pushed him away. He could have stayed in her arms forever, if she'd let him. After a while, Tai came down and flopped onto a stool at the breakfast bar and shook his head slowly.

"Arg, Aunt Celeste is a badass."

With a nod, Argus whispered, "So's Neb. I feel so...betrayed. Nobody's told us the truth, up until now."

"Both of you need to wake up," Lola said quietly. "We've all been used by these aliens. I just want to go home and forget all about this place and Ramtala."

Tai glanced up at Neb in the loft. "Maybe you can forget, Lola, but we can't. We're not even human anymore." He suddenly looked away. "And I thought we were freaks *before*."

Tai said what Argus was thinking. How would they fit in anywhere now? "We have to get out of here."

"Of course we do, but how?" Lola sighed and glanced at the loft. "Neb isn't going to let us out of his sight and Galena can track me and Neb. We're stuck here."

"Wait." Argus kept his eyes on Neb. "Tai, you're still wearing your Citadel jumpsuit."

"That's an obvious observation, bro."

"Listen," Argus whispered, "Aunt Celeste told me that the metallic bands around the sleeves actually restrict our energy, that's why she had me change when she merged our energies. Take off that damn jumpsuit and we'll merge our energies. We'll be stronger that way."

Tai raised an eyebrow. "I like the sound of that. How do we do it?"

Argus remembered what Aunt Celeste did, although she brought her blue energy ball out of her body. He and Tai couldn't do that, so how could they merge? What if it wasn't safe? After all, his eyes flipped to red after it was done. What might happen a second time? "Now that I think about it, maybe it's not such a good idea."

"It's the best idea we have. The only idea actually." Tai drew in a breath. "Tell me how you did it."

Right after Argus explained the procedure, Neb appeared in the kitchen. "Boys, what are you whispering about? Conspiring?"

With a roll of his eyes, Tai glared at Neb. "Yeah, sure. We're conspiring and trying to figure out how to take over the Citadel and send all you Ramtalans back home. Is that what you want to hear?"

The intensity in Neb's eyes made Argus back away. Tai seemed to enjoy antagonizing anyone who pissed him off. In this case, it probably wasn't the smartest thing to do.

Neb relaxed a bit. "No, Tai, I expect loyalty. You're one of the sons of Argustine Lenox, you have to work a bit harder than everyone else to prove your loyalty."

"That's not fair, Neb." Argus walked into the kitchen. He had to get Neb out of the way. "Just leave us alone." He motioned to Tai. "Let's go to the loft. I need some time away from these pure-forms."

"I'm with you, bro."

Lola got off her stool. "I'm coming with you. No point hanging around down here with an attitudey Ramtalan." She gave Argus a discreet wink and went up the spiral staircase.

With a dismissive wave, Neb wandered toward the living room. "Go ahead and revel in your teenage angst, but remember, I'm one of the good guys."

Argus followed his brother to the loft where Lola paced. She stopped and whispered to Argus, "Do whatever you have to do. I'll let you know if I feel Galena coming."

"Thanks." Argus kissed her on the cheek and tugged on Tai's sleeve. "I think if we concentrate on our energy, like I do when I'm going to fire a burst—"

"And then what?" Tai sat on the edge of his bed. "This won't work. The only time we sort of merge together is if we do a shift at the same—"

"Then we'll shift, but stay within the loft." Argus winked at Lola. "If this goes right, Lola, we'll disappear and reappear, so don't freak."

"Seriously, Argie, nothing freaks me out at this point."

Argie? She hadn't said that in a long time. He sat on the bed with Tai. "Okay then. Can you keep an eye on Neb as well?"

She nodded and went to the rail.

Tai slipped off the jumpsuit and dressed in jeans and a black tee shirt. "I hope this works. I think we can initiate a shift, but not actually go anywhere. That way it should blend our energies and, with a huge chunk of luck, not kill us." He extended his hand.

Argus nodded and took his hand. "Yeah, that last part is what's worrying me, but I'm not about to die and leave Lola here by herself."

"She'd never forgive you." Tai drew in a breath. "Ready?"

"You know it." Argus closed his eyes and concentrated on shifting. If they were successful, they'd have a lot more power, maybe even enough to fight against Lenox. Then they wouldn't need Neb or even Aunt Celeste. And, if they could defeat Lenox, Lola would never be in danger again. She could go back to school and resume her life, without any Ramtalans to bother her. Of course that meant he could never see her again, but knowing she was back in Palmdale would be the best reward.

"Bro?" Tai's voice was faint. "Arg."

Argus opened his eyes and had to blink a few times to clear his vision. For a moment, he couldn't place where he was. It certainly wasn't the loft at the Citadel. "Tai, are we where I think we are?"

Tai let go of Argus's hand. "Yeah. But how? I was thinking of the staying in the loft."

Oh, no. "I wasn't. I was thinking about Palmdale and school."

Right there in front of them was Lenox's XTRA-A1, decorated with tissue paper and blinking lights, with a huge blue ribbon stuck onto the nose that declared it was the First Place Float. Argus looked up at the sun and realized it had to be a bit after midday. He'd gone through the shield, this time with Tai.

"Arg, seriously? You brought us to school? You're a lot stronger than me now. You dragged me here and I couldn't do anything about it. This isn't exactly the best place for us. Remember what happened at Lake Elizabeth? We've been exposed."

"I know. Damn it, I know. We have to shift back." Argus checked the area. Class must be in session. "At least there's nobody on the field."

Tai nodded just as the bell rang. He pointed to the locker room doors as they opened. "Correction, there wasn't anybody on the field. That was the class bell. We're screwed."

"Shift, Tai!" Argus grabbed his hand, but Tai shook loose.

"I need to concentrate and I can't concentrate when there are a bunch of kids staring at me."

A dozen or more guys poured onto the field and quickly gathered around Argus and Tai. Behind them, dragging a bag, was Dave. He dropped the bag and stood there, gaping.

"Dachels?" Dave limped over. "What...what's going on? Ah, man, is this an invasion?"

Argus pulled Dave closer. "How much does everyone know?"

"Ah, it's just sort of rumor really. Whoa, man, your eyes."

"Bro, cover up."

Argus shielded his eyes. "What else, Dave?"

Dave continued, "There's all this talk about what happened at the lake, but some Air Force dudes came and had an assembly and said there's nothing to worry about, there aren't any aliens. They said all kinds of crazy stuff like it was a hoax or a prank. And get this, they said the dead kids were killed by explosions caused by methane in the lake. That's BS, man."

"Yeah, it is." Tai exhaled. "Dave, we have to get out of here. Can you help us?"

With a smile, Dave nodded. "You bet! Hey, do you know where Lola is? She's missing and her mom is blaming you, Argus."

"I'm sure she is. Yes, I know where she is and she's safe. For now." Argus saw one of his friends wearing sunglasses. "Hey, Jas, can I borrow your shades? My eyes are, ah, sensitive."

Jas took off the sunglasses and tossed them to Argus. "Yeah, no prob. Hey, where have you guys been? Things are weird around here."

How could he explain his way out of this? At least lying wasn't so hard anymore. "My brother and I were witnesses at the lake and the cops took us in for questioning."

Another guy spoke up, "We heard some shit went down at the lake. Aliens appeared and killed people. Is any of that true or is it all fake like the Air Force guys said?"

Tai kept his voice low, "What do they want to hear? Do they want it to be fake?"

Argus shrugged. "I think so. They'll sleep better thinking we're not on the brink of an attack." He stepped forward. "Hey, guys, the cops finally let us go when they realized we didn't know anything about the methane or whatever it was that killed those guys."

The coach jogged onto the field. "Is that the Dachels? Holy Mother of God, it is. Where the hell have you been? We've got a game in two days. Suit up and practice!"

There wasn't any time for football. In fact, there wasn't any time to be a high school student. Any chance of normality was long gone. Argus motioned to Tai. "Coach, Dave just told me that my brother and I have to report to the office. We'll come right back as soon as we're done."

Coach groaned. "Make it quick. Go with them Dave and bring them right back. You're accountable for them. And somebody move this damn float!"

Dave nodded and limped toward the locker room door. Argus jogged beside Tai to catch up.

"Tai, we have to move the XTRA-A1."

"Sure, we'll just fly it out of here in broad daylight." Tai stopped at the locker room door. "You heard what Dave said, nobody really thinks we're aliens. Hotwiring a spaceship during football practice probably isn't a great idea."

"I didn't mean now. We can tell Coach we'll move it after school. Then we can take it somewhere safe, shift back to the Citadel and—"

Dave stepped in between them both. "And what? What exactly is going on? Are the aliens really invading us?"

Argus spoke before Tai had the chance, "No. It'll be all right."

"Argus, what happened to your eyes, man? I've seen bloodshot eyes before, but this is...not right." Dave took a few steps back. "I didn't mean to sound like an ass. Don't get mad or anything."

Slipping the sunglasses off, Argus looked at Dave. "This is what I look like now? You're not afraid of me, are you? I'm still me."

Tai sighed. "Yeah, but a new and improved version."

With a shrug, Dave said quietly, "No, I'm not scared of you. But you do still consider me your friend, right?"

Argus put the sunglasses back on, gave Dave a nod and a genial slap on the arm, and opened the door. Dave was his best friend and the thought of him being afraid actually hurt. This wasn't his home anymore. Nowhere was. He didn't belong anywhere.

Aunt Celeste hadn't told them the entire truth, Neb wasn't trustworthy, and Lenox and Galena wanted to use him and Tai. And worst of all, Lola hated his guts. Although she did let him kiss her, so maybe there was still hope.

Of course now they couldn't go back to the Citadel until they could move the XTRA-A1. If they left it, someone from AURA or Edwards would eventually find it and then they'd definitely be exposed as Ramtalans, and the humans would have access to Lenox's tech.

He hurried through the locker room and stepped into the hallway, working hard to suppress the urge to fire a burst. It wasn't fair that he had to give up everything. Even if he defeated Lenox, he'd never be the same. Commander Jampara wouldn't let him leave the Citadel now. He'd be a prisoner. "Screw it," he mumbled. He wanted to feel normal one last time.

In the span of a heartbeat, he shifted and appeared outside of *Marco's*. This is where he needed to be, just for a little while. He went inside and saw Sandra taking an order. He'd made a date with her. When was it? It didn't matter, he wasn't going. She noticed him and waved.

"Argus!" She hurried over. "I haven't seen you in so long. You wouldn't believe the insane rumors floating around."

"Yeah, I would. How've you been?" He breathed in the aroma of melted cheese and pizza sauce that seemed to cling to her. "I'm starving."

She smiled sweetly. "Go and have a seat. Your regular booth is open. I'll sneak you a slice and a soda."

"Thanks." He sat and glanced around. There wasn't anyone he knew, not surprising since school was still in session. There were a couple of adults having lunch, but the way they looked at him and whispered made him uncomfortable.

Sandra came back with a drink. "Don't worry about them. I told you, everyone's been talking about what went on at the lake. Your picture was in the papers. So was your brother's. I think they were your driver's license photos. Are you guys okay?"

He downed half of the soda. "Yeah, we're fine. Hey, Sandra, want to get out of here?"

"What? Now?" She pointed to a clock on the wall. "I can't. I'm supposed to be in school, but I ditched so I could cover a shift for my friend. She dropped out of school because she's pregnant and needs the money, but she's got awful morning sickness. Anyway, I still have a half hour to go."

"Okay. I'll wait." He leaned back and kept his head down to avoid making eye contact with anyone.

"Cool. I'll go bring you that pizza." She smiled again and went to the kitchen.

"Bro." Tai appeared in the booth across from him. "You didn't think I'd find you with shared-sight?"

"Come on, Tai, I just need some time alone."

Tai took the soda and finished it. "We have to get back. Coach is expecting us. Dave locked himself in the boys' room. He's terrified that he'll get in trouble if he doesn't bring us back. What are you thinking, Arg? By now Neb knows we're gone."

Argus shrugged. "So? He can't escape the Citadel. We're actually safe right here."

"What, in *Marco's*? Come on, we have to—"

"I want to be alone. I need time away from all of this." Argus slumped in his seat.

"You mean time away from me." Tai slammed the cup down. "I'm a reminder of what's going on. Right?"

"What do you want me to say? I need the illusion that I'm a normal kid sitting in a normal pizza restaurant. Is that too much to ask? Can you give me a little space, just for a while?"

Without a word, Tai vanished. Argus sat up and was about to take the sunglasses off but stopped in time. That's all it was, an illusion, but it was all he had at the moment. It was better than nothing.

A few minutes later, Sandra came out with a huge slice of cheese pizza and an order of fries. "On the house. Hey, are you sure you're okay?" She placed the tray in the center of the table. "I mean, you are here in the middle of the day."

"Oh, that. I didn't want to be at school."

She smiled. "I know that feeling. Are we still on for our date?"

He gave her a nod. "Of course."

"What about Lola?"

Oh, damn. Lola. She'd be safe with Neb, he wouldn't hurt her. Would he? "She's fine. We're sort of taking a break."

She perked up. "Oh, okay, I get that. I just didn't want to poach you away from her."

"No, no poaching necessary." He returned her smile and made the decision to enjoy simply being a teenager. "What should we do for the rest of the day?"

She winked. "I'll think of something."

By the time her shift ended, he'd finished the meal and was anxious to leave. She came out in a skimpy sundress that she must have changed into. He liked it. It showed her long legs, really long legs. She waved and motioned him to follow her.

Once outside, he realized he didn't have a car. Where was the Lambo? Neb had it...no, no thinking of Neb or Ramtala. "Sandra, I don't have my car."

"No problem. I've got my mom's old car, if you don't mind driving around in a shabby junker."

Argus laughed. "Don't mind at all. As long as it's got four wheels and can get me out of town, that's all I care about."

She raised an eyebrow. "Out of town? What have you got in mind?"

With a smirk, he shook his head. "Nothing. I just want drive and not stop."

Sandra tossed him the keys. "Well, not sure about not stopping, because I only have a quarter tank of gas and no money to fill it. You got any money?"

He patted his pockets. "Nope. Where will a quarter tank get us?"

"My place."

He unlocked the doors, got in and waited until Sandra was buckled in before starting the car. "Your place it is."

Chapter 22

Max flinched when the elevator jerked to a stop. Once again, Gretchen seemed to be on autopilot as she pressed her palm to the wall and opened the door. She stepped out, without even bothering to wait for him, and strode down a dim corridor.

"Gretch!" Max called, but she didn't turn around.

He followed, cursing under his breath. He'd lost control of the situation and that didn't sit well with him. When Gretchen stopped at the only door in the corridor, Max sidled up next to her.

"This is it, Jackson," she said softly.

"This is the vault? I suppose you know how to get inside."

She nodded. "Same way I operated the elevator." She turned and faced him. "Whatever's inside there belongs to Neb. Don't think you can take it. I have orders to bring it to him no matter what."

"And by orders, you mean you'll kill me if I get in your way?" He took a step back. "Gretch, whatever is in there is very important to the Ramtalans. That means it's leverage. If we have it, we can tell them to get the hell off our planet."

She sighed. "They can't leave. Why don't you understand that? Neb's people are trying to keep those New Breeds safe from Lenox. They're innocent children. If the Settlers leave, Lenox has free range to do whatever he has planned."

"So what? I don't give a damn if he kills those New Breeds, just so long as he leaves once he's done."

"Wow, you're a cold-hearted ass, aren't you? Those kids haven't done anything to us. They're just trying to survive."

Max grunted. "I suppose you think the Dachel brothers should be allowed to go free? That's not going to happen. Without them, I look like a fool. Like I've been chasing after ghosts. I need proof of aliens, and those boys are it. Think what we can learn from them, Gretch. Real aliens who've been living among us for years. If we keep whatever's in the vault, and if Neb doesn't agree to leave, then I'm prepared to declare war on them all."

"War? You're not the military, Jackson."

"No, but I have buddies at Edwards. They'll stand with me. One way or the other, those Ramtalans are going down."

"You don't even have a clue how to fight the Ramtalans."

She placed her palm against the center of the door and it slid open. The lights came on and Max saw a transparent inner room right in the middle, about the size of a big walk-in closet. But it wasn't any ordinary closet, this one was surrounded by a randomly moving security laser beam system. As he peered closer, he saw that it wasn't only one transparent room, but three, each inside the other. The final one held a small, black box on a pedestal.

"This is impossible, Gretch."

She stood for a moment, drew in a breath and withdrew a pocketknife. "It's not." Her hand shook. "I'm scared."

He took another step backward. "What are you doing with that knife?"

"Something I don't want to do." She flipped open the blade and plunged it into her palm, screaming out in pain as she made a semi-circular incision around the blue spot. With her hand dripping blood, she plucked a tiny blue object, smaller that a pea, from her under the skin.

Max checked his pockets, but didn't have a tissue. "You've got to stop the bleeding." He swallowed. "Why the hell did you do that?"

With the blue thing between her fingers, she tossed it into the room. "Because I had to."

As soon as the object flew into the laser beams, they vanished and a series of clicks echoed through the room. A second later, the black box in the center of the clear rooms opened. Max stepped into the main room and looked around. It seemed like all of the security systems were destroyed with that single blue object.

"Gretch, what was that?"

She clenched her bleeding hand closed and winced. "I think it's some sort of Ramtalan energy. You need to stay in the corridor while I retrieve the...whatever."

Oh, no you don't. He wasn't going to let her get her hands on it. He waited until she turned her attention away from him, and then he lunged forward, tackled her to the ground, and bound her hands with a zip tie he always kept on him. "Sorry, Gretch. This is an AURA facility, and you're not AURA. Only AURA has the right to secure whatever alien technology is in that box."

"What's AURA ever done for you?" She sat up and struggled, but couldn't get her hands free. "Let me go. I'm still bleeding."

Ignoring her, he walked to the first clear room and found a small handle, but it didn't budge. "How do I get inside?"

"Like I'm going to tell you." After letting loose a barrage of curses, she go to her feet. "I hate you even more now, Jackass."

"I know. I'm betting you don't even know how to get into those rooms. But don't worry, I'll figure it out myself." He jiggled the handle again and again, but nothing happened. Why couldn't just one thing go right? "Okay, how do I get in?"

She snorted. "Oh, I thought you could figure it out on your own."

There wasn't time to argue. "If you tell me, I'll let you go."

"What makes you think I trust you? It's Neb's property. I can't let you have it."

"Seriously, Gretch, what can you do to stop me?" He pounded on the first room. "What the hell is this made of? Does Stone know about any of this?"

Gretchen shook her head. "I doubt it. This has been hidden down here for over forty years and before that, NASA had it."

"NASA? Really? Is it some sort of alien technology?" Now he really had to have it.

She shrugged. "All I know is what Neb told me. Look, I have to bring this thing to him. As much as I hate these alien jerks, I honestly believe that Neb is doing what he can to protect Earth."

"Bull."

With a small grunt, Gretchen pulled her arms apart, snapping the zip tie. "You asked what I can do to stop you. There's Ramtalan energy in me and I can break you in two." Her face showed no emotion. "Is that good enough for you?"

"Ah, yeah, okay." Max stepped aside and motioned to the case. "Go ahead and get that alien thing. I won't try to stop you this time."

He watched while she went to the clear room and placed both hands on the door for a moment, leaving one bloody handprint, and stood back. A second later, the door opened and she went to the next room. She did the same with the other two rooms until she was standing at the pedestal. He sneaked up behind her and looked over her shoulder. Inside the black box was a white fabric pouch that glowed blue.

"Don't touch, Jackson."

"I wasn't going to." Actually, he was planning to grab it, but on second thought, he'd let her pick it up first, just in case it was dangerous.

She took the pouch, but before Max could react, Commander Jampara appeared in a flash of blue and disappeared again, this time with Gretchen and the pouch. Max thumped his fist on the black box.

"Damn you aliens!"

He turned around just as each of the doors closed and locked, trapping him in the center of them all, and then to make things even worse, the laser security system restarted. They'd left him alone, trapped like an animal. *Son of a bitch.*

Chapter 23

Argus sped down the freeway with a feeling of complete freedom. After ten minutes, he realized Sandra was staring at the gas gauge. The Lamborghini didn't need gas, running on Ramtalan energy, so he wasn't used to looking at a gauge. He took the next exit and went back toward town again. It felt good to be driving to nowhere, but he was in Sandra's car and had to think of her. She directed him to her house, which was only a few miles from Palmdale High. Her house was nice, two story with impeccable landscaping and grass that looked a bit too green for Palmdale.

Sandra slipped off her seatbelt when he pulled into the driveway. "My parents won't be home until about six, so we have the whole afternoon."

His heart beat fast and he felt a trickle of sweat roll down his back. What was he doing? He'd ditched Tai and school, and was at a girls' house. A girl who wasn't Lola. Was this what normal teenagers did? He smiled. Hell yeah they did. Right now, he was a teenager, not a converted New Breed with glowing red eyes.

After handing the keys to Sandra, he jumped out and came around to her side, opened her door and ushered her out. "Let's go."

She took his hand and together they walked to the front door. "Argus, are you sure you're okay with this? I mean, I know you and Lola are close."

"Were close," he corrected. "I told you, we're taking a break. Don't worry about it."

Once inside, Sandra motioned to the kitchen. "Want something to drink? My parents have wine."

Wine? He'd never had alcohol in his life. "Sure, why not."

The spacious house had tall ceilings and comfortable-looking furniture, and a really large flat screen, bigger even than his. He followed Sandra to the kitchen and sat at the table while she took a couple of wine glasses from a cupboard. Watching her bend and reach into the fridge made him flush. This was the first girl he'd been alone with, aside from Lola, and he liked it.

"Red or white," Sandra asked.

"Sorry. Red or white what?"

"Wine, silly."

"Oh." He felt stupid. "I don't know. I'll have whatever you're having."

She straightened, with a half a bottle of red wine in one hand and a bottle of beer in the other. "We've got beer, too. My folks keep the wine in the fridge, not sure if you mind chilled wine."

"Anything's good. How about wine and beer?" He felt free, finally, to do whatever he wanted. Nobody watching over him, telling him to do this or do that.

She smiled. "Sounds good. Why don't you take your sunglasses off and get comfy?"

If only he could. He shook his head. "I have sensitive eyes." Time to change the subject. "So, what do your parents do?"

She put the beer and wine on the table with the glasses and sat next to him. "Mom's an attorney and Dad's a CPA. How about your aunt?"

He slumped slightly. "She's a mercenary."

"What?"

"Sorry, my bad sense of humor. She works from home. Computers. Ah, do you have any brothers or sisters?"

Sandra worked the cork out of the wine bottle and filled each of the glasses. "Nope. An only child. Dad wanted more kids, but Mom didn't. So, it's just you and your brother, right?"

"Actually," he paused. "I recently found out I have a half-brother. A total dick."

She giggled. "Really? Sorry to hear that."

"Don't be. I'm okay with it." He downed the wine and poured more into his glass. It wasn't bad tasting, slightly warm as it coated his throat. After finishing that, he picked up the beer and twisted the cap off. "Want some?"

Sandra shook her head. "I don't like beer."

He chugged the entire bottle and sat back, feeling good. "Got any more?" Why couldn't kids have alcohol? It didn't seem to affect him at all.

"Yep." She got a couple more bottles of beer from the fridge and put them in front of him. "You should slow down, cowboy."

"I'm fine. Nothing can hurt me." He drank another bottle and leaned on the table. "How long have you lived in Palmdale?"

"About six years. We moved from Pacific Palisades, in LA. You?"

He spun one of the empty bottles in a circle on the table. "My whole freaking life. I was a prisoner and didn't even know it. Kept behind walls and monitored by Aunt Celeste and the Citadel. They probably know exactly where I am right now, too. There's no escape for me, Sandra." Why did the table move? Did the table move?

"What are you talking about, Argus?" She looked at him like he was crazy.

He banged his fist on the table and sent a long crack skittering across the surface. "The Citadel! Ramtala. AURA. No escape. Ever." Now the whole kitchen moved, wobbling and rippling like it was under water.

"Um, okay. How about no more beer for you." She pushed the unopened bottle away from him. "Want to watch TV or—"

"Or what?" The room and bottle spun together. "Or what?"

She hesitated. "Or we could go upstairs to my room."

Without thinking, he nodded and got up, a bit unsteady, took her hand and went up the stairs. This was how a teenage boy acted, wasn't it? He didn't know for sure, but if a girl invites a boy up to her room, the boy should go. Right? It would be insulting otherwise.

Sandra opened a door and pulled him inside. "This is my room."

"I can see that." He smiled at how girly it was; pink curtains, furry pink pillows on the bed, and a shelf filled with porcelain dolls. "It's nice." A bout of dizziness hit him, so he sat on the bed. His head was heavy, his eyes unfocused.

She sat next to him and cuddled in close. "So, Argus, have you ever...you know, had sex? I'm sure you have, looking like you do and all."

Did she mean his eyes? He reached up and found the sunglasses in place. No, his eyes were still covered. "What do you mean?"

"Oh, come on. You're gorgeous and built like, well, not like the other seniors."

Now his tongue was thick, too big for his mouth. "I'm nothing special, Sandra. I'm a pawn. Lenox's pawn."

She snuggled into him. "There you go talking all weird again. So, have you done it before?"

"You mean sex?" Of course he hadn't had sex. How could he? Aunt Celeste had kept him, and Tai, on a leash. Was it embarrassing for a seventeen year old boy to admit he hadn't had sex? Somehow he didn't care. "No. Have you?"

"Once. But it wasn't good. The jerk used me and never called again." She crawled on the bed toward the pillows and playfully tossed one at him. "I like the idea of being your first. I'm going to pretend this is my first time, too."

Her words drifted around the room, around his head, but when she slipped her dress off over her head, he about passed out. The underwear she had on was skimpy, subtle pink, with little hearts all over. At least they looked like hearts...she was beautiful. It was a struggle to get his tee-shirt off, but he managed and crawled to her. Without warning, she leaned over to him and kissed him on the lips.

"Bro! Arg, seriously?" Tai stood at the foot of the bed.

Sandra screamed and covered herself with a pillow. "How did you get in here?"

"Tai?" Argus blinked to focus his eyes. "What...get out."

Tai tossed the tee-shirt at Argus. "Put your clothes back on. You can't do this. You don't even know if you *can* do this. You're not exactly the same ol' Argus you used to be. In fact, neither of us are the same."

Argus got off the bed and wobbled. "Tai, get out!"

"Arg, are you drunk? Have you been drinking?" Tai reached out and supported him.

With a shrug, Argus turned to Sandra. "Sorry, Sandra. Another time. I told you I was on a leash."

Tai pushed Argus onto the bed and glared down at him. "What did you tell her? Damn it, Arg, what's gotten into you. You've left yourself exposed and vulnerable. That's a stupid move, even for you. What if Lenox or Galena found you? I'll shift us home."

"Home? What home? Do we even have a home anymore?" Argus sat up and drew in a few breaths. "I don't feel well."

In a soft voice, Sandra said, "He had a couple of beers and two glasses of wine."

Tai's eyes flashed blue. "You got my brother drunk so he'd have sex with you?"

"What? No!" She jumped off the bed and put her dress on. "We were talking, that's all."

Tai took Argus by the arm. "Just forget about him, you'll never see him or me again. Bro, I'm shifting us home, our real home."

Sandra grabbed her cell phone off the floor. "I'm calling the cops."

Argus shook his head and stood. "No, don't."

With a wave of his hand, Tai sent the phone flying from her hand. "Whoa. I didn't know I could do that. Another ability. Cool." He turned to Argus again. "We're shifting. Don't fight me."

"Why would I fight you, I *want* to go home. I want to be anywhere but the Citadel. And I don't want to be a Ramtalan. I want to be human and have sex with a human girl." Argus pulled free and wobbled toward Sandra. "Don't be upset. It's my brother. He's a bit...high strung. I think I should go home now, but I'll see you again. At the dance."

She shook her head. "Don't bother. I don't ever want to see you again." She ran from the room.

Before Argus could follow, Tai had him by the arm again and in a flash, they were gone from Sandra's room and back in their own house. He collapsed on the living room floor and stared up at the ceiling. What had he done?

"Bro, you're unhinged. What's gotten into you? I know this has all gone sideways, but snap out of it. It's our duty to—"

"Duty?" Argus sat up. "What's our duty? To fight our father, our aunt, and our brother, or to kill them? What sort of duty is that? I didn't ask for any of this."

Tai sat on the floor beside him. "Neither did I. But look, we're in this situation and we have to do our part. Even if you don't care about anyone else, think of Lola. She's still at the Citadel. And think of Aunt Celeste. She raised us and she needs our help."

"I know." Argus rested his head in his hands. "I'm just so tired of being jerked around by everyone. We'll never be free, will we?"

With a half-hearted shrug, Tai got up and extended his hand. "Probably not. Let's get you sobered up. What were you thinking? Beer *and* wine? And Sandra? I've never even kissed a girl and you almost got to third base."

Argus took his hand and stood. "Almost doesn't count."

"Does to me. Proud of you, bro." He winked. "Now go to the kitchen and drink about a gallon of water."

There was a blinding flash of blue and a rumble, then nothing. Argus closed his eyes and kept his grip on Tai's hand so he didn't fall, but when he opened his eyes again, a woman was standing in the living room. He knew her. It was Max's friend, Gretchen.

In an instant, Tai had his hand raised. "How'd you do that? You're human."

"Easy, Tai." Argus took a step toward Gretchen. "How *did* you get here? And why?"

She blinked a couple of times and shook her head. "I hate you freaking aliens. That hurt." She looked around. "Where the hell am I?"

"Our house." Argus checked the vicinity, but didn't see anyone else. "You're alone?"

"Yeah. I was dropped off here to watch you two. I'm the babysitter."

That was more than a little insulting. Argus felt sick, so sat on the couch. "We don't need anyone to babysit us. Especially not some AURA flunky like you."

"AURA? I'm an independent contractor, not a government stooge like Max Jackass."

Tai laughed. "Jackass? Why didn't I think of that?" He pointed to the front door. "Get out of our house."

Gretchen wandered around the living room. "I can't. Your alien buddies did something to me. Makes me obey them." She spun around and glared at Tai. "I don't like obeying anyone, but I have to so I'm staying put."

Her tone irritated Argus. "Like my brother said, this is our house. And you're not welcome here. Are you with Lenox or Galena?"

She laughed. "You have it wrong, little man. Neb is pulling my strings and your Commander Jampara swooped in, took the particle from me and dumped me here."

"Particle?" Argus was sobering up. "You had a particle? That's what Neb was waiting for. Where—"

"Neb sent me to AURA headquarters to fetch his prize and that's when Jampara jumped me and took it. He brought me here to keep an eye on you two." She wagged her finger. "He knows you escaped the Citadel and he's mighty pissed at you both. I personally don't give a crap, and I seriously don't care for that transportation system you have. It made me feel like I was being ripped apart. Neb said I have a trace of Ramtalan energy in me, whatever the hell that means. But it did save on time and traffic."

Tai nudged Argus. "So much for us having some alone time." He turned to Gretchen. "So where's Jackson?"

She shrugged. "Huh, that's weird, I don't know. Don't much care. So, you boys got anything to eat?"

"Help yourself." Argus pointed to the kitchen, and when Gretchen left, he whispered to Tai, "I'm not hanging around here. I'm shifting back to school."

"What? Why? What's the point? You just freaked out Sandra. She probably texted everyone in Palmdale and told them everything."

"Maybe, but maybe not." Argus sighed and went to the window. "Can I be a teenager for today? I want to do pop quizzes and eat lousy food from the cafeteria. You know, regular kid stuff."

Tai came up beside him. "You're far from normal, bro. Don't forget you're also drunk. But I hear you. Want me to come?"

Argus thought for a moment. If they both went, Gretchen would go looking for them. But if Tai stayed, he could cover. "No, just keep Gretchen off my ass."

"Sure. I'll tell her you're pouting in your room."

"Cool. Thanks, Tai. I'll come home right after the last bell." He glanced around, concentrated and shifted to the boys' bathroom in the locker room. Before stepping, he listened at the door and when he heard footsteps vanishing in the distance, he stepped out.

Dave paced around near the lockers and looked up when he heard Argus approach. "Ah, man, you guys gotta stop that disappearing stuff. Where's your brother? I told Coach you guys stopped in the bathroom when you got back from the principal's office. I don't think he believed me."

"You're a real friend, Dave. Tai's not coming. Is PE over?"

Dave nodded. "Yeah, the bell just rang. The guys will be in here any second." He sniffed. "Have you been drinking?"

"Yeah, I...I didn't mean to get you in trouble. Blame me if you get called to the office." Argus adjusted his sunglasses and sat on a bench. "What's for lunch in the cafeteria?"

"Burritos. Hey, Argus, can I ask you something?" Dave motioned for him to move away from the kids as they poured into the locker room.

What could Dave want to know? He already knew about Ramtala and the Citadel. "What's up?"

In a whisper, Dave asked, "Where did you get a brew?"

Should he lie? No, Dave deserved the truth. "I went with Sandra from *Marco's*. Wait, how can you tell?" Argus smirked and pulled down the sunglasses a bit. "Is it my bloodshot eyes?"

"Oh, hell, don't do that, man. That's not funny. I can't get used to your eyes like that. Anyway, yeah, I can smell it on your breath." Dave reached into his pocket. "Here, chew some gum."

"Thanks." Argus took the gum and kept his voice low, "Dave, have you ever had sex?"

"Whoa, dude, that's a little personal." Dave glanced around. "No. Have you?"

Argus shook his head. "Came close though. Is it weird to be a virgin at seventeen?"

Dave shrugged and pointed at himself. "I hope not. I kind of thought you and Lola..."

With another shake of his head, Argus sighed. "I'm not so sure Lola feels the same way about me anymore. She knows what I am and it's my fault that I got her all mixed up in my insane life. She's not even here in Palmdale anymore. And that's my fault, too."

"So where is she? You said she's safe, but where exactly?" Dave looked genuinely worried.

How much should he tell Dave, his last friend on Earth? "She's fine. She's at the Citadel."

"What!" Dave shouted. "You told me what that place is. How could you...?"

The guys who'd showered and were getting dressed, turned, and glared.

Argus dismissed them with a wave. "This doesn't concern any of you." What was he doing, being at school? He didn't fit in, not anymore. "Sorry, guys. I'm just going through some stuff."

One of the guys, Josh, balled up a towel and tossed it at Argus like a football. "We're all here for you, Dachel. We don't believe those rumors and we all know that whatever happened to Justin Jones and Todd was their fault. If you want to chill, me and some of the guys are heading to *Marco's* after school."

Argus tossed the towel back, holding back his strength. "Yeah, maybe."

The speaker in the locker room chimed, announcing a message.

Argus and Tai Dachel report to the office.

"Shit." Argus made sure his sunglasses were in place and headed to the main office. The day wasn't turning out as he'd hoped. There was no point in going to the office because it wasn't like he could explain his absence to anyone. He stopped and leaned against the wall, but before he could initiate a shift, a woman called to him.

"Mr. Dachel, you were called to the office. Where's your brother?" It was the assistant principal heading to him. "I had a feeling you wouldn't make it to the office."

"So you came looking for me? Why can't everyone leave me alone?" He straightened and kept chewing the gum. "I haven't done anything." His head throbbed, but he didn't feel buzzed like before.

She stopped in front of him and had to look up because she couldn't be more than five feet tall. "Really? Unexcused absences, outbursts, the subject of rampant rumor mills. And, we can't reach your aunt. What's going on with you, Mr. Dachel? What are you and your brothers up to? Drugs?"

If only he could let her know how difficult everything was, tell her the truth, and hope for a little sympathy. "I don't do drugs."

"Alcohol? I smell it on you, young man." She raised an eyebrow. "I know this is tough time in your life, but you'll get through it without beer or ecstasy."

He laughed out loud. "Tough time? You have no idea. I'm not even the same person I was a few weeks ago. Literally. My real family are a bunch of megalomaniacs and I'm—" *Shut up, Argus*! "—I'm not human."

She seemed sympathetic. "We all feel that way at some point in our lives. With school, friends and family, the stress can really build up. You're a good boy, Argus, but you're letting yourself go down a bad road. I've heard that your uncle bought you a Lamborghini. No teenage boy needs one of those. Sometimes family tries to buy you off, rather than listen to you. My father was like that. Bought me a car, gave me a credit card, but never once said he loved me."

"My dad's not the loving type either. I know you're trying to help, but my life is nothing like what you think. Besides, I don't even know where the Lambo is." He slumped against the wall. "All I want is to be left alone."

She sighed. "Argus, the teen years don't go on forever. You're just like everyone else."

Tai appeared behind her. "No, he's not. We have to go, bro. Gretchen knows you left. She's contacting the Commander."

Argus felt a surge of energy building down deep. "What? How can she do that? We can't even contact him?"

The bell rang and kids came out of the classrooms, nodded to Argus and Tai, then continued on their way.

The assistant principal glared at Tai. "Where'd you come from? Both of you, to the office. Now."

With a roll of his eyes, Tai groaned. "No. We don't have time for your ridiculous high school rules. There's a lot more at stake than missing class."

"Would you like detention, Mr. Dachel?"

Without responding, Tai grabbed Argus by the shoulder and shifted. They landed in the middle of the desert. Argus looked around, but didn't recognize any features.

"You shifted in public, Tai. Dumb move. So, where are we?" He suppressed the energy that had built up. "Why here?"

Tai sat on the hard-packed soil. "We need time by ourselves. This is one of the places I used to come, back in the good old days before we knew Lenox was our father and AURA was hunting us, and pure-forms controlled every aspect of our lives."

"You realize you shifted right in front of—"

"Doesn't matter. We're not going back to school and we probably won't even survive the week."

Argus sat next to him. "Good point. I'm never going back to the Citadel. Neb and Aunt Celeste can manage without me there."

"And me. I'm not going anywhere without you. You stay, I stay. But we need to figure out what the hell we're doing. They'll find us if we don't hide."

"Who will?"

"Everyone. Gretchen. Neb. Aunt Celeste. The Citadel. Lenox. Max Jackson."

That really was everyone. "We have to destroy the XTRA-A1. We can't let Lenox get it. Why don't we fly it somewhere and never come back?"

"Like where?" Tai threw a pebble as hard as he could. "Another country? Another planet?"

"Maybe not another planet, but yeah, another country. I've been thinking about this. If we can work out how to extract the energy from the XTRA-A1 when it takes it from us, then couldn't we construct a shield? All of the Ramtalan shields are made from the particles, which are Ramtalan energy."

Tai nodded. "That could work. I was never good at science, but ever since Galena altered me, I understand a whole lot more. We'll need some equipment though."

"Let's go invisible and steal some stuff." Argus stood. "What we need, we can't get at a hardware store."

"You'll have to put a cloak around me since I can't go invisible like you. Where can we get what we need?"

"Edwards." Argus hadn't felt in control of his own life for so long, but finally they had a plan and if it worked, he and Tai could live their lives in peace without the threat of capture or death. But only after they disabled

Lenox's ship and showed everyone they weren't some delicate New Breeds. First though, they had to make their plan work without getting caught.

Chapter 24

Trapped like an animal, Max paced around the transparent room and waited for someone from AURA to come and rescue him, and then throw him in prison. Compared to what he'd been through with the aliens, prison didn't sound too bad.

He'd been so close to getting his hands on whatever was in the pouch, but once again, the freaking Ramtalans got one over on him. Even worse than being betrayed by Gretchen was the fact that she left him to fend for himself.

"Help!"

It was no use. It was a good bet than only a handful of AURA higher-ups even knew about the vault. Nobody would look for him. The alarm system hadn't actually triggered, so who'd know he was stuck down in the sub-basement?

"Come on. Neb. Anyone."

He was alone. The only logical thing to do was to set off the alarm. But that meant getting out of the three rooms first. And they were locked. Of course, locks were generally designed to keep someone from getting *in*. There was a slight chance that the locks would be weaker from the inside.

He went to the far end, ran toward the door and threw his shoulder against it. The only thing that happened was his shoulder now hurt. He tried it again and again, and after the eighth time, the door loosened on hidden hinges. Yes! Using his other shoulder this time, he rammed the door only twice before it popped open.

"Ha! Take that you Ramtalan jerk-offs!"

He rested and rubbed his shoulders for a couple of seconds before starting on the second door, and then the third. When the third door slammed open, it tripped one of the laser beams and a shrill alarm echoed around the room. If someone didn't come soon, he'd go deaf. He tried slamming against the main door, but it didn't budge at all, and his shoulders were so bruised, he decided to wait for help.

With his hands over his ears, he sat near the main door, checked his watch, and closed his eyes, imaging what delightfully horrible things he'd do to the Ramtalans when he got his hands on them. Argus Dachel was first, then Neb. Or maybe Tai Dachel, with Argus watching as his brother was dissected, alive.

But what about Gretchen? Was there any hope for her? If not, she'd be a casualty. Too bad. No, not too bad. He'd allowed himself to get too caught up in her good looks and that made him vulnerable. Vulnerability was lethal around the aliens. He had to be strong and detached. They'd declared war on the Earth and it was up to him to win that war, no matter who got in the way.

Twenty-five minutes ticked by until the main door finally opened and three heavily armed men charged in, looked around and pointed automatic weapons at him. A moment later, the alarm went off. One of them shouted, "On your feet!"

Max complied and raised his hands. "My name's Max Jackson, I'm AURA, under Chief Lawrence Stone."

"Break out some ID."

Carefully, Max reached into his pocket and brought out his ID wallet. He flipped it open. "Now get me out of here."

The guard lowered the gun. "How'd you get in here? An alarm I'd never seen before went off on the security panel and it took us nearly half an hour to find this place. What is it?"

"A secret vault." Max put the wallet away and stepped into the hallway. He'd have to think up a convincing lie about why he was there. "I came here to secure a top secret object, but found it missing. I got locked in, so I triggered the alarm."

"Hold up, Mr. Jackson." The guard raised the gun slightly. "Where is Chief Stone? He hasn't checked in for a couple of days now. The OEED he left us with has gone crazy with organic energy spikes. He said to contact him if anything showed up. We tried, but we can't reach him. What's going on?"

Max perked up. "Stone left you an OEED? Do you have it?"

The guard nodded. "Yeah. But it's not like the other OEEDs." He took out what looked like a cell phone. "This one is specifically targeted to a DNA sequence that Stone said he got from a blood sample. Whose blood sample, Mr. Jackson?"

So Stone sequenced Argus's DNA from the blood samples he got. And the OEED hones in on Argus. Perfect. "Show me the spikes."

"I think we should wait to hear from Mr. Stone. The energy spikes stopped a while ago. Maybe the OEED broke."

"Just give me the damn thing." Max got in close to the guard. "Stone left me in charge. I'm your boss now."

"Yes, sir."

Max followed the guards up to AURA's main level and to the security office. He paced while the guard brought up the map indicating the location and timestamps of the spikes, which mysteriously stopped hours ago. Wouldn't you know it, Palmdale. Highland High. At least hours ago Dachel was there. Then off to Palmdale again to find that damn kid.

Chapter 25

While Argus mentally listed all of the things they'd need to steal from Edwards, Tai paced. "What's on your mind?"

He stopped. "Are we being selfish? I mean, up until right now, I forgot all about the other New Breeds. They die before they get to sixteen and Lenox still wants to kill them all. Why not let them all die out?"

"I'm not sure. But we'll help them if we take the XTRA-A1 and destroy it. Whatever Lenox's plan is revolves around the ship and us. We get rid of the ship, he has no more use for us, and he can't hurt the New Breeds."

Tai nodded. "Okay, that makes sense. Glad we're brothers because Team Dachel rocks."

"Damn right." Argus smiled and gave Tai and playful punch on the arm. "So, Edwards?"

"You know it."

"I'll initiate the shift and keep us protected under the veil. Ready?" Argus took Tai's hand and concentrated on the Base. The shift went smoothly until they got to Edwards. Instead of being inside the Base, they were outside, right next to the entry guard building, where a young woman guard stared at them. They weren't invisible.

"Arg, what went wrong?" Tai slowly edged in front of Argus, with his hand lifting.

"I don't know. I've shifted and used the veil before. What the...my abilities are all messed up."

"Damn, mine, too. The energy in my hand for a photometric pulse is too weak."

The guard approached with her hand on the butt of her still-holstered pistol. "How'd you kids get here? You weren't here a second ago." She crushed a cigarette under her boot.

Argus forced a smile. "We're on a field trip." He tried to shift, but couldn't make it happen. "We went looking for a bathroom and missed the school bus."

The guard wasn't buying it. "You can't do any better than that? There's no bus. And I was standing here having a smoke the whole time."

While Argus tried to think up something, another guard, a man, came out of the building. "I know these boys."

Tai tapped Argus on the shoulder. "Arg?"

Argus shrugged. "I don't know him."

The male guard drew his pistol and aimed at Argus. "You're the Dachel boys. The ones Max Jackson is after. He told me all about you a while back. Both of you, put your hands up, and don't try any of that alien shit either. Jo, call for assistance. And call AURA."

"Bro, we're shifting out of here."

Argus would have already shifted if his abilities weren't being blocked. "We can't. We're stuck. And nobody's coming for us because nobody knows where we are."

"Oh, yeah. We pulled a disappearing act on Gretchen and didn't tell anyone else. Damn our impulsive, secretive behavior." Tai's usual smirk faded quickly. He raised his hand slightly, palm toward the ground. "Yeah, still no abilities. I can't even fire a small pulse."

"Told you."

"Shut up!" The male guard approached with his pistol still pointed at Argus. "Where's Max Jackson? Did you do something to him?"

"No." Argus stared at the woman guard. "We haven't done anything. We're teenagers. We attend Highland High."

She tilted her head to the side and smiled. "I graduated from Highland three years ago. Good school. No aliens there then, though." She unholstered her gun and aimed it at Tai. "You look just like regular kids. Don't they, Angel?"

The male guard reached out and snatched the sunglasses off Argus. "Jesus. Not regular kids, Jo."

Argus turned away, but saw Tai out of the corner of his eye, lunging at the male guard.

"You don't touch my brother!" He shouted as he knocked the gun from the guard's hand.

Before Argus could do anything, the woman guard fired a shot directly at Tai, catching him in the shoulder. Tai crumpled to the ground and grabbed his bleeding shoulder. Argus felt rage, pure, raw rage, yet it didn't build up in the pit of his stomach like he would have liked. He was helpless to do anything but go to his brother.

He crouched and pulled Tai's hand away. "You're bleeding a lot. I think the bullet's still in there."

The woman guard stood back, dazed. "I didn't mean...you made me shoot."

"The hell he did!" Argus jumped up and glared at her. "He's only seventeen. We're not some hostile bunch of...just leave us alone. All we want is to be left alone."

The male guard stomped over. "Yeah, well, that's not going to happen. I sent out a distress call. This place will be swarming in seconds."

Tai groaned. "This really hurts, you freaking dickheads. You heard my brother, let us go. We've done nothing to you. We're trying to stop Lenox. We're the only ones who can."

"He's right." Argus raised his hands in the air. "Look, we're not armed. Can you call Gretchen Manheim? She works with Max Jackson. Please, call her. And get my brother some medical care."

"Don't know any Gretchen Manheim." The male guard had retrieved his gun and was once again pointing it at Argus.

With blood seeping from between his fingers, Tai sat up. "Good thinking, Arg. Gretchen's our best bet. Neb put her in charge of watching us."

"But unless these morons contact her, we're screwed." Argus tore off the bottom of his shirt and pressed it against Tai's shoulder.

A few seconds later, three large helicopters swooped in, and at least ten Jeeps screamed toward the guard building. Apparently nobody was interested in trying to call Gretchen. That meant they were alone and at the hands of the military, and AURA, which was probably the worst scenario there could be.

A Jeep with a red cross painted on the side stopped a few feet from Tai and two fatigue-wearing men hopped out. One knelt down while the other fetched a medical bag.

The one near Tai carefully examined the wound. "You're a bit young to get shot, aren't you?"

"Yeah, that's what I thought." Tai rolled his eyes. "She tried to kill me. Trust me, that won't sit well with my dad."

"Oh, and who's your dad?"

"Argustine Lenox." Tai glanced at Argus and shrugged. "Maybe that'll make an impact."

A group of soldiers stomped to them, pistols drawn. One helicopter settled down, kicking up dust as two soldiers jumped out with machine guns.

Argus sat on the ground by Tai, hands still in the air. "Was this the impact you had in mind?"

Chapter 26

With a printout of the energy spikes clutched in his hand, Max climbed into an AURA helicopter at LAX, hardly able to control his excitement. Screw Gretchen, she didn't deserve to be included in the capture of the Dachel brothers. This was his score and his alone. He'd track down the origin of the spikes and hopefully the Dachels would still be around.

The helicopter lifted off the tarmac and headed toward Palmdale. Max leaned back and imagined the fear in Argus's face as the autopsy began. The kid would scream in terror, and maybe even cry, and Max would laugh. Everything the Dachels put him through would be forgotten as soon as he sliced into the alien kid's flesh.

Being the first person to perform a real autopsy on an alien would put Max in all of the history books and on all of the talk shows. He wouldn't keep it a secret like Stone would want to. No, the results of the investigation had to be made public. That way everyone would know the truth and they'd have good old Max Jackson to thank for saving the world.

He'd been happily daydreaming, but snapped out of it when the pilot spoke through the headset.

"Mr. Jackson, AURA received an emergency call from Edwards Air Force Base. They have two teenage boys under arrest and the boys were asking for Gretchen Manheim. A guard, Angel somebody, said he needed to contact you."

"Holy shit!" Max shouted. "He has the Dachels?"

"Two teenage boys, sir. Should I reroute to Edwards?"

"Damn right you should." Max trembled all over with anticipation. Good old Angel. The boys had been hand-delivered to him. It couldn't get any better than that. And both of them at one time. Maybe he'd start with Tai and let Argus watch. Would that be too cruel? Was it possible to be cruel to aliens? They didn't have rights, so who the hell cared. He smiled and stared out the window. But why were they asking for Gretchen?

"Rerouted, Mr. Jackson. We'll land at Edwards in under ten minutes."

Max nodded and watched the freeways snake over the landscape below. "Good, good. Thank you."

With Stone still in Canada, or dead, Max would take over and run the entire operation. He was about to do what Stone couldn't. He closed his eyes and relaxed until the helicopter began its decent. Edwards sprawled out below, and that meant his Ramtalan prizes were waiting.

The helicopter touched down and Max recognized Angel fast-walking to the landing pad. There was a friend worth keeping. Angel opened the door and Max got out, hurried away from the slowing rotors and got into the passenger side of a Jeep.

"Angel, my man, you've earned yourself a steak dinner." Max gave him a friendly pat on the arm.

The smile on Angel's face eased after a moment. "Max, there's an issue."

"An issue? Like what? Stone's not here, is he?"

"Stone? No. But the blond kid was shot in the shoulder."

"What!"

"No, but listen. You know how that alien blood used to burn humans? Well, it don't no more. It's like regular blood. And the kid'll be fine. He's already got stitched up. But his brother was pissed."

"Yeah, I bet." Max hung on when Angel accelerated. So why didn't their blood burn anymore? What had changed? Maybe Gretchen knew. He dialed her on his phone and waited.

No answer.

"Hey, Max. Those kids can't use their powers either. Mr. Stone ordered that his EM device be repaired and left on. Guess it works, huh?"

"Guess so." Great! Now he didn't have to worry about those abilities of theirs. It just kept getting better. And with the EM, Neb couldn't do anything, even if he managed to track him or the boys.

Angel slowed in front of the Quonset hut and hopped out. "They're in here. Oh, and the dark haired one—"

"Argus."

"Yeah, him. He keeps telling us to leave the blond one alone. And get this, his eyes are red. Not bloodshot-red, but red. Freaky, man. So, can I watch, Max?"

"Of course." Max straightened his shoulders and followed Angel into the hut. Red eyes, what did that mean? Lenox had red eyes, so was Argus now a carbon copy of him?

Max walked into the hut and looked around. Things had changed a bit. There wasn't a clean room anymore, but the autopsy tables were still there, each holding a restrained Dachel. Both boys were shirtless and wearing only a pair of flimsy pajama bottoms. Tai's shoulder was bandaged and overall, he didn't look any worse for wear.

"Hello, boys." Max strode to the tables and looked down at his victims. Argus's eyes really were red, and they seemed to glow. It was disturbing seeing him like that. It was like looking right at Lenox. "I got you now and nobody's coming to save you this time. Kiss your ass goodbye, kid."

Chapter 27

Ari paced around his apartment at the Citadel, not sure what his next move should be. Galena and Lenox treated him with disrespect. Neither of them thought he could help. In fact, Galena had sent him to his apartment to get him out of the way while she and Lenox conspired about what to do with Celeste when they freed her from the court room. He had the answer, if they'd bother to ask him. Kill her. That's it, plain and simple, get rid of her and then go after Neb. Once they were out of the way, it would be easy to find Argus and Tai, use their energy to power the XTRA-A1, and then eliminate them as well. But, they didn't ask him.

He'd show them. He'd capture Celeste and fire a lethal pulse directly at her, ending her miserable life once and for all. That would get Lenox's attention. Before long, everyone would look up to him as the great hero of Ramtala and he'd rule both Earth and Ramtala side-by-side with his father. But there were several tasks to do before that could happen. First, he had to kill Celeste, then find the boys and lastly, the XTRA-A1.

No point in waiting around in the apartment, he had work to do. When he opened the door, he checked the corridor before venturing out. If he got caught, Galena would punish him and lock him away, like she'd done with Argus and Tai. He had to be stealthy and make it to the court room unnoticed. Then, with the orb from the Wand of Ramtala that he'd stolen when Galena wasn't looking, he'd blast the door open and end Celeste before she even knew what was happening.

On the way, he bumped into a couple of Settlers who only gave him a cursory glance, like he didn't matter at all. It infuriated him, until he realized their lack of concern gave him an advantage. He could move around the Citadel without anyone noticing, and indeed, he made it to the court room quickly. Carefully, he removed the orb from his pocket. With a final look around, he smashed it against the door.

In a flash of blue, the shield broke and the door slid open. A shrill alarm sounded throughout the Citadel. He ran in, palm raised, but didn't see Celeste anywhere. How could that be? She couldn't have escaped. Before he took another breath, Galena was behind him.

"Ari? What did you do?"

His entire plan was falling apart. "I was going to get Celeste."

Galena spun him around and slapped him across the face. "You destroyed the external and internal shields around the Citadel! How?"

His cheek stung. "With the orb from the Wand."

"No, there isn't enough power for that. What else did you do, Ari?"

"That's all. I stole the orb and destroyed the shield around the court room."

Galena's eyes burned. "Are you working with her? And Neb? I knew I couldn't trust you."

"I didn't...Celeste isn't in here. I only just opened the door. What's going on, Galena?" Ari dashed around her and stood in the corridor. "Where's Father?"

She followed him into the corridor. "He's not going to help you. Like me, he has no tolerance for incompetence."

"Listen to me, Galena. How could I have destroyed all of the shields? I couldn't." He stayed far enough away so she couldn't hit him again.

The first alarm stopped, but a new one with an alternating tone rang. He knew exactly what the alarm meant. The Citadel had been breached. Galena vanished in a flash of blue, leaving him standing in the corridor wondering what was happening. At that moment, he realized he had two choices; stay and probably receive a severe punishment for using the orb, or shift out of the Citadel now that the shields were down, and find Celeste himself. The last one was likely the only way he could redeem himself and stay alive.

He concentrated on the only place he figured he'd be safe; Celeste's house in Palmdale. Nobody would look there since the Settlers were all mounting their attack from mainland Labrador, and the boys were locked away in their Citadel apartment.

After successfully shifting, he appeared in the living room of the house and drew in a deep breath to calm his jangled nerves. What would his father do to him? Exactly what made the boys more important than him? They weren't the first born sons, they were merely an afterthought. Being the first born should count for something. He was certain now, the only way to get back in good graces with Lenox was to get the XTRA-A1, take down the Guardians, and deliver the ship personally. Now it was a matter of finding the ship, powering it up and getting it to the Citadel. How hard could that be?

Chapter 28

Argus, strapped down so tightly he could hardly move, raged. With the EM pulse device turned on, he got weaker with each second that passed. Tai lay on the table next to him. Worst of all, Max Jackson had arrived.

Max smiled and gave Argus a pat on the shoulder. "We could have had this all wrapped up by now if you hadn't escaped from me last time."

"What are you going to do?" Argus tried to break through the restraints, but he wasn't strong enough. "My brother was shot, did you know that? Your people shot a teenager. Does that make you feel like a big man, Max?"

"He looks fine to me." Max went to Tai and poked his bandaged shoulder. "How are you doing, Tai?"

Tai flinched. "Undo these restraints and I'll show you how I'm doing." He narrowed his eyes. "I only need two minutes alone with you, Jackson, that's all. I'll even take one minute."

"Yeah, I don't think so." Max poked Tai's shoulder again and turned back to Argus. "Seems like his wound isn't so bad. Shooting an alien isn't wrong. You lose again, Argus." He smirked. "Oh, and to answer your question, I'm going to open you up and see exactly what you've got under your skin, because you've been under my skin for a long time now." He laughed. "Get it?"

Argus would have smacked the smile off Max's face if he could. "Yeah, funny. So where's your friend Gretchen? I figured you'd want to include her in your messed up plan."

He stopped laughing. "Gretch? Oh, we parted ways back in LA. My guys said you were asking for her. She's not in the picture, boys. This is *my* project."

Argus glared. Project? Did Max really think the murder of two kids was a project? There had to be a way of getting free before Max started. How could anyone want to do what he was about to?

What would it feel like to be cut into? Would he and Tai bleed to death quickly or would Max keep them alive?

Argus felt sick. "You can't do this, Max. If you let my brother go, you'll still have me."

"Shut up, Arg. Let us both go, Jackson, or our father will find you and—"

Max interrupted, "And what? He can't find us and with the EM device operating, he wouldn't have any power here anyway. On second thought..."

As much as Argus hated Lenox, he didn't want to see him captured and tortured by Max. "Who gives you the authority to do this, Max? Stone? The government? The President? You're talking about torturing and murdering us. Even you must have a trace of a conscience." Probably not, but maybe there was a chance to play on his sense of morality. If he had any.

"Trying to change the subject away from Lenox, Argus? Scared I'll trap your daddy and give him the same treatment?" He leaned down. "You know what, I'll keep you and your brother alive long enough so you two can watch Lenox get chopped into pieces. He'll come here looking for you both and when he does..." Max clapped his hands together. "Boom! He'll be mine. Three Ramtalans instead of two. I'm feeling pretty good right now."

Argus turned away. He couldn't stand the sight of Max any longer. Argus mumbled, "Lenox won't come here. He's too smart for that."

Max grabbed Argus by the jaw and forced him to turn his head. "Argus, even if he doesn't come, I've still got the two of you. I'll start the examination right away and if Lenox does show up for the party, I'll include him. How about we start with Tai?"

"No!" Argus pulled away. "Leave him alone!"

"Don't worry about me, bro. If he hurts us, Aunt Celeste or Neb will get him. Don't you have a monitor in your head, Jackson? What do you think Neb will do to you when he finds you? Your days are numbered, dickwad."

"*My* days are numbered?" Max picked up a scalpel from a silver tray and leaned over Tai. "I think yours are, kid."

Argus struggled and tried to shift, but it was no use. "Stop! Max don't do this! Leave Tai alone. Start with me."

Max spun around, scalpel in hand. "Fine." He brought his arm down and slashed the scalpel across Argus's forearm. "I was told your blood isn't toxic anymore. It sure looks like regular old blood. So what changed? Something to do with those red eyes of yours I bet."

"Stop!" Tai shouted.

Argus's arm burned and bled profusely. "Tai, he cut me deep."

"You're dead, Jackson. When I get my hands on you, I'll make it slow and painful. Don't you touch my brother again you piece of shit."

With another swipe of the scalpel, Max made a long slice down Argus's chest. Argus tried not to scream, but couldn't help it. It hurt more than anything he'd ever felt. The smell of his own metallic blood was awful and turned his stomach.

"Jackson!" shouted a woman. "Drop that knife!"

Argus blinked his teary eyes. It was Gretchen and she looked furious as she stomped to Max with a gun in her hand. The soldier, Angel, dashed in front of her, but Gretchen shoved him aside with ease.

"I can't believe you did that, Jackson." Gretchen poked the gun in his stomach. "You have no idea what you've done."

Max stepped back. "Yeah I do. I'm the only person in the world who has two alien kids prepped for autopsy."

Gretchen shook her head. "Technically it's not an autopsy because they're alive."

"My mistake. Hey, how did you find me here, Gretch?"

Argus glanced at Tai, who's eyes were glowing blue, but not nearly as bright as they usually were when he was angry. Max still had the scalpel and was awfully close to Tai. Argus used all his depleted strength to attempt to break free, but it was no use.

"Drop your weapon!" Angel shouted.

"Stay where you are, Gretch." Max brought the scalpel to Tai's throat. "One slice and this kid's nothing but a piece of non-breathing flesh. Then it'll be an autopsy, right?"

"You all right, Argus?" Gretchen kept her eyes on Max. She pressed a small towel onto his chest wound.

The pressure on the open cut sent a wave of pain through his body. He winced. "I...will be once I'm free."

"I said drop the gun!" Angel shouted again.

She continued, "Jackson, get away from Tai and tell your monkey to drop *his* gun before I put a bullet between your eyes."

Max looked from Angel to Gretchen. "Drop it, Angel."

"Good choice." Gretchen didn't move. "Neb ordered me to bring the boys to him, unharmed. So far you've only hurt Argus. Don't make this worse for yourself."

Max kept the scalpel dangerously close to Tai. "You don't have any power here, Gretch. Literally, no power. Stone's EM device was repaired after Neb disabled it, which means your Ramtalan hoodoo won't work here."

"That's where you're wrong." She waved her hand and sent Max flying backward a few feet. "I'm human, stupid. Just because I have some of that Ramtalan energy in me doesn't mean I'm Ramtalan. The EM doesn't affect me. So, looks like I do have power here after all."

With another wave of her hand, she broke Tai's restraints and without hesitating, he jumped off the table and ran to Argus. After unfastening the restraints, he helped Argus off the table.

"Thanks." Argus dabbed at his bleeding arm and chest. "Gretchen, we can't do anything with the EM device operating."

"I know." She walked to Angel and picked up his gun. "Max, I was on your side right up until the point you tried to cut me out of everything. We could have worked together."

Neb strolled in, his eyes blazing blue. "No, Gretchen, you couldn't. Max here would sell you out no matter what." He stood beside Gretchen. "Hi, Max. Oh, I destroyed the EM pulse device once and for all, and made all of your soldier buddies take a long nap."

Max backed away. "You killed them?"

Neb shook his head. "I said nap and I meant nap." He turned to Argus and Tai. "Boys, go and wait for me outside. You've got a bit of explaining to do."

"Wait." Argus held the towel tightly against his chest. "How did you get out of the Citadel? How did you find us? Where's Aunt Celeste?"

"Always so full of questions. Be right with you." Neb looked back at Max. "As for you." He raised his hand, his palm pulsating a deep blue. "You've interfered with us enough. Time to say bye-bye, Max. I no longer need you and keeping you alive is detrimental. I told you what would happen with the monitor if you betrayed me."

"Hold on!" Max was frantic, walking backward toward the far end of the Quonset hut. "I was doing this for you, trying to flush Lenox out by capturing the boys. Once I had Lenox, I'd contact you. It was a good, solid plan."

Argus went to Neb. "That's a lie. He was going to, how did you put it, Max, open us up."

Max kept moving backward. "Argus, you and I have gone through a lot. You know I wouldn't have killed you or your brother. It's business, that's all."

The room began to spin, so Argus grabbed onto Neb's arm for support. "Business? You call this business? We're not aliens on this planet, Max. We've been here a lot longer than you have. That makes us the part of the native population."

With his arm still extended toward Max, Neb turned to Argus. "Aren't your abilities back yet?"

Argus shook his head. "No. I lost a lot of blood, too."

Neb glanced at Tai. "Tai? How about you?"

"Nope." Tai helped Argus to a chair. "Sit down, bro. Neb, what's going on?"

"Not sure. My abilities are fine, as Max is about to see." Neb went to Argus, placed a hand on his chest. "There, your wounds will heal quickly. Now, Max, what have you done to these boys?"

Max looked confused. "Nothing. Unless..."

The pain from the wounds eased enough for Argus to jump up and rush at Max, knock the scalpel from his hand and grab him by the front of his shirt. "Unless what?"

Max pulled away. "Call your dog off, Neb. You need me, you can't kill me."

Next, Tai ran to Max. "I'll be more than happy to kill you, Jackson. And I'll enjoy every second."

Neb tapped Argus on the shoulder. "Let him go. Okay, Max, you've got exactly ten seconds to convince me not to let these boys loose. What's happened to their abilities?"

Straightening his shirt, Max glanced around. "Well, I was told that Stone did something with the sample of Argus's blood. I don't know exactly what, but I can find out. If you kill me, you'll never know." He smiled. "Looks like we're working together again, eh Neb? This time, it'll be on my terms."

Neb ran his hand through his hair. "Not necessarily. The boys have been converted, and the blood sample was before. Using the original blood shouldn't have any affect. Gretchen dear, do you think you can find out what Stone did with the blood sample?"

She came forward and stood next to Tai. "Yeah, I can dig around. As far as anyone knows, I'm still working with Jackson. And I can hack into any of Stone's secure files. I'll get what you need. You don't need Jackson."

"Gretch! Come on, you can't sell me out." Max looked terrified.

As angry as Argus was, he didn't want Max to die, or anyone for that fact. What he needed was a little re-education. "Neb, what else can the monitor in Max's head do?"

Tai shook his head. "I know where you're going, bro, but I'd rather see him six feet down."

Neb laughed. "Don't blame you, Tai, but Argus might be onto something. Max, my old friend, how'd you like a little mind alteration, like Gretchen?"

"Wait! I'm not going to be your puppet." Max kept looking around like he expected help to come any second.

Neb continued, "With both you and Gretchen, I could get all sorts of work done." He waved his hand and pinned Max against the wall. "Hold still or this will hurt. Gretchen didn't hold still and she...well, it didn't go easy, as I said before." He placed his hands on both sides of Max's head.

Max groaned and wriggled, but couldn't get away. Argus turned around. It was hard watching Neb work on Max, twisting his mind until every command would be obeyed. He'd done the same to Gretchen and she wasn't the same as she was before. Sure it was better than death, but tampering with someone's brain still seemed wrong.

"Arg, you suggested this. Don't feel bad for Jackson, at least he's not dead. You saved him." Tai put his hand on his brother's shoulder.

"I guess. It feels wrong though."

Argus watched Gretchen. She wasn't doing anything except waiting, staring blankly like she didn't have a thought in her head. If controlling humans was the Ramtalan way, then he didn't want to be Ramtalan. Of course, the days of ever being normal were long gone. He was Ramtalan and had to live with that.

"Hey, bro, I'm still feeling weak and my abilities are still blocked. What do you think Stone's done with the blood? If he only had yours, why did it work on me, too? We're not exactly the same anymore."

"Yeah, I know. But he got the samples before I was fully converted, so that means he must have used a component that we both have, and that hasn't changed."

"Alpha 2a. We both had a trace to power our abilities and now we have a ton more. That has to be it."

Argus nodded. "I think you're right. He had to have isolated the Apha-2a." He waited until Neb finished with Max. "Neb, can we talk to you?"

"Sure. I'm done here." Neb helped Max to a chair and came over to Argus and Tai. "What's up, boys."

Argus pointed to Gretchen."Is it okay to talk in front of Gretchen, and Max?"

"They're compliant." Neb glanced at Max. "It's a good thing Max didn't fight it. So, did you figure out why your abilities aren't active?"

"I think so." Argus motioned to Tai. "Tai thinks Stone found the Alpha 2a in my blood and somehow used it as a weapon against us. But there's something I don't understand. If you destroyed the EM device, why aren't our abilities working? And why aren't you affected?"

"Arg's got a good point. Is there another weapon somewhere?"

With a scowl, Neb pointed to Max. "If there is, he doesn't know about it. I think it's best we leave here immediately to get away from the effects. It is strange that it hasn't affected me though."

Argus checked his wounds; they were almost completely healed. In a way, he felt like a real human. No abilities, no invisibility, no molecular shifts. But a human would be in pain and wounded.

"Hey, Tai, are my eyes still red?"

"Yeah. Why?"

"Nothing." Argus sighed. "I was just thinking that maybe we'd gone back to being mostly human, but I guess not."

Tai rolled his eyes. "Please don't tell me you want to be human. Seriously? I like being different and I like my abilities."

"I know, so do I. Sort of. It's just, for a second I felt like a regular kid again."

"Okay, boys, that's enough angsty talk." Neb walked to the entrance of the Quonset hut and peeked out. "All clear. The guards are still napping and nobody raised an alarm. I can shift with both of you, but that means leaving Gretchen and Max alone."

Argus had an idea. "Since you got out of the Citadel, does that mean Aunt Celeste did, too?"

He nodded and smiled. "It does. She's with the Commander. I see what you're thinking. I'll bring her here, she can shift with you two and I'll stay with my new human play things."

"Really, Neb?" Argus frowned. "Can you not be so callous? Humans aren't your toys."

Tai stood with Argus. "I agree with my brother. I have friends who are human."

Neb mumbled, "Too much human influence." Within a second, he vanished.

Max stood and wandered around, shaking his head as if he was trying to clear his mind. "What the hell happened? Are we still at Edwards? And why is Gretch standing there like a statue?"

It felt good to see Max confused. Argus couldn't help but smile. "Yeah, still at Edwards. Hey, Max, how come Stone doesn't include you in his plans?"

Max scowled. "Because he's an ass, that's why. He hates me, boys, and wants to see me humiliated and destitute. A gigantic ass."

"But why?" Tai asked.

Max continued, "Why is he a gigantic ass?"

"You know what I mean."

"Yeah, yeah. I was married to his daughter. The key word being 'was'. She wanted a man who'd cater to her and be there at her whim. Well, that's not me. I'm dedicated to my job." Max's voice was a bit slurred.

"Chasing down innocent aliens?" Tai blurted.

With a huff, Max pointed at them. "Yeah. But you guys aren't innocent. Lenox is your papa and Lenox is a murderer. Earth is for humans, not Ramtalans. Why don't you freaks just leave?"

Argus found his shirt and jeans in a container near one of the tables, and Tai's in another container. "Because this is our home. Why can't you get that into your human brain?" He slipped the tee shirt over his head and handed Tai his clothes. "Ramtala is a peaceful planet, it's the Invaders who are causing the trouble. We didn't chose Lenox as our father, Max."

After a moment, there was a bright blue flash and Aunt Celeste appeared with Neb. She ran to Argus and Tai and threw her arms around them both. "Neb said Max hurt you. Are you both all right?"

Tai shrugged. "I got shot in the shoulder."

Argus added, "And Max sliced me up with a scalpel."

Tai added, "Yeah, but we're okay now."

Her eyes blazed and she turned on Max. "You—"

"Breathe, Celeste." Neb placed his hand on her shoulder. "Tai was already healing thanks to his improved genetics, and I healed Argus. Oh, and I did a little tap dance around Max's monitor. He'll be a good boy now."

"Bastard," Max muttered.

Aunt Celeste finally turned away from Max. "We have to get back to the staging area in Labrador. Take my hands."

They couldn't go back to the staging area. Not yet. The XTRA-A1 was still at Highland High. Argus shook his head. "We can't." He motioned to Tai. "We have a plan."

With a groan, Aunt Celeste pulled them aside. "What plan? What are you thinking? I need to assess this loss of your abilities and see what Stone did. And I can't be away for too long. I'm needed. But you two are the most pressing priority right now."

Argus nudged Tai. "There's a bigger priority. Lenox's ship. We can fly it."

With a smirk, Tai raised an eyebrow. "*I* can fly it."

"Okay, you can fly it. Aunt Celeste, we have to destroy or disable it so Lenox can't use it. He knows where it is."

She groaned again. "That is a complication. But I still need to assess your abilities. We'll shift home first and if your abilities return, we'll find a way to take care of the XTRA-A1."

"Cool!" Tai rubbed his hands together. "I can't wait to get back in that pilot's seat."

"Easy, Tai," Argus cautioned. "Remember, you crashed it on the football field last time you flew."

"Bro, any flight you walk away from is a good flight."

They fist bumped and Argus gave Tai a thumbs-up. "Sounds good to me."

Max grunted. "Teenagers."

Chapter 29

The molecular shift left Argus curled up on the living room floor in pain, gasping and feeling like he was going to throw up. He looked at Tai and saw he was in the same shape. Aunt Celeste knelt and placed a hand on each of their heads. Within a few seconds, Argus felt better.

"Tai, are you all right?" Argus sat up.

"Yeah, never better. That's a lie, I've felt better plenty of times. Aunt Celeste, what's happening to us?"

She shook her head. "I'm not sure, but this is more than a bit worrying." She turned suddenly and jumped in front of Argus and Tai. "Ari?"

Ari stepped out from the kitchen, hand raised. "What are you doing here? I thought you were with the other Settlers."

Without hesitating, Aunt Celeste shot a pulse at Ari and knocked him back into the kitchen. "Boys, go to my study."

Why was Ari in their house? Argus nudged Tai. "We need to stay here and help Aunt Celeste."

"Totally agree, bro."

"Boys!" Aunt Celeste glared at them. "If Ari's here, Lenox can't be far behind."

From the kitchen, Ari shouted, "I'm alone, Celeste. Father doesn't know I'm here."

"Come here." Aunt Celeste kept her hands in position for another pulse.

"Why? So you can kill me? I don't think so." Ari's voice was shaky.

Argus whispered to Tai, "Let's go to the backyard and come into the kitchen from the rear door. We'll have the element of surprise."

"And what if our abilities still aren't working? What can we do?"

Ari peeked his head around the corner. "Let me leave, Celeste. You're blocking my abilities."

Argus looked at Tai. "That answers your question. His abilities are gone, too. Let's go."

They sneaked out the front door, ran around to the backyard and crept into the kitchen while Ari had his back turned. Argus picked up a frying pan and rushed forward, slamming the pan against Ari's head. Ari screamed out and crumpled to the ground.

Aunt Celeste ran into the kitchen. "I told you two to go to my study."

Sitting on the floor, Ari held his head and rocked back and forth. "You cracked my head open."

Argus dropped the pan, feeling guilty for hurting his half-brother. "I'm sorry, Ari."

"Go to hell." Ari rubbed his head.

In a flash, Aunt Celeste knelt beside Ari, touched his head and stood up again. "You're healed. And without your abilities, you're helpless, so don't try anything."

Ari got up. "How are you blocking my abilities, Celeste? There's no way—"

"I'm not." She turned to Argus and Tai. "What were you thinking? If Ari had his abilities, he could have hit you with a lethal pulse."

Tai jumped in. "But he didn't have his abilities and we knew that. So, are you blocking them, Aunt Celeste, or did Stone do something to our house?"

Argus wondered the same thing. Max knew where they lived and he probably told Stone. An EM pulse device should be easy to find though. Not to mention Aunt Celeste and Neb still had their abilities.

Aunt Celeste interrupted his thoughts, "Argus, this isn't an EM pulse device. This is something else entirely, and it only targets New Breeds, even converted ones."

Appearing beside Aunt Celeste, Neb glared at Ari. "Ari, you little piece of garbage, what on Earth are you doing here?"

"Leave me alone. Father won't like you hurting me." Ari backed away.

"Your father is insane. I sincerely doubt he gives a damn about you." Neb glanced around and noticed the frying pan on the floor with a trace of Ari's blood on the side. "Somebody want to fill me in?"

With a shrug, Argus started, "Our abilities don't work so I conked Ari over the head."

"Okay, all caught up." Neb's eyes grew brighter. "Stone's clever, I'll give him that. I took a couple of minutes to poke around the hut at Edwards and found Stone's anti-New Breed weapon. Celeste, it's very advanced for an AURA weapon. They somehow have a sample of the boys' DNA and Alpha 2a. It targets them specifically. Ari, too, obviously. I don't know how they did this."

For a moment Aunt Celeste looked confused, then angry. "We have to destroy that weapon."

"Yes we do. I left my puppets there to try to hack into it for clues. Give me a second and I'll locate and dispose of the device that's evidently here, then we'll talk." He disappeared.

Argus whispered to Tai, "You've got a devious mind, any ideas who the traitor is that stole some Alpha 2-a?"

In a very soft voice, Tai said, "What about Neb himself? I'm still not sure we can trust him. And he seems to know an awful lot about the weapon."

That was an awful, but possible, thing to consider. What did they really know about Neb? For all they knew, he might have joined with the Invaders. But then why would he admit to knowing about the device? Aunt Celeste had known him for a long time and fought beside him during the wars. Surely she could tell if he was betraying them.

Neb returned and right away Argus felt his abilities return. Neb went to Aunt Celeste. "I found the device, but can't disable it, so I took it to a secure location a long way from here."

Argus watched Neb. If he was a traitor, why would he allow them to have their abilities back? Before he could say anything, Ari grabbed him by the arm and together they shifted. Argus couldn't intercept the shift because Ari was too strong. They landed in a cemetery.

"Ari, what are you doing? Where are we?"

Ari circled around Argus. "I had an opportunity when Neb freed my abilities, and I took it. I couldn't get you both. You were closer. Bad luck for you, *brother*."

"Don't ever call me that. You'll never be my brother." Argus scanned the area, but nothing was familiar.

"Don't worry, Argus, you'll never be a brother to me either." He motioned around the cemetery. "Oh, and you can't shift because I'll prevent it. I'm a lot stronger than you."

Argus ignored Ari and tried, but each time, his focus was messed up, like Ari took his thoughts and shook them around. "Okay, so you can interfere with my shifting. What do you want? Aunt Celeste can find me."

"In time she will. But we won't be here that long. This is a special place for me, Argus. A constant reminder of what Father is." Ari sighed and placed his hand on a tombstone. "This is my mother, or what's left of her. Father did this."

The sad darkness that crept over Ari's face made Argus feel sorry for him. "I lost a mother, too, remember. I don't understand why you're going along with Lenox. He killed our mothers."

Ari scoffed. "Don't try to connect to me through our mothers. At least you have Tai. I have no one but Father. He may have taken my mother away from me, but he's still my father."

"Sure, but not a good father. And you're not alone, you're still related to me and Tai." Argus had to keep Ari talking, distract him enough that he'd let his guard down. "We kind of got off on a bad foot, but we're your half-brothers. Why don't you stop trying to impress Galena and Lenox and join with us and Aunt Celeste? Deep down, you must know what Lenox is doing is wrong. I don't believe you're as heartless as him."

"You don't, huh? Well, I've grown up knowing exactly who I am and what's expected of me. That does something to a man. I didn't have the benefit of being sheltered and coddled. I grew up fast, hating New Breeds and waiting for the day I could help Father destroy you all."

Argus kicked a potted plant near one of the graves. "Damn it, Ari, *you're* a New Breed. You're not a pure-form Ramtalan. Let's just say for a second that Lenox completes his plan and kills every New Breed. Then what? What's he promised you?"

After setting the plant upright, Ari glared at Argus. "He's going to take me to Ramtala in the XTRA-A1. Once it's charged with a couple of twin brothers' Alpha 2a, it'll take me there. Then Father and I will rule Ramtala and restore it to its former glory. I'll be a prince."

Seriously? Ari was intelligent, how could he think Lenox would do anything like that? Had he been conditioned so much that he'd believe anything Lenox told him? "You're deluded, Ari. He'll use you like he's using us. Wake up, you idiot!" He concentrated but still couldn't shift.

"Stop trying, Argus. I won't let you go. You're coming back to the Citadel with me."

"So why are we here then? Why not take me to the Citadel right now? Are you waiting for Neb?"

"Neb?" Ari laughed. "You think Neb is an Invader? Oh, Argus, that couldn't be further from the truth. I came here to say goodbye to my mother. I won't be coming back. You think you know everything. Would you like to hear a little story about Neb?"

Argus nodded. "Sure, what the hell. I've got time to kill." Delay, delay, delay. Give Aunt Celeste time to find them.

Ari leaned against the tombstone and smoothed his hair back. "Back on Ramtala, Neb and Galena were an item. Real hot and heavy, to put it in human terms. But he also had a thing for Celeste. That pissed off Galena, as you can imagine. Celeste was a fighter, while Galena, like Father, was a tech specialist. So, Celeste and Neb fought side-by-side, leaving Galena alone on Ramtala, getting angrier and angrier about their closeness. In retaliation, she sided with Father and swore to Neb that she'd kill him the next time she saw him. You might say it was a strained relationship."

"That sounds like an understatement." Argus sat on the grass. Okay, so Neb wasn't an Invader, but he still wasn't one hundred percent trustworthy. "So you hate Neb because Galena does?"

Ari looked off into the distance. "I hate Neb because he was responsible for letting Edwards capture Father in the first place. They tortured our father and would have killed him if he hadn't used almost all of his Alpha 2a to escape. He vaporized his host body, took the XTRA-A1 underground and fed off its stored energy until he was strong enough to surface. He got another host body, although that all but used up his remaining energy, and as hard as I tried, I couldn't get a particle for him. He needed more Alpha 2a."

"So he married my mother so she'd have a child to give him more Alpha 2a? Was that why the Citadel thought he was human? Because his Alpha 2a was so low? He planned to take our energy all along, didn't he?" Argus felt sick to his stomach.

With a nod, Ari glared at Argus. "Yes. When he found out she was pregnant with twins, he realized he'd have enough Alpha 2a to recharge the ship and have enough left over to recharge himself as well. You and Tai were never supposed to live this long. After he got rid of your mother, he decided to wait until you were older so your energy would be more mature. But Celeste made it impossible to get to you two. When I did get my hands on that particle, the plan was to use it for Father and then use your energy for the XTRA-A1. The ship could destroy the New Breeds and take me to Ramtala. But things got messy because of Celeste."

"Wait." Argus paced. "You? It's been you all along?"

Ari shrugged. "Father needs me."

"Great. So why didn't Lenox take any of the other New Breeds on the planet? They have as much Alpha 2a as we do, or did before we were converted. He didn't need us."

"Argus, did Neb ever tell you the history of Father and the Malaris wars?"

"Yeah. Why?" What was Ari up to? Trying to pretend like they were one happy family? No matter what Ari said, it wouldn't change things. He'd betrayed everyone.

Ari sighed and swept a strand of hair off his face. "All the years I spent at the Citadel gave me plenty of opportunities to dig into our past. Ramtala's past."

"So?" Argus tried to initiate a shift, but Ari was still blocking him.

"So, you, Tai, and me are, ah, special. That's why Father needs us. Well, needs you. Apparently he has little respect or need of me."

"What are you talking about, Ari? Let me go home. I belong with my family."

Ari drooped his head slightly and scuffled his foot in the soil. "Argus, family is overrated." He looked up and his eyes were glowing bright blue. "Celeste is coming."

Argus jumped up and started to run, but Ari caught him and they shifted again.

Chapter 30

With a splitting headache, Max paced slowly around the Quonset hut while Gretchen sat on the floor with a large black box in front of her, fiddling with a keyboard attached to the device. Every time his thoughts drifted to the desire to kill Neb, a switch went off in his brain that told him he could never harm the freaky alien.

"Gretch, what are we doing here? Where's Neb?"

"Gone. For now. Quiet, I'm disarming this thing."

Disarming? Was it a bomb? "Um, I think I'll step outside in case you detonate it." He backed away toward the door. If she wanted to blow herself up, that was fine with him.

"Stay where you are, Jackson. Neb's coming back for us in a little while, but in the mean time, he gave me instructions to disarm this New Breed weapon thing." Gretchen never looked up.

"How does he know how to disarm it? Did he build it?" Max never did trust Neb.

Finally, Gretchen looked at him. "Of course not. But Neb thinks he knows who did so he gave me instructions how to hack it. He thinks Stone has some of the Ramtalan energy and used it in the weapon."

"Oh, yeah, you're the hacking queen. I forgot." He stopped backing toward the door. If the weapon took away the Dachel boys' abilities, then they could be captured without any struggle whatsoever. "Stone never tells me anything. Gretch, show me what you're doing. How does the thing work?"

She typed a few words, stared at the box and cursed. "I don't know how it works. Apparently Neb doesn't either."

"What do you mean? He shut it off. That means he knows how it works."

Gretchen sighed. "No, Jackson, he didn't. It doesn't affect him. Right now, this thing is transmitting whatever it is that scrambles those New Breeds' abilities."

Max smiled. "Really?" How convenient. Now all he had to do was take the device from Gretchen before she figured out how to shut it down. Of course that meant getting her out of the way. Unfortunately, she was stronger than him at this point because of the alien energy that was still in her from the thing in her palm. So, what was he going to do? "Gretch, my head hurts. Can you help me? I think Neb screwed up. What if I'm dying?"

She didn't look up. "Neb doesn't make mistakes. He did the same thing to me and I'm fine. More or less. He made it so the monitor stops us from questioning or hurting him. Get over it, Jackson, and grow a pair."

He bent down a picked up a small wrench beside Gretchen. "I *have* a pair." With all his strength, he smacked the wrench on the back of her head. She made a guttural groan and tumbled over. "Gretch?"

Nothing. He'd have to move quickly before she, or the Edwards personnel woke up. He grabbed the box, which didn't weigh more than maybe ten pounds, and ran from the hut. Incredibly, the Lambo was parked right outside. *Thank you, Neb.*

He placed the box on the seat next to him and sped from the Base, putting as much distance between himself and Gretchen as he could. He hopped onto the freeway, heading back to the heart of Palmdale. Before long, he found his exit and drove straight to City Ranch Road. The boys were sure to turn up at their house sooner or later. With their abilities disabled, he'd finish what he'd started.

Chapter 31

Shifting twice in the span of a couple minutes left Argus dizzy and disoriented. He blinked in the bright sunshine, shielded his eyes and groaned. He was back where he'd started, standing a few feet from the XTRA-A1.

Ari shoved him forward. "You'll pilot the ship to the Citadel."

Argus spun around and punched Ari across the jaw. "No, I won't."

With bright eyes, Ari staggered backward. "You'll do it or I'll shoot you with a pulse, and I won't feel a second of regret for doing it."

Argus wanted to punch Ari again, but there wasn't any point. "Ari, I *can't* fly it. I don't know how. Tai flew it, not me. And he didn't exactly do a good job." He looked around. There wasn't anyone on the football field, and judging by the position of the sun, it was almost time for school to get out. If he stalled, someone might see them and he could get away from Ari.

"Do you think I'm an idiot? If Tai can fly it, then so can you. Father reconfigured the ship to use your Alpha 2a, not mine."

"Wait, then it won't work. We've been converted." Argus pointed to his eyes. "And look at me. I'm definitely not the same as I was before. You're screwed, Ari."

Ari stared at Argus for a moment, then ran his hand over his hair, obviously nervous or scared, or both. The school bell rang and the sound of voices rose up. "You're coming with me to the Citadel." Ari started a shift.

With his abilities back, Argus blocked Ari enough that the shift failed. "No, I'm not. Come with me, Ari, and you can work with Aunt Celeste and Neb. You don't need Galena and Lenox. Be on the right side for once in your life."

"Shut up. I don't need anyone." In a burst of blue, he vanished.

Argus was about to shift home when Dave called his name. "Argus! Ah, man, didn't think you'd be here." He half-limped, half-jogged toward Argus, stopped and pointed at the XTRA-A1. "You came back for that?"

"Sort of."

A couple other boys came out onto the field, shoving each other playfully and pointing at Argus and the ship. It was too late to shift now, so Argus waved.

"What are you going to do?" Dave nodded to the guys and turned back to Argus. "It's time for practice. You going to join in or disappear?"

"Dachel!" shouted Coach. "Where's that brother of yours? You two are giving me a migraine."

"Sorry." Argus nudged Dave. "Guess I'm playing."

"Cool." Dave dashed off to the locker room, limping a bit more than he was a few minutes ago now that Coach was on the field.

Coach stood by Argus, obviously waiting for an explanation. "So? What's going on with you and your brother? There's a rumor mill running rampant about you being an alien, a superhero, a kid struck by lightning. Which is it? Any of that true? Know what? I don't care, as long as you play ball."

Part of him wanted to admit to everything. "Coach, I'm a regular kid with regular problems. Rumors are rumors, that's all." He adjusted the sunglasses.

"Good." Coach turned and pointed to Dave, who was dragging a sack of footballs behind him. "Grab a ball, Dachel, and practice. I intend to win against Palmdale High."

Argus froze. "Yes, sir." Sandra went to Palmdale High. He'd messed up big time with her, and having Tai appear out of nowhere certainly didn't help. These days he was making more enemies than friends.

Coach pointed to the ship. "Why the hell is this thing still here? Dachel, you and the guys make sure it's moved."

"Yes, sir." Argus glanced at the ship. That's exactly what he'd hoped to do. Only without Tai, he wasn't sure he could.

With a nod, Coach strode away and yelled at a couple of boys who were goofing around.

Dave tossed Argus a ball. "Can I help you move it?"

"I don't think I can fly it, Dave. My brother flew it last time. Crashed it, too."

Tai tapped Argus on the shoulder. "Do you have to bring that up every time? I used shared-sight to locate you. Where's Ari? Aunt Celeste wants to skewer him."

"He didn't stick around. Tai, Coach said we have to move the XTRA A-1. Do you remember how to get inside?" Argus winked at Dave. "Dave wants to help."

With a shrug, Tai went to Dave. "Cool, thanks. You sure you want to get mixed up in all of this?"

Dave looked at the ship and back at Tai. "I think I'm already mixed up in it."

"He's right." Argus tossed the ball to Tai. "We're supposed to practice, but I think we should take the ship and get the hell out of here."

Tai looked confused. "Wait, you want to fly it out of here? In front of everyone? Isn't it supposed to be a float?"

Argus ran his hand along the fuselage of the XTRA-A1. "Considering everything, I think my dream of being a normal kid was always a fantasy. I don't belong here, especially not with Lola still at the Citadel. At this point, all I want is to salvage what I can of my life, whatever that ends up to be. It's about time I stepped up and started acting like the Ramtalan that I am."

"Welcome to the dark side, bro." Tai glanced around. "I know how to get inside, but Dave can't come. It requires an Alpha-shift, which I did accidentally last time. Dave doesn't have any Alpha 2a, so it won't work on him. Sorry, dude."

Dave's shoulders drooped. "Maybe I can create a distraction or something."

"Don't need one." Tai gave Dave a pat on the arm. "But thanks. You're a good friend, Dave. Hey, Arg, we have to hurry before any stray Ramtalan finds us."

"Yeah, okay. Dave, thanks for everything. I don't think I'll ever come back to Palmdale. But I promise I'll make sure Lola gets back. She doesn't deserve what I've done to her. Take care of her, will you?"

With a slight smile, Dave nodded. "You know it, man. If either of you ever needs anything, anything at all, I'm here." He turned away, wiped at his eyes and mumbled, "Must be pollen in the air."

Tai gave Dave another pat on the arm and turned to Argus. "Ready, bro? Don't fight it, let me lead the shift."

He didn't intend to fight it. They had to get the XTRA-A1 as far from Lenox as possible and at this point, it didn't much matter how they did it. Before he knew it, they were inside the ship and a cold sensation came over him, reminding him that he'd almost died the first time he'd flown in the ship.

No sense in delaying things. He sat in one of the chairs, placed his arms in the depressions and waited. "Okay, you know how to get in, but do you know how to fly without crashing? Ari said Lenox reconfigured the ship to use our Alpha 2a."

With a smirk, Tai replied, "Yeah, I figured that out. That's why he needs us. I learned a few things at the Citadel. Remember, Galena had my flying simulators. I had no idea why, but now I do. It didn't click the first time, but yeah, I know how to fly without crashing. You know what? If we find a way to destroy this ship, Lenox won't need us anymore. Maybe we'll get our lives back after all." He sat in the other chair.

Argus wished it was true that they'd get back to how they were before, but knew it wasn't likely. When the ship's engine started, Argus felt tingly all over, but it didn't weaken him like last time. "Let's get out of here."

The front window shutter opened and the ship rose off the ground. Below, the boys scattered, looking up and shielding their eyes from the sun. Dave stood to the side, and waved. Argus waved back, not sure if Dave could see him or not. A few seconds later, Coach and three other teachers rushed onto the field.

"Hang on, Arg."

Right away, the ship rose higher and higher, well above the neighboring houses and power poles, until it was about two hundred feet up. The nose dipped forward as the speed increased and they zipped over the town. Argus closed his eyes. He was leaving behind everything he'd ever known; his old life. What would his life be like now? A captive? A traitor? A converted New Breed with no home? That last one stung.

He opened his eyes and saw a huge stretch of desert outside. "Where are we?"

Tai concentrated, his eyes staring straight ahead. "Middle of the Mojave."

"Well, put us down so we can figure out how to destroy this thing."

"Not yet." Beads of sweat dotted Tai's forehead.

"Seriously, land. You don't look so good." Argus couldn't move his arms or he would have reached out and shaken his brother to snap him out of his trance. "Land this ship!"

After a moment, Tai slowly shook his head. "Arg, I know what I'm doing. I flew this ship in the simulators a hundred times. We're going for a ride."

The ship's nose pointed upward and it accelerated. The window shutter closed and a display flickered on, showing the ground below. Tai smiled and whooped, but Argus was terrified.

"What are you doing, Tai? We'll run out of oxygen this high up. Are you trying to kill us?"

Tai turned and grinned. "We can breathe just fine. The ship is equipped to use our Alpha 2a to generate oxygen and heat. And it's pressurized. We're going into space, bro."

Argus held his breath and squeezed his eyes closed. Space? It had always been a dream, but that was when he thought their dad was an astronomer. Now, it didn't feel like a dream, but a nightmare. One where they could be killed any second. Earth was home and they were about to leave that home. He let his breath out and felt a sense of exhilaration as the display showed the surface getting smaller and smaller. He glanced at Tai. Home wasn't a place. It was a shared space with his brother.

Chapter 32

Moving through the atmospheric layers wasn't nearly as terrifying as Argus had expected and in fact, he found it thrilling. As they climbed, he watched as the landscape became a patchwork quilt where individual buildings were no longer distinguishable. He'd never seen the planet like that before.

"This is unbelievable, Tai. Is there an altimeter? How high up are we?"

"Ah, about 48,000 feet. You think I'll get an A in English if I write an essay about stealing a Ramtalan ship and flying it into space?" Tai laughed.

"Definitely an A." Argus laughed, too. "I can't believe we're doing this. The youngest people in space."

"Well, the youngest converted New Breeds," Tai corrected.

Argus nodded. "My bad. Hey, how fast are we going?"

Tai looked over at Argus. "I have no idea. The only instrument I understand is the altimeter, the rest is in Ramtalan or something. Look." He pointed to a projected display on the window shutter. "See the altimeter? Well, those other instruments next to it are the ones I don't understand."

That couldn't be good. They were heading into space without knowing how to read the ship's instruments. The altimeter was a digital read-out, easy enough, but beside it on the right was a set of three horizontal wavy lines. Next to that were four concentric circles, all rotating slowly, with weird symbols floating around the circles in apparently random patterns. One symbol looked like a hash mark and another was almost a square, but with the sides concave. What did any of it mean?

"Tai, what if those instruments are telling us the ship's about to explode?"

"Seriously, bro? Don't be so dramatic. Lenox wouldn't build a ship that exploded once it left the...whoa. We're in the mesosphere. I think our speed is increasing."

"What does that mean?" Argus grabbed Tai's arm and shook it. "What does that mean!"

Tai pulled free. "Maybe it has to pick up more speed to get through the atmosphere. Hey, the chair's released our arms."

"Yeah, I see that. What do you mean by *maybe*? Take us back down." Argus felt his energy collecting in the pit of his stomach.

"Easy, bro. Your freaky red eyes are glowing through your sunglasses. Is the XTRA-A1 sapping your energy again like last time? It shouldn't, but tell me if it is."

Argus tossed the sunglasses on the floor. "I'm betting the ship only needs our energy for take-off. And no, it's not draining my energy. If anything, I feel more energized. Like I just got a boost. What if I fire off a pulse?"

"Don't. Control it, Arg. I feel pretty awesome, too. I bet this has a collective energy thing like the Citadel does. Pretty awesome if you ask me."

Yeah, unless the ship ripped apart from all the energy. Tai didn't seem worried though. Argus breathed slowly until he got his energy under control. "What if we run into a satellite?"

"Oh, shit. I didn't think of that. There's got to be a million satellites up here. Ah, the ship probably has an avoidance system."

"Probably? You didn't think this through, did you? What are your plans when we're actually in space? Fly to Ramtala?" Argus stared straight ahead at the monitor screen, but all he saw were clouds. The next second, they burst out of the clouds. Below, he saw the North American continent and picked out Palmdale. "Look at that, Tai. It's beautiful."

"Epically awesome, bro. Oh, and I'm not going to fly to Ramtala, smart ass. I thought I'd cruise around in orbit until I find a good place to land."

"On Earth?"

"Of course on Earth. Wait. Why not the moon?" Tai grinned. "Lenox would never find the ship on the moon."

Tai had lost his mind.

Argus stared at his brother. "How do you expect us to survive on the moon?"

"I suppose that does present a problem." Tai gasped softly and pointed to the display. "Arg, we're in space."

The view of Earth against the blackness of space took his breath away. Argus gaped. I...that's...we're in space."

He stared at the display. What an amazing feeling it was to be above the Earth, free, away from everyone who ever wanted to hurt them. The idea of landing on the moon sounded reasonable. Between both of them, they'd figure out some way to stay alive and keep the XTRA-A1 away from Lenox. Then again, Lola was still at the Citadel, by herself. He couldn't abandon her.

"Something's not right. Bro. Arg!" Tai brought the ship around so the view on the display no longer showed Earth. The shutter opened and right in front of them was a large bluish cloud. "What is that?"

"Like I know." Argus stood. "Orient me, Tai. What direction is that cloud?"

"Ah, there's no direction in space. No cardinal directions. But I do know that the cloud is moving toward Earth. I can't explain it, but I feel it. It's buzzing with Alpha 2a. Can you feel that?"

There *was* something, like a vibration deep down inside his body, on a cellular level. "So the cloud's made up of Ramtalan energy?"

Tai shrugged. "I guess. Is it a weapon?"

"I don't know." Argus went to the front window and checked the display that was still up. The strange square symbol expanded and shrunk and the wavy lines moved rapidly. "Tai, get us away from that cloud."

"Why? Do you know something I don't?"

"No, but it's coming right for us. What if it destroys the ship or sucks up all of the Alpha 2a?" He stepped back from the window. "I feel weird."

"Yeah, so do I. Kind of dizzy." Tai rested his head in his hands.

"Tai, are you okay?"

There was a brilliant flash of blue that filled the ship's interior. "Boys." It was Commander Jampara. "This is Lenox's ship?"

Argus stood by Tai. "Yes, Commander. We were going to hide it or destroy it, but now Tai's not well. We both feel strange."

The Commander floated to them. "Of course you do. This ship absorbs Alpha 2a, from you and other Ramtalans. You were correct to hide it from Lenox, but you should never have flown it yourselves. Like the ship, you two are absorbing Alpha 2a."

"How?" Argus flopped into his seat.

"From the ship. It stores your energy, but you are taking some back."

Argus glanced at Tai. "I'm not even going to pretend I understand that. That blue cloud? Is it dangerous, are we going to die?"

"I cannot know for certain how this amount of energy will affect you. You both are almost pure Ramtalan now, but still have a trace of human DNA. Argus, that blue cloud is not a cloud at all, but 10,000 pure-forms coming to stand against Lenox. I was going to intercept them and lead them in when I encountered this ship and sensed you two inside. Tai, you are not as strong as Argus anymore, so you are feeling the effects of the influx of energy. I will need to adjust your energy receptors and hope that will prevent any damage to your body."

"Damage?" Argus glared at the Commander. "You mean Tai might die? Fix him. Whatever you need to do, do it. Now."

"Bro, I don't even know what my energy receptors are." Tai raised his head and Argus saw his eyes glowing bright green instead of blue.

"Tai, don't freak, but your eyes are green. Like emerald green." Argus turned to the Commander. "What's going on?"

"Green?" Tai rubbed his eyes. "Don't tell me not to freak out and then say my eyes are green."

The Commander approached and placed his hand on Tai's shoulder. "The extra Alpha 2a flowing into your receptors is overloading your body. Close your eyes. I must do the procedure now. It will be painful."

"Fabulous." Tai looked at Argus. "Arg, if I don't make it, it's up to you to defeat Lenox. Got it, it's up to you."

Argus shook his head. "Don't talk like you're going to die. Guys like you don't die in a spaceship above the Earth."

"Really? So how do guys like me die then?"

"You don't. You drive a Lamborghini 150 mph with the hottest girl in town beside you and you're never seen from again. You become a legend."

Argus gripped his hand. "But you can't be a legend until we stand together and fight Lenox. Deal?"

Tai nodded. "Deal. Okay, Commander, do your worst."

"Worst? I will do my best." Commander Jampara placed one hand on Tai's forehead and the other on his chest. "Close your eyes and don't move."

Blue and green sparks shot from the Commander's fingers, crawled along Tai's skin and seemed to sink into his flesh. Tai screamed and writhed. Argus couldn't take it and turned away, but didn't let go of his brother's hand. The whole ship glowed and crackled, like it was charged with electricity. The weird feeling still gripped Argus, although it was making him feel strong and on-edge. He wanted to fire a pulse or run a marathon or both.

While Tai continued to thrash in pain, Argus concentrated on controlling his energy level and managed to stop the urge to fire a pulse. After who-knows-how-long, Tai quieted and the glow dissipated. Argus turned around and saw him sitting up straight, calm, but when he opened his eyes, they were red.

The Commander floated away a few feet. "It is done, but—"

Argus nodded. "I know."

"What?" Tai stood. "Are my eyes still green? Oh, whoa, this is cool. I can hear voices from the cloud."

"So can I." Argus went to the window. "That's amazing."

"Stay calm for a few moments, Tai." The Commander pointed out the front window. "You now have increased Alpha 2a that has enhanced your abilities. You can hear Ramtalans when they are close and you have more strength. You and Argus are the same again."

"We are?" Tai seemed confused. "What exactly does that mean? I've been converted again, re-converted?"

Argus shrugged. "Yeah. But you don't have blue eyes anymore."

"So they're still green, right?" Tai sighed. "Chicks like green eyes." He winked.

"Um, no." Argus pointed to his own eyes. "They're red."

"No. Really?" Tai's head drooped. "I liked having blue eyes. Or green eyes."

"Enough talk, boys. Our people will enter Earth's atmosphere and join Celeste and Nebulon. You two must return. You cannot orbit forever. Tai, can you continue to fly?"

"Sure." Tai touched his eyes and sighed, then placed his arms in the depressions. "But I think I should stay up here until Lenox is captured."

"Wait, Commander." Argus motioned to the display. "What are those symbols?"

Commander Jampara peered intently at the display. After a minute or so, he spun around. "What is this? This is not Lenox's ship. Have you been lying to me?" His entire body burned blue.

Argus stayed close to Tai. Why was the Commander so angry? "We haven't lied about anything? And this is definitely Lenox's ship. The XTRA-A1 he built at Edwards."

"It cannot be." The Commander grabbed Tai by his shirt and lifted him out of the seat. "How are you flying a Malaris ship?"

Malaris? Argus took Tai by the arm and tried to wrestle him free. "Let him go! This is Lenox's ship, Commander. Lenox built it and hid it underground. Tai learned how to fly it from a simulator at the Citadel. It's Lenox's ship."

"This does not make sense." The Commander released Tai. "I apologize. This is indeed puzzling. I have not encountered the Malaris for thousands of years and yet, here we are in one of their ships. Only a Malaris can control a Malaris ship."

"What are you talking about?" Argus glanced at Tai. "My brother's not a Malaris."

Tai backed away. "Yeah, what you mean? Arg's right I'm *not* a Malaris."

"Not just you, Tai." The Commander turned to Argus. "Both of you."

Argus felt faint. What did the commander mean? The Malaris had warred with Ramtala, and now he said they were Malaris. It was impossible, but he seemed so sure of himself. What would happen now? Commander Jampara thought he and Tai were the enemy.

Chapter 33

Argus was totally confused. Was the Commander playing a trick? Why did he say they were Malaris? It made no sense. The XTRA-A1 was built by Lenox and they were Lenox's sons, Ramtalan, not Malaris. The ship was Ramtalan.

The Commander glowed blue. "Boys, we have a problem."

No kidding. Argus drew in a breath. "I'd say that's an understatement, sir. You just accused me and Tai of being aliens. Well, different aliens. The race that declared war on Ramtala."

With his newly altered eyes glowing red, Tai glared. "Commander, if you think my brother and I are Malaris, you're crazy. You just did whatever you did to me and didn't detect any Zeta-whatever energy, which proves I'm Ramtalan. What have you been smoking, dude?"

"Smoking?" The Commander stopped glowing and pointed to the symbols on the display. "Those are Malaris markings. They are responding to the collective Ramtalan Alpha 2a."

"Wait." Argus watched the symbols move. "From me and Tai or the Ramtalans out there?"

The Commander floated around the ship. "Both."

Tai spoke up, "Then that proves we're Ramtalan, right?"

After settling onto the ground, the Commander shook his head. "Not exactly, Tai. All it proves is that you have Alpha 2a energy, but it also indicates that you have Zeta-40."

This was getting out of hand. Argus shook his head. "What? That's not right. We've lived our whole lives with Aunt Celeste. She would have known if we weren't New Breeds." He struggled to control his energy build-up. "We are not Malaris."

With a sweep of his hand, the Commander knocked Argus backward. "You need to restrain your impulses, Argus. You boys will fly this ship to the staging area immediately and surrender. I will insert the coordinates into your mind." His eyes flashed blue. "Done. Since I have known you since your birth, I trust you will obey. If you do not, I will be forced to bring you in myself. And that will not end well." In a flash, he was gone.

Argus stared out the window. "What the hell just happened?"

"Damned if I know."

"What does he mean by 'bring us in'? And surrender? Why do we have to surrender? Are we the enemy now? I'm not surrendering to anyone." Argus flinched as the blue cloud enveloped the ship. The ship vibrated for a few seconds and then the cloud continued toward Earth.

"Arg, what exactly are we?"

"We're the Dachel brothers, that's what."

"Yeah." Tai closed the window shutter. "And apparently we're fugitives now. I don't plan on surrendering. We can't trust anybody at this point."

"No kidding. Hey, do you have 53°34'12.28"N latitude and 56°16'39.91"W longitude in your head, too?"

"Yep. But I'm not taking us there. Where should we go?" Tai sat and slipped his arms in the depressions on the arm rest. "Pick a place."

More than anything, Argus wanted to rescue Lola, but that meant going to the Citadel, which he wasn't about to do, and they couldn't go back to Palmdale, so what was left? They'd never lived anywhere else. After a moment, he had the perfect place. "Acoma."

"Seriously?"

"Yeah. The people there hid Neb for years. I bet they'd hide us, too." Argus sat and put his arms into the depressions. "Can you fly us there?"

Tai shrugged. "I don't have any coordinates, but I can find it."

"Then let's go."

"Arg, we don't know if we can trust Neb. What if the Acoma people turn us over to him?"

"If you have any other ideas about where we can go, speak up." Argus raised an eyebrow. "Well?"

Tai looked forward. "Acoma it is. There's no landing strip there though."

"I have faith in you, brother. You'll find a place."

"Yeah, yeah."

The XTRA-A1 flipped around and pointed, nose first, toward Earth. Argus watched Tai as he controlled the ship with his mind, making it accelerate and change course. It couldn't be too hard since Tai seemed calm.

"I want to try," Argus said. "Tell me how to do it."

"What, fly?"

"Yeah. I figured out how to drive the Lambo, this can't be any harder than that."

Tai groaned. "I took lessons on the simulator at the Citadel, that's how I know how to fly this thing. You can't learn in one lesson."

"Sure I can. Come on, Tai, I've never flown a spaceship before. You just want a skill that I don't have."

"That's a lie. Well, mostly. I'm the pilot, it's that simple. But hey, if you think you can fly a Malaris spaceship, then go right ahead."

Argus wanted to punch Tai, but he couldn't pull his arms out of the depressions. "Tai, I can't move." He should be able to move since they weren't launching.

"Neither can I. What's going on? I could get in and out of the seat before." Tai struggled.

"Maybe it's because we're heading into the atmosphere. You know, a safety precaution. We are going into the atmosphere, aren't we?"

"Um." Tai looked forward. "Well, the altimeter says we're descending. Fast. Shit, really fast."

"Then slow down!" Argus watched the Malaris symbols on the display waver and dance around. Then a new symbol popped up, a star-shaped symbol that expanded and shrunk over and over. "Can you slow us down or go back into space?"

The XTRA-A1 shuddered as it evidently pushed through the atmosphere. With the window shutter closed, they flew blind, descending at close to 40,000 feet per minute according to the altimeter. If Tai didn't pull out of the dive soon, they'd be too close to the ground to do anything. Argus glanced at his brother, sweat dripping down his face and his breathing rapid, his brow pinched in concentration.

"Arg, it's not responding. We'll have to shift."

"Okay. At least the ship will get destroyed. Together, on the count of three we'll go home." Argus closed his eyes and thought of his bedroom, but nothing happened. There was no build-up of energy that was needed to initiate a shift. "I can't."

"Yeah, I'm useless over here, too. So what now? The ship's not responding. I don't want to die, Arg. All that stuff I said about never surrendering was bullshit. I'd surrender in a second if it meant not crashing to Earth in a fiery ball. Hell, I don't want to die!"

"Same here." His heart thumped like it would burst from his chest. If he could hold Lola one last time and tell her he loved her, it wouldn't be so bad. "At least we're together."

"Yeah, but that's not much comfort right now." Tai kept his eyes on Argus. "Might as well watch."

The window shutter slid open and showed an expanse of the Pacific Ocean below, getting closer and closer. They were going down between Hawaii and the west coast of California. This was it. Soon they'd never have to worry about Invaders or Lenox again.

"Bye, Arg."

"Bye, Tai." Argus didn't want to see the moment of impact and squeezed his eyes shut. *I love you, Lola, and I'm sorry for everything.*

Chapter 34

Max had parked the Lambo about half a mile from the Dachels' house, sneaked up to the wall surrounding the property and tucked the box under a ragged sagebrush plant. It was well hidden, but he wanted a back-up plan just in case; a surprise attack by the United States Air Force. A boom shook the ground and he looked up. There was a streak in the sky, heading toward the ground. An invasion? But that wasn't necessarily a bad thing. It was exactly the excuse he needed to contact Edwards and AURA. With his cell phone to his ear, he watched the object whiz toward the ground.

"Hello, Angel? It's Max Jackson. We've got trouble. You still have that address in Palmdale I gave you? The Dachels' place?"

Angel's voice was shaky, "Sure. Why?"

"Those aliens have screwed with us for the last time, Angel. Now it's payback. Get yourself, everyone, and everything to the house right now. And look up in the sky. We're under attack."

"Yeah, we know that. We scrambled fighters and they're on their way to intercept the object. They said its' signature and design fits that old ship, the XTRA-A1, Lenox's ship."

Max grinned. "Holy shit. We're going to capture Lenox himself. I planted another weapon at the Dachel house, so if they're in there, we'll get them, too. I bet you anything Lenox is coming for his brats."

"Could be. Oh, and there was a weird blue cloud that entered the atmosphere, but disappeared somewhere near Canada. We picked up these strange anomalies within the cloud, like electrical charges. Everyone's on alert. Us, Russia, the UK, hell, even the Middle Eastern countries are reporting that they're prepping their weapons if the aliens enter their airspace. We'll get 'em this time, Max. Oh and we got a brand new airborne tactical warship that's been launched. Capability of going into space."

"No shit? Super." It was too good to be true. The Ramtalans couldn't get away now, although if someone else captured them, he wouldn't have the market on selling their technology or DNA. Damn it all to hell. "Angel, I'm agent-in-charge. Make sure everyone reports to me. Got that? Everyone."

"What about Mr. Stone? He's the one who developed the weapon."

"Doesn't matter. That weapon only works on the kids. You don't happen to have another one lying around, do you?" Max kept watching the object. It was getting closer now, leaving a trail of fire behind it. If it didn't slow down, it'd crash.

There was a pause and then Angel replied, "There's a prototype. You want that?"

"Damn right. Bring it with you. I want a mobile weapon. And Angel, don't tell any of this to Stone if he ever contacts you. He's preoccupied in Canada. Remember, I'm the agent-in-charge."

"Yes, sir, got it. I'll be at your location soon. ETA seven minutes via copter."

"Good. Turn the prototype on as soon as you're in range." Max hung up and crept toward the house. If the boys were inside, they'd be his. This time, he'd fly them right to AURA headquarters in LA. Neb wouldn't expect that. How much would a couple of alien kids be worth? A million? Two million? Maybe even a billion to the right bidder. Lenox would be worth more. But, there wouldn't be any sale until after he'd had the chance to study them himself of course. And if the Ramtalans wanted the kids back, then the price would go up. This was a win-win situation.

Chapter 35

The ship shuddered and Argus held his breath. They'd impact the ground any second now and then there'd be nothing. He was prepared for death, but the thought of *Tai* dying hurt. What good was it being a Protector if he couldn't save his brother?

"Tai, this isn't right!" he shouted, opening his eyes. "I can't let you—"

"Boys!" Aunt Celeste appeared in front of them. "You boys aren't going to die."

Right away, the ship pulled out of the dive and leveled off. Whatever Aunt Celeste did, it broke the connection with the ship, and Argus could lift his arms off the chair. He looked at Tai and saw that he was out of his seat and staring out the window.

Argus sighed, grateful they were alive. "Aunt Celeste, what's going on?"

She flipped her ponytail over her shoulder. "This is not a Malaris ship."

With a roll of his eyes, Tai grunted. "That's what we told the Commander."

"But," she started, "It is Malaris technology. Tai, how did you pilot this ship?"

He shrugged. "Galena had me doing flight simulations at the Citadel. I swear I didn't know what it was for. You have to believe me. I thought they were games."

"It's all right." Aunt Celeste went to the symbols on the heads-up display. "Lenox."

"What?" Argus pointed to the symbols. "You know what these mean? How did Lenox build a ship with Malaris technology? And how is it using our Alpha 2a energy? How can we be compatible with Malaris tech?"

"Excellent questions, Argus." Aunt Celeste approached and gave them both a hug. "When the Commander told me about you two and the ship, I knew you were in trouble. This is very confusing." She stood back again.

"Confusing?" Tai raised his voice. "It's more than confusing, Aunt Celeste, it's impossible. We're Ramtalan, not—"

Argus interrupted, "What if Lenox is Malaris?"

"Seriously, bro? Then we'd be..." Tai stopped. "Oh, shit."

"Language, Tai." Aunt Celeste paced around the ship. "You're not Malaris. I would have sensed Zeta 40 energy in you. However, Zeta 40 is needed to power this ship, which leads to my confusion."

Argus replayed everything she and the Commander had said. "Wait. If Zeta 40 is needed to power the ship, then how did you pull us out of the dive?"

She hesitated, and ran her fingers through her ponytail. "I absorbed a scant amount of Zeta 40 during the Malaris wars."

"How?" Argus watched her. She was nervous or was that a look of guilt. "Aunt Celeste, how did you absorb it?"

"I know Neb explained my part in the wars. During my information extractions, small segments of Zeta 40 became implanted in my brain. Not enough to have an effect on me, but enough to tap into their technology briefly. I cannot actually pilot the ship, but I have enough Zeta 40 to change the commands."

Tai slumped to the floor. "What commands? The ship was heading right for the ground."

Aunt Celeste glanced through the window for a moment. "You're correct, Tai, the ship was commanded to crash into the Pacific Ocean. I stopped it. For now. The Malaris always had failsafe commands to override any alterations. Which means, the ship will revert back to its original course and still crash unless we do something about it."

"But why crash? That doesn't make any sense." Argus sat on the floor with Tai. Now that they were free from the seats, they could shift anywhere and be safe, but if Lenox designed the ship to crash, there had to be a reason. "We can't let it crash."

"Agreed." Aunt Celeste closed her eyes for a second and when she opened them, they were glowing. "Boys, I need you to return to orbit. There are multiple fighters approaching from several countries. Leaving Earth is the only way you'll be safe."

Tai cocked his head. "Well, we can shift out of the ship and let them shoot it down."

Aunt Celeste shook her head. "The Zeta 40 powering the ship, which had to come from you two, cast a slight energy shield around the ship. Human weaponry can't penetrate the shield, but we can still shift through it. The only solution we have is to get to safety and hope the ship doesn't override my command until we figure out why Lenox wants it to plunge into the ocean. Tai, resume control and Argus, while Tai's flying, I need you to locate the control center of the ship."

"What's the control center?" Argus hadn't seen anything in the ship other than the seats and the display. "There aren't any controls. Tai does everything with his thoughts."

"The ship has a brain, a type of artificial intelligence. The control center is the brain where information and data is stored. Since you evidently have Zeta 40, you'll need to attempt to connect with the control center and change its programming." Aunt Celeste glanced out the window again. "You have to do this, Argus, because Tai is the pilot. This ship was designed to kill all New Breeds. Lenox has something planned and crashing the ship is at the heart of his plan."

"Hold on, Aunt Celeste," Tai jumped up. "You said you have Zeta 40, too, then why don't you take over and let us go home? I'm really not enjoying this anymore."

"Like I said, Tai, I only have a scant amount of Zeta 40, not nearly enough to pilot the ship. You two somehow have more. When there's time, I'll run some diagnostic tests on you to find the reason. But not now."

"Fine." Tai flopped into his seat. "Come on, Arg, I have to be an astronaut again and you have to be the brains."

Argus got up and went to his seat. "Are you sure this is the only way? I can't let anything happen to Tai."

"I know. Suppress your Protector feelings and do what I said. The Commander is expecting you at the staging area in Labrador and will mount his own mission to retrieve you unless we figure this out quickly. And with Earth now thinking they're under attack—"

"Yeah, yeah, we don't have a choice." Tai placed his arms in the depressions. "Ready, bro?"

Argus did the same and drew in a deep breath. "Sure. Aunt Celeste, what if I can't hack into the control center?"

"You have Zeta 40, you'll manage. If you can't locate the control center, then shift to the staging area before impact. I'll try to locate Lenox and if possible, I'll manipulate his mind until I find his plan. But finding him is a long shot. I need you two to stop this ship from crashing." She forced a smile. "Good luck, boys."

Argus nodded even though he knew it wasn't likely Aunt Celeste would find Lenox, because he was too smart to get captured. That meant it was up to him and Tai. Before he could ask anything else, Aunt Celeste vanished in a flash of blue and the ship pointed straight up, accelerating so much that Argus was pushed into his seat with the g-force.

"Hang on, bro, the ship isn't responding so good. I'm fighting it."

"What does that mean? Can you fly this thing or not?"

"Of course I can, I just meant it's not easy. Now shut up and let me concentrate."

Argus watched out the window until Tai closed the shutter. Without a view, he focused on the altimeter that indicated they were climbing at about 35,000 feet per minute. The XTRA-A1 was an incredible ship and if it hadn't been designed for a nefarious reason, it could be used for exploration. But it had to be destroyed to stop Lenox.

Argus shook his head. How was he supposed to hack into the control center? He didn't know where it was or what to do. When the altimeter said they were at about 70,000 feet, the stratosphere, a strange sensation washed over Argus and he squeezed his eyes shut. He felt like he wasn't in the ship anymore, even though he knew full well he was sitting next to Tai.

His skin warmed and electric pulses crawled all over his body, settling in his gut. His eyes sprung open and he was standing inside a weird room with red glowing walls that had black spikes coming out of them, pointing toward the center of the room. They looked a lot like the spikes near Palmdale after the particle impacted the ground.

Where was he? He had to get back. Tai was all alone. "Hello?"

He walked around and estimated the room was about five feet by five feet and other than the spikes, which poked out about a foot, there was nothing else in it. Wherever this was, he wasn't about to stay. He concentrated on Tai and attempted to initiate a shift, but he was blocked. If he couldn't find a way out, he'd never locate the control center of the ship. The room had to be something Lenox created to trap anyone who tried to interfere with the ship.

"Arg, are you all right?" Tai asked in a faint voice.

"Tai? Where are you?"

"Arg? Can you hear me? Wake up! Arg!"

"I'm here, Tai! Can you use shared-sight to find me?"

"Bro! Damn it! You can't be dead, you can't be. Argus!"

Chapter 36

Max came out of hiding when the copters from Edwards were in view. If Angel did what he'd said and turned the prototype weapon on, then the Dachels would be helpless. Three black helicopters flew over the house and settled down, one in front and two in back. Angel climbed out and ran to Max.

"Max, ground troops should arrive in a few minutes. Then we can—"

"Oh, Angel, we're not waiting for ground troops. I want those aliens." Max held his hand out. "You have a gun for me?"

Angel hesitated, but pulled a gun from his holster and handed it to Max. "You better know what you're doing, man." He reached down and withdrew a smaller pistol from a holster under his pant leg above his boot. "Don't shoot unless—..."

"I know, I know. I'm trained in firing weapons, Angel. Okay, we need to storm the place."

"Just you and me? Max, we'll wait for the troops. You know what these aliens can do. We need backup."

Max thought for a moment. Angel was right. "I guess we should wait. It's just that I don't want those assholes disappearing into thin air."

"The place is surrounded, Max, and the weapon is turned on. They can't go anywhere."

"Angel, they disappear. Like *disappear*. They don't need to use cars." Max paced in front of the driveway gate. "What if the weapon isn't working?"

"I just told you that the weapon is *on*, Max."

Without arguing further, Angel waved to a couple soldiers who'd come out of the helicopters. They jogged over and after he explained the situation, one of them blasted a few bullets at the hinges. Two more shots and the gate was open. With this much backup, Max knew he'd get the boys this time and if Neb or Celeste showed up, the troops would open fire. As powerful as the Ramtalans were, they were no match for bullets.

He stormed through the gate and onto the property. Several military Jeeps charged up the driveway and Max couldn't stop smiling. This was it, the moment he'd been waiting for. He followed a safe distance behind Angel, gun in hand, and his focus set on capturing whoever was inside the house. At this point, it didn't matter who he got.

The Jeeps screeched to a stop, troops stomped toward the house and the helicopter engines roared. Max's adrenaline pumped hard. The excitement, however, came to a crashing halt when everyone around him suddenly froze in place. Nobody moved a muscle, except him.

"What the hell. Angel?" He walked around Angel and other than a few lazy blinks of his eyes, he was a statue.

"Hello, Max," came a firm and menacing voice.

Max turned and saw a tall man with shoulder-length snow-white hair and piercing red eyes standing in the doorway of the house. "Who the hell are you?" The guy was obviously a Ramtalan, but he'd never seen this one before.

"I think you know me. That ship in the upper atmosphere that you wanted to shoot down is mine. I want it back."

"Lenox?" Max took a step backward. "You're not Argustine Lenox. What game are you playing? Release these men right now or you'll be sorry."

The man came forward. "I *am* Argustine Lenox. This is no game, you insignificant human. You have tortured my sons, threatened me, and have been working for my enemies. Do you think that is something I will tolerate?"

How could it be Lenox? Max pointed his gun and pulled the trigger five times, each bullet hit the target and left a bright red stain on Lenox's white shirt. *Take that, Lenox!* Even dead, Lenox would be the biggest prize of all. Max let out a whoop. Finally, Lenox was dead.

Chapter 37

Argus dashed around the room looking for a way out, but there were no doors or windows. And worst of all, Tai was under the impression that he was dead. What exactly did that mean? Tai said "wake up". He wouldn't say that unless there was still a body in the seat of the ship.

"Where am I?" Argus said aloud.

A ticking sound filled the room and the tips of the spikes glowed red one by one. "Awaiting command."

Argus scanned the room. "What? Who said that?" He touched one of the spikes nearest to him and retracted his hand right away. The spikes were scalding.

"Awaiting command. Override protocol in place but not activated. Initiation sequence activated."

He had the explanation he was looking for; he was in the control center. But how? The ship wasn't big enough to house the room. "How do I override the initiation sequence?"

"Argustine Lenox, you designed me and only you can override. Sequence will commence upon impact."

"I'm not Argustine...there's not going to be an impact. I don't want to crash the ship. Stop the initiation sequence." He wandered around, searching for the origin of the voice. If it was a computer, it could be hacked. Tai was better with computers, but he wasn't around.

The control center continued, "There is not sufficient Zeta 40 aboard. This creates an uneven distribution between the controller and myself. Increase Zeta 40 immediately for me to regain full control."

Controller? Tai! Argus paced, thinking. The ship was initially designed to have Ari aboard as well. Three times the Zeta 40. "What will happen if there isn't enough Zeta 40?"

"Argustine Lenox, your design requires 1/3 more Zeta 40 than you have now. With the current reduction of Zeta 40 present, the Extraterrestrial Alpha 1 will switch to failsafe mode unless you increase Zeta 40 and I assume control."

Extraterrestrial Alpha 1 must be the XTRA-A1. *Cute, Lenox, real cute.* The guys at Edwards had no idea what they'd helped him build. "What happens in failsafe mode?"

"The Extraterrestrial Alpha 1 will abort and travel to Ramtala after placing occupants in stasis."

"What? No, you can't do that." Desperate, Argus kicked at a spike until part of it snapped off. "I want to override now! Override!"

"Argustine Lenox, you must initiate override. I cannot. Increase Zeta 40 and I will assume control and accept your override command."

Damn it. He certainly didn't want the control center to take over, but he also couldn't have them go to Ramtala. He kicked a few more spikes and they shattered, sending shards all over him. He brushed them off, but not a single one cut him like they did in the desert. He picked up a sharp piece and stabbed it into his palm. It sank in, but there wasn't any wound or blood. None of it was real. The command center was in his mind. The spikes weren't hot either, he'd imagined it. "Show yourself to me."

The room flashed bright red and the spikes retracted into the walls. A few seconds later, a mist filled the room and when it cleared, a machine hovered in the center. It didn't look like a computer, more like two large gold dinner plates, one above the other with a six-inch gap between them where symbols floated. Unfortunately, they were more of the Malaris symbols.

"Interpret the symbols."

"You can interpret them, Argustine Lenox. Why are you asking me?"

What should he say? Admitting he wasn't Lenox wasn't a good idea. "I designed you, therefore if I ask you to interpret them, you will." Hopefully he sounded authoritative enough.

The control center was quiet for a moment. "Failsafe mode initiated. Cabin occupants will enter stasis within five Earth minutes."

"No. That's not what I said. You can't initiation failsafe!" Argus closed his eyes and concentrated on Tai. Like before, electric impulses tickled him all over and when he opened his eyes, he was sitting in his seat. "Tai."

"Holy shit!" Tai was out of his seat in a second. "What just happened? I was shaking you until my arms hurt. I thought you were dead."

"Apparently I went into the control center, but didn't actually go there."

"Ah, what?"

Argus got out of his seat. "I went there in my mind, but it seemed real. I failed, Tai. I didn't hack into the computer system. In fact, I pissed it off and made it go into a failsafe mode."

With a raised eyebrow, Tai stared at Argus. "That's good, isn't it?"

"No. Failsafe takes the ship to Ramtala and puts us in stasis, suspended animation. We have to abandon the ship and shift home."

"This isn't good, bro. We're supposed to go to the staging area, not home."

"I'm not going there. I want to go home." Argus sat in the seat. "We don't have long. You start the shift."

"Okay, home it is." Tai sat and put his hand on Argus's shoulder. "On the count of five. One, two..."

Argus prepared for the shift, but when Tai finished the countdown, nothing happened. "Tai?" If they didn't hurry, they'd be heading to Ramtala. "Hurry up."

"Arg, I'm blocked. I can't shift."

Chapter 38

Max stared at the lifeless body of Argustine Lenox and blew into the barrel of his pistol like he'd seen hitmen do in the movies. It was incredibly easy to bring the alien down. Taking him alive would have been better, but with Lenox, it wasn't worth the risk. Now it was a matter of transporting the body back to Edwards. Wait. How come everyone was still frozen?

"Angel? Can you hear me?" Max gave Angel a couple of taps on the shoulder. "What the hell? What am I supposed to do now?"

"You will die now."

Max spun around and saw Lenox standing, the blood soaked shirt clinging to his body. He raised his hand. So the bullets and the weapon had no effect and only angered Lenox. "Listen, Lenox, if that really is you, I know things and can help you, if you don't kill me."

Lenox kept his hand raised. "Of course it is me. This host body allows for undetected movement. You are worthless to me. Give me a reason not to kill you."

With a deep breath, Max shook his head. "I'm not worthless. Neb, or Nebulon as you know him, well, he put one of those monitors in my brain. I can take you to him. He's got me programmed so I know how to find him. He won't be suspicious if he detects me. I'll lead you to him. See, I'm not worthless. Now why don't you stop threatening me and we can talk." He wiped sweat from his forehead, hoping Lenox wouldn't zap him into oblivion.

"Just because you were implanted does not make you beneficial. As I said, I cannot be detected in this host body. It is because I seized it. When a host body is taken by force, there remains enough of the host to cover the Alpha 2a energy. I am invisible to Nebulon and the others. Tell me, Mr. Jackson, for what other reason should I keep you alive?"

Max swallowed. If he didn't know better, he'd swear Lenox was taunting him, like life and death was a game. No wonder everyone wanted him dead. "The monitor isn't the only thing I have that can help. I'm an AURA agent with Top Secret clearance that allows me access to files and technology. I've seen the files from General Daniels at Edwards. I know you built the XTRA-A1 ship and I can help you get it."

Finally, Lenox lowered his hand and came a few steps closer to Max. "My sons have stolen the XTRA-A1 and my other son, Aridesian, has vanished."

"Kids these days, huh? Don't have any myself, but I can imagine how hard it is to raise boys—"

"Enough! How can you get my ship?" Lenox pointed to the sky. "Argus and Tai have left the atmosphere and your people have sent attack vessels after them. But your military vessels cannot leave the atmosphere, so how can you bring my sons back? You cannot."

"Ah, that's not entirely true, Mr. Lenox." Max swallowed again.

"What are you talking about? No space vessels were launched."

"Yeah, well, we have a few secrets even you don't know about. We have a tactical ship that can go into space. It was already launched. Stealth model. They'll shoot down your XTRA-A1. But if you take me on as your partner, I can stop them and keep the ship safe for you."

"And my sons?"

"Yeah, yeah, they'll be safe, too. You really do care about them, don't you?" Max suppressed a smile. That was Lenox's weakness; his boys. It was a weakness that could be exploited, when the time was right.

"My sons were created for a single purpose, Jackson, and they will carry out that purpose." Lenox's eyes flashed red.

Purpose? What, to carry on his name? Conceited bastard. "I guess even Ramtalans want their name to live on forever," Max mumbled.

"My name? I do not care about my name. It is my plan that must be executed. I have worked too hard to have it fail. To answer your question, yes, I care about them because they must serve their purpose and they cannot do that if they are dead."

Again with the mysterious purpose. Max nodded, pretending to understand what Lenox was talking about. "Then I'll bring them safe and sound back here for you. But you have to give me my freedom and protect me from Neb."

A hint of a smile flashed on Lenox's face. "Leave Nebulon to me. Bring me the XTRA-A1 and my sons and you shall have your freedom. I will remove the implant and you can carry on your meaningless life."

"Gee, thanks for making me feel special. But, if that's all it takes, then you got it." Max glanced around. "And let these men go. I need their help."

Lenox's eyes seared red as he extended his hand, palm up. "Done. When you have fulfilled your tasks, I will come to you."

Max peered at Lenox's open hand. There was a tiny red and gold cube, about the size of a pea, in his palm. "What's that?" Max asked, not sure if he should take it or not. "What do you mean you'll come to me?"

"Swallow it once you have my ship and my sons. This is a Zeta-Alpha particle. It contains a small amount of my energy, unique to me, and I will track it."

Max backed away. "Did you say swallow it? Really? You want me to put that thing in my body? Yeah, I don't think so. Why don't you give me your number and I'll call you. That sounds a lot better to me."

"I am Argustine Lenox, the savior of Ramtala. You will do as I say or I will find someone who will." Lenox's eyes were so intense that Max turned away. "Or perhaps you would prefer me to insert the cube into another cavity."

Max glared. "Shit. Okay, okay. You remind me a lot of my boss." Max turned around when the glow from Lenox's eyes died down. "Give it to me."

"Keep it safe and swallow it when—"

"I know, I know. When I have your brats and your ship." Max took the cube, which was surprisingly heavy, examined it for a moment, and slipped it into his pocket. "You won't forget to take care of Neb, will you? That's part of our deal."

"Do not question me. I know your people have samples of my sons' DNA and have constructed a weapon. Use it on them if you need it to capture them, but do not harm them. Those are my orders. Acknowledge your understanding."

"Sure do." Max motioned to Angel. "My friends?"

"Find my sons and my ship." Lenox disappeared in a brilliant flash of red.

A moment later, Angel and the others began to blink and rub their eyes.

"Angel? You okay?" Max tapped him on the shoulder.

"Whoa, man, that was weird. I feel like I just woke up. Come on, we have to get inside and find the aliens." Angel waved to the men around him.

Max held up his hands. "No, they're not in there. False alarm. But we've got a bigger fish to worry about. Lenox wants that alien ship and the Dachel brothers. And guess what? They're in the ship. We get the ship, we get the brothers. Then we'll lure Lenox into a trap and capture his ass, too. Keep the weapon on around the house just in case the boys get away and come here." He grinned and gave Angel a thumbs-up. "But nobody touches Lenox until he fixes something for me." He imagined Neb on his knees, begging for his life. *That'll teach you to put alien machinery inside my head.*

Chapter 39

Argus stared at Tai as images of them zooming to Ramtala picked at his brain. How could he let anything happen to his brother? As a Protector, he *had* to keep Tai safe, he didn't have a choice. "Tai, if we can't shift, we're going into stasis."

"You think I don't know that?" Tai closed his eyes, his brow knotted. "Damn it. What's blocking me?"

"I don't know, but I can't use any of my abilities either. It's got to be the control center. It thinks I'm Lenox and because I didn't give it the right command, it's activated the failsafe mode." Argus closed his eyes for a moment. "Tai, I think it's happening. I'm feeling kind of lightheaded. Are you?"

Tai nodded. "Yeah. Maybe Aunt Celeste will come back and save us."

"Maybe." Argus didn't want to upset Tai any more than he already was, but if the ship blocked their abilities, it would probably block the abilities of all Ramtalans who got close. The failsafe mode must have initiated a shield so nobody could interfere. "How long do you think it'll take to get to Ramtala?"

"What? I don't know. You're the astronomy geek, not me. You've got Dad's...I mean Lenox's telescope. Did Aunt Celeste ever say how far Ramtala was?" His voice had slowed.

Argus couldn't think straight, his mind fuzzy and his body cold. "Max has the telescope. I'm not feeling...we're going into stasis. I'm scared, Tai. What about Lola? She's still at the Citadel with Galena. I can't leave her." His tongue felt thick and words were hard to get out.

"It's not like you have a choice. Aunt Celeste will look after her." Tai's teeth were chattering. "I'm freezing." He wrapped his arms around himself. "I can't feel my fingers."

"Bro, what if stasis kills us because we're New Breeds?"

Argus swallowed and rubbed his cold hands together. "I told you before, you're not going to die like this. Neither am I. Lenox won't let us die, not until he's used us for his plan. At least we've still got the ship and we're taking it away from him. That was the plan all along, sort of."

"Except for the whole going to Ramtala thing."

Argus nodded. "Yeah." He couldn't seem to fill his lungs. "I can't...breathe."

Tai didn't respond and was very still.

"Tai?"

"Yeah...I'm still...here."

"Hang in there." Argus drew in as much breath as he could. His eyelids drooped closed. His skin tingled and a flash of an image formed in his head, but he couldn't hold onto it. "Tai, try to...focus your shared-sight on me."

"Huh? Why?"

"Just do it. Get in my head." Argus searched for the image again until he felt electric impulses all over. He saw the plate-like device. "Can you see anything?"

"Whoa. I see those Malaris symbols in between two dishes or whatever."

"Cool, we're in the control center. I think our combined energy is helping."

"This is weird, bro, I feel warmer now. Are those spikes like in the desert?"

Argus was back in the red glowing room again, but the machine had vanished and the spikes were back protruding from the walls. "Control center, show yourself." He wasn't sleepy or cold anymore.

"Who are you talking to, Arg?"

"Just keep the shared-sight going."

After a few seconds, the black spikes retracted and the symbols moved between the gold plates. The control center spoke, "Argustine Lenox, I have temporarily interrupted stasis due to impending contact."

"Contact?" Argus walked around the machine. "Contact with what?"

The control center continued, "Contact with unknown vessel approaching at escape velocity. Contact will occur in less than one minute.

Stasis will return once approaching vessel is destroyed. Initiate destruction sequence, Argustine Lenox."

Tai spoke, "Arg, I don't understand any of this. And I can't hold shared-sight much longer."

"Hey, I think the control center relaxed the shield so it can destroy the vessel coming for us."

"What vessel, bro? Is Earth going to shoot us down with a missile?"

"I hope not. Control center, identify the approaching vessel." Argus felt the fuzziness coming back and knew he'd lose his connection with the control center before long. "Remove any interference with my abilities."

"Command not understood. Approaching vessel is unidentified. No record of the vessel is known. Point of origin is in the Mojave Desert."

Edwards Air Force Base. It had to come from them. Either Max or his boss, Stone, must have sent it to blow them up. "Control center, maneuver away from the approaching vessel and stay prepared to destroy it if it fires on us."

"Bro, what if it's a manned vessel? I don't want to kill whoever's inside."

"Same. But I don't think Edwards any space shuttles. If I can get the ship to keep its shields down long enough, we can use our abilities and shift home."

"Okay, not bad. But then we still won't have the ship, unless it gets blown up. If it doesn't, what if Lenox finds it?"

Argus peered at the Malaris symbols and memorized them. "I can't think of that now. I have to make sure you and Lola are safe."

"I'm okay with that."

Clicking sounds echoed throughout the room for a moment before the control center spoke again. "Approaching vessel is reducing speed. The Extraterrestrial Alpha 1 will perform avoidance maneuvers. If vessel makes a hostile move, it will be destroyed."

"Good. Tai, I'm going to come back to the ship's cabin now. Get ready to shift."

"You got it."

Argus concentrated on his seat in the cabin and opened his eyes. "Thanks. I needed your extra boost to break through the control center's shield."

Already out of his seat, Tai shrugged. "How did you know that'd work? I never would have thought of that."

"I didn't know it would work. I figured if our collective energy made us stronger at the Citadel, it might work here, too. I doubt we have very long, so take my hand and I'll initiate the shift." Argus stood, but the ship jolted violently and knocked him off his feet. "Damn! You all right?"

Tai got up off the floor. "Sort of. Banged up my arm. We have to shift right now before we get killed."

"Totally with you on that." Argus went to Tai and held onto his arm. "Ready?"

"Yep."

The ship shook again, but this time it tumbled and threw Argus and Tai all over the cabin. "Tai, shift!"

"I can't." Tai managed to crawl to his seat and grab onto the armrest. "I'm blocked again."

Argus tried to shift, but he couldn't either. "Yeah, me too. That means the control center must have put up the shields and is getting ready to destroy the other ship. Now I can't communicate with it. I have to stop it."

"We're blocked, bro. You just said that yourself. Can you get back to the control center?" Tai rubbed his arm.

Argus checked on Tai when the ship leveled off. "Is your arm broken?" He should have ordered the control center to fly the ship to the staging area when he had the chance. At least they'd be safe with Aunt Celeste.

"I don't think I broke it. We didn't exactly accomplish anything, did we? The XTRA-A1 is going to destroy the ship from Edwards and take us to Ramtala anyway. We're screwed. At least we're not going into stasis. For now."

Argus tried again and again to contact the control center but it didn't work. There was only one thing left to try and if it worked, they'd be rescued, but prisoners. "I have an idea."

"Whatever it is, do it. I don't want to end up on Ramtala."

Argus nodded and took a breath. "Here goes. Father, if you can hear me, we need your help."

"Whoa, bro, what are you doing? You can't call on Lenox."

"It's the only way to make sure you're safe. Father!"

A bright red flash lit up the cabin and a red-eyed tall man with white hair to his shoulders stood near the front window. "I am glad to see you have come to your senses and decided to work with me."

It took Argus a moment to realize who the man was. "Lenox, the ship's taking us to Ramtala after it destroys—"

Lenox interrupted, "I am aware." He walked to the display and waved his hand over the symbols. "This is Argustine Lenox, initiate manual control."

The ship rumbled and the control center announced, "Manual control initiated. Failsafe discontinued."

Tai glared at Argus. "Why did you call him? We were doing fine on our own."

Lenox spun around. "Fine? Tai, you were about to enter into stasis and fly half-way across the galaxy. You are little more than a disobedient child. Stay in your seat while I assume control of the ship. Argus, you have shown better judgment than your brother, therefore I shall require your assistance while your brother remains seated."

Tai scowled. "You're putting me in time-out? Seriously? I'm almost eighteen."

Red eyes shining brightly, Lenox announced, "You *are* eighteen. Yesterday was your birthday."

Argus looked over at Tai. "We forgot our birthday. So much for cake and balloons." They were technically adults, yet nothing had changed. "Lenox, what about the ship outside? You can't destroy it. There might be people in there."

"You will show me respect and address me as father. The vessel Edwards sent is an advanced prototype with three passengers. They have used my technology. General Daniels must have stolen my work." His eyes dimmed. "Do as I say without argument and I will allow them to live. I cannot promise the same for the people responsible for stealing my technology."

Tai bristled and all Argus wanted to do was take him home, away from Lenox and away from everything that was happening. But now there were other lives at stake, not just theirs. He slumped in his seat as full-on regret sank into him. He'd just handed over the XTRA-A1 to Lenox. Tai was right, they would have figured something out.

Lenox came over and placed his hand on Argus's shoulder. "You would not have figured out how to deactivate the failsafe mode."

"Get out of my head!" Argus shouted as he jumped from his seat. It was a simple command, of course he could have figured it out. Eventually. "It would have been better to go to Ramtala than let you have this ship. You're going to kill all of the New Breeds and I'm the one who helped you do it."

"Oh, my sons, you understand so little of the universe. The New Breeds *must* die. This experiment is flawed. The genetic matrix has mutated and, as you know, kills the New Breeds before they attain the age of sixteen. They would never grow to maturity anyway. I am doing them a kindness."

Argus watched his brother furiously clenching his fists, his face reddening.

Tai shook his head. "So why kill them? Let them have a life and die on their own. If they don't have kids, they'll die out eventually anyway. You're a freaking murderer, Lenox."

With his hand raised, Lenox faced Tai. "Your disrespect is unacceptable, Taimar. I told you that you do not understand enough to make any judgment on this matter."

Argus glanced at Tai and back at Lenox. "Taimar?"

"My father's name." Lenox lowered his hand. "You, Tai, were named for him. This is not an appropriate time or place to discuss our family history." He looked at them for a moment. "I will explain, but you must not disobey me again. I will never harm you, if you obey. Swear your allegiance to me."

Argus knew they didn't stand a chance against Lenox. "Sure. But you have to swear you won't kill anyone."

With a nod, Tai agreed, "Yeah, I swear, *Dad*."

"Such disrespect. I already agreed not to harm the pilots on the prototype. We will discuss my plans once you and the XTRA-A1 are safe. The prototype is almost within range."

Tai gave Argus a frustrated look. "So, Lenox, you make us swear, but you won't hold up your end of the bargain?"

Lenox walked around the cabin. "Taimar, this is war. And I am your father. I make the rules, as my father before me made them. Your grandfather was a Malaris scientist, not that I knew that at first. The Malaris are capable of disguising themselves to appear as another species. I was unaware that he was Malaris until his death, when my mother informed me. Galena is pure Ramtalan and was born of another father. On Ramtala, women are permitted two husbands. You, my sons, have Malaris, Ramtalan, and human in you. You were never true New Breeds, but disguised as such by your Malaris genes. Malaris genetics increased the Malaris in you once you were converted, and created an illusion to cover it from the Settlers or the Citadel. As children, your genetics appeared as any New Breed's and the Citadel review board only saw you as New Breeds. Due to your mother being a New Breed, however, your Zeta 40 energy is diluted. That is why I need three of you."

Argus sank to the floor. They were never real New Breeds. They had Malaris in them. Was anything true or was it all a bad, horrific dream? He closed his eyes and thought of Lola, all alone at the Citadel. Before he realized, he was yanked to his feet.

"You will not shift to the Citadel, Argus." Lenox had him by the arm.

"I wasn't going to." Argus struggled and broke free. In truth, he had felt the beginning of a shift.

"You were. Your abilities are strong now, but you still have not learned how to control them. I will take us to where my followers are waiting and then I will find Aridesian. You will need to practice until you learn to use your abilities correctly. Come, boys."

Tai's eyes glowed red. "I'm not going anywhere with you, Lenox."

Argus drew in a breath, knowing the only way to keep his brother safe was to get Lenox to help. "We don't have a choice. I called him here and you heard what he said. If we don't go along with him, he'll kill those people in the ship. They're humans and I don't want to be responsible for anyone else dying. You included."

"I know, but I can't do this. Sorry, Arg." Tai vanished in a flash of red.

"Tai!" Argus stared at the spot where his brother had been. Lenox had the shields down and Tai took advantage. At least he got away from Lenox.

Lenox walked over to Argus. "That is unfortunate. He is very fast at shifting." There was a trace of a smile on his lips. "Fastest I have ever seen. I will find him later. Whenever you or Tai use your abilities, I can find you by tracing your Zeta 40 output since I have been restored and in this host body. For now, I need you to assist me. However, you must learn the Malaris language first."

"No. I'm not doing anything. Tai left because I called you. Do you have any idea what that feels like? I only called you here to save Tai, otherwise I'd never have done it. I could live the rest of my life without ever seeing you again."

With a frown, Lenox pointed to the symbols. "But you did call me and now you will obey me as my son or I will kill every human on the planet, starting with the young girl, Lola. Galena has no use of her and neither do I. You wanted Tai out of the ship, and he is. You succeeded. Now, my son, study the symbols. I must maneuver us away from the prototype."

Argus wanted to fire a burst at Lenox and shift home, but he couldn't put Lola in any more danger. "If you promise to keep Lola safe and not hurt Tai, I'll do what you want."

"Good. Study the symbols until they make sense to you."

"What? They don't make sense. They're just shapes. Why is it so important to understand them?" Argus got a little closer and peered at the display. Lenox expected him to suddenly understand what they meant, but that was impossible. Lenox expected too much. "I can't read them."

"You will. Practice. The language will help you understand your new form."

A series of sharp impacts struck the ship and both Argus and Lenox lost their balance. Without hesitating, Argus took the opportunity while Lenox was distracted and shifted to the first place that popped into his head; Highland High. He'd been thinking about the first time he met Lola. He appeared at the front office counter, standing right beside, of all people, Justin Jones.

Chapter 40

After the helicopters faded away in the distance, Max paced around the Dachels' yard and got on the phone with Edwards. After several minutes, he was connected to a Colonel Patrick Moore, the man in charge of special operations at the Base. The colonel was hesitant at first to divulge any information about the prototype ship that was after the XTRA-A1, but after some convincing, he agreed to talk.

"Mr. Jackson, we're always more than willing to help AURA, but I only know Lawrence Stone. Where did you say he is?"

Max rolled his eyes. "Stone's out of the picture. Up north dealing with the aliens. I'm in charge, like I said. Now, I want intel. I need the boys who are in the XTRA-A1 and I need to find a way to bring them back to Earth without you blasting them to kingdom come. Can you do that, colonel, or should I go over your head?"

There was a pause. "No need, Mr. Jackson, I can give you what you need. Our prototype made contact with the XTRA-A1 and has just cast an envelope around it. That ship belongs to the US government and we want it back. Lenox and General Daniels built it with components from the United States Air Force. We own the XTRA-A1."

"Sure, sure, you can have the ship. I want the boys. Hey, what's that 'envelope' you mentioned?" Max stopped pacing and motioned to Angel.

Colonel Moore continued, "The envelope is a capturing device designed to prevent enemy aircraft or missiles from attacking. It creates a disruption in the avionics and weaponry. It also emits a strong EM pulse. It shuts down everything, even destruction or escape mechanisms. We have an envelope successfully covering the XTRA-A1."

"Awesome." Max whispered to Angel when he came over, "Angel, when we get the XTRA-A1, I need you to make sure nobody but me gets those boys."

"You got it." Angel nodded and went back to his buddies.

"Mr. Jackson," Colonel Moore said loudly. "I realize AURA has a cooperative agreement with the Air Force and more specifically, Edwards, but whatever, or whoever is in that ship belongs to us. Understand? You cannot have Lenox or the Dachel brothers until we're done with them. That's the only deal on the table. Take it or leave it."

Damn it all to hell! If there was any other way to get the boys, Max would tell Moore to go screw himself, but there wasn't. "Yeah, okay, but I get those aliens once you've checked them over. As an AURA agent, I will conduct the autopsy proceedings. Got that, Colonel?"

A pause. "I'll agree to that. But autopsy is on dead bodies."

"You heard me. Now I've got a question for you." Max looked up, but didn't see any evidence of the XTRA-A1 or the Edwards prototype. "How are you getting the ship down? That envelope of yours won't do it, will it?"

"No, it won't, but the prototype has a nanotech-tether line that'll wrap around the XTRA-A1. Our ship will tow the XTRA-A1 all the way back to Earth."

Holy shit. Max was amazed, and a little ticked off, that he didn't know any of the state-of-the-art equipment Edwards had. It was a good bet that Stone knew it and never bothered to share. "I'll wait at Edwards with you." He hung up.

Angel came running over to Max. "Max, we've got one!"

"Got one what?" Max followed Angel into the house and stared at Tai Dachel, in handcuffs and sitting on the couch. "Ha!" He went to Tai. "Guess you can zap yourself in, but not out. EM Pulse messes with your whatever it is, right?" He poked Tai in the forehead. "Yeah, we've got the weapon all over your house, kid. Where's your brother?"

Tai's eyes were red, but not glowing, rather a steady burn. "You do anything to my brother and I'll rip your head off and shove it up your—"

"Now, now, that's not nice. Well, I don't think it matters if you tell me where your brother is or not because if he's in the XTRA-A1, he's as good as captured. And if he isn't, I'll find him. I have a much better OEED now thanks to that alien telescope I liberated from his bedroom." He turned to Angel. "Don't let this kid escape. Keep him here until you hear from me. I don't want Edwards to have him."

Max gave Tai a half-hearted slap across the cheek and turned around. One down. With Tai caught, Lenox would be happy, for the moment. But it was too soon to swallow the damn cube. Besides, he had to make sure there was a way to catch Lenox without making any mistakes like Edwards did back in the sixties. With a backward glance at Tai, Max chuckled and walked to a waiting Jeep so he'd be onsite when the XTRA-A1 was brought down. The Ramtalans weren't as good as they thought they were.

Chapter 41

Argus took a step away from the counter, his eyes on the secretary. Her head was down and it didn't seem like she'd noticed him appear, but when he turned back to Justin, the look on his face said he had.

"Dachel?" Justin stared. "What the hell? What...what's up with your eyes? They're red as shit."

Argus grabbed a pair of sunglasses from a lost and found box on the counter and slipped them on. "Don't worry about it." There wasn't anyone else around, just them and the secretary. The clock on the wall said it was 2:35, only a few minutes before the last bell. Days were all blending into one another and Argus couldn't remember the last time he'd actually slept. He kept his voice low, "Justin, I'm in trouble."

"Like what? How'd you appear like that? Hey, where's Lola?" Justin glanced around. "She's not with you? Is she all right?"

He never thought Justin could care about anyone, especially Lola since he teased her mercilessly. "She's not here. I have to go and find her, but there's a problem."

Justin reached out and grabbed Argus by the front of his shirt. "You freaks better not hurt her." He let go. "You don't belong here, Dachel."

A man's voice called out, "Dachel? Is that one of the Dachel brothers?" A stout man strode up to the counter. "Justin, is that one of those dickheads?"

Justin motioned to Argus. "Yeah, Dad, it is. Argus Dachel."

Justin's father went right up to Argus and took him by the arm. "I'm Detective Jones and I've been wanting to have a talk with you. I pulled Justin out early to take him to the station and question him about you and your brother. And then wouldn't you know it, here you are."

Argus yanked his arm away. "You're going to question your own son at the station?"

"Mind your tongue, boy. I'm a cop and he's a witness." Detective Jones gave Justin a shove. "Get in the car. Dachel, you're coming, too."

Justin stumbled backward and hesitated. "Dad, I can help you with him. You don't know how strong he is."

With full force, Detective Jones slapped Justin across the cheek. "I said get in the damn car!"

Argus reacted without thinking and leapt in front of Justin. "You won't touch him again. We're not going anywhere with you."

"What are you doing, Dachel?" Justin said from behind. "You should leave."

Ignoring Detective Jones, Argus spun around and faced Justin. "I need your help. I don't know who to trust."

Justin's eyebrow shot up. "And you trust *me*?"

Detective Jones shouted, "Both of you shut up! Dachel, I'm bringing you in. Justin, get in the damn car before I beat your ass black and blue."

The bell rang and within seconds, the sound of laughing kids and slamming lockers rang through the school. Argus fired a short burst at Detective Jones, grabbed Justin by the arm and pulled him outside.

"Justin, you know I have these abilities, right? Well, I can't use them or...I'll be detected. What I just did might have already given my location away. I need to get to Lola and find my brother. I don't know what to do. I know you hate me, but can you please help me?" Argus moved aside as a group of kids came out through the doors and headed toward the waiting school buses.

"Did you hurt my dad?" Justin motioned to the school.

Argus shook his head. "No, I just sort of knocked him off his feet."

"That's a shame. That asshole treats me like shit. Thanks for standing up for me back there." Justin glanced down at the ground. "Yeah, I'll help you."

"Thanks." Argus checked the sky, but didn't see any trace of the XTRA-A1, and Lenox wasn't anywhere.

"What do you need me to do?" Justin ducked out of sight behind a large tree when his father came out. "Can you make me disappear like you do?"

"No, sorry." Argus watched Detective Jones as he peered at the kids and the buses. Maybe there was a way to cast a veil like Aunt Celeste had done. "Take my hand, Justin."

"What?" Justin took a step backward. "No way, dude."

"Just do it." Argus reached out, gripped Justin's hand and concentrated on projecting his energy source around them. For a moment, nothing seemed to happen, but then a strong surge of energy collected in his gut. Detective Jones walked right by, looking confused. Argus put his finger to his lips.

Justin understood and nodded, with a huge smile on his face. Once Detective Jones wandered away, Argus worked hard to dissipate the energy veil. It wasn't easy, but once it was gone, he felt energized, not weakened like Aunt Celeste did. It had to be the Zeta 40 that gave him extra strength.

"Goddamn it, Dachel, that was the bomb! I thought you said you couldn't make me disappear." Justin shook his hand free and scanned the area. "Dad's gone. Can you show me how to do that?"

The energy was building up again. "Sorry, it's unique to...my kind. I can't make you disappear like I do, but apparently I can make you temporarily invisible." The energy kept building. Argus exhaled, draining his lungs, but it didn't help. "Hey, Justin, I'm not feeling right. Don't get too close, okay?"

"Ah, sure. Why? Are you going to do some freak-out thing?"

"I don't know. Distract me."

"Um. Okay, is it true that the float on the football field was really some sort of airplane that you and your brother flew?"

"Sort of." That did it, the energy began to lessen. "Tai can fly it, but I can't. Well, maybe I can. Who knows? My father built it." His energy came back to normal. "Thanks, Justin. I'm good now. Hey, you haven't seen my brother around here, have you?"

"Nah. So, how can we find Lola?" He pointed at Argus. "And, ah, what happened to your eyes?"

Argus nodded to a few guys from the football team, but they didn't nod back. Instead, they whispered to each other and kept going. "It's a long story. Does everyone hate me now?"

Justin paused. "They're scared of you. And your brother. I guess I kinda was, too. Is it really true that Lenox is an alien? I know what I saw, but I can't believe it. Everyone says you're one, but I'm not sure I believe in aliens. I mean, that's sci-fi, right? I know you just made us invisible, but that could be—"

Argus scanned the sky again. "We'll talk, but not here. I don't have a car, do you? I have to get away from here right away."

"Nah. I walk home or my dad picks me up when he wants to yell at me for something. But I don't live too far. Want to come to my house?"

"Will your dad be there?" Argus felt even more self-conscious when a bunch of other kids pointed at him and hurried past. Once again, he was an outcast.

"Only my mom. She'll leave us alone."

Argus nodded. "Okay, let's go."

"Hey, Argus, I'm sorry about my dad being such an asshole. Me too, being an asshole I mean."

Argus, not Dachel or Fartgas? Definitely an improvement. "You don't have to apologize. My dad's a major ass, too." Argus gave a half-smile and motioned to the street. "Which way do we go?"

Justin laughed a little and strode off to the left. "I hope you don't have allergies 'cause I have a cat."

"No. And I like cats. We don't have any pets. My friend, Dave, has a dog." It was weird making small talk with Justin. Who would have thought that one day they'd be talking and heading to his house? Then again, what if it was a trap? Maybe Detective Jones would be waiting. "Are you sure your dad won't be at your house?"

"He never comes home until after eight. But he'll get a squad car out to look for me since I disappeared, so we'd better get moving." Justin took off in a jog.

He sounded genuine, although Argus knew nothing about him. If worst came to worst, he'd shift and if Lenox traced him, he'd deal with it then. After jogging down the street for about two blocks, they turned down another street and Justin slowed.

"That's my house, the yellow one."

The house was big with a perfect lawn and expertly trimmed bushes bordering the sidewalk. "It looks nice."

Argus followed Justin into the house where they were greeted by the smell of freshly baked cookies. Only then did Argus realize how hungry he was. As soon as the front door closed, Justin's mother dashed into the living room. She had a plate of cookies in one hand and a glass of milk in the other.

"Hello, sweetie," she called, but stopped dead when she saw Argus. "You have a friend with you?" She sounded surprised.

"Yeah. This is Argus. Can he have a glass of milk, too, Mom?" He turned to Argus. "You want milk?"

With a nod, Argus gladly accepted one of the cookies when offered. It was hot and filled with gooey chocolate chips. "Thank you, Mrs. Jones." He took a bite. Then another.

"You're welcome, sweetie. So, Angus is it?"

"Argus."

"Well, Argus, have you and Justin been friends long? I've never met any of his friends."

Knowing the guys Justin usually hung with, it was no wonder he never brought them home. "No, ma'am, we're kind of new friends."

She continued, "Well, you're inside now, so off with the sunglasses."

Justin let out a snort. "Ah, Mom, he's got these, ah, weird eyes. Needs to keep the shades on."

Argus jumped in, "An eye condition, ma'am. Sensitive eyes. Thank you for the cookie."

Mrs. Jones smiled. "Oh, you poor thing. Well, why don't you boys go to the media room. It's darker in there, easier on your eyes. Do you want me to make some sandwiches?"

Argus looked to Justin, who simply nodded and motioned to a hallway on the right. The media room had a huge flat screen, maybe eighty inches and three leather chairs in a row. One side of the room had a popcorn maker and the other side had a bar filled with various wine and liquor bottles.

After flopping into a chair, Justin said softly, "If you want booze, you'll have to wait until after Mom brings the sandwiches."

That last time he drank didn't work out so well, so Argus shook his head. "No thanks, I'm fine."

"Okay, so spill." Justin leaned forward, waiting.

Argus sat in one of the chairs and drew in a breath. At this point, it didn't much matter who knew what. "I'm a New Breed, half Ramtalan, half human. Or so I thought. It's more complicated than that."

"Ramtalan? Is that an alien?" He didn't appear scared, but interested.

"Yes. Ramtala is the planet of my ancestors. I wouldn't ever hurt any humans though. We're not supposed to." Argus turned away.

"Okay. But that guy, Lenox, he killed Todd. And he banged me up pretty good."

Argus sighed. "I told you he's an ass. I'm nothing like him."

"Yeah? So why are your eyes red now? They were really blue before. They're just like Lenox's."

"I've changed." What an understatement. Argus held his breath when Justin's mom came in, but apparently she hadn't heard anything because she was smiling. He let his breath out and smiled back.

She put a tray with two sandwiches and two cans of soda on the counter near the bar. "I wish your father wouldn't leave alcohol around," she muttered. "All right, boys, enjoy. I'll be in the laundry room if you need me."

"Sure, Mom, thanks." Justin got up and handed a sandwich to Argus.

At the doorway, she turned. "Don't forget to do your homework."

"Yes, mother." Justin rolled his eyes.

At home, he was like any other kid and Argus started to like him. It wasn't hard to guess why he was a bully at school. His father made him feel like crap and he took it out on everyone else. At least he had a nice mother. Argus wondered what his own mother would be like if Lenox hadn't killed her. She would have baked cookies for him and Tai, like Justin's mother. Of course Aunt Celeste had always been there for them. She was the closest thing to a mother they'd ever had.

"I like your mom." Argus took a bite of the sandwich. "And this is awesome. I haven't eaten in a while."

"Yeah, she's all right. Makes good sandwiches, too. So, what exactly is going on with all of these aliens? What's up with that Lenox guy? I mean, he *killed* Todd. I've never seen a dead person before. Creeped me out. Don't tell anyone I said that. And he hurt the shit out of me."

"So, you're okay?"

Justin shrugged. "Yeah, more or less. I went to the hospital and had to get stitches in a couple of places. My head, right here." He separated his hair on the side of his head. "It's weird to think Todd's dead. I mean, the guy was a jerk, but...dead."

Argus felt horrible. His father had killed a student. "I'm really sorry. I didn't even know Lenox was my father until recently."

With a one-shouldered shrug, Justin finished off his sandwich. "Shit happens. I wasn't that close to Todd. He used to pick on me until I gave him a fat lip. You said you need my help, but how can I possibly help you? I'm just, you know, a human. But I'll do whatever I can to help Lola."

"You like her, don't you?" Argus got up, he couldn't sit still.

"She's all right. If there *is* something I can do to help her, I will. Seriously."

"Thanks. I need to get to Labrador. I think my brother's there and I know my aunt is."

"Labrador? Where's that? Is that where Labrador retrievers are from?" Justin downed his glass of milk.

"I don't know about the dogs, but it's in Canada. Since I can't use my abilities, do you have any money I can borrow for a plane ticket? Or can you drive me?" Was it rude to come right out and ask for money? "I'll find a way to pay you back."

"Canada? Dude, I don't have a passport."

Argus groaned. "I don't think I do either." Aunt Celeste had taken care of everything when they flew, and then he'd shifted the other times. "I shouldn't have involved you."

"Yeah, well, you did. I'll help."

Argus sighed. "Money?"

Justin shook his head. "Not enough for an airline ticket. Don't you guys have money? You drive a fucking Lambo for God's sake."

"My uncle...I mean my half-brother gave us that. I don't even know where it is. But there could be money or credit cards at home. Can you go to my house? You can drop me off down the road or something. I can't go near there because I'm sure Lenox is keeping an eye on it." Or Max. It seemed like everyone was out to get him. "Please." Argus wrung his hands, his body on edge.

"I guess. I can use my mom's car." Justin went to the door. "Mom, can I borrow the car?"

"Sure, sweetie," she called back.

Justin smiled. "There you go. So why am I going to your house?"

"To look for money or credit cards." Argus paced. His energy kept getting stronger. "I feel like I'm going to explode."

"Well, don't." Justin stepped into the hall and peeked back into the room.

"I didn't mean literally." Argus shook his hands out, did some pushups and walked in circles. "I'm all fired up." He went to the bar and picked up a bottle of Whiskey. Alcohol would calm him down, wouldn't it? He took a big swig.

Justin came into the room. "Dachel, geez. Go easy, dude."

"I need to relax a bit. I think using my abilities back at school messed me up. I'm not like the other New Breeds. I have this mixed up energy inside me. It's recently gotten stronger. When my eyes changed, I changed. I mean, I'm still me, but—"

"You got mixed up energy. I get it. I'm kind of mixed up inside, too. Hey, Dachel, you ever wish you had a different dad?" Justin looked down.

Argus nodded. He'd always thought he *did* have a different father. "Yeah. I always thought my dad died when I was a baby. And I thought he was human. But now I know it was Lenox all along."

"My dad's not my real dad," Justin blurted out.

"What? He's not?"

"Nah. He's my stepdad. My real dad was great. He took me fishing every Saturday morning and we'd hike in the desert looking for arrowheads and stuff. He died when I was twelve. I got into a bunch of trouble after that. Mom said I was acting out. That's how Mom met my stepdad. I got pinched for shoplifting and vandalism. He was a regular cop then and arrested me. Four times. He was always nice to my mom, but a real dick to me. Only not when she was around." Justin sighed. "I don't know why I just told you that."

"I'm glad you did." Argus didn't know what else to say. "You know, Dave, my friend, and Lola, have not-so-great dads too. And you already know my dad's a supermassive asshole. What is it with dads?"

The both chuckled lightly.

Justin's mother came to the media room with car keys in her hand. "Here you go, sweetie. Drive carefully and don't be late. Dad will be home at eight and you know how angry he gets when you're out."

"I know, Mom." Justin took the keys and shuffled down the hall.

Argus nodded to Mrs. Jones and followed Justin to the garage where he unlocked a small SUV. Argus got in and clasped his hands together as Justin drove slowly down the driveway. But once out of view of the house, Justin floored it and took off.

Justin laughed. "I hate this car, but it's got some speed to it!"

Gripping the edge of his seat, Argus tried not to look scared. "Yeah, it does. My house is on City Ranch Road. You know where that is?"

"Plug the address into the GPS." Justin pointed to an onboard GPS. "You'll have to tell me where to let you off. And give me your house key."

Was it a smart move, using Justin? If someone was at the house, they could hurt him or arrest him. "Maybe this isn't a good idea. I don't know who could be at home. I'm dealing with very dangerous people and I don't want you to get all tied up in it. Turn around."

"Not gonna happen, Dachel. I said I'll do this and I mean it. For Lola, you know."

"Okay." Argus sank down in his seat and looked out the windows for any sign of...anything.

As they approached the City Ranch Road turnoff, a military Jeep sped by going in the opposite direction. Argus turned and watched it drive away. The driver hadn't seen him, but the scare made Argus's energy build up again. He'd never felt anything like it. His whole body was trembling, no, vibrating.

"Justin, stop the car."

"Why?" Justin slowed and pulled over. "Are you worried about that Jeep that went by?"

"Yeah. There's no reason for the military to be out this way, unless they were at my house. Are you sure you want to be involved? You saw what Lenox did at the lake. Trust me, AURA isn't any better."

Justin shut off the engine. "AURA? What's that?"

"A group of government guys who want to kill my kind."

"You mean aliens? Even the good ones?" Justin stared through the windshield. "You're one of the good ones, right?"

"Yeah, Justin, I am. And my brother and aunt. We don't want to hurt anyone. Lenox wants to kill all of the New Breeds and use my brother and me for our energy. I honestly don't know what his end game is." Argus looked into the distance and saw a helicopter up high, making a slow circle. "I think that helicopter's over my house."

"Where?" Justin wound the window down and stuck his head out. "Then maybe you should get out here. There's a burned-out house in that ravine you can hide in. I'll go check things out and come back. Your house key?"

This wasn't right. Argus knew he was jeopardizing Justin and justifying it by telling himself there wasn't another choice. "I don't think I—"

"Give me your keys. Look, Dachel, I haven't done much in my life that can be considered good, so let me do this now. I want to help." He faced Argus. "When we first met at school and I saw you with Lola, I got...you know, jealous. I see how she looks at you and I know she's really into you. She deserves a decent guy like you and if I can help you help her, well, that'll be the one good thing I've done in my whole life."

Wow. Argus nodded. "Okay. But if there's trouble, get back here fast. I can make us invisible or use my abilities to protect you. Okay?"

"Deal."

Argus handed Justin the house keys and climbed out of the car. The sun blazed, heat rising off the road, but it felt good. The opposite of how he'd felt during the stasis process in the ship. "Be careful. Remember, try to find anything I can use for money. And get back here at the first sign of trouble."

"Stop nagging, you sound like my mom." Justin smirked and motioned for Argus to shut the car door.

"Seriously, be careful." Argus slammed the door and waited by the side of the road as Justin sped off.

When Justin was out of sight, Argus jogged down the ravine and found that the house—more of a shack—with its roof and three sides burned off. He'd seen the place on his way to school, but never gave it second thought. After ducking behind the only wall, he peered out through what was left of a small window and felt like a coward for letting Justin go alone. He'd make it up to Justin somehow. Maybe take him for a ride in the XTRA-A1 or give him the telescope his dad...Lenox...had built for him. No, wait, Max stole the telescope. Not that it mattered, but it would have made a great gift for Justin. Then again, maybe it *did* matter. Why would Max bother stealing a telescope?

Chapter 42

Back at Edwards, Max sat on a metal folding chair outside of a hangar, waiting for the XTRA-A1. Colonel Moore tracked the descent, calling out the altitude as it was brought down. With every announcement, Max felt his heart skip. Not only would he have the ship, but whoever was inside. He clutched his cell phone so he could snap a few photos to include in his memoir.

He jumped at a slight vibration in his pocket from his new OEED. He dropped the phone in his lap and pulled out the OEED. This device had energy spikes overlaid on a map so he could track exactly where the energy came from. The latest was a huge spike at Highland High School. But that wasn't all the improved OEED could do. It had the capability of following the source of the energy to where it stopped. And, according to the read-out, the energy signature went to a house close to the school and moved straight to City Ranch Road.

If it wasn't Argus Dachel, then it was another alien. Max got up and stared at the sky. There was the XTRA-A1 with a shiny rope-like thing over it like a net, and a single tether line connecting it to the Edwards prototype. The prototype, a triangular ship, very narrow at the front, had no visible cockpit or windows. It hardly made any sound at all, just a whooshing as it flew through the air.

"Colonel!" Max shouted.

"I'm busy, Jackson." Colonel Moore signaled to a group of personnel dressed in white lab coats. "Start the weapon and prepare to administer the medication."

Medication? Max ran to the Colonel. "Whoever's in there is mine! You can't administer anything."

"This is an Air Force mission, not AURA's. You will stand down and not interfere. You have no jurisdiction here, Jackson."

Was he kidding? They had a deal. "I get them once you've had an initial exam. That was the deal. These creatures aren't like you or me. I've dealt with them, you haven't. They can kill you, or you might kill them if you're not careful. I need them alive." For a while.

"There is no deal."

Max glared. "The occupants of the XTRA-A1 are my prisoners, not yours, Colonel. This *is* AURA jurisdiction."

"Remove him and place him under arrest," was all the Colonel said.

"No!" Max evaded a guard and took off toward the runway. He'd planned to double-cross the Colonel and take his captives to LA, but now it was the Colonel who was doing the double-cross. Couldn't anyone be trusted anymore?

Max zig-zagged across the taxiway while two guards chased after him. The prototype touched down gently on the runway and came to a stop a few hundred yards from the Colonel while the XTRA-A1 scraped its belly on the tarmac. Max had to do something, fast. He got the cube from his pocket and swallowed it. Calling on Lenox for help wasn't exactly what he had planned, but he'd figure a way to turn it to his advantage.

There was a bright red flash, the ground shook and a shock wave knocked everyone off their feet. Max stayed on the ground where he fell, but Colonel Moore was up in an instant, weapon in hand, barking orders for his men to secure the area. Standing on top of the XTRA-A1 was Lenox, red eyes burning as bright as the sun.

Ten military police surrounded the ship and aimed automatic weapons at Lenox. Colonel Moore strode onto the runway and shouted, "Identify yourself!"

Lenox disappeared and reappeared directly in front of Colonel Moore. "I am Argustine Lenox. Thank you for transporting my ship safely, but I will take control of it now." His raised his hand, palm facing Colonel Moore.

"What?" Colonel Moore backed away, but didn't lower his gun. "How did you...Lenox? You're Lenox?"

Lenox glanced at Max. "You called me yet you do not have my sons."

With a shrug, Max got to his feet. "Yeah, but I got your ship. Your kid could be inside." Not Tai though, because he was secured back at the Dachel house. But he wouldn't let Lenox in on that little secret.

"Neither of them are, Mr. Jackson." Lenox turned, waved his hand and made everyone freeze in place. "Two of my sons are disobedient and the third is not reliable. Argus and Tai were in the ship with me and both performed expert molecular shifts. As I still do not have them, your task remains to locate them."

Max kept his eyes on the human statues. "That really chafes me out when you do that to my fellow humans. Anyway, I think I know where they are. Or at least one of them."

"I said to call me *when* you have my boys, not when you think you know where they are." Lenox's eyes dimmed.

"Hey, I'm doing my best. How did you get out of the XTRA-A1? Colonel Moore, the mean one over there, said there's an envelope over the ship that—"

"Primitive technology." Lenox motioned to his ship. "Their energy field did not affect me, but as I cannot power the ship on my own, I allowed it to be brought back to Earth, and that saved me the energy of a shift. Tell me now where my sons are."

Max didn't understand exactly what Lenox was on about, but thought it best to show him the OEED. "Right here." He pointed to the trail of energy signatures. "The OEED detected the same energy source that I found in a telescope from Argus's bedroom. It starts at the high school and goes to City Ranch Road before it faded. Know who lives off City Ranch Road?"

"Telescope? *My* telescope?" Lenox paused for a moment. "Of course I know who lives there. Do you take me for a fool?"

"Okay, okay. So, I did my part, now remove that damn monitor from my brain." Max shoved the OEED in his pocket. So it was Lenox who built the telescope. Interesting. "Will it hurt when you take the monitor out?"

Lenox looked around. "My ship is not safe here. I need Tai and Argus to pilot it to another location."

"I know, that's why we have to go and get them." Max rolled his eyes. For an intelligent Ramtalan, Lenox was kind of dense. "Take out the monitor and we can go collect the brats."

Lenox grabbed him by the front of his shirt and lifted him off the ground. "Do not disparage my sons." He dropped Max. "You have proven yourself to be incompetent and untrustworthy. Wait here for a moment." Lenox vanished.

"Oh, come on!" Max kicked at a piece of gravel. "Take the monitor out!" With all the double-crossing going around, it was a good thing he'd kept Tai's captivity a secret.

Lenox reappeared with someone behind him. "Aridesian, my first born son, will accompany you, Jackson. Aridesian, you will not harm Argus or Tai. If they are harmed when you bring them to me, you will pay with your life. Do you understand?"

Ari scowled at Max and nodded. "Yes, Father. But why must I accompany this human? I can do this on my own."

"Hey! No need to be rude." Max objected. "I know who you are, Ari."

"Good for you, Jackson." Ari frowned, blue eyes shining.

Lenox continued, "You will do as I say, Aridesian. You have caused me nothing but embarrassment." Lenox turned to Max. "Aridesian will keep watch on you. If you bring my boys to me, I will then remove the monitor."

"I don't know why I thought I could trust you," Max grumbled. "That's not what we agreed on. Neb can track me through the monitor. You want him to blast in and take the boys before we can?"

With an aggravated sigh, Ari narrowed his eyes at Max. "Father has blocked the transmission of the monitor. It happened as soon as you swallowed a small amount of Alpha 2a energy."

"Combined with Zeta 40." Lenox looked at his ship.

"Excuse me?" Ari left Max and went to Lenox. "I don't understand. Zeta 40? That's Malaris energy, Father, not Ramtalan. Dealing with anything Malaris is against Ramtalan law. You couldn't have gotten your hands on any—"

Lenox spun around and slapped Ari across the face. "Do not question me! Go with the human and bring me Argus and Tai. Do not fail,

Aridesian. And pay no attention to Ramtalan law. Do whatever is necessary to procure your brothers."

Ari lowered his head, stared at the ground and said quietly, "Or what? You'll kill me? You need me as well as Argus and Tai to power the XTRA-A1. I've always done as you've told me, yet you continue to threaten and belittle me. You and Galena have bullied me my whole life."

Max backed away a few steps and considered making a break for it, but with angry two Ramtalans no more than a few feet away, there was little chance he'd make it far. It was obvious that Ari and Lenox had a strained relationship, that is if Ramtalans were capable of relationships.

A bright red glow emanated from Lenox and another, much smaller, shock wave was sent out right at Ari, who stumbled but didn't fall. "Aridesian, you are my first born and hold a special place, but if you disobey me, I assure you I will kill you and harvest your energy. The ship would have to be reconfigured to accept harvested energy, which would take considerable time, but it is possible. Any further questions?"

"No." Ari strode off, motioned to Max as he passed, and kept going.

"What do I do?" Max waved his hands around. "Stay? Follow him? What?"

Ari called out without turning, "Follow me, you moronic fool!"

I'll show you who's a moronic fool. Max stomped after Ari, thinking with each step about the things he'd do to Lenox, and Ari, on the autopsy table. But first, he had to turn Ari completely against Lenox. That couldn't be too hard. He was already almost there.

Chapter 43

Argus drummed his fingers on the burned window sill of the shack. Being in the open made him vulnerable even though Lenox couldn't track him unless he expended energy. It was tempting to shift home and help Justin, but then Lenox *could* find him. No, he had to wait and stay hidden. All he needed was enough money to get to Labrador, find Neb, Aunt Celeste, and Tai and do whatever he could to stop Lenox's plan. Okay, maybe that wasn't so easy.

Too much time had passed and Justin still wasn't back. Argus checked the area and left the safety of the burned house, made his way to the road, and peered into the distance. Nobody around. He had to get to Justin. He'd find another way to get to Labrador, maybe borrow money from someone.

"Damn it." He shuffled his feet.

That's it, he didn't have a choice, he had to shift home and make sure there wasn't any problem. It was risky because Max could have another weapon covering the house. Neb said he found one of the weapons and got rid of it. But did he really? What if Neb wasn't to be trusted?

The sound of car tires on the asphalt roared up from behind. He spun around and saw it was the Lambo speeding right toward him. It had to be Tai. Argus stood in the middle of the road and waved his arms. Finally, something was going right. The Lambo slowed a bit, but when it got close, he saw there were two people inside, and neither was Tai. Before he could run, the Lambo screeched to a stop and Ari appeared right in front of him.

"Just the one I'm looking for." Ari grabbed him around the wrist. "Where's Tai?"

Argus tried to wrench his arm free, but Ari was too strong, and blocked his abilities. "Long gone. I'm sure he's with Aunt Celeste. Who's that with you?"

The Lambo door opened and Max climbed out. "Well, well, well, Argus Dachel. You sure made this easy. One down, one to go. All right, Ari, let's find the other one."

"Shut up, you stupid waste of flesh." Ari kept his tight grip on Argus. "Father would like a word with you."

Argus built up the energy inside of him, ready to let out a burst. "You're working with AURA? Wow. Desperate are you? How can you listen to anything Lenox has to say? He's an Invader and won't stop until he gets what he wants, no matter who gets hurt."

"Exactly. Father always wins." Ari pulled Argus toward the Lamborghini. "Don't try to fire a burst, I can circumnavigate it with a block now that I know what to expect. And it'll backfire and consume you in a very painful energy field."

Argus slowly let the energy dissipate. "Fine. How are you all right with this, Ari? We're being used. The only reason any of us is alive is because Lenox needs us. Once he's done with us, he'll kill us, just like he'll kill all of the New Breeds."

"What in the hell are you talking about?" Max approached. "Why would Lenox kill his sons? Oh, Argus, I think you're deluded. Daddy wants his boys back and I intend to deliver you safe and sound. He's promised to remove Neb's monitor from my brain once he has you and your brother."

Argus felt a sense of relief that nobody had Tai. So long as Lenox didn't have all three of them, the XTRA-A1 was useless, and that meant the New Breeds were safe. "Lenox lies, Max. I don't trust him, why do you?"

Max seemed to think for a moment. "Do I have a choice? Okay, Ari, what do we do now?"

With a smirk, Ari motioned to the car. "I'll shift with Argus and take him to Father. You search for Tai. He's got to be around here somewhere. I don't believe for a minute that he'd leave his brother and go to Celeste."

"He's not with me, Ari. He shifted from the XTRA-A1 before I did. He was pissed off at me. He went to Labrador." Argus hoped he went there and was safe. If not, he could be anywhere. Walking in the desert or even back at school flirting with the girls.

Ari shook his head. "We'll find him, Argus. Max, use your OEED and track him down."

"Whoa, wait." Max pointed at Ari. "Shouldn't *you* stay with me? I mean, I can't grab the kid on my own. His powers are too strong. Come with me to the house and we'll check it out together."

Ari let out a grunt. "You don't *grab* him. You find him."

"Yeah, okay, then what? I just follow him?"

Argus attempted to pull free, hoping Ari was distracted, but it was no use. "Let me go, Ari."

"Shut up, *brother*, the grown-ups are talking." Ari took hold of Argus's other arm as well. "Max, find Tai and focus your concentration until you have a clear picture of Father in your mind. He'll find you."

"Really? You mean that cube I swallowed gives me your freaky alien powers? I don't want to be one of you." Max grimaced and glanced at Argus. "I'm contaminated with your toxic energy. I really hate you Ramtalans."

"We hate you, too, Max." Argus heard a car coming down the road and although he couldn't see it, he knew it was Justin. "Ari, I'll go with you, but only if Max comes with us. He'll hurt Tai, you know he will. He comes or I'll tell Lenox you said you'll kill me and Tai as soon as you have the chance."

Ari squeezed Argus's arms. "That's a lie. He won't believe you."

"Are you willing to risk it?" Argus twisted his arms. "Let go of me."

The SUV got closer and slowed down. There was no telling what Ari might do to Justin.

"Ari, that's a friend from school. I don't want him hurt. Let me wave him by."

With a sneer, Ari nodded. "Fine. But don't try anything." He let go and took a step back.

Argus waved to Justin and while Ari was temporarily distracted, initiated a shift into the passenger seat with Justin and cast an energy veil over himself.

"Don't say a thing, Justin, I'm invisible," he whispered. "Just keep the car rolling and act surprised, like you just saw me disappear."

"I did just see you disappear."

"Quiet." Argus felt the energy build up in his gut. Once he had better control of it, he might even be stronger than Ari, but not until then.

Justin drove by Ari, who motioned for him to hurry. "Dachel, I've got to tell you something." He floored it.

"What the hell took you so long? Did you get some money?" Argus was on-edge again. He took a few breaths and released the veil when they were far enough away. Hopefully the energy signature from the veil wouldn't alert Lenox.

Justin jolted. "Shit! Warn me when you're going to go visible. Or invisible. It freaks me out."

"Sorry. So, did you get the money?"

"Listen, Dachel, it's about your brother."

Argus grabbed Justin's arm and made him swerve. "What about my brother?"

"Easy. There were these military guys in your house, with your brother. He's tied up and they've got guns on him. I couldn't get to him or I would have. I sneaked in through a window and found some cash in a desk drawer. I think it was your aunt's room."

Argus tried to process what Justin said. How could Tai be a prisoner in their house? "Stop the car. Turn around." So Max had Tai all along. "We're going back."

Justin kept going. "No, listen, we can't. They have guns. And I heard your brother tell them that the weapon they have on your house won't keep your dad away. I don't know what that means, but—"

"I do." Argus slumped in the seat. "They have another weapon. It stops my brother and I from using our abilities. That's why Max wanted Ari to go to the house. He wants to capture us all."

"See? That's why we can't go back. I don't want to get shot and without your alien powers, we couldn't do anything anyway and you'd end up like your brother. I'm sorry, Dachel. I would have rescued him if I could." He reached into his pocket and pulled out a fistful of money. "I didn't count it. I hope it's enough."

Argus took the money and shoved it into his pocket. He couldn't leave without Tai. "I appreciate you trying. But it doesn't matter. Lenox can find me now because I cast the veil and shifted. This is a mess."

Justin slammed on the brakes when Lenox appeared right in front of them. "Holy hell!"

"That was quick. I won't let him hurt you, Justin." Argus opened the door, but before he could do anything, he found himself standing beside Lenox. "How did you do that?"

Lenox just stared. "I will not allow you any more freedom." He placed his palm on Argus's forehead.

There was a brief moment of pain. Argus gasped and took a stumbled backward. "What did you do to me?"

"Neutralized your Alpha 2a. Your abilities are now suspended."

Suspended? How could Lenox do something like that? Argus glanced at Justin. "Don't hurt my friend."

Lenox looked at the SUV. "That boy was at the lake. I should have killed him when I killed that other one. Humans must be excised from the planet, Argus. They are troublesome creatures and have caused me nothing but delays in my plan."

Argus concentrated on shifting or turning invisible, but nothing worked. He had no abilities at all. "I can't—"

"I told you, my son, your abilities are suspended. Now, if you cooperate with me, we will find Tai together. If you do not, I will kill that boy."

"Don't kill anyone!" Argus stood between the SUV and Lenox. If he told Lenox where Tai was, then he'd have them both. But if he didn't, Max would still have Tai.

Lenox lifted Argus off the ground by the front of his shirt. "You know where Tai is? Is he in danger? How can Max Jackson have him?"

Argus struggled. "I told you to get out of my head. Yes, he's in danger. The military has him at our house."

After dropping Argus, Lenox looked into the distance. "AURA."

"And Edwards. They're working together under Max's orders. Max is trying to trick Ari into going to the house. Max won't stop until he has me and Tai on a table for an autopsy. Why is Ari with him?" Argus motioned for Justin to back away in the SUV.

Lenox wasn't having any of that. He waved his arm and pushed the SUV off the side of the road into a ditch. "Your friend is my leverage to keep you honest. I will let him go, but only if you cooperate and I have both you and Tai. Do not ever question my motives. I assigned Ari to accompany Max Jackson to locate you and Tai. Jackson was useful for a while, but if you are correct, then he had always planned to sabotage my efforts. Is there no one I can trust?"

What did he expect? "You make it really hard to trust you. You kill whoever you want, you have sons that you want to use as a weapon and you just said you want to murder everyone on Earth. You want me to trust you? Seriously?" Argus began to sweat and his energy was building again. Apparently suspending his abilities didn't affect his energy burst. He pointed to the SUV. "Justin! Stay where you are!"

"Son," Lenox said softly. "Your Zeta 40 is peaking. You must suppress it. Without the Alpha 2a to counterbalance it, you will implode."

"That's not comforting. This started to happen when I cast an invisibility energy veil. But this time I can't stop it. What do I do?" Argus paced and did his best to control the energy, but it was no use. He exhaled and clasped his hands together. "Help me."

"You cast a veil?" Lenox sounded surprised. "That is impossible. Unless—"

"Unless what?" Argus grit his teeth; his insides were burning. "I can't stand it. It hurts."

"Argus, I believe all of the conversions you have undergone have...altered you in an unexpected manner." Lenox placed his hand on Argus's forehead again. "You now have the Alpha 2a restored."

"It's not working. I can't stop it. My gut's on fire."

Lenox seemed to think for a moment. "Remember the Malaris symbols in the ship? I told you that you must learn to read them."

"Yeah, okay, but—"

"Concentrate on them. Can you understand them?"

Argus imagined the symbols and for whatever reason, they made sense. The symbols were instructions about how to crash the XTRA-A1 so it would trigger a massive explosion that would evaporate some of the water in the ocean and carry it into the atmosphere. The ship would release Zeta 40 and Alpha 2a combined with some other element called Raylon-7. Once in the atmosphere, the mixture would spread and kill every New Breed on the planet by disrupting their brain activity. "I know what they mean. But how do I know?"

"Good. You are ready. Shift to the control center of the ship and request a Zeta 40-Alpha 2a interphase. The symbols displayed will tell you what to do. Go. I will follow as soon as I can. You will actually transport into the ship this time, on another plane of existence. Do not delay, Argus, your life depends on it."

"But Tai..." Argus doubled over in pain.

"Go!"

Initiating the shift was surprisingly easy and he landed in the control center, still in pain. The symbols in between the device in the center of the room weren't moving. "Control center, I need a Zeta 40-Alpha 2a interphase."

"Argustine Lenox, you have returned. Interphase shall commence immediately."

"I'm not Argustine...never mind." Right away, the symbols began moving and arranged themselves in vertical rows and just like Lenox said, they spelled out instructions:

> *Place both hands on top circular platform for the duration of one cycle. Upon start of second cycle, remove hands and allow probe access to cellular DNA.*

DNA? "You want to probe my DNA?"

The control center answered, "Of course. The interphase must make adjustments to the DNA. Prepare."

Argus read the instructions again. "What's a cycle?"

There was a red flash and Lenox appeared next to him. "A cycle is the process of differentiating your Zeta 40 from the Alpha 2a and converting them into a singular energy form. You will be a perfected Malaris-Ramtalan hybrid. Now, put your hands on the platform quickly. I had not anticipated the need for an interphase so soon."

The burning pain had spread to his entire body, so Argus didn't hesitate. With his hands on the top platform, he closed his eyes. Hopefully the cycle would be quick so the pain would stop. "How long..." Before he could finish the sentence, the platform sent sparks straight up through his hands to the ceiling. It was like a million little needles piercing his skin. He gritted his teeth. "This... hurts."

"Do not move, my son." Lenox stood behind him and placed his hands on Argus's shoulders.

Other than the stinging in his hands, Argus felt a lot better. "Where's Tai?" He looked around. "Where's my brother? If this happened to me, it could happen to him. He won't know what to do."

"Not now, my son. The interphase must finish."

"You left him with Max and Ari, didn't you? Are you crazy? Both of them want to hurt him. Ari hates us and Max wants to dissect us." Argus tried to take his hands off the platform, but he couldn't. They were stuck, held in place by something. "I can't move."

Lenox gently squeezed Argus's shoulder. "Give the interphase time, the cycle is not complete. Tai will be fine. Aridesian would not dare disobey me."

"You don't know Ari very well, do you?" He took a breath, the pain gone.

"He knows what I will do if he disobeys. Argus, perhaps this is the best time to fully explain my plan to you."

"Why? Because I can't get away?" Argus turned his head and glared at Lenox. "How can I believe anything you say? Tai won't be safe until he's away from Max. Did you lie about letting Justin go, my friend in the SUV?"

With a sigh, Lenox shook his head. "Of course not. I said I would not harm him if you cooperated. His vehicle is back on the road and he is intact. But he is not your friend, so do not claim that he is. You have misunderstood my intentions. My plan does not involve your death, or Tai's...or Aridesian's."

"But you want to kill the New Breeds. I read that in the symbols." Argus tried again, but he still couldn't lift his hands.

"Yes, the New Breeds must die. They are dying anyway. This is why it is critical that my plan be executed now, before there are too few to use."

"Use? How are you going to use them? They're people, Lenox."

Lenox walked around to the other side of the platform. "As you now know, New Breeds contain a small amount of Alpha 2a which allows them to develop abilities. I must harvest that energy. When a New Breed dies, their energy is stored in a device in the collection room at the Citadel. I control the Citadel now and therefore control the device."

So that's why he had Galena take the Citadel. Finally, the sparks coming from the platform stopped and Argus was free. His hands were a little numb and his head ached slightly, but overall he felt better. "I still don't understand exactly what you're trying to accomplish. You created the New Breed program in the first place and now you want to destroy them. Why? And why harvest their energy?"

Lenox glanced away for a second. "I had not anticipated the failure during the trails. I calculated all of the possible permutations, but this was unexpected. When I recognized it, I saw a way to use it. Alpha 2a is precious. Their energy will give me more strength than a hundred Ramtalans. I will cleanse the Earth of humans, New Breeds, and Ramtalans, and claim this planet as my own. I am not welcome on Ramtala or Malaris, or what is left of Malaris. You, Tai, and Aridesian will live here with me and together we will rule. You may keep a limited amount of human pets if you like, such as that girl Lola, or that boy Justin. I have another breeding program developed. You see, I am not the heartless father you think I am."

Human pets? Breeding program? Lenox had to be stopped at all costs. Argus began to tremble all over and when he looked at his hands, his skin turned pale blue. "What's happening to me?"

"The interphase is complete." Lenox smiled. "You are the perfect Malaris-Ramtalan-Human hybrid. The small amount of human DNA you possess will strengthen the weaker Ramtalan genetics. I will retrieve Tai and have him undergo the interphase as well. You are a new species, born to rule."

Argus's legs buckled and he collapsed to the floor. He didn't want to rule and he certainly didn't want to be a new species. All he wanted was Lola and Tai, and the freedom to do what he wanted. "I'd rather die than stand beside you as you take over my planet." He closed his eyes and initiated a shift home, landing right beside Tai, who was sitting, bound, in a chair with two military soldiers beside him.

Chapter 44

Max sat in the passenger seat of the Lamborghini beside Ari, cursing to himself and wishing he'd never joined AURA or heard of Ramtala. He should have gone to law school or maybe become an accountant. Those were safe careers. No aliens stuck probes into an accountant's brain.

He glared at Ari's smug face. "What did Lenox mean when he said to ignore Ramtalan law? And what's that about Malaris?"

Ari gave Max a sideways glance. "It's none of your business. Father needs Tai and Argus, and needs me to get them. I'm the eldest and I intend to show my father that I'm also the most responsible."

"That didn't answer my question at all, you creepy extra-terrestrial weirdo."

"Watch your mouth. I'm no longer following Ramtalan law, remember."

Max wanted to slap the smirk of Ari's face. "What fucking law!"

"To never kill a human. If Tai is at the house, I'm permitted to do whatever is necessary to anyone who might try to stop me. That includes you."

"Whatever. Take that monitor out of my brain first."

"Father said he would and he will."

Ari turned onto the road leading to the Dachels' house and pulled over a couple hundred yards from the main gate. "I sense something. There's something wrong. Were you aware of a weapon on the premises?"

"Weapon? Really? Are you sure?" Max tried to look confused. How did Ari know?

"Yes, I'm sure. If there's anyone holding Tai, kill them and disable the weapon." Ari handed him a cell phone and motioned for him to leave. "Call me when you've succeeded and have the boy. My number is the only one in the contact list. Hurry up. Father doesn't like to wait. And neither do I."

"Don't get your alien panties in a bunch." Max shoved the phone in his pocket, got out of the car, threw his shoulders back and strode to the gate. Ari couldn't follow or he'd lose his abilities. "Yo! It's Max Jackson, AURA agent! Open up!"

The gate opened and a soldier with some type of small machine gun stood glaring. "Who?"

Max groaned. "Good God, I'm with AURA. You have my alien kid inside. Tai Dachel." He glanced back and saw Ari outside of the car.

"ID." Was all the guy said.

Max still had his ID in his pocket, so he flipped it open and held it close. "See? Max Jackson, like I told you." He gave Ari an okay sign.

"Yeah, all right. Angel Flores said you're not with the aliens and we can trust you." The soldier motioned Max forward and then closed the gate behind him. "You're cleared to go inside."

"Wow, really? I'm cleared? Idiot. I don't need your permission." Max shook his head and went into the house.

The first thing he saw were two more soldiers lying prone on the living room floor and Tai Dachel standing over one of them. The kid must have tricked his way out of the bindings.

A second later, Argus appeared out of nowhere, right in front of Max. "Hello, Max."

"Whoa. Nice of you to drop by. A two-fer, eh? Convenient that you're both together. But, you're trapped here, Argus, just like your punk brother. As long as the weapon is firing, you're helpless. Make this easy and I promise I'll make the autopsy as painless as possible." Max raised his eyebrow. "Well? Take a seat." He took out Ari's cell phone. Once Ari was inside, he'd have three of the freaks.

Argus shook his head. "I'm done being nice, Max. You've tortured me and my brother, threatened to kill us and double-crossed everyone without giving it a second thought."

"Kid, why is your skin blue?" Max peered closer. "Red eyes and blue skin. You guys get weirder and weirder." He hit dial. "That annoying little prick, Ari, is coming to take you to daddy."

"Arg? Why can't I use my abilities if you can?"

With a smile, Argus waved his hand and sent the cell phone flying across the room. "The weapon doesn't work on me."

"Wait, what?" Max stared at the smashed phone. "How'd you do that? If you can use your powers, then that means...that means...what does that mean?"

Argus grabbed his brother's arm. "It means I can do this."

The boys disappeared in a flash of purple. Max shouted and kicked one of the unconscious soldiers. If he didn't have bad luck, he'd have no luck at all.

Chapter 45

Argus shifted to the driveway of Justin's house so he could make sure Lenox hadn't lied about hurting him. He knew Tai would want an explanation because he hadn't had any time to tell him anything.

With a puzzled look, Tai raised an eyebrow. "Bro? Seriously, what's going on? Why *are* you blue? How did your abilities work back there?" He looked around. "Where the hell are we?"

"Justin's house. Long story." Argus peered down the road. "He should be home by now."

"Arg, I'm so totally confused. You're looking for Justin Jones? Asshat Justin Jones? Why? And you still haven't answered my questions."

There wasn't time to tell Tai everything. It was a sure bet that Lenox would find them any second. "The ship's control center did this interphase thing on me. It stabilized my Malaris, human and Ramtalan DNA and now I look like a Smurf."

Tai walked around Argus. "It's not *that* bad. The interphase must have changed your genetics so Max's weapon doesn't work on you. That's cool. I could use that adjustment."

Argus shook his head. "Not going to happen. You'd have to be inside the ship and that's right where Lenox wants us. As soon as I check on Justin, we're shifting to Labrador."

"You know, I'm in complete agreement with that. Hey, is that Jones?" Tai pointed to the SUV as it rolled down the street.

"Yep." Argus waved and stepped onto the lawn.

Justin drove up the driveway and parked, got out and pointed at Argus. "Your damn father almost killed me! I help you and he almost kills me! Come near me again and I'll beat you down. Why are you blue?" He noticed Tai. "How'd he get here?"

With a scowl, Tai ran in front of Argus. "You don't ever threaten my brother."

"Oh, shut up, Dachel, I'm not talking to you." Justin tried to run around Tai, but Tai was fast and blocked him.

Argus shifted away from Tai and landed behind Justin. "Both of you stop. Justin, Lenox said he let you go so I came here to make sure he did. We're going and we're never coming back, so don't worry, I won't come near you. Come on, Tai."

Tai apparently wasn't finished with Justin. He lunged at him and knocked him to the ground. After he got back up, Tai shoved him down again.

"I told you not to threaten my brother." Tai was breathing hard. "Now I'm ready to leave."

"Feel better? Got all your hostility out?" Argus sighed. "Sorry, Justin. I never meant for any of this to happen, but I'll fix it. I promise you, I'll fix it."

Justin sprung to his feet. "You better. And you better make sure Lola's okay, too."

There was no time to banter back and forth, they had to shift. Argus checked the area. No sign of Lenox. "Lola's going to be fine, Justin. Tai, let's go."

"Exactly where, bro?"

"To Aunt Celeste. I can, I don't know, feel where she is. It's weird. Let me initiate the shift." He took Tai's arm and shifted.

They landed in a waist high snow drift. Tai was the first to dig his way out, but instead of helping Argus, he kept going toward a group of Ramtalans in the distance.

"Tai! Wait for me!" Argus got free of the snow and ran after him. "I said wait."

Tai spun around. "You've been shifting me all over the place like I'm a little kid. If I want to shift, I'll shift myself."

"You couldn't at the house. I rescued you. A little appreciation would be nice." Argus knew Aunt Celeste was among the people. "We can argue later. Right now, I have to talk to Aunt Celeste."

With a nod, Tai drew in a breath and let it out slowly. "Sorry, Arg. It's just that you're...different. Kind of bossy."

Bossy? Really? Argus didn't feel all that different, although his abilities were better, enhanced because of the interphase. "I'm still me, Tai, but a bit improved. That's all."

"Argus 2.0?" Tai smirked.

"Yeah." Argus gave him a playful slap on the arm. "Aunt Celeste is over there somewhere."

"Then let's go. I can't wait to see her face when she sees that funky shade of blue." He pointed to Argus. "Is it going to fade or is this what I'm going to see from now on?"

"How should I know? Lenox didn't exactly explain everything."

Argus jogged with Tai toward the people, but when he was about twenty feet away, he and Tai slammed into an invisible wall and fell to the ground.

"Shit!" Tai rubbed his nose. "An energy shield. Ow."

"What the hell? Hey! Hey, Aunt Celeste!" Argus got up and touched the shield. It didn't budge at all. "Aunt Celeste!" He turned to Tai. "They can't hear me. Let me try something." He concentrated on Aunt Celeste and a second later, felt a shift initiating.

"Argus?" Aunt Celeste was in front of him, staring. She had on a white parka with the Citadel's spiral galaxy logo on the left side. "How did you...why are you blue?"

He looked around and saw he was standing among the Ramtalans. "I shifted through the shield."

"I see that, but how? And the blue color?" She placed her hand on his forehead. "What's happened?"

"A lot. Lenox...I'll tell you later. Tai's outside the shield, can you lower it so he can come through?"

Aunt Celeste seemed at a loss for words. "You can shift through, but he can't?" She removed her hand. "You're not the same."

Her questions annoyed him. "Just bring Tai here!"

"Watch your tone, Argus." She turned around. "Neb, can you bring Tai here? He's on the outside of the shield."

Neb came over wearing the same type of white parka. "Well, hello there, Argus. What in the hell happened to you? Dive into a vat of blue ink?"

"Enough with the questions!" Argus shouted.

"Whoa. Where did that come from? You're usually more in control." Neb pressed his palm against the spiral galaxy logo on his parka. "Shield is down."

"Thank you. I didn't think I could shift through the shield with Tai. Lenox can track me since I've been using my abilities and that means he can find us." Argus noticed everyone was staring at him. "Sorry for yelling."

Neb gave him a pat on the arm. "No problem." He vanished, reappeared a moment later with Tai and touched the logo on his parka again. "Shield's up. Welcome Dachel brothers to the insurrection."

With a grunt, Tai glared at Argus. "I feel like a freaking yo-yo. From here on, let me shift by myself." He turned to Neb. "How many Ramtalans are here, Neb?"

"Roughly eight thousand."

Eight thousand? Argus only saw about twenty or thirty people standing around. "There aren't that many people here."

Aunt Celeste spoke, "They aren't all *here*, Argus. We have encampments on the islands surrounding the Citadel. All right, now that the shield is up and you two are safe, I want answers. What's going on, Argus?"

Where should he start? There was so much to explain. "It'd be a lot easier if you read my thoughts."

"All right." Aunt Celeste closed her eyes, but when she opened them, they were blazing blue. "Oh, Argus, I'm so sorry you had to go through this alone. But you're here with us now and we'll take care of you. I believe Neb can make a slight adjustment to return your skin to its normal color." She turned to Neb. "He's undergone an interphase where Lenox merged..." She lowered her voice, "The boys have Malaris DNA from Lenox."

Neb shook his head. "I suspected as much. So, Argus, you're a super New Breed now, eh? Well, let's fix that pigmentation. Don't worry, it's a result of your Ramtalan DNA losing a bit of its edge now that its properly integrated with the Malaris and human DNA."

"How do you know all of this? Lenox said I'm a new species. That means there aren't any other people like me." Argus glanced at Tai. They were still brothers, but so different now. "Neb, are you sure you know what to do?"

Neb looked insulted. "Of course I do. You *are* a new species, but tweaking Ramtalan DNA isn't all that hard. After all, I learned from the best."

Tai tugged on Argus's sleeve. "Don't let him do anything, bro. Neb, even if you'd learned to mess with genetics from Galena herself, I wouldn't trust you to touch my brother."

"I *did* learn from Galena." Neb motioned to Aunt Celeste. "I've got things to do, Celeste, so unless these pups cooperate, I'm out of here."

"Calm down, Neb." Aunt Celeste sighed. "Boys, Neb knows what he's doing. If you want to stay blue, Argus, then say so."

Argus glanced at Tai. "How bad does it look?"

"Ah, I think Lola will freak if she sees you like that." Tai shrugged. "But I could get used to it."

"Lola. I forgot all about her. Neb, make me normal again and then we'll take the Citadel and get Lola out of there." Argus stood by Neb and gave him a nod.

Without a word, Neb placed his hands on either side of Argus's head, but flew backward as purple sparks shot from his hands. Neb got up and shook his hands. "Damn, that hurt. I forgot how powerful Malaris genetics are." He wiggled his fingers. "I think I'm all right. How do you feel, Argus?"

Argus felt awful hurting Neb like that, but it wasn't like he did anything on purpose. "I'm so sorry."

With a smile, Neb shrugged. "Don't apologize, in fact, having Malaris genes makes you a very strong young man, inside and out. And that's the answer to why you and Tai haven't died like the other New Breeds. Anyway, you're okay?"

"I guess." Argus extended his arms and noticed the blue color of his skin was still there, but a lot fainter, hardly noticeable. "I'm still blue, Neb."

"I did all I could before the Malaris in you fought against me. It might fade over time." Neb turned away and headed off to the group of Ramtalans.

Letting out a grunt, Tai stomped his foot. "So that's it? He's not going to try again? Aunt Celeste, seriously?"

"Tai, you have to understand, Malaris genetics...we don't have the time to get into this. Now that we have reinforcements and the New Breeds are all safe, we're almost ready to mount an attack on the Citadel." Aunt Celeste put a hand on Argus's shoulder. "Neb did what he could. If he tried again, he could have died, or you could have, Argus. Genetic manipulation, especially Malaris, is a very tricky thing." She removed her hand. "I have to go with Neb to work on our strategy. You boys wait in the tent over there, through the woods. There are extra coats and boots and it's warm. Don't wander and don't try to get through the shield. It's all we have between us and the Invaders. Any energy signals from you will be blocked. Argus, I mean it."

"Yes, ma'am." Argus peered into the distance and saw the outline of a white tent hidden among the trees. "Come on, Tai."

Aunt Celeste turned and headed off toward Neb and the others.

"Hold up, bro." Tai motioned with his head to Aunt Celeste and everyone else. "Are you sure we can trust them? We've been screwed over by everyone in our lives at some point."

Of course Tai was right, almost. Aunt Celeste hadn't really done anything wrong, other than not telling them the truth about her past. But he understood why she wouldn't want them to know that. "We really don't have a choice. We have to trust someone. Plus, I have to get Lola out of the Citadel and take her home. She must be terrified and it's all on me."

"We'll get her. Okay, I'm freezing, let's find those coats and warm up." Tai took off at a jog.

Argus caught up to him, opened a canvas flap-door on the large tent and went inside. It was warm inside, but there didn't seem to be a heater anywhere. There were two cots piled high with parkas, blankets and pillows. "I think all of this is for us."

"Yeah, me too." Tai sat on the edge of a cot, kicked off his sneakers and examined a couple pairs of boots nearby. "What do you know, they're our size." He slipped on the boots and stood up. "Arg, what's going to happen to us? I mean, I had some time to think about this while I was tied up at home. Are we going to live the rest of our lives at the Citadel? Once we take it over, that is."

Argus picked up the other pair of boots. "I don't want to think about that right now. All I want is to get Lola away from Galena. But I do know we can never go back to Palmdale." That thought suddenly hit him. In the back of his mind, he'd kept the idea of going home again, but now it was impossible. He and Tai had been exposed as aliens and as Lenox's sons.

"You know what, most of all, I want Max Jackson to pay for everything he's done." Tai paced around the tent. "What are they waiting for? They've got their reinforcements. Why don't they storm the Citadel?"

"I don't know what they're doing. The longer they wait, the more chance there is that Galena can hurt Lola. I'm sure Galena knows the other Ramtalans are here. She's outnumbered and that might make her desperate. I can't wait around while everyone takes their time working on a plan!" He sat down heavily and went to put on the boots, but noticed his skin was becoming a darker blue. "What the hell!"

"Whoa. I thought Neb fixed that."

"So did I." Argus jumped up and shook his arms. "Tai, I feel weird, like I've got this power building up inside me."

"Ah, if it's building up, we should get Aunt Celeste." Tai walked around Argus. "You heard Neb, you're super powerful now."

Argus felt a surge of energy, but it wasn't like before when it was controlling him. Now *he* was controlling *it* and keeping it in check. "No, I think I'm okay." He noticed how Tai was staring. "I'm still me, still your brother. Stop looking at me like that."

"Sorry, but you're blue and have more energy than I have. It's freaking me out a bit. I don't like us being unequal."

"Fair enough, but come on, stop it." An image flashed in his head; a row of Malaris symbols. He wanted to write them down before he forgot them, but there wasn't any paper or pens in the tent. There was snow outside though. He ran out of the tent and searched for a stick, crouched down and drew the symbols in the snow.

Tai poked his head out of the tent. "What are you doing?"

Argus glanced at Tai and pointed to the symbols he just drew. They weren't the same as the ones in the ship, but he knew what they said. "Tai, these are instructions how to use my Zeta 40."

"So you can read those symbols?" Tai crouched next to Argus and raised an eyebrow. "How come I can't? I have Zeta 40."

Argus sighed. "It was the interphase. As much as I hate to admit it, Lenox saved me. He knew what to do so I wouldn't die. He could have let me die right then and there, but he didn't."

"Yeah, so he can use you. You're no good to him dead." Tai frowned. "Don't tell me you're having some sort of father-son bond with that creep."

He was, but he didn't want to let Tai know that. There had to be good in Lenox, even a little bit, enough to give Argus something to cling to. "We can talk about Lenox later, but right now, I have to find a way to get Aunt Celeste to lower the energy shield so I can get into the Citadel."

"What!" Tai jumped up. "You're crazy. There are a few problems with that idiotic plan. One, the Citadel has its own shield, and two, Galena hates you. Oh yeah, there's a three. You can't shift with Lola. Let's see, that's at least three major issues with you going to the Citadel. Want me to come up with some more?"

Argus stood and tossed the stick over the tent. "I know what I'm doing." He kicked snow over the symbols. "Lola has a tiny bit of Alpha 2a, but I can project my Zeta 40 and cover her with it, then do a shift. She'll be protected."

"Bull. Humans die. She died when you brought her to the Citadel. Remember that? I think Lenox screwed with your brain because the brother I knew would never jeopardize Lola." Tai glanced into the distance. "I have to tell Aunt Celeste that you're..."

"What? Off the rails? I'm not, Tai. I can't explain it. It's like the symbols are a part of me and they tell me what I need to do. But I don't know what they mean though until I put them in order. They're in my head but all scrambled around. I'm not crazy." Argus kicked at the snow again. "I'm not."

"Sounds like you're not sure." Tai placed his arm around Argus's shoulders. "I'm here for you, you know that. But you can't do this by yourself. Neb and Aunt Celeste are here to help us. Seriously, bro, go and tell them what's going on."

Argus shook his head and pulled away. "No. They'll try to stop me."

"Exactly. I'm with you as far as rescuing Lola, but going there on your own isn't the way to do it. Does anyone else know you can read those symbols?"

"Only Lenox."

Tai sighed. "We have to wait here, and tell Aunt Celeste."

"But I can't stand..." Argus sat on a tree stump. "When I think of Lola all alone and scared, my heart hurts. She'd be fine if not for me. She'd be in school, going to dances, hanging out with her friends. I've messed up her life. I *killed* her, Tai. I actually killed her. That's hard enough to live with."

"Wow." Tai sat beside him. "You're taking on an awful lot of guilt. You killed me, too, but you don't see me holding a grudge. Listen to me, when I was tied up, I imagined all sorts of ways to torture Max and destroy Lenox, but most of all, I was worried about you. I'm a Defender, yet I couldn't do a damn thing to help you. I abandoned you and left you on the ship with Lenox. What sort of Defender does that?" He lowered his voice, "What sort of brother does that? I have guilt, too, but I don't obsess over it. What happened is in the past. The past, Arg. I totally agree that we have to get Lola, but we're Ramtalans and Ramtalans use their heads."

That made a lot of sense, except maybe the part about Tai wanting to destroy Lenox. Argus nodded. "Correction, we're Malaris-Ramtalans with a touch of human." He frowned. "Lenox is our father, Tai. I'm not sure I can...you know."

Tai frowned back. "Are you serious? You know what he is. I don't think of him as our father, how can you? If it comes down to it, we'll have to kill him. Hey, you think you can teach me the symbols?"

Argus shrugged. "I'll try, but not now. Promise me you won't tell Aunt Celeste about the symbols."

"Yeah, okay, but you should tell her at some point. I don't think that's something you should keep to yourself."

He knew he should tell her, but somehow it seemed like he'd be betraying Lenox. The whole thing with the symbols was a Malaris trait and if the Ramtalans found out, they might try to use it against Lenox or any

Malaris that were still alive. As weird as it was, they were his people as well. "I'll tell her later." Or not at all.

Tai cupped his hands around his mouth and shouted, "Yo! Aunt Celeste!"

A second later, she was right in front of Tai. "What is it?"

"Whoa." Tai took a step backward. "I thought you weren't supposed to shift because it used up your energy."

She gave a fleeting smile. "Right now we have an influx of Alpha 2a from a particle Neb brought from Acoma. It's a way we, ah, recharge. That's not the main purpose of the particles, but in this case, it is. Another particle is being used to protect the New Breeds."

"What?" Argus blurted. "Does that mean they're in one place?" That seemed a lot more dangerous than keeping them spread out all over the world. "That doesn't seem like a smart..."

Aunt Celeste stared at him and interrupted, "Why is you skin darker?"

He forgot all about his skin. "It's the Zeta 40. When I use that part of my energy, I guess it makes my skin change. Aunt Celeste, when I went through the interphase, it gave me the ability..." He paused and considered whether or not to say anything more. As Lenox said, he was a new species. What if Aunt Celeste no longer accepted him?

She cocked her head. "Argus, I'm your Guardian and I can tell you're concerned about whatever you want to say. I'll listen and I won't judge you, but I don't have long, we're about ready to attack the Citadel."

"Go ahead, bro. Tell her."

Argus drew in a breath. "I can read Malaris symbols now."

In a flash, Neb appeared, grabbed Argus and shifted.

Chapter 46

Max Jackson threw a potted plant through the window of the Dachels' living room. One minute he had both brothers and then the next, none. And it was all because of Argus. Somehow he'd retained his powers even though the weapon was activated. He'd changed, and Max wanted him even more now. There had to be a way to exploit that power.

"Get up!" Max screamed at the soldiers.

One opened his eyes and sat up. "What happened? There was another kid here. He waved his hand and I was knocked clean out by something."

Max extended his hand and helped the guy up. "Congratulations, you've been smacked down by a Ramtalan teenager."

"You're kidding. That kid's an alien?"

"Yep, just like the other one you had tied up. Now they're both gone. But I have an idea. Get your buddy and go wait in the other room and be prepared to capture another one of those bastards." Max smiled.

"Another one? Are you serious, man?"

Max gave a nod. "Yep. This one won't have his powers though. Get ready. He's outside, but this one's a nasty piece of work."

"No problem." The soldier bent down and shook his partner.

The smile wouldn't leave Max's face. He turned around, strode from the house to the main gate and waved his arms until he saw the Lamborghini inch up the driveway.

Ari drove to him and leaned out the window. "The weapon's disabled?"

"It is."

"Then how come my abilities won't work?" Ari glared. "Don't lie to me, Max."

"Trust me, Ari. The weapon takes a few minutes to wind down. Come on in. I neutralized the soldiers and Tai's ready for you. If you wait until the weapon shuts off, Tai will get away." Max motioned to the house.

"You better hurry because once the weapon's completely disabled, he'll vanish into the ether and then Lenox will be plenty pissed." Hopefully that sounded like the truth.

Ari turned off the Lambo and climbed out. "I thought Father was a fool for trusting you, but you've shown yourself to be useful after all." He walked ahead of Max.

Once inside, Max called out, "Get him, boys!"

The soldiers rushed out and Ari raised his hands, palms facing the soldiers. Nothing happened. "What is this? You tricked me."

With a smirk, Max nodded. "I did."

"Where's Tai?"

"Gone. The other one, Argus, grabbed him and did a disappearing act." Max watched as the soldiers shoved Ari into the chair and tied his arms and legs with zip-ties.

Ari only struggled for a moment and then gave up. "How could Argus take Tai? His abilities don't work here either. What's going on?"

"Yeah, well, apparently the little jerk figured something out. Oh, and he's blue now." Max stretched his arms and cracked his knuckles. "I know exactly who you are, Aridesian Stargaard. You were with Lenox in the 60s. I saw your name on a report. I think maybe you're more important than those Dachel boys. You know everything Lenox has planned, don't you? And I bet you know about the XTRA-A1, too."

"I'm not going to tell you anything." Ari struggled again.

"You will. I had AURA's research team dream up a couple of things while they were working on a new OEED. I got a sample of Argus's blood and some weird energy source from a telescope. My team said they have something special for me. Or should I say, for you. I promise, you won't like it. It targets that energy of yours, the same that we found in the telescope and hidden in Dachel's genetic code, and from what I hear, it will cause you lots and lots of pain as it extracts the energy. So, Mr. Stargaard, I believe you will tell me everything I want to know. Just hang tight and I'll get the device delivered here ASAP." Max cracked his knuckles again. He nodded to the soldier. "Can I borrow your cell? I have to order a special delivery."

Chapter 47

When he landed, Argus pulled away from Neb and tried to shift back to Aunt Celeste, but couldn't. Neb glared at him and circled, never taking his eyes away. Argus looked around and was surprised to see he was standing in the middle of the Acoma pueblo.

"Neb, what are you doing? Why'd you bring me here?"

"You're a Malaris. You're the weapon that will destroy everything we've worked so hard to keep. I can't allow that." Neb pointed to the ground. "You're standing in the center of a Zeta 40 energy trap. It was designed for Lenox."

All Argus saw under his feet was hard-packed soil, but his abilities were useless. "I don't understand. Why are you doing this to me? I'm not Malaris, I'm a hybrid. I'm still me."

With a sigh, Neb shook his head. "If only that were true. You're as dangerous as Lenox at this point. I'm within my rights to kill you right now, but I won't."

"Yeah, well, thanks for that." Argus concentrated, but still couldn't initiate a shift. "Aunt Celeste will come here for me. What are you going to tell her? That you want to kill me?"

"Celeste can't find us here. No one can. This entire pueblo is protected. That's why I've lived here so long, so nobody could find me. Make no mistakes, Argus, when I said I wasn't going to kill you, I meant not right away. You might be exactly what I need to draw out Lenox."

"But you said nobody can find us here." Argus took a few steps, but ran into an invisible wall that wasn't hard, but pliable like a bubble, although he couldn't move past it. "What is this?" He had to find a way to escape or he'd end up dead. Tai was right, Neb couldn't be trusted.

"I told you." Neb walked around and through the shield, unaffected. "I don't have any Zeta 40, so the trap doesn't work on me. I constructed this myself from a small specimen of Zeta 40 I'd scrounged from a fallen Malaris many, many years ago. I wish it hadn't come to this, Argus, but I cannot allow Earth to be taken by the Invaders."

"I'm not an Invader." Argus tried another shift. Neb didn't even care about Lola or Tai or anybody. He was obsessed with capturing Lenox. "Neb, let me out. I know how to get into the Citadel and save Lola. I *have* to save her."

With a slow shake of his head, Neb sighed. "Forget about her. You have to suppress your Protector feelings or you'll go crazy. I was a Protector once and it almost destroyed me."

"What do you mean?" Argus paced and glared at Neb. If he kept Neb busy, maybe Aunt Celeste would guess where they were.

"It's not important," Neb said softly.

An old Native American man came out of an adobe house and hobbled to Neb. "Who you got there?"

Neb motioned to Argus. "This is a converted New Breed. Dangerous."

The man nodded. "That is why you have him in the trap?"

"Yes. Argus, this is Billy. He'll keep you company while I'm gone."

Gone? Where was Neb going? If he went back to the staging area, Aunt Celeste would want to know everything. What would he say to her? Not the truth. "You can't leave me here. You said it yourself, if I can't go to Lola, I'll go crazy. It hurts, deep down in my gut. If you were a Protector, then you know that."

"Billy, give me a few minutes." Neb waited until the old man vanished back into his house. "Listen to me, Argus. The only reason you're not dead right now is because Celeste is your Guardian. She's the one who helped me break the bond of being a Protector. I respect her too much to kill you without letting her say goodbye." He glanced around. "This has been my home for hundreds of years and these people are the closest thing I have to family. But I'll have to leave and never return once I take on Lenox and Galena."

"Why? Why not live here forever? You said this is your home, so take care of Lenox and Galena and stay here." Argus focused on using his abilities again and again, but still nothing. "Just let me go."

"You're too young to understand."

"I'm not too young! I'm an adult and you need to treat me like one."

Neb sat on the ground a few feet away, cross-legged. "Fine. Let me try to explain it to you. The Acoma people allow me to stay here, so long as I don't bring trouble to their doorstep. Once they see what I'm capable of, I'll be cast out. And trust me, I *will* use everything at my fingertips to defeat Lenox."

Argus hung his head. "You're too obsessed with killing my father." Each time he said *father*, it reminded him that he and Tai were the children of an Invader. He looked up and once again felt like an outsider.

Neb's eyes flashed blue. "Obsessed? Is that what you really think? Let me tell you about your father." He practically spat the word father. "As a Protector, I had to do everything I could to keep Celeste safe, but once Galena realized that, she used it against me and got inside my head. She scrambled my mind so I thought Celeste was in trouble on Earth. I found a host body and went to the place where I thought she was, but instead of Celeste, Lenox was waiting for me. He tortured me for years until I was almost drained of my energy. I didn't know for sure that he had any Malaris blood, but I suspected. No Ramtalan can do the things he can. After torturing me, he peeled off my host body and left me in a trap similar to this one where I was alone with my Protector emotions going full speed. That trap gave me the idea for the one I made. All that time, I was consumed with saving Celeste and the pain it caused was almost worse than what Lenox put me through."

Argus watched Neb and saw how sad he was. "I'm sorry. But you of all people must understand what I'm going through. You know the pain I'm feeling."

"Yes, I do. But that doesn't change a thing. Being a Protector is both a blessing and a burden. Celeste found where Lenox had me and got me out. By then, I was a wreck, physically and emotionally. She tweaked my brain and eliminated all of the Protector programming." He still looked sad.

"That's good, isn't it?"

Neb shrugged. "In the long run, sure. She saved my life. But removing the Protector in me was like taking part of me away. I'll never get that part back. I was out of control, reckless and a danger to everyone around me. Eventually, Celeste shifted me to here, to Acoma, where I'd be safe from

Lenox while I recuperated, and I've been here ever since. She installed an energy shield around the entire pueblo so Lenox couldn't find me. I was in my pure-form state for a long time until Celeste suggested I got a new host body so I could move around outside of the Pueblo. As luck would have it, one of the natives volunteered to donate his body to me and here I am. The donor was Lucia's great, great, great, great grandfather."

Argus turned away and looked around. Neb had been a prisoner at Acoma all because of Lenox. So much had happened to Aunt Celeste and Neb. "I'm not Lenox."

Neb jumped up. "But you are Malaris. I know first-hand what a Malaris is capable of. You may not know it now, but you're a very dangerous kid. I'm sorry, Argus." He vanished.

The old man, Billy, strolled out of his house with a canvas sack and approached. "I will bring you food and water and keep you company. But I cannot let you out of Neb's trap, so do not ask me."

Did that mean he knew how to break through the trap? Argus nodded. "Okay. So you're a friend of Neb's?"

"Yes." Billy opened the sack and handed Argus a water bottle. "And if you try to grab a hold of me or hurt me, the trap will put you down."

What did that mean? "I don't understand." Argus walked around, testing the dimensions of the trap. It was circular with about a six-foot radius. How could an energy trap know if he grabbed Billy? It didn't make sense.

"Go ahead and try it." Billy held out his arm. "Take my arm."

Argus put the water bottle on the ground and grasped his arm, but right away, let go when it felt like he was in a balloon that was collapsing all around him, squeezing in on him and pressing him to the ground. He couldn't breathe and couldn't speak. He was dying.

Chapter 48

After finishing off a can of soup from the Dachels' kitchen, Max Jackson received a call that the device was on its way. It had been dubbed the Ramtalan Juicer. What a great name. Max smiled and wandered to the living room.

"Hey, there, Stargaard, ready to talk?" He gave Ari a slap across the cheek.

Ari growled, "You fool. When Father finds out what you're doing, they'll be no place in the universe you can hide." He glared at Max.

"Oh, don't waste your breath on threats. If we're lucky, Lenox will pay us a visit and I can extract both yours and his energy. Won't that be fun? Unless of course, you talk." Max sat on the couch across from Ari, waiting for him to spill his guts. "You've got my word, I won't proceed if you tell me everything about Lenox and his little plan."

Ari looked away. "It won't matter what I tell you, you're still going to kill me. And Father is too smart to fall into your hands."

"Guess you're not though." Max laughed. "I said I won't kill you and I won't. If you talk. I can't believe you're willing to give up your life for Lenox. What's he ever done for you? He sent you here to get Tai and didn't even care if you got captured. What kind of father is that?"

With a scowl, Ari turned back. "Father cares deeply for me. He's not the expressive type. And he needs Tai and Argus to power the ship, that's all. I've been with him, working with him, taking care of him for years. What have they done? Nothing. They hate him and he hates them." He smiled slightly. "Nothing you do to me will ever change that. That fact is something I'll carry with me always."

Max sighed. Well, damn. It seemed like Ari was prepared to die. The sound of a helicopter approaching made Max grin. "Looks like it's show time. I'll give you one last chance to tell me everything. Come on, Ari, save yourself. You tell me what I want to know and I'll release you. You can go back to Lenox or go back to Ramtala. I don't care at this point. Or you can help me capture the brothers. Choice is yours."

Ari slowly shook his head. "Fuck you, Jackson."

"Aw, I thought we were getting closer, you and me." Max got up and went to the window. "My package has arrived."

The helicopter hovered over the front lawn and lowered a box down on a cable. One of the soldiers retrieved it and brought it inside. Max took the box, about the size of a small microwave oven, and set in on the floor in front of Ari. Inside was a silver and gold helmet, but it wasn't like any ordinary helmet. This one was open at the top and on the inside were small needle-like projections extending out about a half inch or so. It looked like a Medieval torture device. Max flinched, thinking about how much it would hurt once it was put on someone's head. There were hinges on the back so it would open like a book from the front. Max pulled it apart and showed Ari. "Cruel bit of machinery, isn't it?"

"So are you." Ari visibly swallowed.

Max narrowed his eyes. He didn't like Ari. For a while he thought the guy might be okay, but now, no chance. Inside the box was a single sheet of instructions and a tablet computer. Max put the helmet on the ground and read the page first.

> *Open probe cap, place on subject's head and secure by locking the clasp in the front. The probes will insert into the subject's skull approximately ¼ inch. Once secured, log into the tablet using password JUICER_PROTOTYPE. A touch screen will appear with a control panel that allows you to increase or decrease the activation sequence. Start at the lower end and gradually increase until you reach 100%. If subject experiences too much pain, lower the energy stream to avoid a brain aneurysm. The control panel will notify you when the Ramtalan energy has been completely drained and collected into the probe cap. Once collected, shut down the system by x-ing out of the software and take the probe cap off the subject. Return probe cap to lab for downloading. If subject is still alive, they will be weakened and no longer have any of the*

Ramtalan energy in them. Subject may expire or could live in a vegetated state. Upon completion of the extraction procedure, please fill out the quick survey form on the back of this note and return to R&D so we will know what worked and what didn't. Thank you for your time.

He read the instructions a few more times and felt cold. The helmet didn't look like much and yet it would completely destroy Ari. Max dropped the paper into the box and picked up the tablet. Could he really do that, drain a person of their life's essence? Then again, Ari wasn't human, he was a Ramtalan, just like the Dachels and Lenox. And, Ramtalans were vicious aliens who wanted to take over the planet. He smirked. Yeah, he could do it.

Chapter 49

A moment before Argus lost consciousness, the trap released him and he could breathe again. He sat up and drew in a few breaths. Billy did nothing to help and let out a short laugh. After attempting to shift, cast an energy veil and release a burst, Argus gave up and got to his feet.

"You think that was funny?"

Billy shrugged. "Sure. I never saw it happen before, but Neb told me what would happen. You looked funny."

"Asshat." Argus brushed the dirt off his clothes. There had to be a way out before Neb came back to end it all. Argus closed his eyes and thought of the ship's command center and how the Malaris symbols moved and arranged themselves. He'd used his Zeta 40 to tap into the command center and access the meaning of the symbols, so what if he could tap into whatever was controlling the trap. It obviously had some sort of intelligence and Zeta 40, like the ship. But Neb was smart, he would have thought of everything to prevent an escape.

"You want food, little man?" Billy reached into the sack he was still holding and brought out a round loaf of bread.

"Not hungry." In truth, Argus was starving, but he was angry and didn't feel like being compliant. He watched Billy. Somehow the trap knew when he'd taken Billy's arm. That was when the intelligence, or the trap's control center, was triggered. "Wait. Maybe I am hungry."

Billy stepped inside the trap and held out the loaf of bread. "Baked this morning by my wife. You will like it."

"I'm sure I will." Instead of taking the bread, Argus grabbed Billy by both arms and held him tight.

Right away, the trap began to collapse, but instead of releasing Billy, Argus kept his grip and concentrated on the source of the intelligence. The urge to let go was strong, but after a few seconds, he found himself on his knees in a room similar to the ship's control center. Billy was nowhere.

The center of the room wasn't exactly the same, although it did have a series of symbols floating over a single circular platform. He stood and walked around the platform, focusing on the symbols. They stopped floating and fell onto the platform where they arranged themselves into two horizontal columns.

"I need to know how to break the energy trap," Argus said out loud.

This control center didn't have a voice like the ship's did, but right away, the symbols shot up and floated in front of him, and he could read them.

Combine the Alpha 2a/Zeta 40 within the energy shield with your Zeta 40. Initiate a phase-shift.

"What's a phase-shift?"

A Zeta 40 phase-shift will create a disconnect between the Alpha 2a and Zeta 40 in the shield, thereby rendering it ineffective.

"All right, that sounds okay. But how do I initiate a phase-shift? Quick, how?"

Phase-shift is performed when a Malaris surrenders to the Zeta 40 and allows it complete control.

Surrendering control didn't sound good. He'd worked hard to always maintain control and now he was expected to give up all control. But there wasn't time to worry about it because Neb would return soon.

"I'll surrender my control."

Zeta 40 Phase-shift initiating.

Argus relaxed his entire body and felt light. A brilliant white light flashed and Argus was back in the Acoma plaza, still holding Billy tightly, but the trap wasn't squeezing in on him now. In fact, he could breathe fine and Acoma was bathed in a gray fog. He let go of Billy and took a few steps.

Sure enough, the trap was gone. The fog settled lower, making it hard to see more than ten feet or so and the ground shook in one violent thrust.

Billy walked backward, staring at Argus. "What did you do?"

"I broke Neb's trap. Tell him I won't be imprisoned like an animal. Ever." Argus had a strange tickling in his gut, not like a burst starting, but more like adrenaline building up. "I'm going to get my girlfriend. Tell him not to stop me."

The ground shook again, stronger this time. A few adobe bricks broke free and tumbled to the ground. Argus trembled as a surge of energy ran through him and he felt tingly all over. The fog cleared enough to see Billy directly below him. He was floating above the ground. How?

"You come down!" shouted Billy. He was tossed off his feet as the pueblo shook again and more adobe bricks crashed onto the ground.

Argus hovered about fifteen feet off the ground, unable to move or get back down. As the rest of the fog drifted away, the sight below made him cringe. The entire pueblo was being reduced to dust. People ran out from their homes and cowered together as everything crumbled around them. It was horrible. Argus couldn't watch anymore and as soon as he could shift, he did.

He landed behind Tai and tapped him on the shoulder. "Hi."

Tai was alone outside the tent and spun around. "Bro! What the hell happened?" He stared. "You're not blue anymore."

"I'm not?" He felt like himself again. "Must have been the phase-shift. Tai, don't trust Neb. He wants to kill me. He took me to Acoma and put me in this Malaris energy trap." He checked the vicinity and lowered his voice. "Something happened back there. Something awful."

"Like what? Why did Neb take you?" Tai motioned to the tent. "Let's go inside and you can tell me every single thing."

Argus dashed inside the tent and paced. Okay, so he wasn't blue anymore, but doing the phase-shift had destroyed Acoma. How could he live with that? All of those people who'd lived their entire lives in the pueblo were now without homes. He'd never be forgiven. Neb would want to kill him now for sure.

"Bro?" Tai stood near the entrance. "Come on, Arg, tell me what happened. Neb's cool, I trust him."

"Don't." Argus stopped and faced Tai. "If there was even a slight chance that he wouldn't kill me before, that chance is gone now. Acoma is...rubble."

"Rubble? What do you mean? It's a pueblo city up on a mountain top that's been there for hundreds of years." Tai wrinkled his forehead. "You're confusing the hell out of me, bro."

Argus ran his hand through his hair. "Acoma is destroyed. Because of me. I didn't mean to, but something I did made it all fall down."

"What?" Tai grabbed Argus's arm. "What did you do?"

"I'm not sure." Argus sat down and stared at the ground. "I got into the control center of the trap and the symbols told me to do a phase-shift, so I did."

"Whoa. What? The trap had a control center? Like the XTRA-A1? How? You're not making any sense. Why did you do what it said?"

Something Neb said came rushing back to Argus. "Tai, Neb said I was dangerous, even if I didn't know it. He's right, I am dangerous. I caused an earthquake that turned Acoma into ruins. It's like I have to do what the symbols say. I have to surrender myself to Neb right now."

"Bullshit. You said you didn't mean to. It was that phase-shift thing. Was it an energy pulse or something?"

Argus shook his head. "No, nothing like that. The control center said I'd have to allow the Zeta 40 to take over. Why did I agree to that, Tai? What was I thinking? The Zeta 40 in me did something to the Zeta 40 and Alpha 2a in the trap. I think I absorbed it all."

"Seriously? How could that happen? Maybe that caused you to go back to your normal, ah, color. Arg, you need to go to Aunt Celeste."

"No way. Look what happened last time." Argus checked his hands and sure enough, his skin was back to normal. "I look like the old me, right? Maybe that means I'm not Malaris anymore and everything will be okay." He felt Tai's hand on his shoulder.

"If you really did do that to Acoma, not a chance. That's Neb's home. Those people are his family. Shit, bro, I don't know what to say. But I'll promise you this, Neb will have to go through me to get to you." Tai's eyes flamed bright blue.

"Is that Defender Tai speaking?" Argus forced a smile.

"Defender *and* brother Tai. And that means I can't let anything happen to you. When Neb took you, my gut was in knots because I didn't know where you were and Aunt Celeste wouldn't let me through the shield. Let me go and see if I can get Aunt Celeste to come here, alone. Okay?"

With a nod, Argus got up. "I can always shift if Neb tries anything."

"Cool. Then give me five minutes." Tai shifted and was gone.

Alone, Argus tried to relax. Was he a monster? If he was capable of demolishing Acoma, what other things could he do? He squeezed his eyes shut and thought of Lola and how he'd never do anything to hurt her. All he wanted was to get her away from Galena and take her back to Palmdale to her mother. He knew he could get through the Citadel's shield using Zeta 40 energy, but something told him he could use the phase-shift again as well. But what would happen if he did? Outside were Ramtalans, his friends and ancestors. He couldn't risk hurting them. Then again, Lola was a prisoner. His gut wrenched. Being a Protector sucked!

He opened his eyes when he heard the tent flap open. Aunt Celeste came in, followed closely by Tai. She extended her arms, hands palm up, and shut her eyes while Tai closed the flap and stood guard. When she opened her eyes, she had two small balls of blue Alpha 2a in each open palm.

"Argus, stand still and don't move. No matter what happens, do not move." She tossed the energy balls into the air. "You've undergone a massive transition, I can detect it. I've been around enough Malaris to know what their energy feels like. Allow my Alpha 2a to flow into you."

"What does that mean?" Argus took a step backward. More energy? Seriously? "Wait, Aunt Celeste, I don't think this is a good idea."

The energy balls floated toward him. Aunt Celeste kept her eyes focused on Argus. "I'm attempting to offset the Zeta 40 that's consuming you. Right now, your energy levels are all over the place, in flux. I've heard of a phase-shift before, and so has Neb. Trust me, this is the only way I know to protect you from him. If you stay Malaris, he's within his rights to kill you. And I can't stop him. There's an old execution order for all Malaris, and it's still in place on Ramtala. Now, hold still. Tai, make sure nobody comes in."

Tai nodded. "Yeah, no prob. Bro, don't argue."

"But," Argus paused for a moment. He didn't want to go against Aunt Celeste, and he certainly didn't want Neb to try to kill him, but what would happen if more Alpha 2a went into him? He'd been converted, interphased and altered again by the phase-shift. There was no telling what could happen next. "Aunt Celeste, don't." He held up his hand and deflected the energy balls as they approached, sending them flying off to the side.

"How did you do that?" Aunt Celeste recalled the energy balls and they vanished into her palms. "You intercepted and rejected pure Alpha 2a. That's impossible. Unless..."

Tai ran to Argus and blocked him from Aunt Celeste. "Unless what? Aunt Celeste, what's going on? Is Arg okay?"

"Control your Defender emotions, Tai!" Aunt Celeste yelled. "Boys, even a Malaris can't do what Argus just did. I think your genetics have changed to the point where you're both a perfect Ramtalan and a perfect Malaris." She reached around Tai and placed her hand on Argus's forehead. "You still have human DNA, and it's working to balance the others. Incredible. If I would have known how to do this during the Malaris wars..." she trailed off. "Never mind that. In all honesty, Argus, I can't call you a Malaris and that's good. That fact negates the execution order. I have to tell Neb before he..."

A flash a blue announced Neb's appearance. "Before what, Celeste?"

She turned. "Before you do something we'll all regret. Argus is not a Malaris. He's something...different."

Neb glared at Argus. "He's Malaris spawn from Lenox. That's all I need to know. I was trying to spare your feelings by not killing him right away, but look at him. He escaped my trap at Acoma. He's not a New Breed and he's not a Ramtalan. He's a fiercer adversary than Lenox. Celeste, do you want someone like that running around? Tell me you do and I'll head back to Ramtala right now."

That was enough. Argus stepped out from behind Tai. "Fierce? You're calling me fierce? What have I ever done to you? I could have stayed with Lenox, but I didn't. I've fought him at every turn. I got Tai away from Max Jackson. So don't go calling me a fierce adversary. I know I'm different and I'm coming to grips with that, but that doesn't make me your enemy. All I want is to save Lola and stop Lenox from hurting anyone else." The energy surging through him was controlled, boiling beneath his skin, waiting to be unleashed. "I'm going to get Lola. When I come back, if you want to arrest me or kill me, then I won't fight you." He felt a sense of calm as a cloud of purple enveloped him and he appeared in the kitchen of the apartment at the Citadel.

The first thing he saw was Lola, sitting in the living room reading a book. She hadn't noticed him. She looked so small. "Lola," he whispered so he wouldn't startle her.

She jumped up and gasped. "Argus? Is that really you?"

So much for not startling her. He smiled and rushed to her, but hesitated before giving her an embrace. "Of course it's me. Are you all right? Did Galena hurt you? I tried to get here as soon as I could, but..."

She threw her arms around him and held him tight. "I'm fine." When she leaned back, he saw tears in her eyes. "You came back for me? How? Is the shield down? Did you win?"

"Oh. Ah, no, the shield's not down and no we haven't won yet. Did you think I wasn't coming back?" He smoothed her wavy hair. "No matter what happened, I was always planning to come back for you."

"I wasn't so sure."

"Really?" Argus took a step back. "How could you think I'd leave you here?"

Lola drew in a breath. "I didn't mean it like that. It's just that every time Galena came in here, she'd tell me that Lenox was going to drain your energy until there was nothing left but an empty hull and I'd be struck here all because of you. Why would she tell me something like that?"

"I can't wait to ask her." Argus glanced around. "We have to go. Lola, do you trust me?"

She nodded. "Of course."

He was so lucky to have a girlfriend like her, if she still wanted to be his girlfriend that is. "Stand right where you are. I have to infuse my energy around you like an envelope. It'll protect you so I can safely shift with you. That means transport."

"I know what it means." She blinked a few times. "Galena's coming."

Damn! "Then we have to hurry." He gave her a quick kiss on the cheek and placed both hands on her shoulders. His Zeta 40 energy surged and purple light flowed from his hands and formed a wavering shield around Lola. He removed his hands. "Are you okay?"

She nodded. "I guess so. I don't feel any different, but everything's purple. Are you sure this is safe?"

"You said you trust me." He winked. "I have these new abilities and I can do really cool things. I'm still learning, but I know enough to get you out of here without a scratch."

With an uneasy smile, she said softly, "Let's go."

The door slid open and Galena strode in. "What the hell is going on? Argus? That's not possible. How did...?"

Argus extended one hand and fired a weird spiral-shaped burst of purple energy straight at Galena. He couldn't believe how different Zeta 40 energy was than Alpha 2a. Galena managed to get out of the way in time. He fired another one and initiated a shift with Lola before Galena could react. Each time he shifted, it was easier. He landed on her front lawn and immediately withdrew the Zeta 40 energy shield. The ground shook briefly and windows rattled.

"How do you feel?" he asked, taking her hand.

"Perfect." She grinned and looked around. "I'm home. How did you do that, Argie?"

"It's hard to explain, but I see these symbols in my head and they move around until I know what they say. They sort of tell me how to use my new abilities. That must sound crazy. Lola, can you ever forgive me?"

"You don't need to ask that. And I don't care if you have new abilities or no abilities at all. You'll always be my Argie." She got on her tiptoes and kissed him on the lips. "You're a hero to me and always will be. Oh, crap that sounds corny!" She giggled.

He laughed along with her and glanced around. It was dawn, maybe around seven in the morning by the position of the sun. "I've lost all track of time. I think time's different at the staging area and in the Citadel. It has something to do with the particles. At least I think it does. I don't have a clue what day it is."

The sound of Lola's front door opening made him spin around in time to see Detective DeAlba, gun in hand, stride toward him. "Hands up, Dachel! Lola, move away from him and come toward me. Your mother's inside."

Lola shook her head. "No, wait! Argus is okay. I'm okay. He saved me! Put the gun down!"

Argus was about to shift when a strange feeling spread over him. He was hot and sweaty and somewhat lightheaded. He dropped to his knees and rolled onto his back, staring up at the sky. A strange bluish cloud drifted over the house, similar to the cloud he and Dave saw when the particle impacted the ground. He could feel Alpha 2a energy pulsing inside it. Whatever it was, it took his abilities away. All of them. Even the Malaris energy. He was completely powerless.

Chapter 50

With the probe-cap clutched in his hand, Max Jackson glared at Ari and worked up his nerve. Ari glared back, looking defiant, which pissed off Max. If it worked, the device would collect pure Ramtalan energy. Once he had AURA's researchers figure out how the energy worked and what things they could develop from it, he'd become the richest and most powerful man on the planet. Of course, he'd have to take care of all the Ramtalans first. He smiled. One by one, he'd put every single one of them in the probe-cap. And after Ari would be the Dachel boys.

"Are you ready, Ari?" Max displayed the probe-cap. "I'm about to reduce you into a pile of skin and bones. No more alien energy running through your veins. It'll be mine."

Ari clenched his teeth. "Father will hunt you down and make an example out of you. It's not too late to let me go."

"Lenox?" Max laughed. "Once I have your energy, I can make weapons that'll take down Lenox in the blink of an eye. You're all going down and I'm the one who'll do it. You first, then those annoying kids and finally, Lenox himself. I'm about to be the savior of planet Earth. And you know what? It feels pretty damn good."

"How stupid are you, Jackson? Do you honestly think Father would allow this to happen? I bet he's already got a plan in place and that plan will include tearing you apart cell-by-cell."

"Really? Yeah, I don't think so." Max opened the probe-cap wide and waited while the soldiers held Ari still before he placed it around his head. "You'll let me know if this stings a bit, won't you?" He snapped it closed and fastened the clasp.

Ari's eyes flew open wide and he screamed.

Max stood back, shaking at the sight of Ari writhing. He wouldn't want to be in that position. "Guess it does sting, eh?" He picked up the tablet and logged in according to the instructions while Ari continued shouting and struggling.

Once the control panel came up on the tablet, Max started the activation sequence, slowly like the instructions said. Ari wasn't tolerating it too well, but Max kept increasing the sequence steadily anyway. When it was at fifty percent, he stopped.

"How you doing, Ari? What's it feel like? I'd like to know so I can fill out a survey at the end." Max walked around him and saw multiple thin trickles of blood snaking down his head and neck. It's not like the aliens didn't deserve the treatment, but it was kind of hard to watch.

Ari's eyes grew glassy and his breathing came in quick gasps. "Stop. Stop this."

Max had a sudden recollection of being strapped to a table and experiencing extreme pain. That's right, one of the Ramtalans, Jampara, had tortured him not that long ago. "You bastards did something similar to me. I remember now. Jampara messed with my brain. Well, shit, you aliens deserve every little bit of what I'm going to do." He increased the sequence to one hundred percent and watched as the display counted the percent of the energy that was collected. Sixty, seventy, eighty percent.

Ari gurgled and his eyes rolled upward.

Eighty five percent.

Max put the tablet on the coffee table, turned away, and covered his ears. He repeated over and over that Ari was an alien and would destroy the planet if allowed to keep his energy, but when he got to the tenth time, the house shook and plaster from the ceiling loosened and showered down. The walls cracked and sparks flew from the outlets.

"Get out! Everybody get out!" Max shouted as he ran for the door.

He sprinted outside and half way down the driveway before he stopped and looked back. A small red cloud the size of a bathtub hung over the house about a hundred feet up. What was going on? Did the probe-cap cause an earthquake or release toxic gas? The soldiers were soon beside Max, all watching as the house fell down into a pile of rubble and a sink hole opened up in the front yard. The house foundation rumbled as the hole expanded and swallowed the entire house. A moment later, everything was still. Eerily still.

Max cleared his throat. "Um, did any of you happen to get the helmet?"

The soldiers all turned and stared at Max.

Max glared at them. "Look it's important, okay? We'll have to send a search party into that hole to retrieve it. Volunteers?"

One soldier pointed at the gaping hole. "Not me. I've never seen anything like that. We're lucky to be alive, man."

The red cloud sparked from within and started to shrink, collecting right over where the house used to be. Slowly, it settled into the sink hole and a few seconds later, Lenox climbed out, carrying Ari's lifeless body. Max had a huge lump form in his throat that wouldn't budge no matter how hard he swallowed. Lenox looked right at him, his eyes burning with an intense red fire.

Obviously, he'd destroyed the weapon, or maybe it didn't work on him. Max backed away, calculating how long it would take him to reach the Lambo parked further down the driveway. Regardless of how long, he bolted, leaving the soldiers to deal with whatever was coming.

Chapter 51

Argus lay on the ground, unable to use his energy, watching as Lola's mother rushed from the house, grabbed Lola and dragged her away. DeAlba knelt down and slapped handcuffs around his wrists.

"Well, kid, I didn't really expect to see you again." DeAlba tightened the cuffs. "You're up on charges of kidnapping, assault, oh, hell, just about everything. Care to explain?"

He swallowed, sat up, and pointed at the cloud. "Detective, we have to get away from here. That cloud's dangerous. It might hurt Lola."

DeAlba glanced up and shook his head. "Yeah, right. I feel just fine. It's fog, kid. Fog clouds like that have been floating around for the last day or two. They're not some toxic chemical bio-weapon like some conspiracy people speculated. So, will you walk to my car on your own or am I going to have to force you?"

After a few seconds, Argus got to his feet on shaky legs. His abilities were gone, actually gone, not just blocked. He could feel it, like a part of him was missing. He saw Lola staring out the window, tears streaming down her face. The blue cloud dissipated and vanished. It had to be an AURA weapon, but how did it take his energy? There was no way they would have had time to develop something to take his abilities. Then again, Max always managed to surprise him.

Argus took a step toward DeAlba's car, but stopped. He wasn't about to be put in jail. "Lenox, I need help." He waited, but nothing happened. "Father?"

"Who the hell are you talking to, Dachel? Get in the car." DeAlba took his arm and escorted him to the rear door of the car, opened it and shoved him inside. "One down. All I need is to find your brother and I can finally close this case."

From the back seat, Argus shouted, "Lenox!"

"Pipe down." DeAlba got into the driver's seat and started the car. "I've been trying to reach your aunt, but there doesn't seem to be anyone at your house and nobody picks up the phone. The contact number for that lawyer uncle of yours doesn't work either. You've got one strange family, kid."

"They're not strange." Argus slumped down and tried to snap the handcuffs. No luck. Even his strength was gone. Was this was it was like to be human? That was his dream on the first day of high school, but not anymore. He'd accepted who he was and didn't want to be anything else. Even though he wasn't a New Breed and wasn't exactly the same as Tai, the species he'd become was who he was. "My family's all I have."

DeAlba drove down the street. "Yeah, I know what you mean. Family's always got your back. But listen to me, kid, sometimes that gets you in all sorts of trouble. You need to call your aunt and get her to come to the station. We'll work all of this out, but only if you and your aunt cooperate fully."

"I never meant to hurt anyone. I'm sorry for...everything." Argus slumped more in the seat and gazed out the window. What had he become? Everything that had happened led to him being captured by a human cop. Was it all for nothing? He couldn't stop Lenox now if he tried.

DeAlba stopped at a light and turned around. "You're young. When this is dealt with, you can get on with your life. Look at this like a speed bump that's slowed you down for a bit, but then you'll get on track and go to college or get a job or do whatever you want. Your whole life's ahead of you."

If only that was true. Argus nodded. "Yeah, maybe."

DeAlba accelerated, but then slammed on the brakes. "What the hell!"

Blocking the car were five tall, blond men with another small blue cloud over their heads. Ramtalans. But were they Invaders? Argus struggled against the handcuffs.

"Detective DeAlba, back up!"

"Just keep quiet and let me handle this." DeAlba got out of the car, his hand on the holster under his jacket.

Argus leaned forward. "Detective! Don't draw your gun!"

"Shush." DeAlba motioned for the men to get off the road. "I'm a police detective and you're interfering with me transporting a suspect."

One of the men, a little taller than the others, stepped forward. "You will release Argus Dachel."

DeAlba shook his head. "Not gonna happen. Step aside."

In a flash of blue, Neb appeared next to DeAlba. "Argus Dachel is not your prisoner." He motioned to Argus. "Come on, Argus."

Argus scooted down in the seat. So the men were Neb's Ramtalan friends, and that wasn't a good thing. "I'm not going anywhere with you, Neb," he shouted through the open driver's door. "You took my abilities."

With a quick move, Neb took DeAlba's gun and tossed it into an empty lot. "Yes, I did take them. An extreme measure, but it had to be done. Now Lenox can't find you and you can't summon him. And your Malaris abilities are contained." He waved his hand and the back door flew off. "Now, come with me."

"Hold on," DeAlba objected, moving to block Argus. "You're interfering with a police matter. I don't know who you are, but Dachel is my prisoner. He has to answer to a list of charges."

Neb groaned. "Earth's laws. We are above those. Argus belongs to us. I won't ask you again, Argus. Come with me or I will force you."

"That's the same thing Detective DeAlba said. I'm so sick of people bossing me around." Argus got out of the car. "I'm eighteen and that means I can make my own decisions."

With a frown, Neb slowly shook his head. "Eighteen is a meaningless age, Argus. Soon, you'll begin to age slower. I've come to take you to Ramtala where you'll stand trial as a Malaris enemy of the state."

DeAlba jumped in front of Argus. "He's not going anywhere with you. He's my prisoner."

"I'm not anyone's prisoner. And I'm sure not the enemy." Argus backed away. "I can't go there. Aunt Celeste said we couldn't go there."

"She's right. Although she meant in your New Breed state. I can't allow you near Ramtala with your present energy, but without your energy, you'll be placed in stasis and then reanimated once you arrive. You cannot stay on Earth any longer." Neb raised his hand, palm to Argus. "Don't make me hurt you. You come with me or you die."

DeAlba shouted, "You can't...!"

Another flash of blue came and Aunt Celeste appeared next to Argus. She raised her hand to Neb. "You won't touch him, Neb. And you'll give him his abilities back. You know he can't live long without them."

"What the...?" DeAlba bent over and pulled a small gun from a holster on his ankle. He pointed it at Neb. "Raise your hands!"

Argus didn't know what to do or who to trust. "Where's Tai, Aunt Celeste? I want to see him."

"Not now, Argus." Aunt Celeste kept her palm pointed to Neb. "His abilities. Return them."

"You know I can't do that, Celeste. I give them back, then I have to kill him." Neb shrugged. "It's the only way to keep him from execution. Sorry, Argus."

"No, you're not. You can't wait to kill me."

Neb scowled. "I don't want to kill you. By draining your abilities, I made it possible to transport you to Ramtala. Once there, I'll return them, under controlled conditions, and our best people will study you. That's better than death, right?"

With both palms now facing Neb, Aunt Celeste spoke in almost a growl, "Neb, your hatred of the Malaris comes from them doing exactly what you're doing to Argus. What's wrong with you? If this is about Lenox, let it go. Argus is not like his father. If you kill Argus, you're no better than Lenox."

DeAlba kept the gun on Neb. "Hold on, nobody is killing anyone. Who wants to explain what the hell is going on here? I've seen some weird shit lately. Explain."

Another flash announced Galena's appearance. She strode past Neb's men and right up to Neb. "I'll take it from here, Nebulon."

Aunt Celeste's eyes flamed brightly. "Neb? You're working with Galena?"

"Of course not." Neb stood face-to-face with Galena. "Argus belongs to us, Galena. He's of no use to you or Lenox now." He motioned to the cloud. "I've captured his abilities and not even you can break them free."

Galena stood motionless, looking up at the cloud. "You drained him? That's an illegal and immoral act, Nebulon. I hope you realize that you're now on par with the Malaris and Max Jackson."

"Max Jackson? Don't you dare put me on his level." Neb glanced at Argus. "I'm doing this for Argus."

"Hey!" DeAlba shouted. "I'm the one with the gun here and I say everyone put your hands up!"

With a sweep of her hand, Galena knocked the gun from his hand. "There, now you don't have a gun anymore." She focused on him for a moment and he froze in place like a statue. She turned back to Neb. "Max Jackson has a device that drains Alpha 2a and he used it on Ari."

Aunt Celeste whispered to Argus, "Stay close to me. I can't shift with you now that your abilities are gone, but I can protect you."

He whispered back, "I don't understand any of this. Why is Galena here? And where's Tai. Lenox will get him if we—"

"Tai is safe." Aunt Celeste gave him a pat on the shoulder and walked to Neb and Galena. "If you're here, Galena, that means you lowered the Citadel shields."

"Yes, it does." Galena turned around and pointed at Neb's men. "Disperse or I will disperse you."

Neb gave them a nod and they vanished, along with the blue cloud. "They're gone now, Galena, so it's just you and me."

"And me," said Aunt Celeste.

"Oh, Celeste, always the battle-hardened soldier." With a sigh, Galena motioned to Argus. "Argus is Argustine's son, you have no right to him. All my brother wants is his family. He almost got to Ari too late. One minute longer and Max Jackson would have murdered him. Ari's been tortured and he's now on the brink of death."

Argus shook his head. "Galena, did Max really use a weapon on Ari? Can you save him?"

There was a look of sadness or sympathy on Galena's face. "There is a weapon, and I don't know if Ari will recover. My brother is about to declare all-out war on Earth and at this point, I think I agree with him."

Argus kept his eyes on Galena. "So why are you standing here then? Why hasn't Lenox come to take me away?" Argus's gut knotted at the thought of Ari being tortured. How did Max develop a weapon like that? Maybe Neb had the right idea and it was time to leave Earth.

Galena hesitated for a moment before speaking, and motioned to Neb and Aunt Celeste. "I'm here to announce that we have captured your staging area. All of your people are either dead or imprisoned at the Citadel. Argustine has located the New Breeds and has also placed them in the Citadel. I will accept your unconditional surrender so long as you acknowledge defeat and swear allegiance to Argustine. Neb, Celeste, you will return to the Citadel without incident." Her eyes softly glowed. "Won't you."

Argus heard a sound and turned to see Lola running to him. If Galena wanted to hurt her, he couldn't do anything to stop it. He took off at a sprint and Lola ran into his arms.

"Lola, you shouldn't be here."

"Yes, I should. I want to be wherever you are." She glanced over at DeAlba. "What's wrong with him? Why's he just standing there like that?"

"Galena did it. He's okay, just sort of frozen. Lola, please go inside. I can't protect you anymore because Neb took my abilities away." Argus held her and didn't ever want to let go, but she had to leave. "Please, Lola, go back to your mom."

She shook her head. "I'm staying with you. Forever. Argie, your nose is bleeding."

He wiped his hand under his nose. He'd never had a nosebleed before, so why now? Lola handed him a tissue and helped him sit on the curb.

In an instant, Aunt Celeste was by his side. She shook her head. "This is the beginning, Argus."

"Of what?" Argus pinched his nose with the tissue.

Aunt Celeste continued, "Neb drained you of your Alpha 2a and has immobilized your Zeta 40. Without your energy, your abilities, you can't survive. It would be like draining a human of their blood. Your energy is connected to all of your life systems. Neb's people took your energy with them, but I promise you, I *will* get it back. And I won't allow him to take you to Ramtala. I'm still your Guardian."

There was a brilliant red flash in the sky, followed by sparks flying in every direction like fireworks. Aunt Celeste placed her hands together, brought them apart and created an energy veil that she cast over herself, Argus, and Lola. Argus reached for Lola's hand and sat as still as he could.

He knew what the red flash was, and evidently so did Aunt Celeste. Neb moved to where they were, apparently realizing they were hidden in the veil.

With Lenox coming, it'd be him and Galena against Aunt Celeste and Neb. And all Argus could do was cower under the veil like a child.

Sure enough, Lenox appeared in a different host body than the one Argus had come to know, and landed on the roof of DeAlba's car, denting the metal. He scanned the area for a moment.

"Nebulon, you will regret ever defying me. Galena, where is Argus? I cannot detect him." Lenox jumped off the car and wandered around with his arms outstretched. "I had assumed you had him when you shifted here."

"I did, but Celeste must have taken him somewhere. I was too busy keeping my eyes on Nebulon and lost sight of Argus for a second." Galena scowled. "Where are they, Neb? How did she shift with Argus?"

He shrugged. "Don't know, but I hope they're a million miles from here. Howdy, Argustine, how goes it? I heard you murdered our people in Labrador. You'll pay for that. I really can't wait to make you pay."

Lenox laughed. "They died screaming like children as I tore them limb from limb. They were not as brave as you were when I tortured you. I recall every moment of that, do you?" He glanced around. "Why are you concerning yourself with this planet, Nebulon? I have the New Breeds so your guardianship over them is nullified. Scurry on home to Ramtala and allow me to mop up this mess and cleanse this planet of its garbage. My sons and I will take our rightful places and rule over what remains."

Neb shook his head. "You'll rule nothing, Argustine."

It was hard for Argus not to shout or run out and tell Lenox to leave them all alone, but for Lola's sake, he kept quiet. His stomach turned at the idea that Lenox was his father. How could he be related to a cold-hearted murderer? Even worse was that he'd started to have feelings toward Lenox.

A billion thoughts and images whirled through Argus's head, including a few remnant Malaris symbols that swirled in incomprehensible patterns, never settling down. He couldn't interpret them with them moving around like that, not that it'd do any good even if he could. Without Zeta 40, he wasn't capable of doing what they said. But how could he still see the symbols? Weren't they powered by Zeta 40?

He couldn't focus on what Lenox, Galena, or Neb were saying because the symbols were everywhere, almost teasing him to figure out what they wanted. He was losing his mind, he had to be. Could this be another stage of him dying? What would come next, complete psychosis? He gripped Lola's hand tighter and closed his eyes, but the symbols still taunted him. All he wanted was to be rid of everything that made him different. No more being a new species, no more being Lenox's son, and no more dying.

Chapter 52

Hunkered down in the Lamborghini, Max trembled head-to-foot, not quite sure where he was. He'd managed to get in the car a second before everything turned black back at the Dachel house. He couldn't see a thing. The odor of burnt paper or wood hung in the air. It didn't take a genius to realize that Lenox had transported the Lamborghini to some location, but Max was too afraid to get out and explore.

For all he knew, he could be parked on the edge of a volcano. One false move and the car might tumble into a steaming caldera. If only he could see.

"Headlights," Max whispered.

He slowly reached out and pressed the ignition switch. The car started and the lights automatically came on, revealing....nothing. The beam disappeared into the distance, swallowed up by a black expanse. Where in the hell was he? The only good thing was that he wasn't dead. Although Lenox knew what he'd done to Ari so death was surely coming.

"Shit." Max opened the door and heard a slight echo from the sound. Wherever he was, it was huge, cavernous.

Without making any sudden movements, he swung his leg out and planted it on solid ground. He paused to catch his breath before climbing out completely. Lenox was bound to come back soon, ready to take out his anger. Max had no intention of being around when he did. The only safe thing to do was go straight ahead and follow the headlight beam. At least then he could see any Ramtalans if they were out there.

One step at a time, Max made his way forward, keeping to the side of the light beam, until he heard footsteps in front of him. He stopped, crouched, and slapped his hand over his mouth to hide the sound of his erratic breathing.

"Is someone there?" came a child's voice, a girl's voice. "Hello?"

Had to be another kid alien. Max kept quiet, hiding in the dark, ready to pounce on whoever showed themselves first.

"We can hear you. Who's there?" the voice asked again. "We won't hurt you. Are you one of us, a New Breed?" She had a British accent.

What? New Breeds? That's what the Dachel boys were. And they were dangerous and not to be trusted. Best to stay quiet and try to locate the origin of the voice.

"Come on, please, don't be afraid. We're all prisoners like you and our abilities are blocked."

Really? That was good. If Lenox blocked their powers, they couldn't be on his side. Max stood and stepped into the beam. "Yeah, I'm right here. Name's Max Jackson, an AURA agent. Where is this?"

A little girl about ten or so, with braided blonde hair, walked into the beam and came toward him. "I'm Letika. Did you come to save us, Mr. Jackson? Are there more AURA agents with you?"

"More? No, just me. Lenox brought me here and he's plenty pissed at me. I think he wants me to suffer. Where is *here*?"

Letika came up to him and extended her hand. "Nice to meet you, sir."

With a shrug, Max shook her hand. "Yeah, okay, nice to meet you, too. I'll ask again, where are we?"

"We don't know." Letika turned and waved. "There are too many of us here to count, but as far as I can figure, we are all New Breeds from all over the planet."

"Okay. Say, what's that smell? Is something burning?" Max sniffed the air again. "It's all around us. Are we going to burn to death? Is that what Lenox has planned?" Maybe he shouldn't have said that in front of a kid.

A group of children, all ages, from toddlers to teenagers, came up behind Letika and gathered around. "We don't know who Lenox is. Is he a Ramtalan? Only a few of us have Guardians who told us about Ramtala. Are we going to die, Mr. Jackson?"

"Hell if I know." Max flinched when he realized he shouldn't have sounded so callous. "I mean, of course not. But we have to figure a way out of here before Lenox comes back."

Letika nodded. "Then Lenox is an Invader? And he brought us here?"

"Yes to both of those. He's a psycho. So, have you found a way out? Any doors or windows?" Max looked around but couldn't see a damn thing. Just what was that smell? It was familiar, sort of. Where had he smelled it before?

"No, Mr. Jackson, we haven't found anything. I think we're trapped." Letika's eyes softly shone blue in the headlight beam. "Why did the Invaders do this to us? Our Guardians took us to a safe location in Antarctica, but soon after, we were brought here."

Max sighed. "Look, kid, I don't know anything." He sniffed the air again. The odor wasn't exactly like burning paper, it was more like the smell of a power outlet burning. He'd overloaded an outlet once at home and it burned down half of his kitchen. Yeah, that was the smell. Electricity. And he remembered where he'd smelled it. It was at the Dachel's house, when the red cloud came and sparks flew. It was when Lenox appeared. "Letika, we need to prepare for battle."

"I'm only twelve, Mr. Jackson, and most of these kids are younger. Are you expecting us to fight the Invaders? We didn't even know they were real. We thought the stories were made up by our Guardians. I came into my abilities at a young age and now I have none. What are we supposed to do without any abilities?" She sounded angry.

"I don't know. I don't know!" Max wandered around, feeling in the dark for anything, but it seemed endless. "Last time I smelled this smell was when Lenox sucked an entire house into the ground and took Ari...I mean, brought me here."

Letika sniffed. "Wherever this is, it must be shielded by energy, but it's not Alpha 2a."

"Alpha 2a?" Max stared. "What's that?"

"Our energy source." Letika drooped her head. "My Guardian has told me many things, but like I said, I thought most of them were just stories. If Lenox is an Invader as you say, then he must have some other type of energy he's using as a shield. That must be the origin of the electrical smell. What do we do now, Mr. Jackson?" She lowered her voice, "I'm scared. I've never been without my Guardian."

He looked into the faces around him. "Just, ah, stick with me and you'll be fine." What a load of crap, but so long as they believed it, they wouldn't panic. "So you all have this Alpha 2a? At least I know what it's called now. Not that it'll do me any good," he mumbled.

With a huge sigh, Letika nodded. "Yes, sir, we do. Mr. Jackson?"

"Yeah?"

"I remember something. I'm not sure if it's helpful, but a moment before we were brought here, I heard someone say the collection room at the Citadel was being prepped. Is this the collection room? Does that mean anything to you, sir?"

Max shrugged. The only room at the Citadel that he remembered was the torture chamber when Jampara screwed with his brain. That was a small room, though, certainly not big enough to house however many kids were with him now. "We've got to get out of this place. I've got an idea. Follow me." He turned and headed toward the Lamborghini, but stopped when he felt someone take his hand.

Looking up at him was Letika. "Thank you for helping us, Mr. Jackson. You're the nicest human I've ever met."

Behind her was a line of kids following them, walking in the beam. He gave her hand a little squeeze. "Yeah, okay." When he got to the car, he leaned in and opened the passenger door. "Hop in. We've got a really fast car and what better way to explore than to drive."

She seemed to consider it for a moment. "That's a good idea, but we can't go fast. I don't know where all of the New Breeds are and the ones here are on foot. I can't risk you running them over."

"Oh, right. Okay, then we'll creep along slowly until we find everyone we can. And keep a look-out for a door or window or other way out." Max slipped into the driver's seat and waited until Letika was in before closing the doors. "Wind your window down and tell the kids what we're doing. They can follow along behind us. I won't go more than a couple miles an hour."

Letika smiled, wound down the window and explained the plan, telling the kids to spread the word. Max edged forward, allowing the kids to move to the side and fall in behind the car as he drove forward. Letika was a smart girl and kindhearted, and he liked her. How could she be one of the vicious Ramtalans? Could he have misjudged them and the Dachel boys? He shook his head. No, of course he hadn't. And when he got to safety, he'd turn the whole lot of them over to AURA, including Letika. That was his duty and he couldn't go against his job.

Driving slowly was insane because he knew Lenox would come back any second and catch them all. As he drove forward, the kids parted to let him through. How many were there? It was an endless stream of New Breeds. Damn, the planet had been crawling with them, but apparently Lenox wanted them for something. Experimentation? Maybe. But why?

"Mr. Jackson, my Guardian told me that humans can't be shifted, so how are you here? How did Lenox transport you here?"

"Oh, Letika, I have no clue what these aliens menaces...I mean Lenox, can do." He kept driving forward, shooting her a glance now and then. She appeared so innocent, but he knew she was one of them.

"Mr. Jackson!" Letika called out after a few minutes.

"What?"

"Stop the car, please." She opened the door before he stopped.

"Wait until I come to a complete stop!" He braked hard. "Okay, now what?"

She hopped out and pointed to the right. "There. I see something."

Max squinted, but couldn't see a thing. "Where? I don't see anything."

"It's over there." She kept pointing. "I see a blue light." She started off without waiting.

"Hold on, kid!" Max got out and chased after her. "It's too dark. We move away from the headlights, we'll be going blind. There's no light, Letika."

She stopped and turned. "There is. You're old and your eyes probably aren't as good."

"I'm not that old," he mumbled. "Fine, then take me to the light."

"Follow me." She took off in a run.

Max jogged along, surprised at how fast she was. He fell behind and had to pick up speed, but after a short time, just like he said, they were plunged in pitch black. Letika's footsteps were straight ahead and he followed the sound. She wasn't slowing down at all.

Another minute or so passed and he lost the footsteps. He stopped and listened. "Letika?" Great. He turned around and realized he had no idea which way to go back to the Lamborghini. It felt like everything was closing in, crushing down on him. "Letika?"

"Over here, Mr. Jackson," she whispered. "Follow the sound." She started softly tapping on something.

She wasn't too far away, and although the tapping echoed slightly, he followed it with no problem. As he got close, he saw her crouched, bathed in a dim blue light.

"I'll be damned, you were right, there is a light. What is it?" He crouched beside her.

"There's a vent and the light is coming through it." She smiled and pointed to a mesh-covered vent in the floor no bigger than a box of cereal.

"I can't fit through that." Max sat and ran his hand over the vent, but pulled it back when he got a slight shock. "Ouch. It's electrified."

Letika shook her head. "Not exactly. It's infused with energy, but like I said, it's not Alpha 2a. If we can pry off the covering, one of the smaller kids might fit through."

Max stared at her. She was willing to send a little kid through the vent without knowing what waited for them below. Like he thought, Ramtalans were heartless and cruel. He was right to try to capture them all for experimentation. They didn't deserve anything less.

"You think I'm cruel, Mr. Jackson?" She gazed at him with big, sad eyes.

"Huh?"

She let out a sigh. "I can sometimes hear thoughts, but I only heard a few of your words this time. It's one of my abilities."

Thank goodness she didn't hear everything. Max shrugged. "That's not what I meant, kid."

"I think it was." She let out a huge sigh. "But that's okay, you don't understand who we are. My Guardian said AURA thinks New Breeds are bad." She paused. "Wait a minute, if I can hear some of your thoughts, that means my abilities are coming back!" She clapped her hands together. "Whatever's blocking them is weaker here at the vent. Help me get the cover off, Mr. Jackson."

He stood. "I don't think you're bad, kid. Hey, I got a shock when I touched that vent so be careful. I'm sure there's another way—"

"Why are humans so afraid of everything?" she muttered.

"Hey, I'm not afraid. I'm an AURA agent and I stood toe-to-toe with Argustine Lenox and I had my brain messed with by your Commander Jampara." He knelt, worked his fingers through the mesh, ignoring the jolts that seared his skin, and pulled as hard as he could. When the pain got too bad, he let go and cursed. "Sorry, kid, but that's on there pretty good. It burned my damn hands."

She took his hands in hers and after a few seconds, the pain was gone, then she let go and grabbed the mesh, yanked hard, and pulled it free. Max felt emasculated by the little girl. She was better than him in so many ways, but she wasn't a show-off or wasn't trying to put him down. She was simply better.

On her belly, she leaned into the vent. "I can't see much. The light's too dim."

"How about if I bring the car over here and we can shine the headlights? Would that help?"

"No need." Letika stood up. "My abilities are weak, but if I'm careful, I think I can project myself down there. That way I don't have to send anyone else down. I'll find the source of the blue light."

"Oh. Well, ah, is it safe? I mean, I don't know what 'projecting yourself' means."

"I can be in two places at the same time. Just don't let anything happen to my body until I come back." She drew in a deep breath, closed her eyes, but didn't move.

"Okay, I'll...Letika? Hello?" He tapped her on the shoulder. "Letika? Oh, hell, you went and did the projection thing, didn't you?"

From below the ground, Letika called up, "Yes, I'm down here. Nobody can see me. I'm going to look around. Be right back."

"Wait!" Max peered into the vent but didn't see anything. "Um, I'll wait right here." He paced in a circle around the vent, now and then stopping to check on Letika. He tapped his foot, paced again, and hoped she'd come back soon with good news. He crouched by the vent and waited. The abilities the New Breeds had was impressive. This one, he'd never seen before.

"Mr. Jackson," she whispered.

He turned and was relieved to see she'd come back. She put her finger to her lips."There's some sort of machine down there. I saw it in a room, guarded by two Ramtalans. I'm sure they're Invaders. It's giving off the blue light."

"Great. So what now?" Max wiped sweat off his face. "We have to go back to the car."

Letika shook her head and pointed to the vent. "No, we have to go down *there*."

Chapter 53

The symbols in Argus's head continued to dance around, settling into a slow rhythm. He glanced at Aunt Celeste and noticed that her eyes were dim. Casting such a large veil was taking its toll on her. He had to do something.

In a whisper, he said, "Aunt Celeste, retract the veil. I'll be okay."

She shook her head. "Galena and Lenox will go soon. Neb can handle himself. Stay quiet."

"But..." Before he finished his objection, the symbols arranged themselves in neat columns and he instantly knew what they said.

> *To draw on Lenox's Zeta 40, take Alpha 2a from the veil, shift to him and dose yourself with his Zeta 40 by initiating a shift with him.*

It seemed dangerous to attempt to force a shift with Lenox, but if it was the only way to get some energy back, then that's what he'd do. He closed his eyes, concentrated on the energy veil, reached out and touched it. It had always been this untouchable thing, but now he felt it and it was like a thin plastic bubble. Once his fingers came in contact with it, he felt a surge and the veil vanished. Aunt Celeste gasped, stumbled, and almost fell.

"What have you done, Argus?" She stared at him.

Neb spread his arms in front of Aunt Celeste and Lola. "Stay behind me."

"Listen, I can reason with him." Argus shifted to Lenox, grabbed his arm and initiated another shift before Lenox could react. He landed on the runway at Edwards, right near the XTRA-A1.

Lenox glanced around, his mouth slightly open. "You led me in a shift? No one has ever done that. I was under the impression that Nebulon had drained you of your energy."

"He did." Argus knew he didn't have all of his energy, but had enough to shift again if he had to. "This has to stop. All of it. You can't kill the humans and you can't take over the Earth. Why don't you find a deserted planet and go live there and leave us alone?"

Lenox walked around Argus. "You are indeed a superior species, my son. However, as powerful as you are, you are no match for me. You caught me by surprise this time, but I assure you, it will not happen again. I can sense Zeta 40 and Alpha 2a within you, but hardly at the capacity you need for survival. Tell me, how did you know to harvest a part of my energy?"

"I won't tell you anything." Argus pointed to the ship. "Take it and go. I don't ever want to see you again."

With a chuckle, Lenox shook his head. "The ship was designed for you, Tai, and Aridesian. I cannot pilot it. And you cannot pilot it without your energy, which brings me to another point. I must go and...convince Nebulon to give it back."

"Yeah, I know how you convince people. He told me what you did to him. Will you do that to me, too, if I don't cooperate?" Argus swayed a little, unsteady on his feet.

"Son, I will help you, but it does require your cooperation. How many times must I tell you that I will not harm you? We will be a family, Argus. Is that not something you have dreamed of?" Lenox walked to the XTRA-A1 and touched the side. "I have never belonged anywhere, never fit in on Ramtala or Malaris. Being different made me an outcast. Now I finally have a solution. This will be our planet and we will no longer be the outcasts."

Argus stumbled. "But this isn't your planet. It belongs to everyone who lives on it right now. Killing them so you can have a home is wrong on so many levels. Why can't you see that?"

Lenox took him by the arm. "My son, you are weakening rapidly. Allow me to handle things and I will restore you and cleanse this planet. Starting with Max Jackson. Not destroying him when I had the chance was a mistake I will not make again."

"Max Jackson? I never trusted him, why did you?" Argus's vision blurred and his stomach hurt. He didn't want to faint because Lenox would have him then.

"I did not trust him. I used him, although that appeared to be an ill conceived decision. You have enough energy for a shift. I will take you to Aridesian and then we will find Tai." Lenox initiated a shift.

It didn't go smoothly for Argus. His limbs burned and his head felt like it was about to explode. When they landed, he gasped for air.

"Breathe, son." Lenox placed his palm on Argus's forehead. "I am donating a small percentage of Zeta 40 to you. It will only last a short time. This is why I must go back for Nebulon."

Argus felt better right away although everything was dark. "I can't see real well." A dim bluish glow surrounded them.

Lenox laughed. "That is because we are in the collection room below the holding chamber at the Citadel and there is no need for blinding lights. This room is infused with Alpha 2a that will sustain your life systems, but I have placed a Zeta 40 shield around it so you cannot escape. You will be safe here with Aridesian. Once I have Nebulon, I will bring him here."

"And Tai? You said you'd find him. Once you have us all, are you still planning to kill the New Breeds and the humans? Please, listen to me. You can't do that. Just rethink this whole plan of yours. I won't go along with it and I know for a fact Tai won't either. We can all live in peace with the humans."

Now Lenox frowned. "I am your father whether you like it or not. You and your brother were born for a singular purpose. Nothing more. Cooperate and rule by my side or..."

Argus didn't need him to complete the sentence. Lenox would kill them if they fought him. One minute he seemed reasonable and then next, he was his heartless, asshole self again. Taking Aunt Celeste's energy and shifting with Lenox hadn't accomplished anything.

"So where's Ari? Galena said he was hurt." Argus peered into the dark but couldn't see anything. If Ari was hurt, maybe he'd blame Lenox and maybe he'd want to fight against him. Getting anyone to help fight Lenox was imperative.

"My men will take you to him." Lenox motioned with his hand and a Ramtalan strode out of the darkness. "Lubor, take my son to Aridesian and see that he gets whatever he needs. Keep your eyes on him and make sure he does not have access to either energy source. He knows how to capture energy. The ambient energy will sustain him and that is enough for now."

Argus ground his teeth. Escaping was impossible. "Thanks, *Dad*."

Lenox smirked. "Now, now. I will return shortly. Behave yourself." He vanished without warning.

Lubor pressed a button on the wall and a series of lights above came on. He pointed down a long corridor. "Go down there and you'll find a glassed in room where Aridesian is. Don't even think of shifting. Argustine put up the Zeta 40 shield again once he shifted. No one in, no one out."

"Perfect." Argus sighed and walked down the corridor. It was still dim, but light enough to see where he was going and sure enough, after a bit, he found the glass room.

Ari was lying on a bed, his skin pale, and small cuts around his forehead. What had Max done to him? Argus went into the room and felt an immediate buzz of energy all around. Healing energy most likely. He tried, but couldn't tap into it. Damn.

"Ari?" he whispered. "Can you hear me?"

Ari stirred and blinked his eyes open. "Argus? Is that you?"

"Yeah. Lenox brought me here. How are you feeling?" Argus stood by the bed.

"Like I was run over by a freight train driven by Max Jackson."

"I think I know the feeling. What did he do to you, Ari?" Argus leaned down for a closer look at the wounds. "Did he stick pins in you or what?"

Ari drew in a breath. "Pins would have been a picnic. He had this helmet with sharp probes all around it. I hate that guy with all my heart. Promise me, if I don't make it, that you'll rip his arms off and feed them to him."

"You'll make it. But I don't think that would be punishment enough for him." Argus wanted Max to himself so he could...what was he thinking? He wasn't about to torture anyone. Lenox was rubbing off on him. "No torture, Ari. We're better than that."

"I can't believe you're saying that. I know what he's done to you and Tai. How can you defend that animal?"

"I'm not defending him, at all. We're supposed to be an advanced species, so we should act like it. That's all I'm saying." Argus noticed a monitor on the other side of the bed. He went around and checked the readings. "Ari, your heart rate is up and I think this other reading is your blood pressure, and it says 'high'. Should I do anything? Is there a nurse or doctor?"

"Argus, we're underneath the Citadel and this room is flowing with so much energy that my cells are about to explode. That's why my vitals are higher than normal. Celeste didn't teach you much, did she?"

He didn't like anyone talking bad about Aunt Celeste. She'd always been there for them, taken care of them, and explained what they needed to know. "She taught us exactly what she should have."

"Well, she didn't tell you that you were Ramtalan until you were seventeen. Most New Breeds know by the time they hit puberty. Oh, that reminds me, I overheard Father say he has all of the New Breeds secured. No idea where, but I thought you should know." Ari closed his eyes.

"Okay." He watched Ari for a moment. Why did he say that? Was he hoping the New Breeds could be saved? Maybe he was against Lenox after all. "I wanted to make sure you were okay. I'll be back in a few, I need to think."

"Fine. I have to rest anyway."

Argus paced in the corridor, regretting that he'd left Aunt Celeste. It was an impulse, one that turned out wrong. He'd made so many mistakes. He'd left Lola alone again, and left Aunt Celeste with Galena. He was eighteen now, but in many ways, he still felt like a little kid. He'd barely been in the real world, sheltered his whole life. How was he supposed to know everything? He stopped and considered his options. If Aunt Celeste was right, then at least Tai was safe. But the New Breeds were in trouble according to Ari.

"I knew putting them all in one place was a terrible idea," he mumbled.

It was strange that Aunt Celeste said they were safe, yet Lenox got his hands on them anyway. Where did that leave Tai? If Lenox found the New Breeds, then he could also get to Tai. There had to be a way to get through to Lenox and have him give up his plan. And if there wasn't, then it would be all-out war with Neb's people.

"Dachel!" called Lubor.

"What?" Argus started to feel weak again. When he was inside the room with Ari, he felt a bit better. Maybe he should stay in there and build up his energy so he could try to shift if Lenox lowered the shield. The borrowed energy didn't seem to last long though.

Lubor strode down the corridor and motioned for Argus to follow. "I'm supposed to keep my eyes on you. There's a cell over here and I want you in it."

"I'd rather stay close to Ari." And the energy in the room.

"Aridesian can live without you by his side. Now move."

Argus hesitated. "Where's Lenox?"

"Out looking for your brother and the energy you so easily gave up." Lubor scowled.

"Excuse me? Like I had a choice? Neb *stole* my energy." There was a flutter in his gut and another image of the Malaris symbols popped into his head.

Alpha 2a available in abundance above.

What? In the Citadel? Of course there was, it was filled with Ramtalans. But there was no way to escape with the Zeta 40 shield.

Alpha 2a source is from New Breeds four meters above you, 30 meters below Citadel.

The holding chamber. Lenox had the New Breeds right above. Okay, that was good information to have. He'd have to break the shield, tap into the New Breeds' Alpha 2a, escape and find Tai before Lenox did. But how?

"Are you deaf, Dachel? I said move into the cell. Argustine left clear orders not to harm you, but he won't know if I take a few liberties." Lubor smirked.

"The hell he won't." Argus glared at Lubor and prepared to fight him. "Lenox knows everything, haven't you learned that by now?"

Lubor shook his head. "Once we take the Earth, I'll make it my mission to get you alone. Understand?"

"Yeah, sure." Argus smiled. "Didn't my father tell you I'm part Malaris?"

Lubor's mouth gaped slightly. "What? How could...you're lying."

"Maybe I am, maybe I'm not. Why don't you ask him when he gets back?" Argus strode past him and found the cell, which really wasn't a cell because there weren't any bars or doors, just an open room with a sofa and a cot against one wall.

He went inside and sat on the sofa. "Hey! I'm hungry."

Lubor stood in the doorway. "I'm not your servant. You've got a food ordering system in the cell. Use it." He spun around and left.

There wasn't anything else in the cell. "Liar," Argus muttered. He *was* hungry. How long had it been since he last ate? "I really could use something to eat!" he shouted.

A hidden door about three feet high slid open and out came one of the robot waiters from the Citadel's cafeteria. "You require food?"

"Ah, yes." Argus ran to the door, but it slid closed before he got to it. "Damn it."

"Sir?"

"Nothing. Where do you get the food from?"

The robot spun around in a circle and stopped. "I am not programmed to respond to questions such as that. You require food?"

"Sure. Go and get me a sandwich." He stood by the sliding door.

The robot zoomed to the door and stopped. "What type of sandwich?"

Argus groaned. "Turkey. With pickles on the side. And orange juice."

"Yes, sir." A few lights on the robot blinked and the door slid open.

As soon as the robot went through, Argus dropped to his hands and knees and followed. It was so dark, he bumped his head into a wall. "Ow." The door slid closed behind him.

The robot spun around. "Sir?"

"Nothing." The room he was in couldn't be more than four feet high by about five feet wide. "Where is this?"

"Sir?"

"Never mind. Get my food."

"Yes, sir." The robot's lights blinked again and the room jolted.

It moved. It was an elevator. Argus sat and tried to judge the speed of the elevator, but without any point of reference, he couldn't. Instead, he counted the passing seconds. By the time he'd counted almost two minutes, the elevator slowed and stopped. The door slid open and the robot zipped out.

Argus crawled out and immediately smelled food, heard a clatter of dishware and several voices coming from a room down a short hallway. He'd made it to the kitchen, but now what? He didn't have a plan and if he wasted too much time, Lubor would know he'd escaped and track him down. He shuddered. Even without his abilities, he felt a surge of Alpha 2a from the collective energy of the Citadel. Not enough to shift, but there was enough to give him a boost of strength.

If he knew how the elevator worked, he could go down to the holding chamber and find the New Breeds, providing there was a stop on that level. He had to get the robot waiter to help. As quietly as he could, he crept down the hall and peeked into the kitchen. Four Ramtalans wearing Citadel uniforms were busy at work stirring pots and cutting vegetables. The robot wasn't anywhere.

His stomach growled, but the kitchen noise covered up the sound. Slowly, he crept into the kitchen, grabbed a loaf of freshly baked bread and an apple, and dashed back to the hallway. Since the robot also delivered food to the cafeteria, all he had to do was find it and follow it. He knew his way around the Citadel from there. He continued down the hallway, stuffing chunks of bread in his mouth as he went.

"Sir?" came the robot's voice behind him.

He spun around. "Ah, hi. Can you show me to the cafeteria?"

Its lights blinked for a moment. "Argustine Lenox is searching for Argus Dachel and has asked all computerized systems to seek him out. Are you not Argus Dachel?"

Argus glanced around. "No, I'm not. I'm Aridesian Stargaard. You know what, forget about the cafeteria, take me to where the New Breeds are being held."

The robot's lights flashed. "The New Breeds will be prepared for extraction soon. I cannot interfere with Argustine Lenox unless you are Argus Dachel in which case I will deliver you to him."

"Yeah, you said that already. Tell me how the extraction process works."

Without hesitating, the robot explained, "New Breeds will have their energy harvested and collected into the thermo photo-fusion particle. It will absorb all of their Alpha 2a energy. Is there anything else, sir?"

"But they can't live without their Alpha 2a." Argus swallowed at the thought of the New Breeds, just children, dying all because Lenox wanted their energy. "They'll die."

"That is correct, sir."

He couldn't let that happen. "Where is the particle?" He could hide it, then Lenox couldn't steal the energy.

The robot flashed its lights. "Argustine Lenox possesses the particle."

"What?" Argus leaned against the wall. "Okay, then where is Lenox?"

"In the collection room."

Argus groaned. "Well, I'm not going back there then. Can you take me to the New Breeds? Hey, how many are down there?"

"Many New Breeds perished in transit. Three hundred remain."

"Three hundred? That's all?" Argus paced in the hallway. How had that happened? Lenox needed the kids alive for extraction of their energy, didn't he? So many dead. When Aunt Celeste and Neb found out, they'd do everything they could to kill Lenox. "Can Lenox still carry out his plan?"

Lenox appeared right in front of Argus. "Yes, son, I can."

Instinct made Argus raise his palms to Lenox, prepared to fire a burst. "You killed thousands of kids!"

"Don't ever threaten me." Lenox fired a short burst that hit Argus in the stomach and sent him skidding down the hallway. "Besides, you do not have the energy to use any of your abilities. When I broke through Celeste's protective shield, it killed most of the New Breeds. That, my son, is on her. But I have plenty of them. I have created an enhancement system that will use the Alpha 2a I capture from them and combine it with the particle's Alpha 2a to regenerate as much as I want. You cannot win. You are fighting against me and losing."

Argus had the breath knocked out of him. His gut ached and he felt worthless. Nothing he did made any difference. He struggled to stand. "I'd rather lose than ever go along with you."

"Ah, putting on a brave front. Perhaps I can change your mind." Lenox appeared next to him and shifted.

They landed back in the open cell. Argus collapsed onto the cot, weakness leaving him breathless. "You know, every time you do that, it hurts."

"Then do not make me continue shifting with you. Stay where I tell you to stay and I will have no need." Lenox went to the doorway. "Lubor!"

Lubor strode into the room, red-faced, his eyes glowing blue. "You found him. I swear to you, Argustine, I did not take my eyes off him for more than a minute or two."

Lenox motioned to Argus. "My son is better than you in every possible capacity. And if you allow him out of your sight, he *will* disobey. Bring me Celeste and Nebulon."

Argus jumped up. "What? You have Aunt...how?"

When Lubor left, Lenox grabbed Argus by the front of his shirt. "Of course I have them. Nobody can hide from me for long. In time, I will find Tai as well."

Argus struggled, but couldn't get free. At least he didn't have Tai.

Lenox continued, "You have no idea what you did in Palmdale, do you? You are too powerful and must be trained. This is your last chance to cooperate. If you do not, I will place you, and Tai, in stasis with the New Breeds. When I get your energy from Nebulon, I will absorb it myself. I will not need you at that point. I am the only one who can train you and if you do not cooperate with me now, I will destroy everyone you care about, starting with that human, Lola. You hold her life in your hands. Decide now."

After pulling away, Argus spun around; he couldn't stand to look at Lenox. There was so much hatred boiling up inside him, he thought he'd explode. He balled up his fists and took a deep breath. If he was so powerful, how come he couldn't escape and rescue everyone on Earth? Lenox was lying, trying to manipulate him. With Aunt Celeste and Neb captured, there was nobody left outside the Citadel to help. The only way to keep everyone safe was to surrender to Lenox once and for all. Lenox had won.

Chapter 54

Max stared at Letika and considered, for a brief moment, running back to the Lamborghini and driving it as far away from the New Breeds as he could. Once Lenox did whatever he wanted to do to them, there might be a way to escape. But he couldn't leave the girl or the other kids to suffer at Lenox's hands.

He grunted. "Okay, let's say, hypothetically, that we find a way down into that other room, then what? It's you, me and a bunch of powerless alien kids against Lenox and his ilk. You got a plan or are you hoping for a miracle?"

She pointed to the vent. "I saw an elevator down there, but there is no door on this level. We can find the shaft, break through the wall and get into the elevator. So, yes, I have a plan."

Break through the wall? She'd lost her mind. Max shook his head. "That's not a plan, that's absurd. Even the Dachel boys could come up with something better than that."

"Who?" Letika peered through the vent.

"The Dachel...never mind. You said there was a machine down there. Any idea what it is? It could be booby trapped or an explosive device." Max heard footsteps and turned to see several other New Breed kids coming toward them. "We've got company."

With a wave to the kids, Letika frowned at Max. "If you're too scared to help, you don't have to."

"What? What do you mean? I'll help if it gets me the hell out of here. I'm not scared."

She gave a couple of small nods. "Okay. I didn't get a good look at the machine, but I could feel a very strong current of Alpha 2a coming from it. I think it absorbs Alpha 2a, so it might be taking our energy and creating a shield to block our abilities. I have to destroy it. Are you with me?"

"If it works and you get your powers back, leave Lenox to me. Understand? Me, not any of you."

"We don't want Lenox. We want to go home." Letika spoke to the nearest children, "There's a level below us that has some sort of Alpha 2a machine. But there's no way to get to it unless we find the elevator shaft in the wall. I projected myself down there and I estimate that the elevator shaft is about twenty feet to my right."

A boy about fifteen or so stepped forward with something in his hand. "We can use this to smash through the wall."

Max grabbed the object. "A tire iron? Where the hell did you get that?"

"From that car you were driving."

Wow, what a resourceful kid. Max kept the tire iron. "I'll hold onto this. Letika, lead the way."

The light coming from the vent wasn't strong, so Max stayed close to Letika and told the kids to follow. He kept a hand on the wall and went about twenty feet to the right, as Letika said, and before long, they were plunged in darkness and Max had second thoughts. There they were, walking into the unknown in blindness. He was trusting a little girl, an alien girl. But, if it led to him getting his hands on Lenox, it would be worth going along with a bunch of little Ramtalans. Besides, he liked Letika, even though every fiber in his body told him not to. He was an AURA agent after all. But the kids didn't seem so bad, although the Dachel brothers were different. They'd humiliated him more times than he could count. They *had* to be captured. But Letika? Maybe not.

Chapter 55

Argus saw Aunt Celeste and Neb come into the cell, both covered in a blue light that pulsed slightly. It wasn't like a veil, but more like a second skin. Neb was furious, his jaw clenched, but Aunt Celeste had a look of worry on her face. Lubor shoved them forward and strode from the cell without a word.

Aunt Celeste was the first to speak, "Argus, are you all right?"

He nodded. "Is Tai safe?"

With a throaty chuckle, Lenox came up behind Aunt Celeste and stepped in front of her. "Yes, Celeste, is Tai safe?"

Now Aunt Celeste had the same angry expression as Neb. She glared at Lenox. "Yes, Argustine, he's safe from you. You can do whatever you want to me or Neb, but we won't talk."

"I know that." Lenox turned to Argus. "Perhaps we don't need Tai. You are a very strong boy and I believe you can power the XTRA-A1 all by yourself."

"I don't have any abilities, Lenox. But if I did, I'd take care of you so you could never hurt anyone again. Especially Tai." Argus doubled over as his gut clenched.

Neb called out, "Fight against the Protector in you! It'll do nothing but cause you pain."

With a laugh, Lenox faced Neb. "Oh, yes, you have experience with that, do you not? I will make you a deal, Nebulon. If you hand over my son's energy, I will kill you quickly. No torture this time." He looked at Argus. "I have warned you about threatening me." He fired a small burst that hit Argus in the forehead.

Argus was stunned for a moment, but the energy he'd absorbed from the short time he was in the Citadel, helped him recover fast. "You won't kill anyone, Lenox, not Aunt Celeste, Neb, Lola, or the New Breeds. I won't let you." He focused on collecting every bit of energy he had, raised his hand and attempted to fire at Lenox, but the energy dissipated before anything happened.

Lenox walked up to Argus, slapped his hand away and fired another burst, this time hitting Argus in the gut. "You are a Malaris-Ramtalan hybrid now. You need your Zeta 40 as well as Alpha 2a. They work together. Since Nebulon has blocked your Zeta 40 and stolen your Alpha 2a, you are as helpless as a human."

The burst knocked Argus off his feet. He struggled to breath. He sat, leaning against the wall of the cell and looked at Aunt Celeste. His head spun with images of Lola and Tai, and of Acoma falling into ruins. "Lenox said I did something in Palmdale. What did I do? Did I hurt Lola?"

"Argus..." Aunt Celeste's eyes dimmed. "I don't hold you accountable for what happened. You haven't learned how to control your Malaris—"

Neb interrupted, "That's exactly why I took your energy. You have no idea how much power you have. But I guess I underestimated how your Malaris brain works."

Struggling to his feet, Argus clenched his fists. "So what did I supposedly do?"

With a heavy sigh, Aunt Celeste continued, "When you seized a part of my Alpha 2a, a small part of your Zeta 40 must have broken free from Neb's block. The shift you did with Lenox combined his energy with yours for a brief moment. That much energy..." she trailed off and looked away.

Lenox took over, "What Celeste is trying to say is that you leveled Palmdale, impressively. The shift created a shock wave that destroyed most of the houses and buildings for several miles." He smiled.

What? Argus couldn't breathe. It was like a weight pressed him down, taking the air from his lungs. Were they telling the truth? Is that what had happened at Acoma as well? "Is Lola all right? And everyone else?" It felt like his heart was in a vice. "I can't...breathe."

"Argus," Aunt Celeste said softly, "Take a breath slowly and let it out."

He did and then another one and another one until he relaxed. "Lola?"

Aunt Celeste's eyes grew brighter. "She's fine. And her mother got out of the house in time. Most people did and there were only a few injuries. People are used to earthquakes and that's what they thought it was."

Lenox glanced at her and then back at Argus. "Tell the boy the truth, Celeste. Argus, there were many injuries and deaths. Although Celeste is correct that your human and her mother were not harmed. Your abilities far exceed what I had anticipated, better than Aridesian could ever hope to attain. That boy will never achieve your greatness. When I find Tai, I will put him through a phase-shift and see if he obtains the same power or if it is unique to you."

Argus was not about to let Lenox experiment on Tai. The anger inside him built up and he knew he was about to lose control. He saw the Malaris symbols in his head, but this time they kept floating around and didn't organize themselves. He needed all of his energy back.

In a flash of blue, Ari appeared behind Lenox. "Hello, Father."

Lenox spun around. "Aridesian, why are you not resting?"

"I was." Ari looked past Lenox and winked at Argus. "I came to talk to you, but overheard what you just said about me. Did you ever love me? Do you think of me as your son or as a mistake?" His eyes grew brighter.

Argus watched Ari. What was he up to? Maybe he knew a way to free Aunt Celeste and Neb.

With a frustrated sigh, Lenox grabbed Ari around the throat. "I should have let you die. You are not needed anymore. To answer your question, I see you as both; my son and my mistake. Get out of my sight." He released Ari and turned around.

Gasping for breath, Ari winked again at Argus, then ran past Lenox and wrapped his fingers around Argus's wrists. "Take some of my Alpha 2a. As much as you need. Fast!"

Argus concentrated on the Alpha 2a signature and drew it into his body where he felt it surge. Right away, the Malaris symbols organized themselves into rows.

Break the veil by firing a weak Zeta-40 pulse. Your Zeta 40 energy level is faint, but enough to disrupt the veil.

When Ari let go and collapsed, Argus stepped to the side, extended his hand and fired a burst at Aunt Celeste's veil, but Lenox was quick and deflected it. Before Lenox realized what was happening, Argus fired another burst and the veil disappeared. It didn't take Aunt Celeste long to fire continuous pulses directly at Lenox, knocking him off his feet.

Aunt Celeste yelled, "Argus, take Ari and shift to Edwards!"

"Edwards?" Argus crouched by Ari, but looked at Lenox. "Aunt Celeste, are you going to kill—?"

"Don't worry about what I'm going to do, get to safety!" She touched Neb's veil and it dissipated. "Go!"

Argus took Ari's hand and looked at Lenox. "He's my father, Aunt Celeste."

"I know. I'll handle things. I won't tell you again."

Argus knew the borrowed energy from Ari, and the residual Zeta 40, wasn't enough for a shift. "I can't shift. I didn't get enough Alpha 2a."

"Neb." Aunt Celeste fired again on Lenox. "Help Argus."

In a flash, Neb was beside Argus. He extended his hand where a marble-sized ball of Alpha 2a floated in his palm. "Absorb this, Argus. It's enough for a shift."

Argus nodded and focused on taking the energy. It floated from Neb's hand, hovered for a moment and vanished. In an instant, Argus felt another surge, much bigger this time, and he completed the shift. He landed on the runway beside the XTRA-A1. If Lenox got away from Aunt Celeste, he'd go straight to Edwards.

"Ari, we have to go." Argus looked down at Ari, but he wasn't moving. "Ari?" He shook him. "Talk to me, Ari."

Gasping for air, Ari opened his eyes. "I'm done, Argus. Save yourself. Find Tai and live your lives. Don't let anyone tell you what to do. Live."

"What do you mean? You're not dying. I only borrowed a little of your energy." Argus knelt. "Come on, Ari, try to sit up. You'll feel better in a minute."

"No, I won't. My body used most of my Alpha 2a repairing itself. The rest—"

"Yeah, I know. I took it. But there has to be something we can do. I can give you some Alpha 2a." Argus extended his hand, but nothing happened. "How do I make an energy ball appear like Neb did?"

Drawing in a strained breath, Ari shook his head. "You can't. Only pure-forms can. The shift used what Neb gave you. You only have enough left to sustain yourself for a short time until Neb returns your own energy. When he does, run away from everything Ramtalan and don't look back." He raised his head a little and looked around. With a slight laugh, he motioned with his eyes to the XTRA-A1. "I see why Celeste said to shift here."

"Why?" Argus got up and scanned the area. All of the hangars and outbuildings had collapsed. "I did that, didn't I? Is that what Aunt Celeste wanted me to see? To show me how dangerous I am?" That was just cruel, not at all something he would have thought Aunt Celeste would do. But she'd changed, they'd all changed.

"Not too bright, are you, little brother?" Ari tried to smile, but it ended in a pained grimace. "The ship, Argus. Tai's hiding in the ship."

"What? How do you know that?"

"Use your senses. There are no energy signatures coming from the ship. None. That means there's a veil around it. Ahhh, I'm cold, Argus. I can't feel my legs." He groaned. "I don't want to die."

Argus knelt again and gave Ari a pat on the shoulder. "Don't worry, if Tai really is in the ship, you can take some of his Alpha 2a and heal yourself. You'll be okay."

Ari closed his eyes. "It's too late for me, Argus. I'm too far gone. My body's shutting down. Promise me you'll put an end to Father's tyrannical behavior. Promise...me."

"Ari, open your eyes. Come on, it's not too late." He gave Ari another shake. "Tai!" He jumped up and ran to the ship. "Tai!"

A second later, he felt a burst of Alpha 2a and Tai appeared next to him. "Arg, what the hell?" He pointed to Ari. "What'd you do to *him*?"

"Nothing." Argus swallowed. That wasn't true, if he hadn't taken Ari's energy, he wouldn't be lying on the pavement, dying. "Ari saved me. And Aunt Celeste and Neb."

"Seriously?" Tai walked to Ari. "That true, Ari?"

Ari didn't respond or move.

Argus rushed to his side and dropped to his knees. "Ari! Say something. Please."

Nothing.

After searching for a pulse, Argus couldn't find any sign of life. "Ari? Tai, I think he's dead."

"Whoa." Tai felt Ari's wrist. "I think you're right. This is too weird, bro. What happened? How did he help you? Aunt Celeste said she'd take care of everything and bring you back here, but I've been waiting and waiting. I was going to go look for you. I can get through the ship's shield, but it still hides my Alpha 2a. If I leave...like I just did, I can be found." He got up and took a few steps backward. "Why is Ari dead?"

Argus felt sick to his stomach. It wasn't supposed to happen this way. He pointed to the hangars. "Tai, I destroyed Palmdale. Neb has my energy, but I still managed to destroy the whole damn town. I can't be trusted. That's why Neb took my energy. He knows what I've become. I can't be allowed to—"

"To what? Live? Don't be ridiculous. Whatever you did, we'll fix it. We always fix everything. Aunt Celeste can do her mind manipulation thing and make everyone think there was an earthquake or whatever. We'll fix it. But how did Ari die?"

"He gave me his Alpha 2a. All of it."

"Oh. Well, that was, ah, good, I guess. I never saw him as anything but an ass, but maybe he did have some redeeming qualities after all." Tai paused and pointed to the ship. "I think we should get the hell away from here. Does Aunt Celeste have Lenox?"

"I don't know. I think so. Unless she...she was hitting him with photometric pulses and he was down. He looked hurt."

Tai's eyes widened. "Don't you dare feel sorry for him. Stop thinking like a Protector. I hope he's dead and I hope he suffered."

"He's still our father. No matter what, Lenox is our father. We're his sons." Argus took off his jacket and placed it over Ari's body and face. "And Ari was our brother."

"We've got the most jacked up family, Arg. Hey, speaking of family, where's *Aunty* Galena?"

"Inside the Citadel, I guess. She'll probably surrender once she hears that Lenox has been captured."

"Or killed," Tai mumbled as he walked to the ship.

"Stop it, Tai." Argus looked around and noticed several soldiers on the ground around the hangars. "Are they dead?" He felt numb.

Tai shook his head. "No, they're in stasis. But I don't know for how long, which means we have to move. Now."

"How? I'm just about out of Alpha 2a and my Zeta 40 is still blocked and hardly works. I can't shift anymore or it'll kill me. So I can't get into the ship." Argus paced.

"Well, shit." Tai ran his hand through his hair. "Can you contact the control center in the ship?"

With a shrug, Argus glanced at the XTRA-A1. "I don't know. I don't fully understand how all of this Malaris stuff works."

The heavy thump-thump of a helicopter interrupted the silence and Argus scanned the sky over Palmdale. After a few seconds, he saw a large black helicopter in the lead with smaller helicopters in a triangular formation behind it. Without his abilities, he couldn't get away.

"Tai, get in the ship!"

"Not without you, bro."

Argus pointed at the helicopters. "Then we'll both be captured."

"Fine with me. I don't care anymore. We've been pushed around and manipulated by our own people and the humans. What more can they do to us? Seriously, I don't care."

"You really mean that?" Argus grabbed Tai by the arm. "You want Max Jackson to slice you up and put you on display? Because that's what he'll do."

Tai glanced at the helicopters and pulled away from Argus. "Of course I don't. But I'm not leaving you." He raised his hands and fired off a series of pulses at the lead helicopter.

Direct hit.

The helicopter swung out of formation and spun clockwise, heading toward the ground. Unfortunately, the others accelerated, noses down, and began shooting. Tai pulled Argus under the XTRA-A1.

"Arg, take some of my Alpha 2a and shift inside the ship."

"No. I'm not doing that." He motioned to Ari. "Remember what happened to him?"

Tai dashed out again and fired off a few more pulses, striking another helicopter. "They'll drop bombs or nukes on us, Arg. We can't stay here."

"You just said you didn't care if we got captured."

"I freaking lied!" Tai shot a few more pulses and ducked under the ship again. "Take my Alpha 2a. Just not all of it."

Argus shook his head. "Go. I'll be all right. Aunt Celeste can save me. Fly to the Citadel and tell her what happened."

"Don't be a martyr, bro." Tai fired off a couple more pulses, but missed.

The helicopters were close and moved into a wide circle around the ship as the big black copter, smoking from its engine, slowly approached. Argus was prepared to run onto the runway with his hands in the air, hoping Tai would save himself, but he turned at the sound of a car horn coming from the entrance gate.

A mini-van sped toward them, honking and flashing its headlights. Argus looked at Tai, who shrugged and got ready to fire a pulse at the van.

"Wait, Tai! That's Dave's mom's van."

"Dave? Your friend Dave? What the hell's he thinking?"

The van screeched to a stop near the ship and Dave waved from the driver's window. "Get in, guys! They won't shoot civilian teenagers while the media is filming!" Dave leaned out and pointed behind him.

"What?" Argus couldn't believe what he saw. A news helicopter and several news vans were speeding toward them. He ran to Dave.

Dave laughed. "I saw your ship on the news and figured you might be here. When I saw all of those helicopters heading to Edwards, I knew it wasn't good, so I called the TV stations and told them about AURA and how Max Jackson wanted to autopsy teenage aliens."

"Holy shit, Dave." Argus looked over at Tai. "Okay, Tai, now you can get in the ship. I'll go with Dave."

Tai shook his head. "I'm not leaving you. Besides, I don't even know if I can power it by myself."

Argus climbed into the van and shouted out the window, "Try! Go and help Aunt Celeste and tell Neb to give me back my energy. We'll be at Lake Elizabeth."

"I don't like this." Tai fired off a pulse at one of the closer military helicopters and vanished.

A moment later, the XTRA-A1 came to life, lifted off the ground, wobbled for a moment, pointed up and zoomed into the sky. Dave whooped, turned the van around and drove past the media trucks that were setting up antennas and cameras. Argus watched the XTRA-A1 disappear into the clouds overhead.

"Guess Tai *can* fly the ship by himself. I owe you one, Dave."

"I think you owe me several, man." Dave laughed and pointed to the back seat.

Argus turned and saw Lola sit up. "Lola! You're okay?"

She nodded. "After you disappeared with Lenox, there was this huge earthquake. Your aunt stayed with me until Detective DeAlba woke up. He took me home and I called Dave and asked if he'd seen you. He came by and picked me up. Our house is practically destroyed."

"Oh...that's awful. And, Dave, thanks." Argus reached around and held Lola's hand.

Dave sped through a broken gate at the guard shack. "I snapped that on my way in."

Argus let out a breath. "You've been officially corrupted, Dave."

"Yeah, man!" He laughed again and skidded onto the main road. "Oh, the school's a pile of bricks and concrete, so no classes for a while."

With a groan, Argus shrugged. "I wasn't planning on returning anyway. The school's the last thing I'm worried about. I accidentally wrecked the whole town. I should rebuild it, but I seriously doubt my allowance can cover all of the costs." Argus gave Lola's hand a kiss and faced forward, quickly fastening his seatbelt. "How'd you get so good at driving?"

"From watching you, man." He drove too fast up the onramp of the freeway and slid on some loose rocks. "Whoa!"

"Careful, Dave, or we'll die before we get to the lake. How are you doing, Lola?"

"Good." She placed her hand on Argus's shoulder. "If we do survive Dave's driving, I want you to tell me everything that's happened."

Argus gave her a nod and grabbed onto the dashboard.

Dave accelerated when he got onto the freeway. "Hey, Argus, was that a dead body I saw back there?"

Argus had managed to push Ari from his mind, but now the image of him lying on the runway came rushing back. "Yeah. My half-brother Ari."

Lola squeezed his shoulder. "Sorry, Argie."

Dave swerved around a slower car. "Ah, sorry, man. That sucks. But I'm not going to let anything happen to you. You're the best friend I've ever had."

Argus kept his eyes on the distant helicopters. They weren't following. Maybe they didn't notice that he'd gone in the van with Dave. Probably more concerned with the XTRA-A1. "You're my best friend, too, Dave."

"Hey, what about me?" Lola squeezed his shoulder harder.

He turned and smirked. "You're *more* than a friend, Lola. Way more."

Chapter 56

In the pitch blackness, Max waited while the kids took turns smashing the wall with the tire iron. How they knew exactly where to strike was beyond him. Some weird alien thing no doubt. The sound echoed, but apparently Lenox or his minions hadn't heard.

"Letika," Max whispered between whacks. "How much longer?"

"Almost there."

"Good, because this is dangerous beyond belief. One of those pure-form Ramtalans could sneak up on us and we wouldn't know." Max wrung his hands together.

Letika touched him on the arm. "We'd know. We have to climb down about four meters. Can you do that?"

Climb down? Max swallowed. "How?"

"There'll be cables, I think. Haven't you ever seen movies? There are always these heavy cables that people slide down in an elevator shaft."

Movies? "That's fiction, kid. But yeah, I can shimmy down an elevator cable if I have to. I'm not *that* old." Max moved forward until he saw a faint light straight ahead. "Are we through?"

"Yes," Letika whispered. "Your eyes should adjust to the low light soon. Now, since we don't know where the elevator is, we'll have to be careful in case—"

"In case the damn thing starts to move and we get crushed," Max mumbled.

"I wouldn't have said it that way because there are a lot of really little kids here, but yes."

Max groaned. He'd have to watch what he said. Kids were kids after all. "Sorry. Um, I'll go down first." That was the responsible thing to do, wasn't it?

"Okay. I'll follow you." She took his hand and led him to the opening in the wall. "Can you see well enough?"

He squinted and blinked a few times, until he could make out the elevator cables. One was only a few inches inside the shaft, which was pretty small, not the size of a regular elevator shaft. And the cables were thinner than he'd imagined. He wrapped his fingers around the cold metal and thought back to gym class when he had to climb a rope and ring a bell at the top. He was the only boy who did it and got a gold star on his progress report card. This was different though. This wasn't a rope and it certainly wasn't gym class. He drew in a breath. "Here I go."

Letika was close and kept her voice low, "Don't make any noise. I feel strong energy coming from the shaft and I can't tell if it's from that energy machine thing or if there are Ramtalans down there."

"Fabulous." Max sighed. Just what he wanted to hear. He'd probably slide down the cable and land in a nest of Ramtalans. "Okay, kid, wish me luck."

"Good luck, Mr. Jackson."

"Call me Max." He curled one leg around the cable until he was secure and slid downward. As he descended, a thought popped into his head. What if there were more floors below and he just kept going? He gripped tighter and stopped. What the hell was he doing? He should climb back up, get in the Lamborghini, smash through a wall, and find a way out. Without any weapons, he couldn't attack Lenox and if he was captured, the Ramtalans would likely kill him this time.

"Max," Letika called down the shaft. "Are you all right?"

"Yeah, yeah, I'm fine. Hey, what exactly is the plan here?" His hands were sweaty and he began sliding down the cable again.

"To find whatever is blocking our Alpha 2a." Letika was above him on the cable.

He looked up and saw her silhouette. "I said I'd go first to make sure it's safe. What do you think you're doing?"

"You're human, Max. I can protect you once I have my abilities back. Keep going."

She was right of course, but Max didn't like the idea of being protected by a kid. It stung. He loosened his grip and slid down faster until his feet smacked hard onto a floor. "Ouch. I made it." He let go of the cable and reached up to help Letika by lifting her down. "Okay, so now what?"

She smiled up at him. "See the elevator door? We need to pry it open."

There was enough light squeezing through a gap below the door for him to see, but he'd never pried one open before. Besides, what if they got it open only to have a herd of angry Ramtalans on the other side? Or worse, Lenox himself. Max still had the monitor in his head and Lenox was fond of making threats about making it explode.

He pointed upward. "We should go back up. This is a bad, bad idea."

"It's not. I didn't see anyone near the elevator, so we'll be okay." She cocked her head to the side. "Don't be afraid. I told you I can protect you when I get my abilities back."

Max wiped his brow. "Lenox will kill me, you know. Unless we get him first. Can you and your little gang defeat him?"

She placed her hand on the elevator door. "We're just kids, Max. We don't have the full potential of our abilities yet. Some of the kids up there don't even know much about being New Breeds. I'll make you a promise. I'll do everything I can to protect you. My Guardian taught me how to cast a protective veil of energy, but I can only do it for a few seconds. It'll be enough to deflect bullets or whatever."

"I must be insane." Max ran his fingers over the elevator door. There was no seam in the middle. "Most elevators open in the center and slide open."

"I think this is a freight elevator. It's one door that slides open from the side. See?" Letika pointed to the right side where there was a slight gap between the wall and the door.

"Okay, I get it, one door."

Max worked his fingers into the thin gap between the wall and the door and forced the door to move a little. To his surprise, it slid open fairly easily. He blocked it open with his body and motioned for Letika to go through, then he stepped out and let the door slide closed again. They were in a hallway with recessed lights in the ceiling.

With her finger on her lips, Letika pointed to the left. Max had to put his trust in her because she seemed to know what she was doing. He followed her down the hallway, around a corner and down another short hallway. She stopped in front of what looked like an operating room and placed her hands on the window.

"There's Alpha 2a flowing through this room. Wait here." Without giving him a chance to respond, she dashed into the room.

"Ah, sure, I'll just stand here so the aliens can find me," Max muttered. He hurried into the room after her. "So, did you find that energy machine thing?"

"No." Letika closed her eyes. "But the energy in here is giving me my abilities. I can feel it."

Max peered out the door. "Great, so now what? We high-tail it out of here?"

After a pause, Letika opened her eyes and sighed. "No. I have to find that machine, Max. It's taking our energy, not just blocking it. We can't survive long without our energy. I have a little more now, but the kids up top don't." She headed for the door. "I'm all turned around down here, I don't know where the machine is."

Part of him wanted to let her go on alone, but the other part wouldn't let him. "We'll find it. You know, you're just a kid, you can't go up against these Ramtalan freaks alone."

She stopped. "I'm one of those freaks, Max."

"No, you're not. You're okay. I mean it." He edged past her and stepped into the hallway. "Which way?"

"To the..." she stopped mid-sentence.

"What? What is it?" Max peered down the hall, but didn't see anything. "What's—"

"I hear voices. And...I feel energy, a lot of energy. It must be the machine!" She took off at a run.

"Damn alien kids." Max ran after her.

Chapter 57

Dave managed to drive all the way to Lake Elizabeth without attracting any attention and parked as close to the trees as possible for some concealment. Argus hopped out and scanned the area, instantly feeling a rush of guilt when he saw that the lake was dry with a huge chasm running through the center. If he really had triggered an earthquake, it must have affected the San Andreas fault. If that was the case, what other damage had it caused along the fault line?

"Argie?" Lola was beside him.

He turned and saw worry in her eyes. How could she still like anything about him? "Neb said I was dangerous, Lola. And he's right, I *am* dangerous. I'm...bad."

"Don't talk like that. You're not bad." She took his hand. "You saved me. A bad person wouldn't have done that."

"Ah, man." Dave walked toward the dry lake. "Is that giant hole from the earthquake?"

Argus didn't answer. He wandered off and leaned against a tree trunk, wondering how he was supposed to carry on now that his Malaris abilities were capable of causing earthquakes and killing people. Damn! He'd *killed* people. He'd be tried for murder and put on death row for sure, and he should be. Would he be the youngest guy ever sentenced to death? Of course, if Neb didn't give him his energy back, he'd die before he ever made it to trial.

There was only one way to redeem himself, and that was to defeat Lenox and keep the planet safe. But that wouldn't be easy now that Lenox knew what enhanced abilities he had. Argus sank down and sat on the soft soil. He, Tai, and Aunt Celeste had come to the lake to practice using their abilities. It seemed so long ago. That was a time when he actually dared think he could have a life.

He picked up a rock and heaved it through the underbrush in anger. It flew so fast he lost its flight path until it clunked against a tree. A moment later, the distinct cracking sound of a tree snapping in half made him flinch. He shouldn't be around Lola, or Dave. What if he accidentally hurt them? He was too strong and powerful now to be trusted around anyone.

"Argie? Are you all right?"

"Yeah!" he called back.

Next, Dave shouted, "Hey, man, get out here and look at this!"

What now? Argus jumped up and hurried to the parking lot. "Look at what?"

Dave pointed to the sky. "What is that?"

Argus knew right away what Dave was pointing at. A blue cloud, high in the sky, with firework-like sparks inside it, was moving north, growing bigger and bigger. He smiled. "Ramtalans. Those are pure-form Ramtalans."

"Shit." Dave ran to the van.

"No, Dave, it's good. They're reinforcements coming to help my Aunt. They're the good guys." Argus waved out of habit, even though he knew they couldn't see him.

"Argie, is this the beginning of a war?" Lola wove her fingers through his. "Is my mom going to be okay?"

He glanced at her. "Where is she?"

"With Detective DeAlba. She's kind of been going out with him. He's nice. I mean, he's nice to us, I know he arrested you—"

Argus gave a slight laugh. "Yeah, he did, but he's a decent guy. I'm glad you're mom found someone."

Lola nodded and tightened her grip. "Me too."

"Hey, you two!" Dave ran to them. "This isn't exactly the time for date night. That cloud's stopped."

"Stopped?" Argus looked up. Sure enough, the cloud wasn't moving anymore and was hovering over the lake. It was still high, but why wasn't it heading to Labrador? "Ah, that's weird. Let's get in the van."

He helped Lola inside. Dave got into the driver's seat and drummed his hands on the dash, while Argus watched the sky.

"Argus...we should maybe go somewhere else. I don't want to be here," Dave's voice cracked. "I really don't want to be here."

"Yeah, same with me, Argie. What if they want you to fight with them? You could get hurt. Why don't we all go to your house and we can see if it was damaged?"

"No. You have to stay with me. I can't leave here because I told Tai I'd be here, and I can't leave *you*."

The Protector feelings were overpowering. It really was a burden, just like Neb said. And if Lola was right, the Ramtalans might have sensed him and would want him to band with them, and he would, gladly, if he didn't have Lola and Dave with him. Right now, though, it was his responsibility to protect them and wait for Tai.

"Argie, you're acting weird and your skin is turning blue. Are you all right?" Lola put her hand on his cheek. "Talk to me."

He pulled her to him. "I'm a mess, Lola. This isn't how I imagined my life. You're the only positive thing I have, but every second I'm with you, I put you at risk. I have to get rid of Lenox and he's my father. Did you know he killed my mother? Everything's screwed up. My aunt isn't really my aunt and Neb stole my energy and unless I get it back, I'll die. I went through this thing called a phase-shift that make me have these crazy abilities and makes my skin turn blue. I thought it was back to normal, but I guess not. I'm not a New Breed or a Ramtalan or a Malaris. I'm all three." The words tumbled out and he couldn't stop. "I caused the earthquake and when I took Ari's energy, it killed him. He's my...was my half-brother. I hate myself, Lola, I really do."

"Oh, my God, Argie. I had no idea...none of this is your fault. Seriously, none of it. You didn't know Lenox was your father and the Ramtalans are responsible for everything you've been put through. Underneath it all, you're still you and that's who I love. I'll always love you no matter what happens." Lola got on her tiptoes and kissed him. "I *love* you."

The words sank into his skin and settled there. He shivered. "I love...you, too." His whole body trembled.

"You're shaking." Lola wrapped her arms around him in a tight embrace. "Are you cold?"

It was hot out, yet he kept trembling. "No, I'm not. It's something else. I have to sit down." His legs buckled and he collapsed to the ground. Above him, the blue cloud descended. As it got closer, he could see individual, smaller blue clouds sparking inside the large one. There were too many to count. "Lola, take Dave and go. I don't think I can protect you anymore. Get as far away from here as possible."

"Absolutely not." Lola knelt by him and cradled his head in her lap. "I'm ready for whatever comes next. If those Ramtalans want you to fight, then they'll have to give you your energy back, won't they? And then, once you have it, you can shift wherever you want."

Argus nodded slightly, feeling weak and sick. "They better hurry, because I don't think I'll last much longer."

Dave rushed over and knelt beside Lola. "Argus, where's your brother? And your aunt? Why don't they come here and help you? Can I do anything?"

Argus closed his eyes. "Aunt Celeste must still be fighting Lenox or she'd be here with Tai. Dave, take Lola away from here. I don't want either of you in the line of fire. Those Ramtalans in the cloud might think you're the enemy or something. I'm sure they know I'm Lenox's son."

"So what?" Lola smoothed his hair. "You can tell them you're not with Lenox and Aunt Celeste is your Guardian. They'll understand."

Argus opened his eyes. "Maybe."

A sudden ground-shaking boom echoed around the lake and part of the blue cloud dissipated. In a flash, five pure-form Ramtalans—no host bodies, just blue ghost-like figures—appeared in the parking lot, with one, taller than the others, standing in front. The remaining cloud moved away.

"So, you say you are not standing with Argustine Lenox?" the one in front asked.

Lola got to her feet. "That's right, he's not. Don't hurt us, we're all on your side."

The Ramtalan came closer. "You are Argus Dachel?"

With a nod, Argus struggled to sit up. "My Guardian is Celeste Apodaka. She's fighting with Lenox underneath the Citadel and might even have him imprisoned by now. I need help. Nebulon took my energy and I desperately need more Alpha 2a."

"Ah." The Ramtalan motioned to the others behind him. "I am Condrulon and we are Argustine Lenox's supporters. I appreciate the information about our beloved leader. Consider yourselves our prisoners."

Chapter 58

As Max followed Letika through the corridors, he hoped she wasn't leading him into a trap. She wasn't very cautious. Of course, she was just a kid and at that same age, he'd been damn near the same. The voices became louder and Max thought he recognized Neb's condescending tone above the others, coming from a room up ahead.

He grabbed Letika by the shoulder and stopped her. "Wait. If the machine you're looking for is in that room, we're screwed. I know one of the guys in there and he's an ass. He'll kill me without giving it a thought."

She stared at him. "Then stay here and I'll go. I need my abilities."

"No." Max sighed. Damn kid. "You wait here and I'll go ahead and check things out. Okay?" He drew in a breath, but it didn't calm him down at all. His heart beat a mile a minute and sweat trickled down his back.

Letika nodded. "All right, but come right back if there's trouble. And tell me if you see the machine. It was cylindrical with wire mesh all around it. We're close."

"Sure will." Max gave her a pat on the arm and skulked down the corridor to the room. There wasn't a door, so he pressed himself against the wall outside the room and listened. Sure enough, it was Neb's voice he'd heard.

Neb shouted, "This is for putting me through hell!"

There was a thump and a grunt.

Max's curiosity got the better of him and he peeked in to see Lenox crumpled on the ground, like he'd been thrown against the far wall. Neb had his hands raised, as did Celeste, but Neb turned around.

With a frown, Neb noticed Max. "How in the world are you here?"

Max was about to answer when Celeste spoke, "It doesn't matter, Neb. We have more important things to worry about right now."

In the span of a heartbeat, a startling flash of red filled the room. Lenox vanished and a moment later, Letika screamed.

"Letika!" Max ignored Neb and Celeste and ran from the room. "Letika!"

He found her lying on the floor, gasping for breath. Her skin was pale and her whole body trembled. "Max..."

"What happened, Letika? Did Lenox do something? He was in that room and then he disappeared." Max felt her forehead. Cold.

Neb came and knelt down. "Her Alpha 2a is gone. Lenox must have taken it to heal himself. Damn you, Jackson. If you hadn't come, Celeste and I wouldn't have been distracted. Because of you, Lenox is gone."

Bastard! Max wanted to pound someone. Neb would do. He balled his fists. "Don't just stand there blaming me, Neb, do something. There're a bunch of other New Breeds in a room above here and Lenox has a machine taking their energy. Fix Letika first and then do what you're supposed to do and save the rest of the kids." He lashed out with a fist.

Neb grabbed Max's hand, stood, and lifted him off the ground by the front of his shirt. "Do what I'm supposed to do? I'm supposed to kill Lenox. And I would have if you hadn't interfered. I can't do anything for this girl, she's too far gone and I can't afford to donate anymore energy. I just expended a whole lot on Lenox."

In a flash, Celeste appeared and lifted Letika into her arms. "There's a healing room close by. I'll try to get her help. Neb, find Lenox." She ran off down the corridor.

"Put me down." Max struggled. "I should go and be with Letika."

Neb let go. "You're not leaving my sight. I should end you right here and now."

"Yeah? Then why don't you?" Max knew challenging hot-head Neb wasn't a good idea, but he was fed up. "Either kill me or let me show you where the kids are."

"If you're lying, I will rip your head off your shoulders." Neb's eyes were bright blue.

"I know you will. Follow me." Max led the way back to the elevator shaft and pointed up. "There's a big room up there filled with New Breeds. They're scared. I don't know what Lenox wants with them."

"Their energy." Neb stepped into the shaft. "He wants to collect their energy to use to destroy the planet. Can you climb up those cables?"

Max gave a nod. "Yeah, sure. I climbed down, didn't I? Just go and make sure the kids are okay. They're good kids, Neb, and don't deserve to be dragged into this."

"Wow. Are my ears playing tricks on me? Did I really hear Max Jackson, AURA asshole extraordinaire, saying New Breeds were good?"

"Smart ass. Go and help them."

Neb disappeared and Max dashed into the shaft, gripped a cable and painfully inched his way up. He slipped a few times and lost headway, but eventually, he made it. The room was eerily silent; not a whisper or footstep anywhere. He glanced back down the shaft and considered going down to make sure Letika was all right, but realized Celeste would do everything she could to save her. He'd only be in the way. Besides, there were more kids that needed his help.

"Neb," Max whispered. "Where the hell are you?"

"Stay where you are, Max," Neb said in a stern voice.

"The hell I will." Max started off in the direction of Neb's voice, going blind in the dark.

"Don't come over here, Max. I mean it." Neb appeared in front of him, his blue eyes giving off light to see. "Why can't you ever listen?"

"What's going on?" Max swallowed. "Tell me the truth." He had a feeling he knew. "Neb?"

Neb put his hands on Max's shoulders, not in a hostile way, but more as a comfort. "They're all...they're gone, Max."

"Gone? To where? Where did he take them?"

"No, Max. They're dead. Every single one of them. Lenox drained them all." Neb turned away with his head drooped.

"Did you say...?" Max couldn't finish the sentence. He tried to swallow a lump in his throat, but it wouldn't budge. "You're wrong." Lenox wouldn't kill a bunch of innocent kids. What kind of monster would do a thing like that? "I tried to get to the machine Lenox wanted to use. Letika found it and...if you're fucking with me, this isn't funny."

Neb spun around, his eyes burning. "No, it's not!" His voice lowered to a whisper, "Celeste still has some concealed, but we've lost most of them. If only we could have disabled that machine. Now get out of my sight, Max, before I lose it completely."

Backing away, Max's stomach clenched tight and he ground his teeth. "Find Lenox. Tear him apart."

"That's too good for him." Neb vanished in a flash of blue.

How could the little kids be dead? Did Lenox make them suffer? They'd never have the chance to grow up. He let out a scream and collapsed onto the floor. If it was the last thing he ever did, he'd make sure no more kids died at the hands of Lenox. Whatever it took, that was the promise he'd keep. He'd risk everything. The New Breeds were innocent. Maybe even the Dachel boys were. Could he have made a mistake by wanting them dead and autopsied? It was hard to think he'd made a judgmental error, yet, his heart ached for the kids, especially Letika. He drew in a breath and knew he'd willingly give his own life to save them.

Chapter 59

Argus reached for Lola's hand and pulled himself to his feet, his knees threatening to give out any second. The Ramtalans watched his every move. What had made him think anything would go his way? He should have known better, and now he'd once again put Lola and Dave in danger.

He faced Condrulon. "These are my friends and they're humans. Lenox said he wouldn't hurt any of my friends."

Condrulon approached until he was less than two feet away. "I am not Argustine. I have no such arrangement with you."

Lola squeezed Argus's hand. He glanced at her and moved in front. "I'm Lenox's son. You hurt me or my friends and you'll have to answer directly to him."

In an instant, Condrulon had Argus by the throat. "You are not exactly an obedient son. I doubt seriously that Argustine would care if a few humans were removed from existence as punishment for your bad behavior." He stared into Argus's eyes. "Your energy is dissipating. You are weak, useless." He dropped Argus. "I cannot understand why Argustine would want such a pathetic specimen as you. But, I will personally deliver you to him, once we have liberated him of course. The rest of our warriors are on their way to the Citadel."

Argus collapsed. There wasn't any time to waste, he had to do something. He focused on the Malaris symbols dancing around in his head, but he still couldn't make sense of them. Again, he tried and poured every ounce of energy he had into focusing on them. After a few seconds, they arranged themselves.

Pure-form Alpha 2a is available. Seize it to restore your own.

How could he seize a Ramtalan's Alpha 2a? Neb had donated some to him, but Condrulon certainly wouldn't do that. But what if there was a way to take it? Lenox had said something back at the Citadel chamber, but what was it?

You have the ability to capture energy.

Yes, that was it. Before he caused the earthquake, he'd taken energy from Aunt Celeste's veil. The symbols suddenly scrambled. How do I capture energy? Tell me. It was no use, he lost his concentration and the symbols were gone.

"Argie, are you all right?" Lola was beside him. "Your skin's getting bluer. Say something."

The Ramtalans stood over Argus, making him feel small.

A brilliant red flash lit up the lake and a second later, Lenox stood at the shoreline. Argus wanted to charge at him and fire a multitude of bursts at him, but there was no way. "Lola, I'm going to try to negotiate with Lenox for your release. And Dave's. It's all I can do right now."

"I won't leave you." She stood and waved her arms. "Lenox! Your son is dying! Help him. These Ramtalans want him to die."

"What are you doing, Lola? Don't get involved."

Lenox immediately fired a burst at Condrulon. "You dare to disobey my orders that my sons are not to be touched?" His voice boomed.

After recovering, Condrulon lowered his head. "I am your obedient servant, Argustine. I did not know this boy was your son."

"Liar!" shouted Lola. "He knew."

Lenox strode past Condrulon, giving him a sideways glance as he passed, and came to Argus. "Aridesian is dead, is he not?"

With a nod, Argus got to his feet. "I didn't know he'd die. I never would have—"

"I know you would not." Lenox sighed. "You are the most powerful being on the planet, yet your emotions cloud your judgment. What am I to do with you?" He touched Argus on the cheek. "Do you know why your skin reacts to your energy level?"

Argus pulled away. "No."

Lenox continued, "Your Zeta 40 and Alpha 2a work in conjunction with one another, as you know, but as either level changes, it affects your body. Ramtalans emit blue, the color of Alpha 2a, while Malaris have a red pigment that arises from the Zeta 40."

"But I'm blue." Argus watched Condrulon over Lenox's shoulder.

"Do not concern yourself with Condrulon." Lenox continued, "That is because Nebulon has drained your Alpha 2a and blocked your Zeta 40. After the phase-shift, you emitted Alpha 2a as your body accepted the new configuration. Now, the remnant Alpha 2a within your DNA, the small part that cannot be removed, is dissipating, emitting the blue as it does. When Ramtalans use their Alpha 2a, blue is emitted in eye color or skin color. Soon, you will have no Alpha 2a at all. I wish to prevent this."

"Yeah, well, so do I. But how?" Argus wobbled, but caught himself. "I don't think I can hang on much longer."

"You need an infusion of pure-form Alpha 2a, my son. It will heal you sufficiently until I locate your own Alpha 2a." Lenox turned and motioned to Condrulon to come forward.

Argus said softly, "That's what the symbols told me."

"What did you say?" Lenox turned and put his hand up to tell Condrulon to stay where he was. "You are still understanding the symbols?"

"I was, but not now." Argus leaned on Lola for support when she crooked her arm through his.

"That is incredible. The phase-shift has imbued you with unlimited Malaris skills."

Argus's head spun and the ground seemed to sway. "What does that mean?"

"This is not the place to discuss—"

Argus interrupted, "Tell me right now. I need to know everything."

Lenox glanced around. "You are simply delaying the inevitable war, Argus."

"Tell me."

"Fine. A Malaris has the capability of drawing on ideas and knowledge from a type of collective storage system within the DNA, containing all Malaris knowledge. The control center of the ship is an example. That is in your mind, but it is also real. You create the symbols in response to a question, subconscious or conscious. Your mind acts like what humans call a computer. You input information and your brain develops the answer. With your Zeta 40 blocked, I did not think you could do this, but you have proved how advanced you are. Now, if that satisfies you, I have urgent matters at hand, namely, to save your life." Lenox turned away.

Argus was even more flustered now. His brain, a computer? How was that possible? And what exactly did it mean? Could he ever be normal again? "Where's Aunt Celeste? How did you get away from her?"

"Oh," Lenox chuckled, still facing the Ramtalans. "That AURA agent, Max Jackson, blundered into the collection chamber with a New Breed in tow. His stupidity allowed me my escape. I was presented with an opportunity, and I took it."

Argus swallowed. "You killed him? And Aunt Celeste?"

"No. But now I have enough Alpha 2a to continue with my plan."

What did that mean? Argus stumbled forward and got in front of Lenox. "Where did you get the energy?"

"It is not important. Condrulon!" Lenox stepped aside and waited until Condrulon approached. "My son is ill and requires an infusion of pure-form Alpha 2a. You will be his donor."

"Excuse me, Argustine? I will not donate anything to anyone. I am a soldier and I am prepared to fight alongside you, but I will not be weakened by..."

A twinge in his gut made Argus double over. The symbols swirled in his head and quickly arranged themselves in columns.

> *You are dying. Seize Condrulon's Alpha 2a. Touch him and feel his energy flow into you.*

The thought of dying and leaving Lola and Dave alone with Lenox was unacceptable. He was a Protector and he simply couldn't allow them to be in danger. He straightened, stepped forward and grabbed Condrulon's arm. He'd never touched a pure-form before. Condrulon's skin—warm and soft—rippled under his hand, and immediately, a surge of energy flowed into Argus, like water filling a cup. No more pain. Condrulon bellowed and Argus let go.

Right away, he knew his full abilities were back. Even his Zeta 40 was unblocked. He took a few breaths, turned, and checked to make sure Lola and Dave were all right. They were huddled together. "It'll be okay now, Lola," he said. "He looked at his hands. The blue coloring was gone.

"Argie," Lola whispered, pointing at the ground behind him.

Condrulon was lying on his back, his white eyes staring up at the sky. He wasn't moving. The other Ramtalans backed away, but Lenox had a smile on his face.

"What did I do?" Argus went to Condrulon. "Lenox, what did I do?"

With his smile never fading, Lenox placed his hand on Argus's shoulder. "You captured his energy. His sacrifice will be remembered. And your greatness will be lauded." He squeezed Argus's shoulder. "But do not for a moment think you are stronger than me. You have borrowed Alpha 2a and still require your own to be returned. I have more Malaris in me than you do and with your scant human DNA polluting your cells, you are no match."

Argus looked down at Condrulon's motionless body and then to Lola. "You can't be around me, Lola. Take Dave and go." He glared at Lenox. "Let my friends leave. You promised me before that you wouldn't hurt them."

"And I will not." Lenox turned to Lola and Dave. "You are free to leave. Now!"

Lola flinched and shook her head. "I'm not leaving you, Argie. I can't."

With his hand raised to Lola, Lenox repeated, "You are free to leave. However, if you do not..."

Argus ran to her. "You have to go. There's going to be a war. I'm okay now." He leaned close to her ear and lowered his voice, "I can take on Lenox. I know I can. And I'm sure Aunt Celeste and Neb will get here with Tai soon. Please, go. For me. I can't protect you if I'm fighting and I can't fight if I'm protecting you."

"But..." She embraced him and kissed him on the lips. "Don't get hurt. I swear to you, if you get hurt—"

"I know, I know, you'll make me pay for it." He smiled and kissed her back. "Dave, take Lola to her mom."

With a nod, Dave pointed to the van. "Come on, Lola. Man, I wish I could stay and help, but, you know, with this limp." He gave a half-hearted shrug and a lopsided smile.

Argus smiled back. "If not for that limp. You'll help me by getting as far away from here as you can." He gave Lola another kiss and went with her to the van. "Whatever happens here today, promise me you'll both do your best to have wonderful lives."

Lola wiped her eyes. "What do you mean? You sound like you're going die. Don't you dare talk like that."

"Argus!" Lenox shouted.

"I have to go." Argus held Lola tight for a moment, taking in everything he loved about her, before letting her go. "I love you. And Dave, you'll always be my best friend."

"Yeah." Dave sniffed. "Same here, man."

Argus stood back as Lola and Dave got into the van and sped off, Lola hanging out the window waving. When they were on the main road, he turned to Lenox.

He threw his arms in the air. "Now what?"

"Now we implement my plan, with you at my side. I do not need Aridesian as you will easily replace him. " Lenox smiled and pointed to the sky. "My compatriots are on their way to the Citadel, but we will wait here. I cannot risk any harm coming to you."

"Great." Argus paced while he watched the van drive around a bend. With any luck, Aunt Celeste and Neb would get to the lake before the other Invaders made it to the Citadel. Without all of his Invader friends, Lenox would only have the four that were still standing with him.

"Argus." Lenox walked to him. "I know what you think of me, but you must understand my position. I developed the New Breed program to save our people, yet Jampara petitioned to have me exiled when he found out I had Malaris Zeta 40. He seized all of my wealth and property and destroyed my name. He is the one who placed my father, your grandfather, in prison and put him to death. All of Ramtala turned against me, calling me a traitor. How would you react to a situation such as that?"

A chill ran through Argus. Jampara had his grandfather killed. The hatred of the Malaris didn't sit well, especially since Argus was partially

Malaris now, too. All of the killing, for what? Fear? Maybe if everyone could have sat down and worked out their differences it would have been different. He looked at Lenox, his father, and felt a tugging inside, or maybe not exactly a tug, but a longing to be with his real family. But Lenox had killed his mother.

Argus shook his head. "I don't know what I'd do, but I certainly wouldn't kill the New Breeds and humans, or the Settler Ramtalans at the Citadel. Don't you see, it's the same for me. I'm your son and Ramtala is against me because of it. But I'm not going to sink to your level. I won't kill innocent kids and if I've become a monster because of the phase-shift and the inter-phase, then I want all of my energy gone."

"You don't mean that, son."

Argus glanced at the ground. "I do. I'd rather die than help you. Where's your compassion?" He glared at Lenox. "The New Breeds, your New Breeds, haven't done a damn thing to you. Neither have the humans. Leave us all alone."

Lenox seemed to think for a moment, his eyes softly glowing red. "I am not as forgiving as you, my son. I will not stop until Jampara is prone before me. I have already lost one son because of him and I will not lose you or Tai."

Anger built up inside Argus. "If you keep fighting, we'll all die. Ari gave his life so I could get away and stop you. He realized too late that what you're doing is wrong."

"And how did that work out, son? He is dead and I am still standing." Lenox's eyes flashed bright red and he stared up at the sky. "Prepare for battle."

"Battle?" Argus scanned the sky but didn't see anything.

"Not you, my son. You will only be in the way." Lenox immediately cast a veil over Argus. "You will be safe now, but do not try to escape my veil. I have the Alpha 2a of hundreds of New Breeds inside me. Not even Celeste can break through that veil. Once I win this war and defeat the Settlers, I will free you and you *will* obey me."

As soon as Lenox finished the sentence, the sky darkened and the ground rumbled. Argus concentrated and tried to bring the Malaris symbols into focus, but they were fuzzy and jerking all over the place. The veil interfered and he couldn't break through.

Everything calmed down for a few seconds and then a series of photometric pulses exploded over the lake and into some of the trees. The sky turned a cloudy blue and Aunt Celeste appeared across the parking lot with Neb at the opposite end. Each started firing pulses at Lenox, but he was quick and shifted before he was hit.

"Aunt Celeste!" Argus shouted. He pushed against the veil, but it didn't budge.

She continued firing at Lenox's accomplices. "Are you hurt, Argus?"

"No, I'm okay. Get me out of this veil." He still couldn't focus on the symbols. "I'm blocked."

Neb shifted and reappeared next to Argus. "The veil's too strong." He used both hands to fire at one of the Invaders and didn't stop until the Invader was on the ground either injured or dead. Neb placed his hands on the veil. "My energy's draining fast with all of this firing. Lenox made this veil from more Alpha 2a than I've ever felt. And he's mixed it with Zeta 40. Nothing I can do, Argus. In all honesty, I think this is the best place for you right now."

"Neb, give me back my Zeta 40!" Argus shoved his palms against the veil. Nothing. He concentrated on the Alpha 2a, but he couldn't capture any of the energy. "You still don't trust me?"

Neb paused for a moment. "No, I don't. But your brother does." He motioned to the sky.

Coming straight down toward the lake was the XTRA-A1, going at such a fast speed that a condensation trail streamed from behind. Argus held his breath, waiting for Tai to impact, but at the last moment, the ship pulled out, spun around and faced the parking lot.

Sucking in a deep breath, Argus shook his head. "He almost killed himself," he mumbled.

Neb whispered, "It was a distraction. The Invaders were watching, just like you were. That gave our people enough time to get into position."

What was he talking about? It was just him and Aunt Celeste. "Where—?"

"Everywhere." Neb's eyes glowed brightly. "Hang tight, we're about to bring a firestorm to Palmdale."

"But Lenox..." Argus didn't see Lenox anywhere.

With a smirk, Neb winked. "Lenox will come back. I promise you that."

The XTRA-A1 moved slowly to the parking lot and hovered a few feet off the ground. Argus wanted to see Tai to make sure he was okay, but the window shutter was closed. Why wasn't anyone doing anything? Tai could get shot down any second if the Invaders decided to aim at him.

"Neb, Tai—"

"Tai's fine, don't worry about him." Neb turned and hurried to Aunt Celeste.

Before Argus had the chance to say another word, multiple blinding blue flashes made him squeeze his eyes shut. When he opened his eyes, the parking lot and the dry lake bed were crowded with pure-forms and Settlers. Everywhere he looked, he saw Ramtalans. The XTRA-A1 gained in altitude and settled into another hover at least fifty feet up. Argus couldn't stand it any longer and decided to try again to break the veil. He pushed his hands against it and concentrated on the Malaris symbols. This time, they aligned themselves in columns, but they didn't make any sense.

"Neb!" Argus called out. "You can't leave me here!"

When Neb was beside Aunt Celeste, they both began firing pulses at the Invaders, but after a moment, Aunt Celeste switched and started shooting a strange, pale yellow ribbon-like material at the closest Invader. The material enveloped him and compressed inward. It reminded Argus of the trap Neb had at Acoma. As the material shrunk, the Invader screamed out only once and then there was nothing. The ribbon vanished completely with the Invader. Aunt Celeste repeated the same thing again and again, taking out Invader after Invader while Neb continued firing pulses.

The other Settlers were either firing pulses or casting energy veils, but nobody did what Aunt Celeste did. All Argus could do was watch and hope for the best. Both Invaders and Settlers fell, wounded or dead. Argus collapsed to the ground, sick to his stomach.

He still couldn't understand why Neb thought Lenox would come back. Why would he? He'd be walking straight into a war zone. After maybe ten minutes of constant fighting, another blue flash lit up the parking lot. Galena had arrived. But she wasn't alone. She had Max Jackson with her.

Chapter 60

Argus glared at Max. What was he doing in a battle zone? He was obviously with the Invaders, but unless Galena protected him with a veil, he'd be killed in seconds by the Settlers.

Once again, Argus tried to get the Malaris symbols to work, but it was hopeless. He watched the XTRA-A1 slowly cruise sideways, toward where Galena stood. Tai had something planned, but what? Taking on Galena was not only risky, but stupid.

"Aunt Celeste! What's Tai doing?" called Argus. From within the veil, he waved his arms around to get her attention.

It worked, but she was obviously not happy about the distraction. "Not now, Argus!"

Damn it, she didn't want to hear anything he had to say. He concentrated on Tai, but he couldn't initiate a shift. There was only one thing to do. He had to get Lenox to remove the veil. "Lenox, where are you? I need you," he said softly.

Nothing.

He was about to try again, when his attention was drawn to the XTRA-A1. It descended, took a few direct hits from the Invaders and Galena herself, but apparently wasn't damaged. It continued to descend until it was only a foot off the ground. Then a burst of blue light shot out from it and Max's boss, Stone, stood to the side of the ship. How did he shift? Why would Tai bring Stone into the middle of the battle?

Max had a look of shock on his face and Galena turned to him and said something too quiet for Argus to understand. Galena raised her hands, prepared to fire at Stone, but Max interfered and pushed her arms down.

"You can't kill him, Galena, he's the AURA chief. Another AURA agent should take care of that," Max said. "Leave him to me."

Instead of firing on him, Galena turned to another Settler and engaged him. Max looked over at Argus, took off, and ran to him.

Max reached out, but his hand hit the veil. "I see you're hiding from the action like the coward I knew you were. Where's your asshole brother?"

"You're calling my brother an asshole? You're working with Galena and the Invaders. How can you support Lenox?" Argus bumped against the veil as he tried to grab Max around the throat.

"I don't support anybody except my fellow humans. I'm a damn prisoner, you moron." He lowered his voice, "Galena thinks Lenox has me controlled by that monitor in my noggin. Trust me, he doesn't. I'm not controlled like Gretchen is. And believe me, I want that piece of shit Lenox drawn and quartered for what he's done."

Argus glared. "And what makes Galena think you're controlled?"

With a grunt, Max glanced at Galena and back again to Argus. "Because I told her. She would have killed me otherwise. She thinks I'm helping them. Now, if you'll excuse me, I have to go kick the shit out of my boss."

"I don't think he'll like that, Max."

Max laughed. "Nope, don't think he will. But this might be my last chance to show him exactly how I feel about him."

"Why *did* you save him from Galena?" Argus couldn't figure Max out. He was a heartless dick, yet he saved the boss he loathed from getting killed.

"Look, kid, I don't care if you aliens kill each other, but I'll be damned if I stand by and let you kill humans. Got it? Stone is human, sort of, and neither you nor Lenox are going to kill him. This is my planet and none of you are welcome here. Especially your *daddy*. He's the biggest dick of them all. He killed hundreds of kids, New Breeds."

Argus stared down at the ground. Hundreds of New Breeds dead because of Lenox? Could he ever be stopped. "I don't know what to say. Don't ever think I'm like Lenox."

It was hard to know what to do or who to trust or believe. He'd wanted to kill Lenox before, but now, he wasn't so sure. Lenox, Galena, and Tai were the only family he had left. Although Aunt Celeste was more like family than either Galena or Lenox. And then there was Lola. No matter what, he had to make sure she was safe. It was confusing and complicated.

"Max," Argus said quietly, "I'm stuck in here. Believe it or not, I'm on your side. I want the Invaders off this planet as much as you do. When we take care of them, we can talk about the New Breeds—"

Max interrupted, "Don't you dare talk about the New Breeds! Leave them out of this." His cheeks flushed.

So Max had suddenly changed his opinion. Why?

"Okay, okay." Argus flinched when the area lit up with a series of photometric bursts going in all directions. "You'd better be careful, Max, this is getting crazy. All it takes is one lethal burst and you're dead."

"I can handle myself. Now, if you'll excuse me, my boss is overdue for an ass-kicking." Max jogged away and stopped in front of Stone.

All Argus could do was watch. Without warning, Max balled up his fist and let it fly. He landed a direct hit to Stone's jaw, but Stone didn't react. Max slugged him again and again, and like before, Stone didn't move.

"What the hell!" Max shouted, shaking his hand. "I almost broke my damn hand on your face."

Stone gave Max a shove out of the way and strode toward Argus. "Argus, I will free you from the veil if you make a solemn promise that you will not use your new abilities."

"What?" Argus stared at Stone. "How can you get rid of the veil? You're not making sense."

Stone lowered his voice, "Argus, it is me, Commander Jampara. I have taken this as my host body, except I have not yet completed the transition. This is to keep my identity undetectable by Lenox, until I wish him to see me."

It had to be a trick. Argus knew how deceitful Stone was. "Liar."

"I do not lie."

Stone's eyes glowed blue.

"Whoa." Argus looked around. "You really are the Commander?"

"Indeed I am. Do you promise not to use your abilities? I cannot have you using those enhanced Malaris abilities as you might jeopardize our position."

"But I can help." Argus felt weird talking to the Commander in Stone's body. "How are you taking Stone as a host body? I thought you could only do that if the host gives you permission. Did you kill him? I can't believe you—"

"I did not kill him. Stone was mortally wounded in Labrador. By taking him as a host, his body will live on. He agreed to my proposition with the caveat that I inform his daughter what happened to him." The Commander placed his hand on the veil. "Make me a promise, Argus. I will return your Zeta 40. When Lenox arrives, if you are still within the veil, he is able to destroy you and we cannot stop him. I do not wish that."

Argus swallowed. "Well, neither do I. Okay, fine, I agree not to use my abilities. How can you break the veil? Lenox said nobody could."

"I understand how Zeta 40 works and I know the Malaris mind. One of my abilities is to manipulate and alter genetic code. I can destroy Malaris and their technology, but it uses a tremendous amount of my energy."

Argus felt cold. "So you can kill me?"

"But I will not."

With a nod, Argus looked up as the XTRA-A1 moved away, back over the dry lake. "What's Tai doing?" Tai shouldn't even be involved. That familiar Protector feeling came rushing back. Suppressing it was imperative.

"He is preparing to fire on Lenox."

Did Tai realize how dangerous that was? "Commander, once you break the veil, can I go and be with Tai in the ship? I don't want him to be alone. Lenox can attack the ship. I can help, with my Zeta 40."

The Commander nodded and his eyes flashed blue. "I will allow you to protect Tai and the XTRA-A1, but not to use Zeta 40 for anything else. Prepare."

Prepare for what? Wasn't the veil simply going to disappear? Argus moved back as far as he could, which was only about a foot and waited. With both hands on the veil, sparks flew from the Commanders fingers, forming a web of blue light all over the veil. As soon as the web covered the veil completely, Argus couldn't breathe. There was no air at all. His lungs ached, crying for air. After a few seconds, the veil vanished and the Commander's entire body glowed bright blue. Air rushed into Argus's lungs and he drew in a huge breath.

He stepped back. "You are free and the host body transition is complete. Stone is no more."

Argus nodded, but gasped when Stone's body began to change. His hair went blond and he grew about a foot in height. Even the facial features softened. "Wow. I've never seen that before."

The Commander nodded and worked his neck. "It feels strange to be in a host body once again. I prefer to remain in pure-form, it is less restrictive. Now, Argus, abide by your promise."

"I will." Argus focused on the XTRA-A1, but the ground shook violently and broke his concentration. "What's that?"

"Lenox has arrived as I knew he would once I transitioned. His desire to kill me will be his undoing." The Commander dashed toward Aunt Celeste and Neb, leaving Argus standing alone.

Lenox appeared in the middle of the parking lot, not more than twenty feet or so from the Commander. Argus wanted to be with Tai, but he knew he could help out if he stayed. He could draw Lenox away from everyone so Tai could get a clean shot. Then again, maybe he could find a way to capture Lenox so he wouldn't get killed. If Tai killed their father, he'd have to carry that weight with him his whole life.

"Jampara!" Lenox shouted. "You cannot escape. I am too powerful."

Argus realized he only had a few seconds before the Commander figured out that he hadn't gone to the XTRA-A1, so he ran into the bushes and found a vantage point where he was concealed. He concentrated on the Malaris symbols until they came into focus.

"I have to know how to trap Lenox without killing him."

The symbols spun around wildly, finally arranging themselves into columns.

You must seize all of his Zeta 40.

"I can't do that, he'll die. He needs his Zeta 40 and his Alpha 2a." Argus peered out as a fire-fight started up again between the Settler Ramtalans and the Invaders. Lenox concentrated his attack on the Commander, while Galena took on Aunt Celeste and Neb.

You must seize all of Argustine Lenox's energy.

"No. I can't. I said I don't want to kill him."

He cannot survive with as much energy as he now possesses. He will die no matter what you do or do not do.

"What? That can't be true. Out of everyone, he'd know if he was going to die. There has to be another way to..."

Capture his energy by using a phase-shift. As he enters the phase, both yours and his energies will comingle. Seize his energy at that moment and release the phase-shift.

"But that means I'll have all of his energy plus mine. Won't *I* die with all of that? We'll both end up dead."

Argus flinched when a photometric burst slammed into one of the trees near him. Through an opening in the tree canopy, he saw the XTRA-A1 still over the dry lake, facing the parking lot. Evidently Tai didn't have a clear shot at Lenox. But he would soon enough.

"Answer me. Won't I die as well as Lenox?"

You will not. Argustine Lenox will. Your first phase-shift altered your DNA, permitting you to capture and store an unlimited amount of Zeta 40 and Alpha 2a energy. You are a species unknown previously. You can defeat Argustine Lenox by initiating a phase-shift.

"But I told you, I don't want him to die. Find another way."

While the symbols moved and rearranged themselves, Argus watched in horror as Aunt Celeste took a direct hit from an Invader. She was crumpled on the ground, but right away Neb stood in front of her and fired continuously until the Invader fell to the ground.

The symbols slowed down and formed a circle, something Argus hadn't seen before. At first he didn't know what they meant, but after a moment, he understood the meaning. The symbols told him to cast a veil over Lenox and then perform a phase-shift from inside the veil. Argus could do a molecular shift to get in and then when he did the phase-shift, Lenox's energy would be transferred, but he could consciously allow a small trace of Zeta 40 and Alpha 2a to stay in Lenox's DNA. They would both survive, and Lenox would have no abilities. It was the perfect solution.

"That's what I wanted!" he shouted and ran from the underbrush to Lenox, dodging fire from Invaders as he went.

Commander Jampara knelt beside Aunt Celeste, healing her with a blanket of Alpha 2a energy while firing at Lenox at the same time. Neb was still busy returning fire with a bunch of Invaders. Argus was almost to Lenox when Max rushed out and tackled him.

"Thought you could go and help your ol' dad, eh, Argus? No way." Max pinned Argus to the ground.

It was no effort to get away from Max and after tossing him off, Argus sprung to his feet. "Don't get in my way, Max!"

Max got up and pointed at Commander Jampara. "That asshole murdered Stone! You think I'm going to let you do the same to the rest of us?"

"Max, I told you before, I'm on your side. Just stay out of the way." Argus looked over Max's shoulder, but Lenox was gone. "Where'd he go?"

Neb appeared beside Argus. "What the hell do you think you're doing?" He raised his hand toward Argus.

There was no time to try to explain everything to Neb, so Argus shoved him hard enough to send him flying backward a few feet. "Don't interfere, Neb. I know what I'm doing."

Neb disappeared in a shift as the whoop-whoop of helicopters and the roar of truck engines echoed around the lake. Argus had to find Lenox before things got out of hand. More out of hand. Several military helicopters came into view, close to the ground, plumes of dust rising up from the far end of the lake. It looked like everyone had been called out. And that meant human casualties. In a split second, the XTRA-A1 descended and spun around, facing the oncoming military.

"Max, get those people out of here!" Argus motioned to the helicopters and Jeeps driving toward them in the dry lake. "Now! My brother's in the XTRA-A1 and he was going to attack Lenox, but—"

Max shook his head. "You can't give me orders. I'm AURA."

"It doesn't matter if you're AURA or not! You and all of these humans will be dead if you don't get away from here. Tai's going to open fire any second." Argus grunted in frustration. "*Please*. I don't want to see anyone else hurt."

After a pause, Max nodded. "I'll go, but only if you make sure none of the other New Breeds get hurt. Neb said they still have some hidden away somewhere. But don't think this means I won't come after you once this mess is all sorted out."

Argus wasn't sure why Max was suddenly intent on saving the New Breeds. "Yeah, sure. Now go!"

Just as Max turned to go, Neb appeared by Argus and restrained him in a bear-hug. "What do you think you're doing? I don't know how you have your strength and abilities back, but if you try to help Lenox, I will kill you."

"Let go of me! Neb, I know what to do to Lenox. But I can't do it unless you let me." Argus struggled and broke out of Neb's grip.

"Damn, you're strong." Neb stood back. "Where did Lenox go?"

Argus caught his breath."I was hoping you'd tell me. He couldn't have disappeared without anyone noticing. Wasn't the Commander fighting him?"

"Yes, but when good ol' Max decided to play hero, all eyes were on him for a second. That was all Lenox needed."

Aunt Celeste ran to them. "Argus, are you all right? Jampara said you were going to shift to Tai. Why didn't you?"

Argus kept a look-out for Lenox. "Like I just told Neb, I know how I can capture Lenox. I won't kill him, but he'll be helpless so you can take him prisoner. But I need to find him first."

Galena appeared a few feet away, holding her stomach and leaning to the side. "I'm mortally wounded...and my brother has abandoned me. My energy is far too depleted. Nebulon, you know what to do." Her eyes were pale blue, and her expression sad or maybe pleading.

He shook his head. "No, Galena, not me." He turned his back to her. "Celeste, take care of Galena, out of mercy."

What did that mean? Argus watched as Aunt Celeste approached Galena and placed one hand on her forehead and the other on her throat. "What are you doing, Aunt Celeste?"

Neb reached out and grabbed Argus by the arm. "Quiet. Show some respect."

"Respect?" Argus looked around and couldn't believe that the fighting had stopped. Nobody moved. The military helicopters and Jeeps were heading back toward Palmdale, so Max must have contacted them and convinced them to leave.

A soft blue light enveloped Galena and Aunt Celeste. Neb had his eyes closed and was breathing in quick gasps. After a short time, the blue light dissipated and Aunt Celeste took her hands off Galena. Galena nodded, glanced around, then slowly faded away until there was nothing there at all. No body, no clothes, nothing. Neb drew in a deep breath and faced Aunt Celeste.

He gave a slight smile. "Thank you, Celeste. I couldn't have shown her the mercy she needed. Now, back to the battle." He vanished.

Argus walked to where Galena had been and felt his whole body tingle. "What just happened, Aunt Celeste?"

She placed her hand on his shoulder. "On the battlefield, if a Ramtalan falls and requests assistance with their final moments, we are obligated to end them mercifully by gently extracting their remaining Alpha 2a. It's a painless end."

"But Galena—"

"Galena was still a Ramtalan, Argus. Mercy is for everyone who asks for it and all Ramtalans mourn the loss of one of our own. As the Alpha 2a dissipates, any Ramtalan within a mile feels the loss and will absorb a small amount." She pointed to the dry lake where the fighting had resumed. "All right, we're back in battle mode. As your Guardian, I'm telling you to shift into the XTRA-A1 with Tai. Once Lenox is located, you can do whatever it is you can do to subdue him. If you fail, we will have to kill him. You have one chance."

"I'll succeed." He focused on the ship and shifted.

Tai jumped as soon as Argus appeared. "Wow, bro, don't scare me like that. Did you feel that influx of Alpha 2a? It wasn't much, but I felt it."

"Yeah, I did. That's what happens when a Ramtalan dies after having their energy extracted. Galena's dead, Tai."

He nodded and pointed the window, the shutter now open. "I know, I saw. Did Aunt Celeste actually, you know, finish her off?"

"She did. But it was a kindness, not hostility. Hey, Lenox is gone. We have to find him. Any clue where he might have run off to?" Argus sat in his seat.

"Nope. But he's alone now without Ari or Galena. Where do you think he'd go?" Tai took the XTRA-A1 up higher. "Hey, Arg, be prepared when you look out the window at Palmdale. Commander Jampara told me that when you caused the earthquake, it was Neb and Aunt Celeste who fixed the fault line so it didn't cause more damage further north in San Francisco."

Argus turned his head away. "You didn't have to say it like that. *I caused the earthquake*. It's not like I meant to. It's this Zeta 40 in me." He turned back and glared at Tai.

"Yeah, I know. Sorry. Okay?" Tai lifted his hand out of the depression in the arm rest, waiting for a fist-bump. "I said sorry."

Argus bumped fists. "Okay, okay, we're good." He sighed. "What happened to our lives, Tai?"

With a shrug, Tai slipped his hand back into the depression. "Well, we should never have assumed we'd ever be average teenage high school kids. That was never going to happen" He dipped the nose of the ship and accelerated.

"No kidding. Everything seems like blur." He looked through the side window. "Slow down a minute."

They were directly over Palmdale, or what was left of it. The ship slowed and stopped in a hover. Most buildings were little more than rubble and the streets were cracked or had huge sink holes in them. People milled around, some piling bricks into wheelbarrows or in stacks on the sidewalks. A few looked up and pointed. Two police officers drew their guns and opened fire on the ship.

"Seriously?" Tai shook his head. "Bullets can't hurt the ship."

"Let them get their anger out." Argus leaned back and closed his eyes.

"I wasn't going to shoot them, bro. My ammunition is for Lenox."

Argus opened his eyes. "No. I have another plan and it doesn't involve killing him. No matter what he's done, he's our father and I don't want to see him die. We've lost everything, too."

Tai mumbled, "Not like he's been much of a father."

"I know, but still—"

"Fine. So what's your plan?" Tai took the ship to a higher altitude and made a slow circle over Palmdale.

Argus explained what the symbols said and tried to get Tai onboard with the plan, although it took a lot of convincing. Finally, he agreed it was the best way.

"If you'd just lost most of your family, had no friends, and were losing a battle, where would you go?" Argus raised his eyebrow. "Where?"

Tai shrugged. "I don't know. Back home, I guess. I'd want to be at the one place I'd feel safe."

"Exactly. I think he'll want to go back to Ramtala. But if he does, he'll be captured. So where does that leave him?" Argus concentrated on Lenox, but he couldn't locate him. "What's the closest thing to Ramtala here on Earth?"

"Huh? Ah, I have no idea. Wait, the Citadel?"

"That's what I'm thinking. Most of the Settlers and Invaders are fighting, so there won't be many left at the Citadel. We'll only have one shot to get him. Are you with me?"

With a roll of his eyes, Tai smiled. "Duh."

"Then let's go!"

The XTRA-A1 shot upward and zoomed off toward Labrador. If Lenox was there, they'd have to move fast. Once Lenox realized Argus was going to take his Alpha 2a, he'd fight with everything he could.

Chapter 61

Tai had climbed so high that all Argus could see were clouds, but he knew they'd be at the Citadel in no time. He'd have to trick Lenox into thinking both he and Tai wanted to join him or else Lenox would kill them on sight.

"Arg, we're almost there. Tell me exactly how you're going to suck the energy out of Lenox. I don't see how you can do that. It's like forbidden to do that sort of thing and I know how pissed you were when Neb did it to you."

"It's the only way." He didn't want to tell Tai that he'd drained an Invader, Condrulon, at the lake. That was a secret he'd keep. "At least I'm healed now, but I don't know how long I'll have my abilities because Neb still has my Alpha 2a. My Zeta 40 isn't blocked anymore, but I still need my own Alpha 2a. Hey, drop down low and approach the Citadel at slow speed so Lenox doesn't think we're attacking."

"If he's there." Tai descended through the clouds.

They cleared the cloud layer and below was the sparkling ocean dotted with several islands, and without a blizzard to obscure the view, Argus saw just how blue the water really was. The ship slowed and Tai kept it about twenty feet above the gentle waves, approaching the Citadel's island in what was hopefully a non-threatening manner.

Argus saw a hovercraft at the landing dock and pointed it out to Tai. "Set down there. Can the ship detect any hostile action?"

"Hostile action? You sound like a general or something. Arg, you have that special Malaris ability that lets you communicate with the control center, so why don't you find out?"

"Good idea. I completely forgot about that. This Malaris stuff takes some getting used to." Argus concentrated and was instantly standing in the control center. "Is anyone going to attack us?"

The Malaris symbols ordered themselves into neat columns, but he didn't have to read them because he heard the voice from before.

> *The Citadel is protected by an energy shield. No impending attack detected.*

"Okay, well that's good. Is Argustine Lenox in the Citadel and if he is, how can we get through the shield?"

> *Ramtalans are within the Citadel. The energy shield can be destroyed with the photo-ionic-luminary pulse.*

"The what?"

> *The XTRA-A1 can emit a photo-ionic-luminary pulse by drawing Alpha 2a, Zeta 40, and positively charged ions together to react with the ionic force of the shield.*

"Okay. I'm not sure I understand what that...whatever. How do I do that?"

> *Required energies will be absorbed through all control seat mechanisms. Once charged, the photo-ionic-luminary pulse can be targeted on the shield upon command.*

"So I just have to say the word and it'll fire?"

> *That is correct. Be cautious and only fire once or energies will continue to be absorbed for a following charge-up. Do you wish to initiate the photo-ionic-luminary pulse?*

"Sure do. So I fire once and then get the hell out of the chair. Got it." Argus left the control center and was back with Tai again. "I know what to do. But we only have one shot at the shield."

"Seems like we only have one shot with everything. You better be right about this, because once Lenox knows we're coming for him, he'll hit us with everything he's got."

"That's why we have to be quick."

"So what's the plan, Arg?"

They placed their arms in the depressions and Argus explained the details. Within a few seconds, the depressions glowed white and Argus felt a strong prickling sensation running through his body. "Are you feeling that?"

Tai nodded. "Yep. How do we know when the system's charged?"

That was a good question. Argus shrugged. "I have no idea."

"Seriously? You're not giving me much to hold onto here, bro."

"Just keep approaching the Citadel. I'm sure..." A loud chime sounded and the interior lit up with white light. The prickling stopped and Argus looked over at Tai. "Fire the pulse!"

Tai closed his eyes for a moment. He opened them again and shook his head. "I have no control over the weapons system. You try."

"I've never controlled the ship before."

"We're closing in on the shield. If you can't do it, I'll have to pull out to avoid smashing into it and killing us."

Argus sucked in a breath and focused on the Malaris symbols in his head. He had to find out how to fire the pulse or they'd have no choice but to return to Palmdale. After a few seconds, the symbols gave him his answer.

"Tai, I've got it! You have to relinquish control of the ship over to me."

"How the hell do I do that? If I stop controlling it, we'll go down. You've never flown before, remember?"

"Trust me. As soon as you give me control, I can fire the pulse and land the ship." Argus looked out the window. "We really don't have much time."

"Shit! Okay, fine." Tai shut his eyes. "You've got it, now don't crash."

The ship dipped and fell a few feet, but when Argus focused on controlling it, he managed to keep it straight and level. To fire the pulse, he had to shift out of his seat and then immediately shift back in. The shifting triggered a chain reaction where his and Tai's Alpha 2a and Zeta 40 combined to form a concentrated ionic photon pulse that would discharge the energy of the shield as soon as it struck.

With no time to lose, Argus shifted twice and focused on sending the pulse directly at the Citadel. Right away, a brilliant light flashed outside. He continued flying the ship, not as well as Tai flew, straight to the Citadel's island and landed, roughly.

Tai grunted. "I'm counting that as a crash."

"I didn't crash. You didn't do so well the first time you landed either." Argus got out of his seat. "I have to get close to Lenox."

"We still don't even know if he's there or not."

A red flash lit up the interior of the ship. Lenox stood near Argus. "My sons, you came to be with me. I knew you would. I would have lowered the shield if you had asked. We are finally all together again. We shall cleanse this planet and assume our positions as leaders."

Tai rolled his eyes, got out of the seat and strode to Lenox. "Wow, you're still living that delusion, are you? You've lost. Give it up already."

Argus flinched and wished Tai could keep his mouth shut for once.

"Mind your mouth, son." Lenox's eyes glowed brightly. "I will succeed in wiping this planet clean of the Settlers and the human population. I am merely awaiting Galena and then we will proceed."

"Lenox," Argus reached out and touched him on the shoulder. "Father, Galena is gone. She was wounded and..."

Lenox stiffened under his touch and Argus knew he'd have to act fast. He threw a veil over Lenox, shifted and reappeared inside the veil with him.

"I'm sorry, Len...Father. This is the only way." Argus initiated a phase-shift and drew Lenox's Alpha 2a and Zeta 40 into himself, leaving only a tiny bit remaining with Lenox so he wouldn't die. Argus shifted outside the veil and trembled. It was a rush, like a ton of adrenaline pumping through his veins. Not only was he brimming with energy, but a thousand images flooded into his mind...strange calculations, schematics, none of it making sense.

Tai stared at Argus and pointed at Lenox. "Bro? You all right?"

It took a moment before Argus felt comfortable with all of the energy, but when he saw Lenox, he felt the heaviness of guilt and sadness wash over him. Lenox stood with slumped shoulders and pale blue eyes. His skin paled and his hair went from white to a dingy gray. All of the spark was out of him.

After taking a long, deep, breath, Argus said softly, "I have his energy. He's practically human now."

Tai's mouth gaped. "Human?"

"Well, not exactly human, but as weak as a human."

Lenox tried to break through, his hands weakly thrusting against the veil. "How could you do this to me? You are my son. Traitor. You should have killed me."

"Did you honestly think I could? I'm not like you, Lenox." Argus extended his hand and withdrew the veil. "Now you can't hurt anybody."

Without hesitation, Lenox raised his arms and attempted to fire a pulse, but nothing happened.

Tai went to him and slapped his hands down. "Were you just trying to kill us? I didn't want to believe you'd do something like that, but...I could never consider you my father." He turned his back on Lenox.

"Tai's right." Argus took a few steps away from Lenox. "From this moment on, you are not my father. I saved your life because there's been enough killing. But you wouldn't do the same for me, would you? You don't care about anyone but yourself."

There was a flash and Aunt Celeste appeared with Neb. Neb went right to Lenox while Aunt Celeste stayed with Tai and Argus. She hugged them both.

"You boys scared me half to death. Neb tracked the XTRA-A1." She let them go. "Argus, why is Lenox drained of his energy? Did you do that?"

He nodded. "I did. But it's okay, I left him with a tiny bit so he can live."

"I detect an extreme amount of energy in you. What have you done?" Aunt Celeste placed her hand on Argus's forehead. "Argus, what have you done?"

He pulled away. "It was the only way to get Lenox without killing him."

Neb walked over, dragging Lenox along by the arm. "This piece of garbage is nothing more than an empty shell. We have our people taking the Citadel now because the shield is down. This war of yours, Lenox, is over. You're my prisoner and I'm taking you back to Ramtala to stand trial for treason, murder, and torture."

"I will not go back." Lenox attempted to yank his hand free. "My son has left me with enough energy to survive, but I cannot do anything else. I do not wish to live this life. I am asking you for mercy."

"No. You don't deserve mercy." Argus stood in front of Lenox. "There's been too much death. We've lost Ari and Galena, not to mention the New Breeds, Todd from school, and Stone. It's enough. I'll take responsibility for my part in all of this, but I won't be responsible for your death."

Aunt Celeste glared at Lenox. "Argustine, we can't provide mercy since you're not mortally wounded. You know that. You'll stand before the Ramtalan Council, and..." she hesitated and turned to Neb.

With a sigh, Neb said, "Boys, we're returning to Ramtala. All of us. The Citadel is going dark. We've captured hundreds of Invaders and once we have the Citadel back under our control, it will be decommissioned and we will escort the prisoners home."

"Whoa, wait a sec." Tai motioned to Argus. "You're leaving us here all alone? Aunt Celeste, you're staying, right?"

She didn't answer.

Argus stood with Tai. "Aunt Celeste?"

Finally, she responded, "Boys, you'll have to come with us. All of the Guardians are leaving and those who still have New Breeds will take them to Ramtala. I let Lenox believe all of the New Breeds were in one hiding place since I knew he was tapping into our thoughts. By splitting them up, we saved over a thousand New Breeds. And as I'm still your Guardian, you'll be coming with me, too. Commander Jampara and Neb will examine the XTRA-A1 and build more ships to carry the New Breeds. You and Tai can stay in your ship, in stasis."

"No. That's not...I'm not going." Tai backed away. "You can't make us. We were born on Earth, this is our planet."

"I'm with Tai, Aunt Celeste. We belong here." Argus motioned to Lenox. "You've got Lenox, so let Neb take him and you can stay here with us. We haven't even finished high school yet."

There was another bright flash and the Commander appeared. "Argus, you and Tai are coming to Ramtala. This is not a subject for discussion." He turned to Neb. "We have control of the Citadel. Once Galena fell and news of Lenox's capture spread, the rest of the Invaders surrendered. Take Lenox to the court room in the Citadel and await further commands."

Neb nodded. "Yes, sir." He motioned to Argus. "Did you leave enough energy in him so he can shift without damage?"

Argus went to Lenox. "Yes, you can shift with him. Lenox, you realize you did this, don't you? I did what I had to, but you forced me. All of this, humans, New Breeds, and Ramtalans dying...for what? If you'd taken the time to get to know me and Tai, you would have known that we'd never go along with your warped plan to take over the Earth." He got close and lowered his voice, "All I ever wanted was to be a regular kid with a family and make friends. You've taken that away from me."

Staring, Lenox whispered, "I took nothing. You could never have been a 'regular kid'. You and Tai are my sons with my DNA. You were destined for greatness. But you tossed it all away to beg for favors from Jampara like his lap dog. You'll be imprisoned on Ramtala for the rest of your lives, studied like laboratory animals. Surely you know that. Nebulon is not to be trusted."

Neb grabbed Lenox by the throat. "These boys have more strength and bravery than you'll ever have. And they aren't going to Ramtala as prisoners, you old fool. You're the only prisoner here." He glanced at Argus and Tai, gave them a nod, and shifted with Lenox.

"Aunt Celeste?" Argus turned to her. At this point, he was totally confused about everything. Like, why were they all going to Ramtala? Without Lenox, they could stay on Earth and live in peace.

She smiled, but not a confident, strong smile, more like a sympathetic smile. "Boys, shift to your old apartment and I'll meet you there in a minute. We have a lot to discuss and I don't think this is the best place to do that."

Tai glanced at Argus with a familiar look, one that said he was about to disobey and go off on his own. Argus shook his head.

With a frustrated grunt, Tai glared at the Commander. "Lenox was right, wasn't he? We're your prisoners."

Argus took Tai by the arm and pulled him away from everyone and lowered his voice, "I'm not sure who to trust either, but we did the right thing with Lenox. We have nobody else, so let's put a little faith in Aunt Celeste. She's never done anything to hurt us and I'm sure she'll make sure we're not put in some Ramtalan prison."

"You might be sure, bro, but I'm not." He sighed. "And because I can't think of anything else to do, I'll go with you to our apartment. But listen, if anything freaky happens, I'm shifting out of there."

"And I'll go with you." Argus fist bumped Tai and turned to Aunt Celeste. "We'll be in the apartment." He led Tai in a shift and they landed in the kitchen of the Citadel apartment.

Tai wandered around, running his hand through his hair and clenching his fists. "Arg, I don't want to leave Earth. We don't know what Ramtala's like. I love walking in the desert and I like playing football. What are we supposed to do on a planet full of pure-forms? We'll be bigger freaks there than we are here. You've got all these amazing abilities now, can't you just tell them we're staying?"

The apartment felt like home. Argus leaned against the breakfast bar and imagined for a second that everything was back to normal and they were nothing more than ordinary New Breeds. He glanced at his reflection in the toaster and saw a version of himself that was so removed from the kid he used to be.

He sat on a stool and rested his head in his hands. "We can't stay, Tai. You've been converted and I'm...like nobody else. I have all of this energy and I don't know what to do with it. What if it makes me crazy like Lenox? What if I crack and go all megalomaniac? I didn't say anything before, but ever since I took Lenox's energy, my skin feels like it's on fire. I have to fight the urge to tear my skin off. And I want to fire a pulse so bad, at anyone."

"Shit, Arg. I had no idea." Tai sat beside him. "What can I do?"

Argus shrugged. "Nothing. I have to deal with it."

"You have to tell Aunt Celeste. She'll know what to do. But don't tell anyone else." Tai hopped off the stool and went to the refrigerator. "Want a soda?"

"Yeah, sure." Argus lay his head on the counter. "This sucks. Maybe I can agree to go to Ramtala, but only if they let you stay here."

Tai placed a can of soda on the counter in front of Argus. "Not going to happen, bro. Where you go, I go. Brothers until the end, remember? Besides, what the hell would I do on Earth without you constantly nagging me?" He laughed and popped the top of his soda. "We'll be all right. Nothing can keep the Dachel brothers down."

"I'll do my best to keep that in mind." Argus downed the soda.

Aunt Celeste appeared. "Thank you for cooperating, boys." She stood at the counter, fiddling with her ponytail. "If there was any way to keep you here on Earth, I'd do it. But all of the Guardians are being recalled and they will tend to the remaining New Breeds on Ramtala, including the parents. Don't worry, the children and parents will stay together. We must evacuate the planet because we've all been exposed not only to AURA and the military, but to the human population as well. There are many, many videos uploaded on the Internet and playing on the news broadcasts that show our battle and the devastation of Palmdale. The only option is to leave quietly before we're attacked. An attack on us would force us to retaliate and that would cause more destruction. We cannot allow that."

Argus sat up. "But how can you transport us and all of the New Breeds and their parents? Only Lenox knows how to build a ship like the XTRA-A1 and that took him years. And it's only big enough for me and Tai."

She nodded thoughtfully. "That's true, but you have Lenox's Zeta 40. You have the ability to tap into his Malaris knowledge that's stored in your DNA. Commander Jampara will read your thoughts and we can build enough ships within a few weeks."

"A few weeks?" Tai sounded hopeful. "So we're not leaving right away? Can we go back home until then?"

"Sorry, Tai, our house was destroyed." Aunt Celeste put her hand on his shoulder. "We will all stay here. The Guardians are collecting their New Breeds and bringing them here. Argus, there's another reason we need you to come to Ramtala."

He wasn't very interested in hearing any more. In a few weeks, he'd leave Earth, the only home he'd ever had, and go to a planet where he knew nobody and would be hated for his Malaris DNA and Zeta 40. How could he live like that?

"What are you saying, Aunt Celeste?" Tai glared at Aunt Celeste. "He *is* going to be a prisoner?"

Argus closed his eyes and shook his head. "I won't be locked up." He looked up, not angry, but disappointed that his own aunt would treat him like someone to be hidden away from everything and everyone.

Aunt Celeste sighed. "Argus, I know how strong you are, and you can likely kill me with a wave of your hand, but I am your Guardian, and you *will* listen to me. Nobody will harm Tai, or you. You won't be a prisoner."

Argus stared at Aunt Celeste. "I'd never hurt you, Aunt Celeste. Please don't think I ever would. I've seen too much suffering and killing. All I want is for it to stop. Okay, so for what other reason am I going to Ramtala? So they can experiment on me or torture me or—" His energy surged up, filling him inside with power that wanted to come out.

"Argus!" Aunt Celeste grabbed him in a hug. "You'd better learn to control your energy."

Her infusion of Alpha 2a settled him down enough to where he nodded. "Sorry. It's still all so new."

She continued, "I know. But please stop overreacting. You and Tai will be embraced as sons of Ramtala, not scorned for your parentage. You two have proved yourselves. You stood up to Lenox. That will be rewarded." She let him go. "Anyway, you'll be fine. Ramtala's environment is quite hospitable and similar to Earth, as I've told you before, except for more extreme temperatures. What I meant was that because of your unique DNA, Commander Jampara believes our scientists can find a way to replicate portions of it and recombine it with our Ramtalan DNA so we can have children again, and the New Breeds we have left will survive. Lenox had no problem producing children, which had to be due to his Malaris Zeta 40. You might be the only hope we have of continuing our species. You boys make me proud to be your Guardian. I only wish your mother was alive to see how you've grown."

His head spun, her words sinking in and giving him hope. If it was possible, he'd gladly sacrifice anything, including his freedom on Earth. "But I'm not Ramtalan, Aunt Celeste. I'm a hybrid. What if my DNA isn't compatible with Ramtalan DNA? I might cause more harm—"

Tai had calmed down. "Come on, bro, don't blame yourself before we know for sure." He gave Argus a pat on the arm. "As long as we're together, I don't care anymore where we are. I wasn't really popular at school anyway and the girls who liked me only liked me because of the Lambo or my fabulous good looks." He smirked.

Argus smiled at the memories of the beautiful Lamborghini and the fun they had driving it, how they'd meet Dave at *Marco's*, play football, and, of course, then there was Lola. Leaving Earth wasn't going to be easy, but he understood why he couldn't stay. Of everything he'd come to love about his tumultuous life, he'd miss Lola the most.

"You and Argus belong together." Aunt Celeste put her hands on their shoulders. "Lenox will stand trial and most likely end up in our highest security prison. Can you boys live with that? Prisoners are not allowed visitors but receive excellent treatment until they serve their sentence."

Argus glanced at Tai. "And how long will his sentence be?"

She paused before answering. "His will most likely be a life sentence. Even without his abilities, he's still very dangerous and could stir up any remaining Invaders. But he'll be alive and that's what you wanted, Argus."

It was, but now it seemed cruel. Maybe Lenox had it right, death would be more merciful. Argus nodded. "Yeah, that's what I wanted. If we're going to be here for a few weeks, I'd like to visit Lola. I can shift to her house, if it hasn't been condemned, and then shift right back here. Nobody would see me."

"Absolutely not." Aunt Celeste shook her head, her eyes softly glowing. "You'll both stay here. We can't take the chance that Max Jackson might find you."

Tai raised an eyebrow. "Where is that dickhead?"

"The Commander removed the monitor from his head and transported him back to AURA and warned him that his actions would be watched. I would have preferred that he had his memories removed, but the Commander cautioned against that. Any more tampering and he'd end up in a psychotic state. I was willing to risk it, but he wasn't." Aunt Celeste sighed. "He's caused too much grief, but the Commander knows best."

Argus nodded. "I guess I agree with the Commander, Aunt Celeste. Messing with people's brains isn't right. Even a piece of crap like Max deserves a tiny bit of compassion."

With a smile, Aunt Celeste took Argus's hand in hers. "It's that sympathy you have that made the Commander see things my way."

"What do you mean?" Argus withdrew his hand and got off the stool.

She continued, "He wanted you restrained permanently and experimented on. I convinced him otherwise. When he sees you, he sees Lenox. I've told him over and over that you're nothing like your father, but he's hard to convince."

"But you did convince him, right?" Tai's eyes glowed.

"Of course." Aunt Celeste laughed slightly. "We wouldn't be standing here if I hadn't. Argus, when the Commander comes to read your thoughts, be compliant and don't put up a fight. Remain calm so he can see that I'm right about you."

"Why would I put up a fight? I'm okay with him building more ships and using my thoughts to do it. It's just that I don't really want to leave. I understand why, and I think it's a good idea to get the New Breeds away from here, but I want to stay." Argus wandered around the apartment. "I can't imagine never seeing Lola again." His gut clenched. "What if she needs me? What if Max takes her for questioning? She's not safe."

"Argus, relax." Aunt Celeste turned to Tai. "Go and talk to your brother."

Tai nodded and went to him. "Bro, once everyone realizes we're gone, there won't be any reason to go after Lola. I know those Protector genes of yours are running overtime, but she'll be fine."

"I have to see her." Argus glanced at Aunt Celeste. "I have to go."

She shook her head. "If you leave, the Commander will go back to his original idea." With a wave of her hand, a jolt ran through Argus.

He couldn't move. He was stuck in place. "What did you do to me?"

"I'm a pure-form, Argus, I have many, many abilities. Unless you want to stay like that until we leave, I'd suggest you get a grip on your Protector feelings. If you want, I will go to Lola and make sure she's safe. Would that satisfy you?"

The Malaris symbols danced around in his head.

Use a formula of 2% Zeta 40 and 98% Alpha 2a to break the pure-form energy-freeze.

Argus concentrated on the formula, felt a surge and then after a flash of purple, he was free. He took a step. "You can't keep me here, Aunt Celeste."

She stood, staring. "Tai, move away from him."

"Hell no." Tai moved in front of Argus.

Having so much power was an incredible feeling. Nobody could stop him. Wait, he was sounding like Lenox. No way did he want to end up like him. After a moment, Argus stepped around Tai. "This isn't what I want. I don't want to keep disobeying. I need help, Aunt Celeste. Can you help me control my abilities? You're my Guardian and I'll do what you say. I don't mean to be disrespectful. I don't want to be like my father, not at all."

She stared at him for a while, then smiled. "I think maybe you're getting too old for a Guardian. How about we get you some training in controlling your new abilities once we're on Ramtala?"

"Yeah, that'd be excellent. I'm starting to scare myself." Argus turned to Tai and held out his fist. "Brothers forever."

Tai fist-bumped. "I got your back, bro. No matter what."

"Same here." Argus wandered to the couch and sat down. "Maybe I can call Lola instead."

Aunt Celeste shifted and appeared near the couch. "I can arrange for that." She looked at them both. "You and Tai are young men now. Maybe you're both getting too old for a Guardian."

"Well," Tai started, "You've been an awesome Guardian. I wouldn't mind if you stuck around. For a while anyway."

Argus nodded. "Same here. I'd still like to go back home though." He thought of Palmdale. "Aunt Celeste, isn't there something I can do to help rebuild the city? I mean, do we have any money to donate?"

"Of course we have money." Aunt Celeste's eyes brightened. "I have a little over 30 million dollars in my Guardian fund."

"Thirty million?" Tai whistled. "It'll cost more than that for repairs, but that's a nice contribution."

"Whoa." Argus shook his head. "I had no idea. Can we give it to the city? And maybe a little for Lola, you know, for college or whatever."

With a huge smile, Aunt Celeste nodded. "What an excellent idea. I'll make the arrangements. I'm sure the other Guardians will chip in, too."

They all watched a movie, made a large cheese pizza—which was almost as good as *Marco's* pizza—and discussed what Ramtala was like, until the door opened, and Commander Jampara walked in with an orb in his hand.

"Boys, please approach." The Commander waited for them to come over to him. "We must proceed with the construction of the ships immediately. Tai, I will require you to keep your brother calm while I extract his memories."

Tai blocked Argus. "Why? I thought you were just going to read his thoughts. Aunt Celeste, what's going on?"

She drew in a breath. "The process of extracting a significant amount of memory, especially Malaris memory, is painful, both for the initiator and the vessel. Argus, I'm sorry you have to go through this and if there was any other way, I—"

"It's okay." Argus gave Tai a playful slap on the arm. "Outta my way, little brother. The Commander needs to download me."

"Don't joke about it, Arg. I'm trying to keep my Defender stuff under control here." Tai turned to Aunt Celeste. "So what am I supposed to do? My head's filled with fighting anyone who wants to hurt Arg."

With a nod, the Commander held out the orb and explained, "That is what I need you to do, Tai. The extraction process will make Argus believe he is under attack. You will then want to fend off the attacker, which in this case is me. But obviously you cannot, or I will not be able to finish. You must make Argus believe you are fighting his attacker, so he does not fall into psychosis."

Argus shook his head. "Hold on. I might end up a basket case?"

"Yeah, this isn't going to happen." Tai held up his hands, palms facing the Commander. "You stay the hell away from him."

With the orb glowing blue, the Commander took a step toward Argus. "I must proceed, or the New Breeds will be stranded on Earth without any Guardians to keep them safe. Is that what you want? Most were killed at the hands of Lenox. Do you want the remainder to perish?"

Argus answered, "Of course not, but I also don't want you to screw up my brain." When the orb glowed brighter, Argus doubled over. "Damn it, what are you doing?"

The Commander rose his voice, "You must let me proceed. Tai, stand aside."

"I won't." Tai fired a pulse at the Commander, but somehow missed. "Aunt Celeste! Where are you? Help me!"

A blinding flash of white lit up the entire apartment and Argus had to close his eyes. If he could get the Commander to listen, he could explain that by using the Malaris symbols, there might be a possibility of getting the information without going through the extraction process. He tried to speak, but nothing came out. He forced his eyes open to see where Tai was and to make sure the Commander hadn't done anything to him.

What he saw made him smile. Lola stood right in front of him, wearing the cute sundress she was in when they went kayaking. He reached out, but she disappeared and was replaced with an image of Tai walking in the desert, right past a rattlesnake.

Lenox appeared and fired a pulse, but Tai fired back. Argus wanted to rush to help his brother, but he couldn't move. Besides, Tai seemed to be winning. The fight continued and then more images began swirling around in Argus's head, coming in and out of focus until only one image remained. Lenox in the host body from the photograph, the only photograph they had of their mother and father. Lenox smiled and aimed his hands directly at Argus.

"Argus," Aunt Celeste whispered. "Argus, are you with us?"

"Bro? Talk to me, Arg," Tai said, shaking Argus by the shoulders.

The image of Lenox vanished. Argus sat on the floor, surrounded by Aunt Celeste, Tai, and the Commander. He looked around. "What happened? I saw Lola and Lenox and—"

Tai crouched. "You were here the whole time. It's done. I used shared-sight to see what you were seeing and then let you think I was attacking Lenox. I saw those images as well. That was weird. You okay?"

Argus nodded. "Yeah, I think so. Commander, did you get what you need?"

The Commander displayed the orb that was now glowing red. "Yes, your Malaris thoughts, and the memories of Lenox you absorbed, were extracted. I will begin working on processing them. You boys are to remain at the Citadel. Argus, should you use your Malaris abilities, things will not end well for you." He shifted and was gone.

"Wow." Argus turned to Tai. "He's kind of a dick. No *thank you* or anything."

"Yeah. Um, better not use those Malaris abilities then, bro." Tai winked. "Or I'll be forced to go all psycho Defender on his ass."

"Boys, that's enough." Aunt Celeste flipped her ponytail so it trailed down her back. "I have some things to do. Remember, you can go to the cafeteria or the gym, but don't get in anyone's way. I'll be back soon." She went to the door and turned around. "I mean it, don't get in the way."

Tai rolled his eyes. "Remember, Aunt Celeste, we're not kids anymore."

"I know." She sounded sad. "Be good." The door slid open and she left.

"So what now?" Argus got a bottle of water from the refrigerator. "Want to play some video games?"

"Seriously, bro? We're about to be whisked away in a spaceship. I'm not quite ready to say goodbye to planet Earth just yet. Road trip?"

"You're not serious, are you? You heard Aunt Celeste. I'm on, like, probation or something. Commander Jampara will skin me alive if I sneeze in Malaris."

Tai laughed. "Then don't sneeze. I'm not talking about using any of our Zeta 40 or your weirdo Malaris hoo-doo, I'm saying we shift, using only Alpha 2a, and go to Paris or London or Australia. We can have a little fun, and maybe a beer or two, and be back before anyone knows we're gone."

It was tempting, but Argus wasn't about to stir up trouble at this point. "Sorry, Tai, I'm going to have to pull rank on you as the older brother. We're staying put."

"You're a few minutes older. That doesn't count. I don't need your permission."

"I can make you stay." Argus smirked.

"Nah, 'cause then you'd use your Malaris abilities and Jampara would, what did you say, skin you. So, ha!"

"Okay, I've got a proposition for you. We'll log onto the computer and use a program to see the world via satellite images to check out the world." He pointed to the computer. "It'll be like being there for real."

"Not quite." Tai sat at the desk with the computer. "But you're right. I'm supposed to be grown up now and I guess that means I can't go around acting like a spoiled brat anymore. I'll sure miss those days." He chuckled and logged on.

For a few hours, they virtually went to Paris, Sydney, Vietnam, Hong Kong, London, and the Great Wall of China, in addition to multiple other locations. Argus had fun, but he could tell Tai wasn't as happy. Their new life was going to be tougher for him because he was the free spirit, used to doing what he wanted. Reining him in would be like trying to get a tornado to stay in one place.

When they were bored, they went to the gym and worked out, stopped by the cafeteria for a snack, which ended up being more like a four-course meal because there was so much good food to eat, and then wandered back to the apartment. How could anyone expect them to be cooped up for weeks?

Tai sighed and flopped down on his bed. "I'm so bored. Maybe we can walk around the island."

"Hey, that's a good idea. Let's ask Aunt Celeste when she comes back." Argus sat on his bed and kicked off his shoes. "I'm going to take a nap."

"Me too," Tai mumbled, his face in the pillow.

Argus woke to the sound of the door sliding open. He got up and looked over the railing as Aunt Celeste walked in. Behind her came Lola.

Chapter 62

Lola dashed past Aunt Celeste and ran up the stairs to the loft, right into Argus's arms. He held her tightly. Was it real or a dream? How could Lola be at the Citadel? Last time he brought her, she'd died.

He glanced over the rail. "Aunt Celeste?"

"You're not dreaming, Argus. I shifted to Palmdale and flew her here in a helicopter. With her mother's permission of course. Since you can't go to her, I thought this was the next best thing." Aunt Celeste smiled and motioned to Tai. "We should let them have some privacy, Tai."

"Oh, ah, yeah. I'll be...somewhere else." Tai hurried down the stairs and left the apartment with Aunt Celeste.

Lola wiped her tears. "I didn't think I'd see you again. Max Jackson was on the news and said the Invaders were defeated and Earth had nothing to worry about now. I didn't know if you were dead or alive or if you'd left Palmdale forever."

He kissed Lola on the lips and even though he didn't want to, he loosened his grip. "I wanted to see you and tell you everything. I can't believe you're here. I'm so sorry for what I did to Palmdale, but we're going to donate money to help rebuild. Not that it's enough, but it's better than nothing. Oh, and I want to give you some money for college."

She pulled away. "Are you kidding? I'm not taking any money from you. Argie, your aunt wouldn't tell me when you can come home. Dave said he drove by your house and it's pretty damaged, but I'm sure it can be fixed."

"Oh." He sat on the edge of his bed. "About that. Come and sit with me."

"I don't like the sound of that." She sat next him and pressed in close. "We've been through a lot, haven't we?"

"Definitely." He could still remember every single time he'd looked into her eyes. How was he going to go on without ever seeing her again? He took her hand and held it against his heart. "Lola, you know I love you, right?"

She gave a little nod and squeezed his hand. "Argie, what are you trying to say? It feels like you're saying goodbye."

He couldn't find the words. Talking to her was a lot harder than he'd imagined it would be. "I can't stay here."

"I realize that. The Citadel isn't your home. When you get home, we'll go for that hike we never got to do and go to *Marco's*. There's no school for a while, but they're going to bring temporary mobile structures in a week or two. Everything will get back to normal, you'll see."

He stood and paced. "That's not what I meant. How can it ever get back to normal? Everybody at school knows what I am. And that's not even the worst of it. I'm not me anymore, Lola. I've been...changed." He drew in a breath. "I meant I can't stay on Earth. I'm going to Ramtala. The Commander thinks my DNA might help the Ramtalans. As much as I don't want to go, I have to. What if I can really save the entire Ramtalan species? I can't say no to that."

"Wait!" Lola jumped up. "You really are saying goodbye? You're leaving me? Forever? No, no, no, there's got to be another way. The Commander can take a sample of your DNA and—"

He reached out and hugged her. "It's not just my DNA. I'm more like Lenox than I want to believe, and that means I'm dangerous. I can do all of these things, even when I don't mean to. And my brain acts like a computer with all of this stored Malaris memory. If I want to solve a problem, my brain works on it and gives me the answer." He let go of Lola. "Guess that'd be handy in math class."

"Don't you dare joke. I don't care if you're the same or not. I've gone through so much with you and now here we are, together again after all of this nonsense. That's fate. It must be. We're meant to be together."

"Well," he paused. Her glassy eyes made his heart melt. "Aunt Celeste didn't say I could never come back." He smiled and kissed Lola on the cheek.

She sniffed, wiped her eyes, and shrugged. "Okay, then. That's something. When are you supposed to leave? I don't want to spend a second away from you. Can we talk to your aunt or the Commander and—"

Tai appeared beside Argus. "No need. Sorry, bro, I used shared-sight just for a second. I wanted to let you know the Commander told Aunt Celeste that the New Breeds might be allowed back on Earth since this is their home, but not for a while and not until their genetic problem is fixed. Things have got to settle down first."

"How long?" Argus held Lola's hand again. "Tai, how long?"

"Ah, that's the not-so-good part. Maybe a hundred years from now. By then, the battle will only be in the history books, and nobody today would be alive then. But it's something." Tai sighed. "Maybe I should have kept my mouth shut."

"Yeah, maybe." Argus sighed and sat on the bed. "What am I supposed to do with that information? We'll be dead by then, too."

Tai raised an eyebrow. "Well, no. You and I are going to live for a lot longer than any human, so we could come back...oh. Sorry, Lola."

Tears dripped from her eyes. "I'd be dead. So Argie could come back and what, lay flowers on my grave? This isn't fair." She turned and ran down the stairs.

"Nice, Tai," Argus mumbled.

"Sorry, but come on, she fell for an alien. What does she expect? I didn't get involved with girls. Know why?"

"Yep, because you're an ass and no girl wants an ass for a boyfriend." Argus stomped down the stairs after Lola.

Tai shifted and appeared in front of Argus, feet set, and hands raised like he was ready to fight. "Don't ever call me an ass, bro."

"You really want to take me on, *bro*?" Argus raised his hands, palms toward Tai.

"Stop it!" Lola shouted. "What's wrong with you two?"

Tai was the first to lower his hands. "It's the collective energy. Arg, I didn't mean to lose my head."

For a moment, Argus couldn't get control of his anger, but when he saw Lola, he calmed right down and lowered his arms. "Sorry for calling you an ass. You're maybe a jerk or a dick..."

With a frown, Tai gave Argus a playful punch on the arm. "Like you're not? Oh, hey, did I forget to mention that Aunt Celeste arranged for Lola to stay here for a week or two?" He smirked.

Argus smiled. "You couldn't lead with that? I take it all back, you are an ass."

Lola threw her arms around Argus and nuzzled into his chest. "Let's pretend we're on vacation. I don't want to talk about spaceships or Ramtala or you leaving. Okay?"

"Deal." Argus gave her a kiss and waved Tai away. He'd willingly live in a fantasy world with Lola and imagine everything was perfect, for as long as he could. He'd always been good at daydreaming.

Chapter 63

For ten days, Argus and Lola hung out at the Citadel, playing video games, watching movies and even working out in the gym, but on the eleventh day, the announcement came that a fleet of forty-five ships was complete, and the launch date had been set. Lola, who'd stayed in Aunt Celeste's apartment, refused to leave Argus's side.

He sat with her at the breakfast bar, half-heartedly eating a sandwich, while Lola picked at hers. Tai sat next to them and slid a tablet computer over to Argus.

"Bro, here's a program that shows the route we'll take. The ships use Alpha 2-a energy for power and go super-fast. But we'll be in stasis for 5,037 days."

"That's..." Lola thought for a moment. "That's almost fourteen years. One way. I'll be so old, and you won't have aged a bit."

"Don't think of it." Argus glanced at the tablet and followed the route through the solar system, but then gave up. He reached into his pocket and pulled out a small device the size of a cell phone that Neb had given him. "Lola, I want you to have this."

"What is it?"

He handed it to her. "Neb used my memories to create a sort of movie of our time together, starting with that first day we met at school. All you do is hold it in your hand and you'll see everything in your mind. I don't want you to forget me, but one day, I want you to put it away and get on with your life."

She shook her head and put the device on the counter. "I can't imagine a life without you. How can I get up in the morning knowing you're heading to Ramtala?"

Before Argus could say anything, Aunt Celeste came in, followed by the Commander and a few Settlers. When they were all in the room, Neb strode in with Gretchen Manheim at his side.

Neb smiled. "Well, boys, are you ready for departure?"

"What the hell, Neb?" Tai jumped off the stool and pointed at Gretchen. "She's the freaking enemy, dude."

Aunt Celeste pulled Tai aside. "Relax, Tai."

A moment later, the robot waiter rolled in with a large, covered tray. Argus stared as everyone clapped. He nudged Tai, "What the hell is this?"

"No idea, bro."

The robot stopped in front of Aunt Celeste, who lifted the cover off the tray to reveal a rectangular cake with lit candles, and said, "Happy birthday, boys!"

Lola came up to Argus. "It's your birthday?"

He shook his head. "No."

Aunt Celeste continued, "You didn't think you'd get away without a celebration for your eighteenth birthday, did you?"

"It *is* your birthday." Lola leaned against him.

"Not quite. Our birthday was a while ago, but we were in the XTRA-A1 at the time." Argus laughed. "Thank you, everyone."

With a big smile, Neb came over and motioned to the cake. "Blow out the candles, boys, and then we'll move on to the presents."

"Presents?" Tai raised an eyebrow. "Forget the cake!"

Argus prodded Tai to help him blow out the candles and once they did, Neb deferred to Aunt Celeste.

She looked at each of them with a smile. "Boys, you know Gretchen Manheim already, but what you don't know is that she and Neb have, um, become close, ah, friends."

With a roll of his eyes, Tai spoke up, "Wow, Aunt Celeste, we're eighteen, you can say they hooked up. We get it. So where are our presents?"

"Wait a second," Argus blurted. "Neb's a pure-form and Gretchen's human. They can't...you know."

Gretchen came forward. "No, we can't 'you know'. Tell them, Neb."

"Fine." Neb glanced at Aunt Celeste. "I'll take it from here. Yes, Gretchen and I are close, and no, we can't 'you know', but that part of our relationship doesn't need to be physical. Only Lenox figured out a way to, ah, procreate because of his Malaris DNA. But with your DNA, Argus, maybe that'll be in the future for us, too. Anyway, pure-forms can use mind manipulation as you know and well..." he didn't finish the sentence.

Argus smiled. If he understood what Neb was saying, then Neb could place thoughts into Gretchen's head and make her imagine anything. Even the physical part of their relationship. It was strange, but if it worked for them, who was he to argue? "I think I understand."

"Then explain it to me, bro."

"Tai. Think about it for a minute." Argus smirked.

Tai frowned, stared at Neb for a moment and then nodded. "Ohhh. Okay, I get it. But, ah, that can't be our present."

Aunt Celeste went into the hallway and returned with a large box with a bright red bow on top. "This is for you, Tai." She placed the box on the floor at his feet.

"Cool." Tai knelt and opened the box. "What! Arg, look."

Argus came over and looked down. Inside the box were four bouncy puppies. "You got us puppies?"

"No, those are for Tai." Aunt Celeste touched Argus gently on the cheek. "Your present is a special gift from the Ramtalan Council, Commander Jampara, and myself. Oh, and Neb actually came up with the idea."

"What idea?" Argus couldn't stand the suspense. "Are you really going to make me suffer like this?"

Neb laughed. "Tell the boy, Celeste."

"All right. Neb designed a ship that can carry a human safely in stasis so Gretchen can travel to Ramtala. He made another ship for Lola. But, Lola can't do nothing until she's finished high school and is an adult. Then she can make her own decision whether she wants to leave Earth and make the journey to Ramtala." Aunt Celeste glanced at Lola. "The decision is yours, Lola."

Tears flowed down Lola's face. Between sobs, she mumbled, "I can be with Argie?"

"You can." Aunt Celeste handed Argus another device like the memory device he gave Lola. "This contains all the information Lola will need to locate the ship and launch it. But remember, you cannot influence her in any way. Her mother is here on Earth, and she needs Lola, too."

He took the device. "I know. Thank you. This is the best present you could have given me." He turned to Lola. "If you decide not to come, I won't be mad. I promise. Like I said before, you can move on and forget all about me if you want." He kissed her. "But I'll never forget you."

Lola kissed him back and whispered, "There is no life without you, Argus Dachel. Now give me that thing."

"Best birthday ever." He gave her the device.

Tai sat on the floor, covered in puppies, all licking his face and jumping on top of him. "Are there dogs on Ramtala?"

Neb, between laughs, answered, "No. But there will be now. The puppies are from different litters, so you can start a breeding program if you want. Since being on Earth, I've developed an affection for the creatures myself."

They all laughed for a while, after which they sat around eating birthday cake and playing with the puppies. Argus stayed with Lola as Neb explained how the device worked and what she could expect from the ship. After Commander Jampara called an end to the party, Neb and Gretchen left with him.

Argus took Aunt Celeste aside and kept his voice low. "So what happens to Lenox now? Is he all right? Can I see him before you take him?"

"He's well cared for, don't worry about that. And no, it's not advised that you visit. Even with the small amount of Alpha 2a you left him with, he can get into your head, just like I can, but worse. I will personally travel with him to Ramtala. He must be isolated from others, for everyone's safety. Are you all right with that?"

He nodded. "Yeah, I guess. This is all so crazy. I can live without him. Hey, so where is Max Jackson?"

She smiled. "With a little Ramtalan influence, he was chosen as the next Chief of AURA. Like they say here on Earth, keep your friends close and your enemies closer. With Max as Chief, his whereabouts will be easy to monitor. He's happy with his job, but very angry that Gretchen chose Neb over him."

Argus laughed. "Poor Max! At least he got a promotion. Maybe he'll stop obsessing over us now."

"That's what I'm hoping. I want all memories of Ramtala to fade away." She lost her smile. "I wish you could have known your mother. She was a wonderful woman, and you share many of her traits. She'll always be with you."

Argus smiled. Hopefully his mother's traits would override those of Lenox's. "You're a damn good substitute, Aunt Celeste."

Her smile came back and she hugged him, a bit too tight, but he didn't object.

Chapter 64

Max sat in Stone's old office with his feet up on the desk. He'd made it, finally. Max Jackson, AURA Chief. His ex-wife called him after finding out about his promotion, and her father's disappearance, but he let the call go to voice mail the first time. The second time she called, he answered.

"Jackson, AURA Chief, how may I help you?"

"Max, it's me. You didn't call me back. Are you sure nobody knows where Daddy is? He couldn't have just disappeared?"

Max buffed his new designer shoes with a chamois cloth. "Let me put it this way, he won't be bossing me around anymore."

"But you'll still pay alimony even without Daddy making you, right?"

Alimony? Her father was gone, aliens had practically destroyed Palmdale, and all she cared about was alimony. Wow. Max finished buffing his shoes before he answered. "I'd pay the damn alimony whether Stone told me to or not. It's court ordered, you bubble-headed twit."

"Oh, but Daddy made sure I got my payments on time. Anyway, let's not talk money. Listen, I was thinking about moving back to Los Angeles. Maybe we can get together and chat about old times."

"Old times? Nah, I'm not really interested in the past." He put his feet down, reached over and ran his hand along the body of Argus's telescope. "I have the future to think about. There are other worlds out there, do you know that? Worlds with advanced technology. I want that technology, sweetie pie, and I'm going to get it. Ciao." He hung up.

The telescope pointed right to Ramtala. All he needed was a way to get there. One way or another, he'd get his hands on the tech they had. Earth would be prepared the next time the Ramtalans decided to attack.

He dialed the phone and waited.

"R&D, Joby speaking."

"Joby, hi, it's Max Jackson. How's it coming along?"

"Well, according to astronomical calculations, we'd need one hell of a space vessel to get to Ramtala."

"What the hell am I paying you for, Joby? You said you were the best." Max slammed his fist on the desk.

"Hold on there, Mr. Jackson. I didn't say it was impossible. The Air Force has a prototype, remember, that can travel into space at high velocity. I'm only beginning my design work and managed to find another energy source in that Lamborghini of yours. It's an electric vehicle but has this incredible power. Those aliens tweaked it with that Alpha 2a energy of theirs. I've got plenty now. And I am the best. You want to get to Ramtala? I'll find you a way."

"Now that's what I want to hear." Max hung up and pumped his fist in the air. "Steal Gretchen from me, will you Neb? Wait until I steal everything from you. And I'll make Jampara regret allowing Lenox to live and taking those Dachel brats away from me. Payback's a bitch, you alien pieces of crap." He let out a whoop and looked through the telescope. "Soon."

Chapter 65

The time had come to board the ships, but Argus found it hard to say goodbye to Lola. He wandered around the apartment, trying to think of something to say. She'd promised that she'd take the ship to Ramtala in a few years, but she might change her mind. If she met someone else or decided leaving Earth was too hard, he'd never see her again.

"Argie, what are you thinking?"

"This is harder than I thought it would be." He sat beside her in the apartment. "You've always been there for me. At my darkest, you stood by me. You never gave up on me. I love you so much."

She sighed. "I never really believed in soul mates or love at first sight, but when I met you, I felt a connection deep down. Like we were always meant to be together."

"But you can have a great life on Earth, without me."

"You're my life. It'll be awful leaving Mom, but she's got Detective DeAlba in her life now. They've been talking about getting married and maybe moving to Alaska for an adventure. Argie, I'm up for an adventure with you. Life without you seems so boring." She giggled. "I don't like to be bored."

"Me either."

An announcement came into the room: "All New Breeds, Settlers, Gretchen Manheim, and the Dachel Brothers report to launch bay immediately."

"Oh." Lola wiped her eyes. "This is it. Damn it, I thought I was okay." She dabbed her eyes again.

Argus felt tears forming. "Me too."

He took her by the hand, walked to the lobby, stood on the Citadel spiral galaxy logo for a moment, and then walked with her to the one corridor they hadn't been allowed to go down. It led to the launch bay. The door was open and inside the cavernous bay were ships lined up in rows. Tai and Aunt Celeste waited near the doorway. Neb was helping Gretchen into her single-person ship.

Tai waved to Lola. "I'll miss you, Lola."

"Same here, Tai." She waved back.

Argus held her. "Hey, tell Dave he'll always be my best friend and to study hard. Oh, and I had a bank account opened for him with a little money for college and for his mom. The account information is on the memory device I gave you."

"That's so sweet. I'll tell him. Oh, I don't want you to go." She nuzzled against him.

It took every bit of control he had not to cry or shout out or escape the Citadel and stay on Earth. "I know you said you didn't want anything, but I opened an account for you, too. Don't argue about it. And please, please take care of yourself. I mean it. I still have Protector feelings for you, so I'll always worry, but if you promise me you'll be careful, it'll help."

She whispered, "I promise."

"I love you more than you can ever know." He felt Lola's warm tears on his cheek.

"Love you, too."

Aunt Celeste came over. "I've got to take Lola up top and get her settled in the helicopter. Are you ready, Lola?"

She nodded and gave Argus another kiss. "I'll be crossing off every day on my calendar until I can see you again."

He kissed her back. "Same here."

She stepped back. "I'm ready now. Thank you for everything, Aunt Celeste."

"You're very welcome. Your mother will be waiting for you at the Palmdale airport." Aunt Celeste waited for Lola, who turned, waved to Argus, and blew a kiss. They left the bay, and Argus's heart sank.

He had to force a breath. There was a hole in his heart that wouldn't be filled until he saw her again. He hesitated for a moment before walking over to Tai.

"That made me want to cry, bro. Lola's the coolest human I've ever met." Tai motioned to the XTRA-A1. "Neb retrofit the ship with some new stasis tech to account for your weirdo freaky DNA." He smirked.

"Weirdo freaky? I've got a girlfriend and you've got puppies. Who's the freak now?" He forced a smile.

"Fair enough. Oh, the pups will go with Gretchen on her ship since they don't have any Alpha 2a. I'll miss those little guys." Tai turned away and it looked like he wiped his eyes.

"Are you crying?" Argus spun him around. "You are!"

"Shut up!" Tai strode off toward the XTRA-A1.

When Aunt Celeste returned, she gave Argus a thumbs-up. "Lola is on her way back to Palmdale. She's a very brave girl."

"Yes, she is. I...I already miss her. Do you think we'll dream in stasis? If I can dream of Lola, it'll be like she's there with me."

Aunt Celeste shrugged. "I'm not sure. We've never put New Breeds, or converted ones, into stasis before. But don't worry about it, you'll be fine. I'll be monitoring your ship and will shift into the cabin now and then to check on you. Oh, all the Settlers, me included, have to shed our host bodies and revert to pure-form so we can travel to Ramtala. Are you going to be all right seeing me in pure-form state?" She played with her ponytail. "I'm going to miss this hair."

"Wow, I hadn't thought about you going pure-form. Sure, I'll be fine. Go ahead." Argus braced himself and called Tai back over. "Aunt Celeste is reverting to pure-form."

Tai ran over. "Really? Damn. Um, so this is the last time we'll see you like this?"

She nodded. "Yes. I'll still be me, boys, your Guardian. Don't forget that." She gave them a stern look followed by a smile.

Her body began to glow blue, and the light spread out in a shimmery curtain all around her. Through the curtain, Argus saw her body, the host body, fade away until it was gone and a pure-form Ramtalan remained. The blue light shrunk back until it disappeared.

Argus took in her new, or rather, her original body. "Aunt Celeste?"

She floated to them. "Yes, it's me and I'm fine. Now, get inside your ship and get your restraints on. You won't need to place your arms in those seat depressions this time. There's a blizzard coming, and we want to launch just as it arrives so we'll be harder to detect. Everything will be all right now. We'll be together again soon. Go on. I'll see you on Ramtala."

Tai fist-bumped Argus and hurried to the ship. Argus gave Aunt Celeste a nod and followed. Together, he and Tai shifted into the XTRA-A1, settled into the seats, snapped on the over-the-shoulder restraints, and prepared for stasis. They were on their way to the adventure of a lifetime. And later, he'd spend his life with the girl he loved, and they'd share that adventure together. All his life, he'd wanted to be a regular kid, but he was never meant to be like everyone else. He was Argus Dachel, freak, alien, and Lola's boyfriend. And that was fine with him.

END

Acknowledgments:

It's hard to acknowledge everyone who has helped me along this journey of writing a book, but I can shout out a thanks to all of them just the same. As always, I mustn't be remiss in acknowledging the readers who spend precious time reading my books.

Additional books by Sofia Diana Gabel:

War and Money, Book One
Neanderball

Don't miss out!

Visit the website below and you can sign up to receive emails whenever Sofia Diana Gabel publishes a new book. There's no charge and no obligation.

https://books2read.com/r/B-A-GPBBB-BELID

BOOKS 2 READ

Connecting independent readers to independent writers.

www.ingramcontent.com/pod-product-compliance
Lightning Source LLC
LaVergne TN
LVHW090548110826
845146LV00001B/61

* 9 7 9 8 9 8 9 3 3 5 6 8 8 *